Rae Desmond Jones wa_ _____ ____ ___ 1941. He began to write poetry and short stories when he was twenty-seven, and went to Sydney University in his early thirties. His first book of verse, *Orpheus with a Tuba*, was published in 1973. This was followed by three other books of verse: *The Mad Vibe* (1975), *Shakti* (1977) and *The Palace of Art* (1981). His collection of short stories, *Walking The Line*, was published in 1979.

Jones is an accomplished reader of poetry and short stories and has read on radio. He shares an LP with Norman Talbot— *Two Voluminous Gentlemen* (1977)—and performs on the video *Rae Jones: Poet With A Tuba* (1985).

He has been involved in a number of urban environmental issues since 1985 and teaches English and History at Granville Boys' High School in Sydney's western suburbs.

IMPRINT

THE LEMON TREE

RAE DESMOND JONES

ANGUS
& ROBERTSON
PUBLISHERS

IMPRINT

AN ANGUS & ROBERTSON BOOK

First published in Australia in 1990 by
Collins/Angus & Robertson Publishers Australia

Collins/Angus & Robertson Publishers Australia
Unit 4, Eden Park, 31 Waterloo Road, North Ryde,
NSW 2113, Australia

Collins/Angus & Robertson Publishers New Zealand
31 View Road, Glenfield, Auckland 10, New Zealand

Angus & Robertson (UK)
16 Golden Square, London W1R 4BN, United Kingdom

National Library of Australia
Cataloguing-in-publication data

Jones, Rae Desmond, 1941-
  The lemon tree.

  ISBN 0 207 16629 3.

  I. Title.

A823.3

Typeset in 11/12pt Times Roman by Midland Typesetters, Victoria
Printed in Australia by Globe Press, Victoria

Cover illustration: Mt Robe, highest peak, Barrier Range *by Sam Byrne*
Oil on hardboard 56 x 59 cm
Purchased 1960
Art Gallery of New South Wales

To my parents

This work was assisted by a writer's fellowship from the Literature Board of the Australia Council, the federal government's Arts Funding and Advisory Board.

I would like to thank Humphrey McQueen and Rodney Hall for their generous advice.

PART ONE

FAST CAR

Chapter 1

John slid along the lino floor on his backside, propelled by his left leg, which he curled under his buttock. He was alone in the corridor. Beyond the door, a long way away, his mother had disappeared. He looked about, inspecting seriously the unusual sensation of being alone. Orange lino, yellow light.

He worked his way to the wall and began to pull himself slowly upright. It was so high he was afraid. His legs trembled and shook. They had never known the weight or the sensation, although it was inevitable and terrible and familiar. He wanted to allow his back to bend, so that he could slump back to the safety of the floor, his buttocks folding. An instinct told him that it was not possible. The floor could be only a temporary refuge thereafter. Instead he moved sideways. A step, then another. Gently then, trembling still, he allowed himself to slide back to the temporary solace of the floor.

He hated the high chair beside the long slab of terrazzo. Diana made large saucepans full of grape jam, fig chutney, marmalade from piles of lemons on a tray, mulberries spilling from the bucket for mulberry jam. He sulked, and as she worked she looked out through the glazed window and talked and sang.

The songs were old. *Mary this London is a wonderful sight, Oh sweet mystery of life.* She gurgled as she sang.

He watched. She may not have been aware, after a while, of his presence. Yet his being there became necessary for the performance. John sat, listening, looking at the different coloured stones in the terrazzo. Physically he resembled Austin, his father. The bullet shape of the head and the chin, strong yet fragile. The patterns of his mind and perceptions became his mother's.

When he leaned forward he could see past the blue cotton curtains pulled to the side of the window, through the windows where they had been slid open at the join, past the haze of flywire. The vines around the house were thick with leaves. The grapes were not quite ripe. The early summer light glowed around the leaves.

He heard the names of Mary and Murray Cox. There were others, vague incorporeal associations with tones of voice, pleasure or displeasure, distaste expressed through the smallest flattening of the voice.

'He came back from the war but I think it done things to him,' she said to the window, and Diana was herself exploring whether she approved or disapproved. 'He doesn't sit around or laugh much like he used to, he was fun, and instead he wanders about the house and he doesn't sleep well—at least that's what she says, although I don't know that you can rely on her—but he got back so I suppose she's glad. She used to say all those things like Austin should go but I wasn't going to let him, there's no use in it, but she doesn't talk that way so much although she's still snobbish like always. Don't know why she thinks she's a bit better than everyone else, but she does, the way she says things so as to correct the way I say things and she thinks I don't notice.'

He was not old enough to walk when he was left alone in the backyard. When there were food shortages and rationing, Diana had started a fowlyard against the back fence. He sat and watched the chickens for a while, then, impelled by a greater curiosity, he pulled himself upright on the wire. Holding his weight on his fingers, with his feet hooked into the lower loops of the wire, he pulled himself along. Beneath his feet, a sharp edge of corrugated iron that had been buried so that dogs could not dig their way into the fowlyard, bit into the soft soles of his feet.

He moved along the wire crabwise. Side to side. He rubbed his face against the wire and put out his tongue. The fowls pecked at his toes. The sensations of pain were new and interesting. The screen door slapped behind him in the distance and he could hear Diana's slippers as they flapped on the ground. He noticed the line of the afternoon shadow where it passed above his navel. The diaper sagged below his waist. He was interested in these things when his mother grabbed him from behind and began to drag him away. He resisted and screamed as a red bantam rooster pecked at his toes.

'I can't leave you alone, not for a minute,' Diana snapped and slapped his fingers.

He gazed at her indifferently. He had made another discovery. He liked the taste of wire.

Diana watched fitfully from the front verandah as he walked unsteadily and cautiously along the path. The path had been guttered by rain and the rocks hurt his feet. Austin was trimming the rosebushes and he dropped the clippings into a small pile near his boots.

John gaped at the jungle down the slope. The cluster of trees, forming an eiderdown of leaves. He knew that if he wandered there, he would be lost. There, the smooth-skinned lemons flashed their colour. When he bent to the side, he could see beneath the branches another land, of grasses and shadow and sand.

He crawled forward. A cluster of ants dragged a grasshopper through the grass. The wings fluttered as they moved.

His father seldom appeared. When he did, he was silent and terrible. John was almost two when his mother disappeared and he found himself alone in the house with the man who looked at him resentfully when he tried to speak. There were times when his father left him, which would have been a relief had it not been for the woman who came instead. Aunt Mary talked sweetly but he disliked her, and the little girl she brought and left him with in the empty room with nothing but an empty vegemite jar and a saucepan was fat and selfish, and he could tell Aunt Mary did not like him when he hit the fat girl with the saucepan and she cried.

The backyard, with its chooks and lizards in the weeds and the ants with their small hole near the washing line and the spider

5

in the corner of the shed, was desolate and alive. The chooks wandered around their yard ignoring him, and the swift indifferent lizards did not attract his fingers, and he mangled the spider's lovely web and the thin strands were sticky and uncomfortable on his fingers.

Then his father came one day, and took him by the hand and led him along the orange linoleum corridor to the small strange bedroom at the front of the house. His mother normally kept a sewing machine there. He could walk. His trousers were made of rough grey cloth, neatly pressed. They were too small and pinched his crotch.

The room was painted green. His mother was in the corner, watching him with an expectant smile. He moved to her, but Austin held him tight and then lifted him and held him above an oval basket. He looked for the first time at his sister's blue eyes and roundish face. Years later, he could recollect the moment clearly. A child, he told himself later, could not have the characteristics of an adult. Yet in his perception of those features, the elements of their relationship were ordained. Her blue eyes were always to remain blue. Not cold pale blue, like Austin's. They were darker. They looked up at him and the rings around the iris expanded and contracted with an inarticulate mixture of resentment and despair. Memory plays tricks, but he recognised his enemy.

His trousers twisted under his crotch. He turned his body and tried to squirm away.

'Play with her,' gurgled Diana from the side, perhaps unaware of the malevolence in her tone. 'This is your new sister. You can play with her!'

Because of the formality of the introduction, and because there was still in him some vestige of trust, he stopped wriggling and extended a finger gently, to the baby's mouth. The toothless mouth opened and closed. He felt the pull as the baby sucked, and he wriggled the finger. Her eyes turned and the mouth moved around and wrinkled. He turned the finger again mercilessly.

6

'That will be enough now,' his mother said, a little disapproving, a little pleased.

He rested back on his father. The seam in the crotch bit harder as the blue eyes flickered after him.

For three summers there were locusts. It was hot. Diana sat on the verandah with Ellen on her knee. They watched as John killed legions of locusts with a sandshoe.

It was hard not to kill the grasshoppers. No matter where the shoe was brought down, he squashed locusts and their sticky insides spread around the sole of the sandshoe. The ones that lived still flitted and skipped over the garden, chewing and stripping everything. The mass of them darkened the sky.

'Get them, kill them,' his mother encouraged and urged from the verandah, as she put Ellen down beside her. She sat with her legs apart and her dress rose over her knees and sagged in between.

The wings of the grasshoppers whirred past his face and tasted metallic.

During the second year, Ellen was big enough herself to thrash at the grasshoppers. By the third year she was ready to compete. She flattened grasshoppers with an old hammer handle turned on its side. It easily killed seven or eight locusts at a slash. Diana remained on the verandah, calling and urging.

'I'm tired of this,' John complained. 'It's boring.'

Ellen looked up at him with pure loathing from under her bonnet. John walked away. Diana watched closely and thought. She wasn't ready to give up power so easily.

'You can kill some more for me,' she slapped the empty cavern where her dress folded between her knees.

John looked at her and did not answer. Any comment could be manipulated. Diana stared as he walked away without offering any opposition. From this, he learned that Diana did not know how to handle silences.

He went to the backyard, to the garage where there wasn't

7

much for the locusts to eat. The grasshoppers bumped against his chest and dropped in front of him, squashed under his shoes. Eating he could taste them still. Metallic.

Murray Cox came back from the war. He visited Austin and Diana. He was quiet and left most of the talking to his wife, who was only too prepared to oblige. When she tried to get Murray to talk about those funny things they did in Cairo that he had said in his letter, or the thing the blacks did in New Guinea that was interesting too, he smiled and told the story in as short and self-deprecating fashion as he could. It took him several years to heal, then he began to believe the reality that Mary had fashioned for him of the war out of his own letters. Yes, there was the evidence. It sounded so cheery and happy and young, and he had been young. By 1948 he was ready to wear medals and march in remembrance parades and he joined the RSL.

John noticed him when he came and sat at the side of the table. His medals had been polished for the day and a hat lolled easily on his lap and sweat stood out on his forehead as he smiled and made jokes. Diana pushed a plate of fruit cake to him.

'Fruity enough thanks, fruity enough,' he leaned forward nevertheless to inspect the cake and his fingers moved although he rested back.

'Lina made it,' Diana said cunningly. 'You know how Austin's mother cooks.'

'I dreamed about it once when I was sleeping in a foxhole in Tobruk.' He smiled automatically his self-deprecating smile. Then he leaned forward and picked a largeish slice of cake.

John stepped from his chair and moved around, to get a closer look at the medals.

'What is that one for?' He pressed quite close, so that he could smell the beer on his breath, and pointed to a star which he thought was quite beautiful.

'The Africa Star, for all those who fought Rommel.' He tried very hard to be jolly.

'They beat him too,' said Mary.

John wanted to touch the star, but did not dare. Austin glared. He hovered, afraid and helpless, held by the magic of the star.

'Do you want to go?' asked Diana, suddenly and shrewdly.

'Murray has gone as far as he can here,' smiled Mary, 'unless he gives in to the unions. No one gets far here without giving in to the unions.'

'Be the editor of the *Barrier Truth* in fifteen years if I was a good boy,' Murray breathed heavily and the medals swayed out from his chest.

'There's nothing wrong with the unions,' Austin flashed from his solitude. 'I've always been in the union.'

'Well . . .' Mary began, then noticed Diana bristle. 'We're going to Sydney, there's opportunities there, and Murray's got a job.'

'That's good,' interposed Diana, then added darkly, 'What arrangement do we intend to make about Lina, then?'

Mary looked at her sister-in-law with scarcely diguised loathing.

'There is the train to Sydney now,' Diana stated with careful neutrality.

Austin had two weeks' holiday. They went to Adelaide and stayed in the spare rooms of an old woman who sat all of the time in a darkened room listening to the radio. Ellen and John were afraid and tiptoed past the room while clinging to the wall. The old woman's grey head sometimes turned above the chair, but she never spoke.

The house was near the beach. They went by bus to the city of Adelaide, then by tram to Glenelg. John loved the rows of red brick houses and the ferris wheel, the dodgem cars and tents with striped canvas, a wharf with silent fishermen and a cannon pointing benignly to the sea from the centre of a park.

He did not have long to play there. His parents, who were as innocently in love with things as himself, pulled him away with his sister. They walked then for blocks past rows of red brick houses, so different to the corrugated iron of Broken Hill.

'We're going to see your grandmother,' Diana said as they arrived at a perfectly typical red brick house.

John was surprised that Lina should live in such a place. He looked closely at the glossy varnish on the curved bricks of the verandah for a clue, then at the cream verandah poles, and the pots of petunias.

He was more surprised when it was not Lina who met them, but a small soft-looking old woman with plastic-rimmed spectacles. The old woman kissed both children, although John pulled away, and she asked Diana whether these were hers, and how she could have such children.

'I don't know myself,' Diana replied drily.

The old woman's glasses were thick and opaque and her eyes seemed small. The house was dark and musty. There were three big armchairs he was not allowed to bounce on, although there were splits in the stitching through which the springs showed and bits of kapok had drifted recently to the floor.

John would have liked to go back to the park and the beach and the cannon that pointed out to sea. He squirmed. The old woman cried. Diana suffered it tensely and tried to make jokes and bring the conversation back to memories, which would allow her to view from some distance the terror of decay. Austin sat, his pale eyes slightly more prominent and staring than usual. He seemed very thin. Ellen sat on his lap and prodded him impatiently with her elbow.

It was December. There was a short summer rainstorm. The rain pelted for a few minutes, then stopped, as inexplicably and suddenly as it had begun. Wisps of steam rose from the earth outside. On the hour, the clocks throughout the house chimed but did not coincide. Dissonance of chimes. The grandmother on the mantel with a dark timber casing, and the grandfather which looked cheap and pale. John's skin prickled.

The old woman looked down and wiped her face with a handkerchief. Diana looked along the corridor, relieved at the interruption.

'I know you came to be happy,' the old woman sobbed. 'It isn't right Diana to be left like this.'

'Since you left the farm . . .' Diana tried to divert the flood.

10

'Not when you brought up a family, it isn't right to be left alone with no one, it just isn't right.'

John climbed down from the chair and managed to slip outside unnoticed, at last. He wandered, running his fingers along the wet timber paling fence and scuffing with his best shoes the concrete footpath.

'She didn't talk like that when she married again, to that old mongrel,' his mother complained as they walked back toward the beach. 'Even though he didn't last long and she has all that money!'

Austin nodded. He was bored. Over the roofs of the red brick houses, John saw the upper part of the ferris wheel stalled in the sunlight. A woman leaned from the topmost cabin and waved to someone below. The man beside her pulled her back. John ran ahead.

'I want to go there!' He yelled to his mother, although he was afraid of heights.

He was lucky. Diana was so intent on other things that she forgot. Instead, he ran through the tents and played on the cannon.

Lina was closer to him. For a period of four to six months each year, she came to stay with them in Broken Hill. There was tension between Austin and Diana at this time.

Lina was almost completely grey, although there were streaks of red in her hair. Small diabetic sores scarred her arms, which she scratched on the side of the kitchen table. At least once a week she made heavy cakes and puddings and dumplings in the kitchen, and nobody else was allowed in.

'Diana,' she called out as she stood in the doorway between the kitchen and the lounge room, 'you don't mind if I use your sultanas. Do you?'

John watched his mother, who was sitting in exile on the lounge, knitting. Her lips puckered. She did not turn as she answered.

'If you really want them that's alright,' conveying clearly

11

through her tone that the sultanas were being kept for some close and important reason.

Lina took John walking. Long walks, beyond the borders of the town, past the scattered fibro houses that were just being built, past the old camel camps, past the bluestone farm on the top of the hill, past the chained dogs and broken-down cars.

The old woman never talked to him, or to herself, the way his mother did. He let her be silent and regarded her with distaste as he followed. She leaned her heavy body forward as she walked, and her dark blue floral dress hung irregularly above her petticoat. He had learned from his mother to watch and listen. The first subject of his lesson was his mother's enemy.

They stopped at a large white rock halfway up a hill. Specks of mica lodged in the seams of the rock although the large chunks had been picked free long ago. The small flakes caught the sun. Not so far away from the town, the hill was high enough for him to sit beside her and look over the smaller hills leading back to the houses. He was not used to trees. There were none. They had been cut down at the beginning, by the first miners and the company, for fuel and shelter. Shadows of swift moving clouds passed between the sun and the hills, clean patterns of light and darkness.

Lina's heavy body slumped and relaxed. She laid two small parcels wrapped in newspaper on a space on the rock, and unwrapped them ritually, exposing two small pieces of fruit cake. Then she looked at him with watering eyes. Carefully he picked the smallest piece, the one nearest himself. She looked at him gratefully.

They ate together.

He walked with her often after that, until age became too much and she stayed back at the house to irritate Diana by occupying the kitchen, or going sulkily into Austin's garden to rip out weeds by the handful.

When children called her names from the street, she chased them and kicked their backsides when she could, even in the presence of their startled parents.

John was her favourite.

'He acts like his grandfather,' she said once, and she treated his moodiness and solitariness and his interest in books with a fond indulgence that would have stunned her husband.

Diana walked around with a permanent headache when Lina was there. Ellen was ignored or pushed aside by the dominating old woman. John felt that he knew her, and trusted her, and was never afraid.

After some months, she left. Each time she left it was harder for her to pull herself up the steps on to the train to Sydney, to Aunt Mary. She turned and smiled down imperiously, any sadness disguised by the net from her hat down over her eyes. A large white brooch held the bodice of the dark blue floral dress, and parcels and bags looped over both of her deeply scarred arms.

Once she sat in the carriage beside the window, Diana filled any desperate emptiness with talk about the weather and the trip, as though afraid that if she stopped talking the old woman would climb from the carriage and stay.

When the train began to pull and puff, she leaned from the carriage and kissed Austin quickly, then Ellen, who was held up for that purpose. When John was picked up and offered, he received a quick, wet slap on the cheeks. Finally another kiss, for Diana, slightly longer, more hesitant and intense.

The old woman scratched a sore on her arm against the window.

'See you again Diana.' She waved to her son before settling back against the cushion. Although he couldn't see her, John kept waving as the train passed through the gates and away. His sorrow was the first secret that he could recall keeping from his mother.

One afternoon the following year, when she had returned, he walked into the room as she was dressing. It was unusual for Lina to be seen without clothes. She was bending, with her back turned. The size of her bottom was frightening enough; but the wrinkled skin, the thighs, at once shrivelled and flabby. Between her legs, two large flaps hung down. Perhaps haemorrhoids, or a prolapse. Testicles. He turned away, appalled and afraid.

Chapter 2

His mother left him at the long brick building and waved from the gate.

'Be good,' she called gaily. 'You're big now.'

As he walked along the verandah, he watched his mother go. There was another room, full of brooms and hoses and buckets. The schoolteacher had turned to talk to someone else. She found him sitting on a bucket.

He looked at her. He was not frightened. He accepted her hand and they walked to a room full of children, where he was introduced. He sat cross-legged on the floor.

At lunchtime, a boy walked up to him with a smile. When he smiled back, he was pushed forward and his face was pressed into the sand. The boy ran away laughing.

During the year he was there, John had his revenge when he smeared dog shit on the boy's shirt. Apart from that he sat cross-legged, trying to form letters which never came right onto a chalkboard.

One day a teacher asked him to read from the blackboard. He could not see the letters. He was ashamed when he had to go to an optometrist, who made him wear ugly round glasses with yellow steel frames.

Already a failure. In the playground, he was not as good at catching and throwing as others.

Another square of concrete, another sandpit. He remained suspicious of sandpits. 'd' and 'b' changed into one another. 'e's looked like 'i's and 't's shaped themselves tenaciously into 'l's. His left hand and his right hand determined to act independently and wilfully. For a while he confused teachers by writing with his left hand backwards. It might have been clever, except that he was equally confused.

15

'The other hand,' the teacher said, 'we can't read it if it's backwards. But then, we can't read it if it goes forward either, can we?'

Diana sent him off every day ironed and starched, with clean socks. He sweated, choked and chafed in those collars and ironed shirts. He looked capable of writing neatly and adding numbers, but he never could. Sometimes the appearance was accepted. He remained for his school years in middle classes, in which he always came last. He felt as inarticulate as any boy who never knew soap and whose trousers hung from his grimy shirts.

His parents suspected he might be a little slow. Austin and Diana were proud of being able to read and write. Neither of them enjoyed reading. To be able to read and write was an achievement, but to enjoy doing it was incomprehensible and perverse.

He sat near the idiot girl and watched her closely for signs of kinship. He walked home with her on some afternoons. She squatted and pissed in the street, and giggled, delighted at his curiosity. She was not at all like his grandmother. He was puzzled and relieved.

They walked around hand in hand. She was happy. She suffered from the slights of others.

'That girl,' Diana said, 'is a . . . nice enough girl . . . but you could get other friends . . . she is a bit simple.'

'I'm a bit simple too,' he answered.

Diana laughed, to soften the comment.

'She's a bit . . . you know' (she twirled a finger in a circle around her ear) 'dumb . . .'

The yellow steel glasses bit on the back of his ear. He twisted the wing with his finger, so that it curled further and the glasses slipped down his nose.

The schoolteacher agreed with his mother. They were separated firmly. He was hurt that she forgot him in a few days. Certain images of her remained, although he affected to despise her.

When the beatings started, John was surprised. Although Austin in the background had seemed fearsome, he had never before attempted prominence.

He was furious when John did not want to help with the washing up. First he pushed. John was stubborn and sullen. Then it was punches. John screamed and tried to run after his flailing arms failed to stop the fists. He remembered falling, then the short sharp kicks around his ribs. As quickly as it began, the beating stopped. He looked up, around the arm he had wrapped around his head. Austin was standing above him, staring at him bitterly, as though he had done a terrible thing.

For Diana, it was a useful threat, and it added to her power. If they did not do something then . . . and both John and Ellen were tied firmly to her.

After the first beating, it became regular. There were no causes, except for black moods, fear, the failure to love. It did not matter how John or Ellen acted. The beatings just happened, and as quickly they were over.

The only time they stopped was when Lina was there. Then, Austin withdrew into the background, as before. Diana competed for favours instead of demanding them.

Austin was depressed. He loved his wife. He wanted to be a good father, but the children resented him. He tried offering toys but they were afraid. It was not fair. They had a duty to him, and he demanded that they love him. When they did not, he was hurt deeper than he could say. All they had to do was give in, to love him; they would not.

He demanded and demanded; he was angry. He hit out. He could keep on and on. They would give in, eventually.

The car was a new opportunity, a fresh start. When Diana worked out that they could afford it, she told both children. For days they sat about, asking him for details.

John imagined a sleek red car with deep leather seats and an armrest that plumped down across the back seat, and a small

17

window where he could sit and put out his head. As he sat at school, he drew the outline of his car on the desk.

The bell finally went. He walked home, consciously stopping himself from running. It was a wintry day but the rolled gravel road was dry. He paddled through a long pool, pushing his toes into the mud, breaching small dams of leaves and stones so that small rivers flowed again.

He heard a car in the distance. Tingling with apprehension, he turned. There was no way he could know. His sense of disappointment made him certain. The car had a very old square chassis and a canvas top. A crank-handle and a water bag swayed together to the creaking rhythm of the engine.

He knew. The disappointment was tangible.

When the car came abreast, he saw his father, sitting straight-backed and proud and foolish. The car braked slowly. Austin gave him a rare spontaneous smile. The door squeaked open. John clambered in, trying hard to swallow his shame.

Austin was still learning to drive. The big upright gearstick ground into first. The car rattled like a tractor. Beaming with pleasure and excitement, Austin took him on a drive around the block, unaware of John's snobbery or the desperate way he feigned interest.

'What do you think of it?'

'Really good.' The false ring of his voice echoed above the racket of the old car.

By the time the car rolled noisily across the rutted tracks of the back lane, Austin was silent. He concentrated resentfully as he turned the rough timber steering wheel and the car ground through the back gate. Diana waited at the back door. She walked forward as the car narrowly missed the clothes line.

'Isn't it good,' she gurgled as she tapped the green hand-painted mudguard with a tablespoon.

Austin stepped down from the cabin. He was ashamed. He wouldn't meet her gaze.

For the two years they owned the 1927 Oldsmobile, John's

snobbery did not diminish. He did not respond to the leather seats or to the solid workmanship of the car. The heavy steel was embarrassing and lumpish. The car was only saved from the tip by his father's willingness to endure the humiliation of driving it. Similar cars had rolled onto their sides or stood on blocks rusting outside town; their canvas coverings flapped in strips in the wind. It was not new!

In summer the scratched cellophane windows were unclipped and put away. In winter they were clipped back on, but the wind came through anyway.

It took them to Adelaide for a holiday. Other cars swept smoothly past them as they chugged along, with John in the back suffering the smell of petrol and dust, and the taste of anger mingled with lemon squash. Ellen's car-sickness thickened the texture.

He was bored and unmoved through the hours of flatness, until the top blew from the radiator. Boiling water and steam sprayed onto the windscreen. Austin worked his foot up and down until the heavy old car finally stopped.

As the car cooled, Diana sat on the running board and offered cups of warm water. Ellen's face burned under her bonnet.

When Diana became bored, John walked away into the bush. Free of his family and the car, he listened to millions of small animals and insects moving. Along the curve of the earth, multitudes of tiny living things feeding and working. On the crest of a small mound, he was part of it. A level of existence, creating and feeding on itself. The breath caught in his chest. He was isolated and alone. The sun was high. The saltbushes extended for miles without moving. Part of the density, a fly buzzed near his lips. The smell of a dead animal permeated and hung there.

Daring much, he stared there for a while. Then, unable to sustain the concentration, turning slowly in space, teased by the inconceivable emptiness, he turned back.

John noticed Diana becoming more tense and excited as they neared the Burra. The old copper mining town he had never seen was filled with associations he had from her, and he was puzzled as he looked around at the low hills and the farms. It lacked the epic size and crudity of the bush.

The farmhouse where Diana had grown up and had her honeymoon was still there, much as it was. The old car slid to a stop and they climbed out and brushed the dust from their clothes.

As John urinated by the side of the road, Diana walked the length of the building and turned back, then stopped with her hand resting on the gate. Ellen followed her and held her hand as Austin lifted the bonnet of the car and allowed the heat to escape from the engine. John was disappointed in the small bluestone cottage with a shed and a heap of rusting iron under a tree.

'The well,' his mother called to him with unmistakable grief, as though he should have known. 'They've closed the well.'

Searching around for the cause of grief, he looked. A flat piece of steel with weeds growing around it. The fences at the back were broken down and the fields were full of weeds. Somewhere on the far side of the hill, the moaning of cattle.

'Why should they do that? The water was so clear. It was sweet water, the best water for miles.'

She leaned on a gate and pointed a finger at another farm, not far away, with a well head nearby.

'That water was brackish and bitter, good for crops and nothing else, and it is still going.'

A curtain in the farmhouse moved. Diana remained at the gate, defying the legitimacy of ownership. The iron blades of the distant windmill turned slightly in an insignificant breeze. The head of the windmill swung away, then back.

The bonnet of the car crashed down. Austin clipped the locks in place.

'Hasn't changed much, has it?' He looked about with a vacuous smile at the hills. 'A bit run down though.'

'You don't know about farming.'

20

He ignored the remark and walked to the far end of the fence. A woman was peeping around the side of the house. She held a baby, and another child peered cautiously around the hem of her dress.

'You mind if we look around?' Austin called. 'This is my wife. She used to live her. She grew up here.'

The woman looked uncomfortable.

'I don't know her.'

'Before you lived here.'

'I don't want to look.' Diana took her hand from the gate and relinquished.

'She lived here,' Austin persisted.

'I want to go. We must go,' Diana pleaded.

'I only rent the place, love.'

Diana turned and led Ellen back to the car. John hung back, watching his father and the woman, who had by then advanced halfway across the front yard, in tenuous possession. The child who had previously held back revealed himself as a boy in sagging shorts below his navel. He moved in front of his mother and watched Austin insolently.

'We only wanted to see . . .' Austin went on. He was without support. Diana had lifted Ellen into the back seat without turning.

Austin trudged back to the car. A strand of barbed wire had pulled the sleeve of his shirt. The woman stayed where she was, stubborn and victorious. The child did not blink as he stared at Austin's receding back.

Austin was doing an inexpert three-point turn when Diana looked cautiously back at the farmhouse.

'Not friendly people,' remarked Austin.

'They don't own it, they only rent,' Diana added with venom and disgust. 'Aboriginals.'

Beyond the bluestone cottage, the pepper trees, the desolate fields, the ruined farmhouse further down the road, there was no flash of the extraordinary. Behind them, pretty vines still grew unattended around the verandah. An overgrown hedge which

21

Diana would have liked to trim and clean. It would have been neat when she threw the bucket of dirty water over it, onto the hired hand. That was 1928.

'My father sent Clydesdale horses to the war in 1916 . . .' she murmured to no one in particular.

The memorial to the fallen stood upright in the town square. Diana stole a glance at the names on the shops as they walked past. The pastry shop was not far away.

Short round-faced people with strong backs. The men wore hats and braces. The women's roundness was emphasised by shapeless dresses and wide hats. They carried gloves in their stong chapped hands.

A man with dusty shoes and an unironed shirt coughed and spat in the gutter. The women steered their menfolk past carefully, holding their arms and gazing resolutely into the distance. One of the men looked up and mumbled a guilty goodday Fred before being towed along.

The man with the unironed shirt cleared his throat again.

A middle-aged woman, thinner than the others, with glasses too small for her round face, stopped and squinted.

'Diana . . . Diana Bock! After all this time!'

Separating, they surreptitiously checked each other's fingers. The woman flapped a glove and held her knuckles out. Diana turned her left hand in the sunlight.

A man shifted uneasily behind, then shook hands with Austin.

'What are you doing Diana? Do you still play tennis? You were so good.'

Diana gurgled, undecided between flamboyance or modesty. The men talked quietly as the women's voices echoed around the quiet square. John and Ellen sat side by side, sharing a sausage roll with a meagre squirt of tomato sauce.

Chapter 3

The old man next door sat on his verandah, which was sideways to the fence. John saw him when he looked through the bent iron or climbed the mulberry tree.

He had a heavy white moustache. All day he sat, or lay on a black iron bed. There was a step leading from the house to the verandah. An icebox covered by hessian bags dripped water on to a tin tray. The old man was blind. His wife had died ten years before, but his son visited every day.

One day John threw a ball into the yard. Then he crept in to recover it. Slowly he went tiptoe through the gap between the creaking sheets of iron. Then a stone rolled under his feet.

'Who is there? Is that you? Who?' The old man's head turned as he waved an arm, and waited.

John reached forward to pick up the ball. There was no noise.

'Is that you?'

John had the ball. All he had to do was run, out the back, not through the hole in the fence. He was fascinated and curious.

As he walked towards the bed, he knew the old man could hear him, but he was still treading softly and quietly. He became aware of noise himself, the small noises that were normally unheard. A piece of timber hanging on a nail, a sparrow, a car in the distance.

He squeezed the ball between his fingers. It was hard for him to speak.

'Yes.'

The man's head turned.

'Boy next door?'

John nodded and mumbled.

'Come . . . over here . . .'

Despite his terror, John went towards him. His steps sounded clear on the concrete verandah. It was cool under the corrugated

23

iron. A vine on a trellis shielded the verandah from the afternoon sun. The old man waited patiently. John stopped a long step away. A long arm sprang out and gripped him firmly by the shirt. John called out.

'Don't be frightened.' The old man didn't let go of the shirt.

When John settled down, the old man drew him close. He could smell the old man's breath and his clothes. John trembled. With his other hand, the old man felt. Starting at his ear, he lightly ran his hand around the face, fitting the palm into every hollow. When John began to sob, he ignored the wetness of his cheek. Then the feeling hand dropped as he maintained a grip with the other.

'I wanted to see what you looked like.' The old man laughed as though he had used the line before.

John mumbled.

'Please,' the old man tried to lower his reedy voice, '. . . go to the ice company . . . tell your father I have no ice left because Jack didn't come today.'

The old man released him, slowly, reluctantly, afraid that he might go away.

'I have no ice left.'

'Yes.' John was now terrified by the old man's embarrassment. He moved back to stand beside the ice safe. He was wet. The icebox dripped loudly.

The old man pushed himself upright and walked to the icebox. He lifted the bags. In the tray at the top a single small sliver of ice was melting away.

'My meat will go off.'

The old man stared at the wrong place.

'Yes yes yes.'

John ran before the gaze could transfix him on the spot. He didn't stop until he was on the other side of the fence. Then he crept back and looked cautiously. The old man methodically scratched his crotch then settled on the bed and put his hands behind his head. Then, with a swift unexpected movement, he turned his head in John's direction. John ducked.

He did not tell his father or mother and went to the ice works himself. It was a long walk to the tall apparatus of gurgling, steaming, silver-frosted pipes.

In the loading bay, a big man in a dirty apron wiped his hand and pointed to an office. There a man in a white shirt and a pressed blue tie listened to his story about the old man who ran out of ice. He took down the address.

'Right,' he tapped the pencil on a pad and slid it between his thumb and forefinger. 'We'll send someone around.'

As John went, he watched the cubes of ice slide from the chute. With sure timing, the man in the apron caught them with his hook and threw them easily and symmetrically, one on top of the other. He achieved this miracle with the smallest shrug of his shoulders. Despite this, his arms, where they came through his singlet, were flabby and fat. Pieces of ice flew from the corners. Now and then, he deliberately broke a rectangle of ice with a stroke of the hook. Then splinters of ice spread around the steel tray of the truck and the concrete floor of the loading bay.

When he noticed John, he bent and scraped up a handful of ice chips and offered them.

'They're alright when you suck them,' he laughed and shoved a piece of ice into his mouth.

His hand as he held it out was as big as a shovel blade. John accepted the ice and licked it. It burned against the inside of his cheek as he backed away. A drop of sweat fell from the line of the man's dark oily hair. He let the chips fall and wiped his brow with the back of his hand. The ice steamed.

Not long after, the old man died. His parents were still sitting in the kitchen talking about it when John stole out and crept to the fence. The old man's son was leaning against the icebox rolling a cigarette when he looked up and stared into John's eyes.

'What do you want son?'

John pulled his head down without answering. The man walked a few steps towards the fence. Then a woman called out.

'There was a kid here,' the man sounded angry.

'Oh come and help me pack this junk,' the woman added impatiently.

There was a pause before the man's steps went away.

By the following autumn no one talked about the old man and his blindness any more. It was another secret that John felt that he was keeping, although he didn't know whether it was really a secret.

In the evening Austin was digging some old bulbs from the garden. A new, flourishing, lemon tree was behind him. John played with a cardboard pirate hat, with peaks at the side and a white skull in the centre. He thought of the man next door and his eyes.

Insects were feeding in the background. There was a question. It was difficult to break the sense of inevitability and express it.

'What happens to people when they die?'

He tried to sound casual.

Austin paused as he turned the shovel. John could not see his face. Behind him, the lemon tree was alive. There was just enough light for him to see the contents of the shovel. Worms, rotting bulbs, ash.

'They rot,' Austin remarked as he let the shovel drop.

There was a mosquito. John turned the pirate hat around in his hand. He felt alone, with his secret unshared, and the fact of death.

When he played in the backyard, he could see the mines. Larger than the poppet heads were the long plateaux of black dust left from the early mines, when what had been a hill had disappeared. Black dust settled over the town each time there was a wind.

There were valuable minerals in the skimps. No one had worked out a way of separating them cheaply.

A smelter shed was set up. A gutter of silver grey mud bubbled as it moved. People were proud of the modern flotation process which smelled, not of earth, but metal. At the end there was more silt, skimps left in a pile to blow with the wind and harden.

26

The wind picked up the red dust from the leached desert earth. It only took a breeze to raise the fine dust, in which nothing could grow. He felt it itch at the corner of his eyes.

At the primary school, he was beaten up with tedious regularity.

He was a coward. Diana dressed him in neat clothes but he was not better than his persecutors. He would have liked to be one of them, and why wasn't he? His father worked in the same kind of job as their fathers did. He was no better at school. Each day he wore clean clothes, and each day the runtish dirty Ellis led his band to rub John's nose in the dirt and belt him and tear his shirt. He would not have minded if they had liked him.

Pushed against a fence, John was easily terrified by bloodthirsty screams of Ellis and his band.

'Ah whyncha fight why donya eh avago try y'self smartcuntwhydonya ave ago gon . . .'

When he fought, the other members of the horde punched him from the side and tore his shirt and hit him with pieces of rock. There was a kind of miserable exhilaration in this. He would have been prepared to go the next day, with torn shirt sleeves like everybody else, covered in dust and mud, and avago at Ellis. Diana did not accept this. Each day, there were newly sewn shirts and washed and ironed shorts and each morning he polished shoes on the tank stand. Then off again to school, a glowing demoralised target.

One day Diana waited around a corner until the horde was all close in a ring around John. The boys did not know who she was. John waited limply to be rescued and further condemned the following day. He was weak with embarrassment.

'You boys,' she stated quite calmly. 'Stand back, against the wall. I know who you are. If you run I'll come and see you at the school tomorrow.'

The startled boys shuffled back against the fence.

'We'll gecha,' Ellis mumbled, and others muttered assent.

Diana looked at Ellis. His courage left him.

'Din' say nothing.' He stared at the ground.

Diana switched a stick against her leg.

'Fight him.'

'Whad?'

'Fight him. You, on your own, without any of your mates. Fight him.'

It was a small boys' fight. Neither of them had the strength or the sense of direction to inflict serious damage. John was astonished to find that he was stronger than Ellis, and his punches were marginally better directed. Ellis's roundhouse swipes were considerably less fearsome than the terrible faces he pulled before releasing them.

When Ellis pushed forward to get a grip of John's hair, John connected a wild flail to the face. Ellis reeled back. Blood ran down his face. Then he cried and spat out a defiant jet of blood. The boys against the fence were silent. They broke up as Ellis began to run.

John walked home, trying to dawdle away from his mother. He felt sick and disgusted.

'You beat him.' Diana reached to touch his shoulder with her hand. Her voice was thick. She had thrown away the stick.

They were going through the gate as he started to cry.

'Now what's that for?' His mother laughed. 'You weren't afraid . . . you won . . . see what you can do if you fight . . .'

He stalked away, unable to explain. He had always fought. She was right. He wasn't afraid.

The park beside the school was all spindly trees and shrubs and patchy lawn trimmed neatly and bordered with bluestone and gravel. The bandstand stood with dignity in the centre. The water bubbler was turned off during droughts. There was a slippery-dip, and monkey bars made of welded pipe. And at the side of the park there were two tennis courts and a hall.

On Fridays and some Saturdays, his parents went dancing at the hall. His mother dressed in pink taffeta with a flower below the shoulder. Austin's cheeks were more gaunt than ever, dressed in a suit with his watchful eyes, determined to enjoy himself.

28

Saxophones and trumpets. Brushes swished across the face of the drums. The grey-haired trumpeter who looked like Harry Truman. The members of the band were forbidden to take off their penguin suits or bow ties, even on the hottest nights.

Harry Truman stepped forward to the microphone and let the trumpet rest on the floor and played the fiddle solo. The three round medals and one star on his chest glittered in the slightest movement. His hair was thinner in the light.

'Now ladies your partners for the Pride of Erin walss, pleez!'

Then stepped back and put the trumpet to his lips. The piano, the drums, the saxophone, introduced and cajoled and encouraged.

When Irish eyes are smilin'
Sure 'tis like the morn in spring . . .

The sweetness touching them, almost every one a Cornish or Welsh Protestant, the ladies with that contented possessive smile, the men with the *oh yes* smiles, the swish of satin and lace as they moved onto the dance floor.

At interval, he slid with the other boys on the sawdust across the parquet. They ran and skidded until they were dispatched into the less stuffy air outside. As he went, he caught the eyes of the trumpeter—a flash of superficial benevolence and deep dislike. The trumpeter stood with his hands in his pockets beside Austin near the door.

'A good looking boy.' He pulled a hand from a pocket and the penguin coat fell loose around his wrists.

Austin looked at John resentfully.

'What you were saying,' Austin threw back his head, 'it doesn't matter what a man believes if he's a decent man and works hard . . .'

He took a sip of beer from a glass.

'If your life depends on a man like it does underground,' the trumpeter commented.

'I'd rather have him there than some others I could think of.'

'Who would you be thinking of Aussie?'

'It doesn't do to say names when you can't prove anything.'

29

'You ought to be willing to say,' urged Harry Truman, whose real name was Silver.

Out in the dark with two boys who were equally anonymous, John played hide-and-seek. Another pair of trousers he was growing out of were tight on his crotch. It was his turn to hide. The dancing started again inside the hall and the band was playing. Outside he was 'it'. Other children joined the game. He ran across an open stretch of grass. While ten was counted loudly against the wall, he rolled under a pine tree. The branches brushed the ground so it didn't look as though there was any room, but underneath a depression had been scooped so that the tree could be watered. He wriggled there. He liked the closeness and the solitude and the smell and prickle of pine needles.

With his head on the side he could see part of the hall through a window, and hear the stomp of the Gypsy Tap. Once he glimpsed his mother spinning past, sparkling and vital and swift on her feet, as she changed partners in the Barn Dance.

Children ran past looking. They looked underneath the cars parked in the road and in the toilets and around the fence and in the gully that divided the park from the school. They called out to each other, then they called his name.

'It's over John,' one called. 'You can come out now. You've won.'

They stood for several seconds, looking about to see where he was going to come from. When he didn't appear they looked for a little while longer.

'We're going to play something else now,' the same voice called plaintively. 'You can't be in it though.'

John did not fall for this ploy either. Several times, someone looked into the branches of the tree, but he remained still although he almost burst from not breathing.

After half an hour, the others were bored. They drifted along the paths, calling out his name. When they did begin to play another game, he did not come out.

Couples stepped from the hall, talking loudly. The women

30

waved to one another and kissed. Doors slammed and cars drove away. Wrapped in his love of isolation, with revenge for succour, he remained where he was. Huddled further into the dust and the pine needles.

His father walked past, not a metre away. Most of the other cars had left. The band packed its instruments into a utility.

'You don't live far away,' said Harry Truman. 'Do you think he might have gone home?'

'He might have,' said Diana.

She stood in the light at the front of the hall with a wrap on her shoulders and looked keenly into the dark.

The lights went out one by one. The band clattered away in the utility. Finally his parents went to the old car and left themselves. No sooner had the old car rattled off than he was bereft and desolate. He felt betrayed.

He wriggled his way from under the tree and walked home. It was not far. His mother was waiting, sitting at the table. Austin stood beside her.

'Where have you been?' Her voice was shrill.

'I walked around.'

He was not watching as his father moved around the room. The first punch connected the side of his head. When he fell to the floor, a barrage of kicks jabbed into his ribs and his back. Diana screamed. John pulled himself onto his elbow. Austin was still wearing his suit. His shoulders were hunched and he was trembling.

'Where did you go?'

'I . . . walked.'

The side of his head did not hurt as much as it might have. His ribs hurt more.

'Don't hit him,' said Diana.

Austin looked at her dumbly, as though to say, 'I'm doing this for you'. The burst of fury was over.

John stood slowly, conscious of the theatre of each exaggerated movement. He swayed with the sharp pain in his ribs. His father looked at him with stupid innocence, wondering what he had done wrong.

'Don't put it on,' his mother turned on him when the moment was past.

He limped slowly to his room.

Chapter 4

The stock and station agent lived with his family four doors away. Their son was about the same age as John, and they hated one another with constancy rare in children.

Neville had a good throwing arm. Neville ambushed him on his way past and caught him with a piece of gravel between his shoulder blades. Then John had the idea of running ahead, into Neville's yard, instead of charging directly with bellows of rage. It was unexpected, but Neville sidestepped. John threw a stone, which struck Neville behind the ear.

Neville stumbled and scraped his knees before retreating into the house. John walked home slowly, to await retribution.

Luck was with him. His parents had gone out and the only adult left was his grandmother. She was enjoying herself in the kitchen, unopposed by Diana. Washing dishes, scraping her arm against the bench. He explained his situation to her.

'You better go out to the garage,' she stated, her slight accent making it sound abrupt.

Neville's parents soon appeared, dressed formidably in suits. This was all that was necessary to cow Austin and Diana. The act would have succeeded, except for Lina. John watched with mingled delight and terror through a nail hole in the garage, as the old woman pursued them across the back verandah.

'As for that little bastard of yours . . .'

'Please, such language!'

'And from a woman . . .' Neville's father halted long enough in retreat to gaze down his nose.

'I say little bastard, and that is as much about his parents as about him!' Her accent became heavier as the language became stronger. 'I see him every day doing what no other in this area would do, day after day, without punishment or fear. No one else would dare to do the things he does . . .'

'How dare . . .'

They wilted before half a sentence was out. The old lady towered, although she was short.

'Throwing stones at adults. No. Not rich, spoiled adults like you. The poor ones who will be frightened of you. Scratching the paint off cars of people that hardly have money to own one. Breaking windows, he stands in the street and laughs at the parents with no fear. No punishment comes from those who ought to do it. That is, YOU!'

At this volley, both parents fled in disarray. As they ran headlong down the front path, still pursued by the old woman, John crept from the garage and down the side of the house to watch. The mother, who was the more spirited of the two, turned to respond:

'What a way to speak . . .'

'He ties tin cans to a cat's tail. I did see this. In the back lane punching a girl three years younger at least than he is . . .'

The tirade was inexhaustible.

'You old bag!' The woman screeched, dropping finally the pretence of gentility.

'Would you like to have a tin can tied to your tail, you snotty-nosed snobbish cat? I would like to do it for you.'

They had arrived at the front gate. The father let his wife through with as much gallantry as he could muster in the circumstances. Then turned to the ancient figure who occupied the centre of the path, throwing gobs of abuse and truth at them.

'You will hear from my lawyer about this.'

'That is just what I would expect. You won't leave kids to settle their differences and you haven't the courage to stand up and settle your own.'

'You are offensive.'

'You are stupid. If you don't teach that son of yours manners and discipline, then he's going to end up in gaol, whether you have the lawyer or not.'

They flew. Lina stomped back into the kitchen without a pause, and immediately began to scrub a big aluminium pot.

Kerry was interested in birds and reptiles. He lived down the road, next to Neville, and he was John's friend.

Although John did not share his interest in the anatomical and physical variations of the natural world, he was happy to spend hours as Kerry expounded on the different texture of feathers by which pigeons could be identified. Or John held the bucket as Kerry scooped hundreds of tadpoles from muddy water tanks.

Kerry kept birdcages along the fence. Neville was never brave enough to let the birds out of their cages, as the response would have been terrible and unpredictable. Sometimes, holes were bored into the cage, and buckets were tipped mysteriously onto their sides and tadpoles flipped their last in the red dust.

Kerry also had a set of tin soldiers. They bombed the soldiers with stones, delighting in the collapse of lines of bearskin hats. It was the lack of artillery that stimulated them. Then John noticed two lengths of pipe around his backyard. Close to Guy Fawkes' night, firecrackers were plentiful.

The pipes were tied to a petrol drum beside John's garage, on an afternoon when his parents had gone on a picnic. They had to experiment to get the range right, and there was confusion amongst the neighbours as a barrage of light gravel landed on their roofs. Three times they had to retire while the disorder settled down, and erect the cannon afterwards. Eventually the distant tinkle and rattle of gravel on Neville's roof sent them into a dance of delight. Then they packed the pipe away, for an hour.

When the pipe was set up again, and the match was struck, they would both stare at the enchanting flame, where it was cupped in Kerry's palm, wavering delicately in the breeze.

On Sundays, when John was not involved in artillery exercises and managed to escape from the twin obligations of mixing concrete and Sunday School, he walked off into the bush. He extended the route that he learned from Lina, who was no longer able to walk so far.

He wandered out through the old rubbish tips, past the slope made entirely of broken glass and old cars and petrol drums.

The leftovers glittered in the sunlight before him, luring him for days when he did not have the strength to get there.

Then he went beyond the ridges of broken glass and rusting metal, into the hills, and the spider webs strung between the bushes which were sticky around his legs.

There were old diggings, and the ruins of a few huts.

A hut which was not empty stood in a small cleared patch on the side of a hill. John passed it a few times at a distance and watched the old man who sat on a box in the shade.

Becoming braver, he walked a little nearer when the man waved. John approached cautiously. The man stood and hobbled a few steps. He seemed very old and stooped, and the varicose veins hung in bunched blue knots from the sides of his legs.

'I'm not going to hurt you know,' he said reassuringly as John hovered, still prepared for flight. 'Old Aubrey never hurt no one. I seen you in town, though, I seen you collecting bottles at the pictures, right?'

John nodded. He had already seen the impressive collection of bottles leaning against the wall of the corrugated iron hut. The old man's eyes flickered shrewdly.

'I can tell you how to make a few bob, if you want to know.'

He waited and let John make up his mind. John looked closely at the hut, surveying the greasy hessian bags over the gap that served as a door at one end and the gap that served as a window at the other. The inevitable water tank, heavily rusted and much repaired, rested on a stand of rocks above the slope. Aubrey himself wore shorts below which splendid varicosities bubbled, and an old green shirt with a yellow palm-tree pattern. The fringe of grease was stiff around the band of his hat.

'How is that?'

'I been living here for sixteen years. All that time I lived on what I got for the bottles. I ought to know by now,' he grinned.

When he smiled the gums receded from the two yellow teeth at the top of his mouth.

'They wouldn't give me a pension that I can live on, because I didn't go to the war. They knocked me back. Reckoned I was medically unfit. So now they won't pay me anything, except a few shillings for food. So I collect the bottles.'

'What's so good about that?' John's curiosity finally overcame his caution.

Aubrey leaned back and gazed at the ground, as though wondering whether to give away such important information.

'Well,' he kicked the ground. 'Well, I go to town three times a week. Twice on the days before the Council comes around and collects the garbage and once Saturdays when everybody goes to the pictures and has parties. I get a lot of bottles around then.'

He paused, and checked the impact of his well-chosen words. Then he grandly hobbled to one side and indicated with his palm the bottles stacked against the wall.

'The garbage!' John commented with distaste.

'But . . . in the garbage, people always throw out sauce bottles.'

'Sauce bottles?' This was a remarkable revelation.

Aubrey nodded and glowed.

'Tomato sauce bottles,' he added eagerly, 'there's always a lot of them stacked about. Now the soft-drink factory, they take sauce bottles because they fit into their machines.'

'You make much from that?' John tried desperately to be cynical.

'I live well enough. Just as well my tastes aren't expensive, not like when I was your age. Women and grog. I don't drink and I don't smoke, because my father told me it was the secret of a long and happy life. He died at eighteen of lung cancer, venereal disease and alcohol.'

John went to see Aubrey on weekends often, whenever he could get away. He saved tomato sauce bottles and took them to him wrapped as a gift. Aubrey said it was alright, John could use the trick himself, if he wanted. And John did notice how often square-edged sauce bottles came with soft drink in them after that.

Most of Aubrey's originality was expended on the first day.

After that, John listened to more or less refined methods of acquiring sauce bottles, and plotted with Aubrey to acquire the pension to which Aubrey was entitled for not going to the war.

An old iceless ice chest propped up one wall of the hut. Apart from that, the hut was empty, except for an old iron bed frame resting on kerosene tins and a striped mattress covered with rags. Near the door, a rough fireplace made of stones and a broken grate where Aubrey boiled tea. Everything smelled of grease.

He enjoyed sitting there, and he enjoyed the walk home, across the hills swishing at spiders, timing his trot to be back home before the sun went down.

One afternoon during the week, Diana came to his room and told him an old man was at the gate looking for him. Diana looked disturbed and puzzled. As he went out, he found his father standing in the way.

'Who is that out there?' Austin bellowed.

John peered around his father's waist. Aubrey stood near the fence at the front, with his bag of bottles on his back. He edged back when he heard Austin's voice, so that he was partly hidden by the lemon tree.

'That's Aubrey!' said John.

'I saw him . . . years ago. Comes from a family of them. No-hopers, the lot of them . . .'

'He smells too . . . He wasn't that bad . . . now he's so old . . .' Diana hated smells, but something else struggled with the dismissal.

'How do you know him?' Austin turned on John.

'When I go walking, sometimes, I see him. He lives on the other side of the old garbage tip.'

'You see him.'

'He talks to me sometimes.'

'What do you talk about?'

'Collecting bottles, and things.'

Diana was looking at him with that teary hurt look she got when he had done something which placed him beyond all power of her intervention or commiseration.

'What else do you do? When you talk about bottles. Do you go inside his place?' Austin was puffing with the effort of self-control. He shuddered visibly.

'No,' John lied.

'Go to your room,' Austin exploded, then went off to the kitchen to find the strap.

Diana pushed past and went out the front. She came back as Austin arrived at John's door.

'I told him he wasn't home,' she said tearfully, just loud enough for John to hear.

'We'll find out!' Austin pushed open the door.

'Don't hurt him . . . too much,' cried Diana, who had developed finely the art of keeping a foot in both camps.

Chapter 5

School. He spent hours watching the dust rise and fall in the playground. The line of trees near the football ground, the open-sided lunch shed, the school bell on a post.

His handwriting started badly and became worse. It should not have mattered. Lots of boys could not write at all. John doodled and drew cartoons. One teacher worried. He took the books and wrote in the margins UNSATISFACTORY! EXTREMELY UNTIDY! LACKING CONCENTRATION! The drawings slashed with red lines.

When his parents thrust the books before him, he was not disturbed at the red lines or the comments. They were a part of the work, a legitimate response.

Judgement was inevitable, and the punishment harsh. The heavier the beatings, the greater his need to create images. Fantasy was hard to ban. His parents spent a great deal of time and creative effort discovering his pleasures, then banning them. They punished daydreams.

He sat in the playground during lunch. Pieter, his slow friend with Dutch parents, sat next to him with one leg pulled under his thigh.

'Tell me about the old man who lives at the tip,' Pieter demanded.

Pieter wanted to know all about the old man. Whenever he was asked, John was so taken with his story that he exaggerated. He mimed the old man's walk with an imaginary bag of bottles over his shoulder. He humped his back and dragged his skinny legs with their swollen veins.

Other boys laughed, and asked for more. He added more detail. As interest quickened, he exaggerated more. Fantastic elements entered into Aubrey's character. Aubrey became prone to remarkable violence, and lived in a shed because he could no

40

longer stand the hypocrisy of the adult world. He kept a gun to frighten away, and if necessary assassinate, unwelcome callers.

'You never told me that!' Pieter exclaimed.

'You never listen.'

The sympathy of the crowd was with him. The stories were good.

He acted Aubrey fluently and easily, giving him an accent acquired as a prisoner of war of the Japanese. Stories of staying alive despite terrible torture. Death, for the others, was a merciful end. Only Aubrey survived with the wounds on his back and legs to prove the tale.

The story continued over a series of lunch hours. Someone called out 'bullshit', whereupon John turned on the offender a gibbering imitation of Aubrey's broken body stretched on a rack to the delight of the depraved Japanese and the equally depraved audience.

'Break it up,' a teacher yelled. 'There is to be no, repeat no, gangs hanging around this vicinity while THERE ARE PAPERS TO BE PICKED UP.'

John was effectively banished to the back blocks. There, behind the toilet, he found himself with an audience of one, the faithful Pieter.

On Sunday, he was sitting with Aubrey outside his hut, when he saw three boys on push-bikes not far away. They cruised along slowly without coming too close.

They caught him on the track as he was going home. They circled him on their bikes before they stopped.

'That the old man you was telling us about?'

He stared.

'Doesn't look much to me. I seen him collecting bottles at the pictures on Saturday. He's been doing it for years.'

'He's got to live somehow.'

'He's done the things you said?'

'Why don't you ask him?'

'What about the medals he got from the war?'

41

A boy from behind asked that question.

'Yes.'

'Where?'

'He got them from the Queen. He keeps them in a little box hidden around his hut somewhere.'

'It was the King then,' the other looked shrewdly.

'Alright, but he got them from the Queen.'

'What they got on them?'

'Coloured ribbons and writing and heads. Some of them are star-shaped and some of them are round.' He remembered his uncle's medals.

'The old bastard!'

'Why does he live out there if he's that brave?'

'Because he goes mad at nights,' John replied deliberately. 'Then he wants to kill because he thinks he's back in the war. So he lives by himself.'

One of the boys offered a smoke. Then they rode away.

A week later he went to see Aubrey. As he approached, he could see Aubrey nailing the rusted sheets of corrugated iron to the timber frame of the hut.

'When I was in town this morning, some kids got in here. Pulled the place apart and broke the bottles, and ripped up the mattress.' Aubrey was almost crying.

All the bottles had been tossed into the air and broken. The pieces sprayed down the hill and glittered in the sunlight.

John helped him work for a few hours. The hut had been torn down, but Aubrey had erected the frame before he arrived. The rebuilding did not take long.

'Lookit that.'

Aubrey pointed to the water tank. The water had dribbled away through a row of .22-calibre holes.

John nodded and kept helping, although it was hot. He said as little as possible.

Each year, there was the Silver City Show. Each year, John and Ellen went on Saturday afternoon. The show was at the beginning of summer, in what would be spring, when the winds were still cold enough to penetrate and the dust drifted onto the window-sills in small ripples each day.

They spent the afternoon wandering through the sideshows, rolling rubber balls into the mouths of steel golliwogs, shooting at cut-out ducks with air rifles and carrying armfuls of plaster dogs. They were ordered to stay together, but this tedious arrangement they allowed to break down as soon as possible.

John liked to watch Jockey Hand's boxing tent, as the boxers in the audience stepped forward in the guise of local lads ready to have a go. He liked the assortment of Aboriginals and Irish light heavyweights on the plank in dressing gowns, swinging bells and beating drums. The big Maori at the end of the row with womanish breasts who beat the drum slowly and watched his set up opponents with a blank unaggressive gaze.

'What do you say to that Johnny?' Hand stood diplomatically between the Maori and Johnny. 'What you say you're going to do to the Big Chief here? You reckon you could survive two rounds with the Chief?'

'Punch 'is fat face in,' grunted Johnny without malice.

The audience looked at Johnny closely. The local lad was quite unfamiliar.

'How long can you last, Johnny? Don't get smart, though. Otherwise the Big Chief is going to get mad. He has a bad reputation when he gets mad, the Chief. His father was a cannibal and the Chief says he always wanted to try white man, but he's never known one that's lasted in the ring long enough to get him mad yet. You think he'd be tender enough for you, Chief? Good for the big pot?'

The Chief grinned weakly.

'He'll carve you into steaks and eat you Johnny. Are you still game?'

' 'E can try,' observed the laconic Johnny.

'The Chief is dangerous and he's getting wild. You insulted his race, and he won't stand for it. You've hurt the savage pride.

43

He'll go for blood in there. How long do you think you can hold him off?'

''E can try whatever 'e likes, but I can flatten 'im in two. I'll put 'im through the top of the tent in three.'

'Oh,' Hand crossed himself and gazed to the heavens. 'Is there a priest out there? To give the local fighter Johnny the last rites before he gets into the ring with the Chief of the Cannibal Islands. Are you going to have mercy on this cheeky local lad, Chief?'

'Wipe him like snot,' the Chief added emphasis by giving one short, hard thump on the drum with the furless drumstick.

'You got to admit that he's game, Chief. Give him credit for that and have mercy.'

The Chief gave a weak smile.

Inside the tent the Chief and Johnny went to some trouble not to inflict any damage on one another, despite the flurry of snarling and insult in the last round so that there would be a grudge fight next time.

However there was a genuine local lad around at the time. Not far beyond his prime, Robert Sharkey had held the welterweight crown for New South Wales. His weight had lost it for him, but his reputation and ability were sufficient to strike terror into the hearts of Hand's band. Sharkey wouldn't be set up, and wouldn't fight an exhibition bout for a cut of what he would get if he won.

When he won, he demanded payment, counted out before the audience, who loved it. Hand was enough of a showman to go along with it, all the time whispering an offer.

'It's easy. We go half and half, and nobody gets hurt . . .'

'Another pound. "A pound for a round", that's the deal isn't it? How many rounds did it take?'

'Six,' the audience obliged.

'You knocked him out in four.'

'You want me to carry your broken down fighters for six? They couldn't stand up for that long.'

Hand paid, grudgingly.

Each afternoon, Sharkey methodically destroyed all of Hand's boxers. The only consolation for Hand was the fact that the tent filled each time Sharkey fought.

Until the year John watched the end of Sharkey's career. For several years, John watched as the invincible Sharkey got older, fatter, drank more. Half drunk, he was still a match for Hand's boxers.

John stood to the side of the tent, where he could see the Chief's tiki tattoo on his fleshy bicep.

'Hand! I'm here! I'm ready to push over your pile of pillows again!' Sharkey's familiar voice from behind the crowd.

Hand winced.

'Everybody has seen enough of you, Sharkey. We know what you can do. Let's see if we can have a few real local lads who want to try. Someone who needs a quid.'

'How many mugs have you set up in the crowd this year Hand? Bring them on. I'll beat the lot of them.'

'Over the other side here, looks a likely lad. Who wants to fight Kid Kelly, lightweight champion on his way up from Brooklyn?'

'I beat all of them, Kelly and that mug over there. He was standing on the platform with you last year.'

Sharkey staggered through the crowd. Everybody stepped back to let him through. He had put on more weight since the previous year, and his face was puffy. He was very drunk. His shirt was open and he could hardly stand up.

Hand looked shrewdly and took the chance.

'To those of you who don't know, this is Bob Sharkey, local champion. One of the finest fighters ever produced in Australia. One of the finest men. He is a classy boxer, ladies and gentlemen. He is here today to do battle against my team of boxers. Let's give the great Sharkey a hand . . . applause . . . for the greatest sportsman to come out of the Silver City . . .'

The crowd clapped. Sharkey stepped forward, bearing the mantle of greatness. He recognised instinctively that he was the champion, the offering, the sacrifice.

'Enough bullshit.' He made an attempt to raise his arms.

45

'Right Sharkey. The first bout for today will be against the Chief. Chief . . .'

The Chief said nothing. He looked with his blank, unaggressive gaze at Sharkey and flicked the drumstick against the side of the drum.

'He should fight someone easier first,' called a man in a hat from the front row. 'A warm-up.'

'What do you think about that Sharkey?' Hand chortled. 'Nobody here could deny that Bob Sharkey is a former champion of the state, the finest fighter ever to come out of Broken Hill. Is it fair to put an inexperienced boy against him, when we have the Chief, an experienced fighter and a worthy match?'

'I'll kill the black bastard!' As he spoke Sharkey fell back. The man in the hat caught him. The crowd rippled and giggled.

Sharkey pushed himself to his feet again.

'Wait until you're sober,' advised the man in the hat.

'This is it, ladies and gentlemen!' Hand called out before Sharkey had a chance to become more sober or more drunk. 'The championship of Broken Hill! Your own, very own, local boy and champion Bob "the shark" Sharkey is going to fight the Chief, the cannibal champion of the Coral Islands, the terror of the white slave traders!'

Shuffling and giggling and talking, the customers queued and paid half price to get in. Normally there were three bouts. This time there was only one.

It was a rambling messy fight. It was also the only genuine fight ever in that tent. Sharkey, drunk and wobbling on his feet, was still skilful enough to stave away the blows of the Chief. Relying solely on his greater strength and better condition, the Chief charged forward, accepting Sharkey's stinging, better directed blows. When he was in close he concentrated on the body, beating and flailing, forcing Sharkey to run.

Between rounds, when the Chief flopped in his corner, Sharkey kept trying to fight. He thrashed at Hand when he was pushed back into his corner.

46

Hand stepped easily to one side and smiled. Sharkey had never been patronised like that before.

The audience cheered, although a few were doubtful. In the fourth round, the Chief changed tactics. After a whisper with Hand, the Chief began to back-pedal and defend and invited Sharkey to chase him. Sweat poured from his huge breasts and he heaved at the exertion. Sharkey's trousers hung low on his hips. Each time he charged, the Chief put out a slovenly imitation of a straight left and moved back.

'Come on, white boy. You catch me!' He jeered.

With thirty seconds to go, when it looked as though Sharkey might survive the round, he dropped to his knees and began to vomit. Beer and mucus on the sawdust. He struggled to get up, then doubled and retched again. Hand began the count as the Chief leaned placidly on the ropes, looking at his opponent with slightly more interest than usual.

There were still a few seconds of the round to go when Sharkey stood. He could not raise his guard. His chin tucked in, but he dribbled. The Chief weighed the situation.

'Watch it,' Hand whispered.

Two more punches and a third as he went down. Hand did not bother to count.

As the audience wandered out, chattering and laughing and wondering at the significance of what they had just seen, the man in the hat dragged Sharkey away. One of the little Aboriginals took his legs. John followed. Hand stood near the flaps of the tent, watching and savouring a moment he must have waited for as inevitable.

'They all end like that. Pisspots and no-hopers. They get punchy, then the kids in the street beat them up for fun. He'll be like that in a few years.'

One of the customers said that. The Chief watched impassively from a chair but Hand looked to the ground and kept his feelings to himself.

The crowd was subdued as the man in the hat and the Aboriginal dragged Sharkey past. Then everyone turned and wandered off, into the maze of sideshows and freaks.

The two men carried Sharkey to the shade of the concrete wall and laid him down. The man in the hat nodded, and the Aboriginal boxer turned and trotted back to the tents. The man fanned Sharkey with his hat.

Sharkey's eyes were bruised and bleeding. His broken nose had been turned to the other side of his face. His cheeks were scarred. Booze and spittle still ran from his mouth and trickled across the dirt to the side. The man with the hat didn't seem to mind. His neat fair hair flopped forward as he kept fanning vigorously with the hat.

'What do you want son?' The man pushed back his hair with his free hand and looked up angrily, as though John was interfering.

'Nothing.'

John turned and walked back to the tents.

Chapter 6

He had to go to scripture classes. After some tentative questions, he went along to the Church of England, where the priest had the reputation of being less boring. Although his collar and tie were always neat, they were more natty and stylish than the clothes worn by the dowdy Baptists and Methodists. After a short reading from the Bible, the priest stalked the corridors of the classroom.

He had a mannerism of looking at one boy at a time as he made each of his points.

'Do you know what this means?' He pinned the boy on the other side of the aisle with his eye.

'N-no,' stumbled the boy.

'It means YOU MUST LOVE ONE ANOTHER.'

As he spoke, he turned his luminous theatrical gaze upon John. John looked back at him and smiled. The show was wonderful. He knew what was meant and he wasn't going to fall for it. The man was disconcerted.

'You must,' he drew breath slowly then gave it his best shot, 'LOVE ONE ANOTHER.'

John beamed.

'Do you not agree?'

'I agree,' John swallowed.

'You must love your neighbour as YOURSELF!'

John nodded, letting him know how thoroughly he enjoyed the performance.

'Do you not? Would you not turn the other cheek? Would you, were you done an injustice?'

John noted that he was being forced into explicit hypocrisy. It was as bad as the Baptists and the Catholics and the Methodists.

'What would you do, were you struck by another . . . boy?' The priest intoned, and his gaze probed John's very soul.

'I would hit him back, if I could, sir,' John replied regretfully.

'That is not the Christian way!'

John had observed that many Christians hit back in a most un-Christian way, but he accepted that it was not Christian to say so. The priest turned away. John became painfully aware that he was not a Christian.

'Don't take notice of him, sir,' another boy spoke. 'He'd run if any of us hit him.'

The priest tried unsuccessfully to disapprove. The complexity of his position was too great. The class laughed. The lesson might have gone on, except that time was short. They all murmured the Lord's Prayer.

As they trooped out, the priest motioned John to stay. When they were alone, he looked at John closely.

'Are you Anglican?'

'No.'

'What are you then?'

'My mother says she is a Methodist.'

'That is where you ought to be,' the priest said majestically. 'Please go there.'

Roger had been a presence in the back of school photographs through his primary school days. In high school, he sat quietly near the front and worked diligently. A thin plastic cord ran from his ear into his collar. He had a way of looking at things through his spectacles and down a needle nose. The kind of boy teachers notice at the end of the year, while fellow pupils forgot him entirely.

Roger's adolescence began early. He was in love with one of the polite, demure, boring girls who sat in unseeing rows on the other side of the room. Sometimes, stirred by Roger's interest, John looked across at them.

The object of Roger's affection was small and dark-skinned with short cropped hair and wide dark eyes. During recess, Roger walked around the borders of the boys' playground, longing endlessly, watching greedily the distant groups of females who laughed with the high-pitched giggles that seemed deliberately to excite him with their indifference. They held their bags close to the slopes of their bodies. Every movement suggested duplicity in a desire not to be approached, which John had been perfectly willing to comply with.

'Fay,' Roger spoke the name with reverence. 'Look . . . she has those great eyes that look through you and make you tingle in the stomach, doesn't she?'

Was that the cause of it? John looked closely at the object of the confidence.

'She didn't get skin like that from sucking oranges.'

'It would be . . . to be on a boat . . . with her, alone. Moonlight enough so I could see reflected in her eyes.'

John swallowed. He recognised his secret life in the tone of naked sentimentality.

'I dream of her some nights. I dream of her smiling. The way she raises that eyebrow when she looks. Last night I dreamed about her open shirt collar.'

The tortured erotic details which he did not try to defend. John listened to the shallowness of his breathing.

'Nothing happens, I just want to see her shoulders. I look at them and I wither. I feel like I want to cry. Does she ever go swimming?'

'I'd go for that,' John lied salaciously.

'. . . in a bathing suit sitting on the side of the pool. Against the blue tiles, with her hair wet.'

'Better without the bathing suit,' John desperately tried to mask the awful, the sentimental, truth.

Roger's small short-sighted eyes did not waver, although John was sure there was a widening of the pupils, a flash of interest. Roger deliberated.

'Did you ever make love?'

'What?' It had never been described so gently before.

'Root. Jiggy jig. Ridgey didge. Box.'

John felt momentarily sorry.

'Yes.'

'How?'

51

'She came to see me when nobody was home.'

'How? What was it like?' Roger's lower lip trembled desperately.

'I was in the bath. She came in without knocking, then stood there, waiting for me to get a hard-on.'

'What did you do? What did she do?'

'I asked her to get a towel. She said "no way, you come and give it to me".'

Roger bent slightly, and adjusted his underpants.

John stared across nonchalantly at a group of girls playing hopscotch. Skirts tucked into pants, their long skinny legs. One, two. One leg, other leg. Legs spread, hands down. Pigtails up.

'What was it like?'

It didn't matter that it was all crap. He knew it and he was still hooked.

'Some of them do it better than others. Feels like velvet when you get in there. They wrap their legs around you and move and it's really great.'

Roger groaned.

'It's good if they hold your balls and play with them, and run their mouth around the end.'

He had heard that description from a boy with a brother who drove taxis.

'What do you do?'

'Let them do it.'

'That all you do?'

'Depends.' John was thinking hard.

The girls had finished their game. One brushed down her dress. Another laughed with her back turned as she tied on a hat.

'Oh no,' the girl called at the end of her laugh. 'She can't do that. She'll be caught . . .'

An indistinct mumble carried away on the breeze.

'You mustn't tell, you simply mustn't!'

The combination of tantalising fragments from the girls and tantalising fragments from John confused Roger.

'What does it depend on?' He asked.

'Depends on what you want her to say to her friends.'

Roger was stunned. John looked into the distance.

'See, they talk. If you're pretty good or you've got a big dick, then you're in. The word goes out and they all come around when the oldies are out for the day. So you get into the bath with your horn and you wait for them to come around.'

'How many?'

'A few,' John said modestly.

'That's awful,' one of the girls called across the playground.

Both of them looked around guiltily.

'Get the message across to Fay that you're alright and you're available,' John said with authority.

'I don't believe that.' From the way Roger turned his eyes, he was desperate to believe.

'Alright.'

'I've never seen you with a girl anyway.'

'They don't want to tell everyone about it. They talk to each other. You know what they'd get if the boys found out?'

'What?'

'Guess!'

'A rubbishing, a belting.'

'Six blokes at a time, behind the drive-in, no choice, or someone tells their mother. Six of them in, all at once. Once someone told the mother anyway, so when she got home from the drive-in with her pants wet she got a belting all the same.'

John laughed callously. Another story told by the taxi-driver older brother and pedlar of fantasy. He told it well. He had no doubt of its accuracy.

Roger turned away to hide the bulge in his pants.

'Yes. One on top, one in the back, one in the mouth, two eh—' He had forgotten exactly where two fitted. 'In the armpits . . .'

'What about the tits?'

He knew he hadn't got that right.

'That's the last one. You can't fit two there,' he tried to sound authoritative, as before. 'That's because there's so many around her head already.'

'Fay wouldn't be in that.'

'How well do you know her?'

'Her father works with my father at the Zinc Corporation. Her father says she comes home twenty minutes after school, then goes into her room and she reads books. She goes to basketball on Friday nights and she practises on Wednesday nights. Her father takes her there, then he goes and has a drink while she plays. Then he comes back and picks her up. And her mother.'

John was impressed at Roger's dedication. Each detail, Roger stroked delicately with his lips as he let it free.

'Margaret calls on the phone sometimes but Fay doesn't sit and talk for hours about anything. Her father says she ought to go out more.'

'What sort of books?'

'True Romance.'

'You ought to find an interest in common. You could see her in the street, say as she waits for the bus, and you could talk about it. Raise it casually.'

John got that one from the advice to the lovelorn column in the *New Idea*.

'Sit there with a True Romance comic on my lap, say "hey you read this one, it's great huh?"'

'I know,' John continued piously, 'you can't be expected to share everything. But compatibility does rest on some commonality of interest.'

'Do you read True Romance?'

'It's lucky for you I don't.' Still John privately acknowledged a problem.

'Do you think she might be interested if she knew when my parents were out?'

John saw certain difficulties already in the confusion of art with life.

'I don't know whether I'm game. Besides I don't have a big dick.'

'She probably likes the serious type. Tastes in partners are diverse,' John quoted carefully.

'I could write a letter.'

'Never commit yourself on paper unless you are sure that this person is a correct choice for you as a partner for life.'

Roger looked at John seriously.

'It would only be an enquiry.'

'On paper, then you might find yourself in court charged with breach of promise.'

'I'd marry her,' Roger looked moony again.

'Can you be sure? Aren't you a little—inexperienced? Oughtn't you gain some . . . some . . . experience of the world before settling down?'

The bell went and the conversation got no further.

Back in the classroom, Roger sat at the back of the class, where John was never allowed. A note landed on John's desk from the rear.

> SHE IS BEAUTIFUL AND I LOVE HER. IF SHE WILL HAVE ME WE WILL LEAVE AND GO SOMEPLACE ELSE WHERE WE CAN MAKE A NEW LIFE AND LOVE ONE ANOTHER AND HAVE CHILDREN. WE ARE NOT TOO YOUNG TO KNOW THAT LOVE MAY LAST THOUGH YEARS MAY GO. THERE IS NOTHING MORE IN LIFE FOR ME IF THIS IS REFUSED. DO NOT STOP ME.
>
> ROGER.

John thought deeply. Then he tore a sheet of paper from his book, and wrote:

> YOUR LOVE FOR FAY IS VERY MOVING. BUT YOU HARDLY KNOW ONE ANOTHER. THIS IS NOT THE BASIS FOR A GOOD RELATIONSHIP. LOVE DEVELOPS WITH TIME. SUCCESSFUL CHILDBEARING BECOMES FULFILLING WHEN THE RESULT OF A UNION WHICH IS KNOWN TO BE COMPATIBLE. WHAT WILL YOUR PARENTS THINK? WHAT ABOUT HER PARENTS? DON'T YOU THINK THEIR FEELINGS AND EXPERIENCE AND UNDERSTANDING SHOULD BE TAKEN INTO ACCOUNT?
>
> JOHN.

Then the fat hand of the English teacher descended and lifted the page from the desk. John stared up aghast, as the teacher perused the note. Revenge was sweet. John had left a wad of chewing gum, well chewed, on his seat the day before. The teacher moved his tiny eyes with malevolent triumph from John to Roger, who kept his head down and quivered.

With his best fruity theatrical accent, the fat English teacher read the notes out loud. He paused, with careful and ponderous emphasis, on the central words. His fair wavy hair flopped across his forehead.

Everyone laughed, with the exception of John and Roger— and Fay. From the other side of the room, she gazed at Roger with an expression of loathing and contempt. The girl sitting next to her giggled and whispered in her ear.

Roger never forgave. He refused to discuss anything with John, ever again. When John pointed out reasonably that it had been his advice not to commit anything in writing, Roger's fury increased. The blow had been too harsh.

'I will hate you forever,' said Roger coldly.

Gareth Ham took notice of John at high school. He was tall and strong. He had a slow smile and a way of speaking, respectfully, with a touch of well-bred English, that made teachers defer. His family were squatters. He received good marks although he did not show any outstanding ability in his classwork, and teachers tended to be tolerant of him.

He liked tearing the wings from insects and watching them stumble across his desk. He loved catching smaller boys and twisting their arms behind their backs. John was a victim.

'Does that hurt?' Ham asked.

'No,' John kicked feebly.

'Sign the paper!' Ham giggled. The arm went higher, and the thumb twisted on the skin.

When he got bored, he let John go, after taking John's lunch. Until the day John put dog shit in the vegemite sandwich. John regretted letting some dirt in with the shit. Ham might have eaten it all and never known about it.

Ham became worse. John asked for punishments to stay in to avoid him. Teachers became disturbed. He failed all his examinations.

One of the teachers sent him to a counsellor. The counsellor was an untidy good guy with leather patches on his elbow and a way of saying 'look, I'm a bit like that myself . . .'

John confided. He was a good guy.

'He's a good lad,' the counsellor simpered. 'Just stand up to him a bit.'

Then he looked at the wall. So John learned that he was not the only victim. But the counsellor was a good guy. He tried. So long as it wasn't tough, he tried.

So somewhere, somehow, a teacher suggested very politely to Gareth that perhaps it would be better all around, and hell who cares, he's a wimp but you better go find another victim for a while.

John learned about this during a particularly vicious arm-twisting session.

'You did. I know you did,' in the silky voice of one born to power. 'You are going to hurt for it. Does it hurt? Does it?'

The school counsellor asked later if it was alright now.

'Yes sir, it's alright now sir. Been resolved.' John smiled at the counsellor blankly.

'That's good.' The counsellor was relieved and reassured. 'It's very good that we were able to settle that.'

John nodded and rubbed his arm.

'I believe he's a good sort of chap. You'll probably get to be friends one of these days. When you grow up a bit. Worthwhile, comes from a family. Not that that means anything. He'll finish his education in England, somewhere like Cambridge.'

He was awed.

'I doubt that I'll get to know him that well,' John interrupted his reverie.

'Oh . . . think about it.' Another scratch at the arm rest. 'You don't get them much better, people from the land. Could do worse. I know you don't like sport . . . I'm a bit that way myself . . . but he's not a bad ruckman, I believe.'

The thought of playing football with Ham almost made John retch.

Ham wasn't in the same class as John. At the next early morning assembly, John looked for him. He was easy to see. He loomed above everybody, including most of the boys in the year ahead of him. Ham's eyes were glassy and he turned a lop-sided smile on John and as he walked away, he plodded. These signs meant trouble.

John hid carefully during the breaks. As Ham plodded slowly around, weaving cleverly and doubling back, John circled slowly in the opposite direction. Finally, he sought sanctuary behind the toilets.

The bell was about to go. Cautiously he moved along the side of the building. As John scampered past the toilet door, Gareth loomed on the step above him. Both arms raised, preparatory to bringing them down to crush John's shoulders beneath their weight. The fork of his legs was on a level with John's waist. He slipped his left palm behind Ham's testicles and punched as hard as he could. The small soft balls squashed against his palm. Ham groaned as he doubled up and folded to the ground. As he writhed, John sank a kick hard into his stomach. Ham turned his face up. He was dribbling. John leaned down and drove his fist into his mouth. As Ham screamed and spat out teeth, John began to dance on Ham's body.

A teacher ran up and tried to pull John away. A teacher who had walked past indifferently before. John spat in his face.

Ham hauled himself to his knees. Then he dropped and curled on his side and held his balls.

'I'll have you expelled,' he groaned.

The teacher grabbed John in a lock from behind.

The next time he went to see the counsellor, he looked hard at John.

58

'I heard you had some trouble with Gareth?'

The leather patch rubbed the top of the table.

'Yes sir,' said John brightly. 'A manly disagreement, settled in a manly way. We're good friends now.'

'We have had a complaint from his father.' The counsellor looked disturbed.

'That's a pity. Adults shouldn't get too involved in young people's disputes—not unless they are really serious.'

'I suppose not.' The counsellor looked thoughtfully through his window, out at the boys punching and lunging at one another near the pepper trees.

Chapter 7

He hated change and he was compelled towards it. To minimise change, John was a destroyer of the status quo, a quivering conservative, a revolutionary beating at the present because it was the mask of the past.

An alteration of timetables, a different teacher, the students, all made him afraid. He made a methodical attempt to categorise people, reading characters in their physiognomy.

He observed the types of chins, noses, the breadth of faces. Large noses did not, as existing stereotypes would have, predispose their owners to stinginess. The reverse seemed to be true. Eyes were important. Eyes that held you without a flicker did not indicate their possessor was gazing deep into your soul. Rather, they wished that you weren't there. Ellen's eyes watched him. She had climbed up to him, then climbed beside him. Then she passed him. Rapid dilation indicated attack was imminent. Through fear of being defeated, he turned away.

Kirk Douglas chins did not suggest inner strength but rigidity.

He spent a lot of time scribbling the essential symbolism of faces. He might have invented an occult system of racial types, except that Austin was promoted to shift boss and given night work. Then his grandmother died. Then began his small rebellions.

Austin was at his end of the table. As John came into the house, Ellen gave him a look.

'Your grandmother is sick.' Diana was leaning her back against the sink.

'How?' John did not know what response was expected.

'She has gone to hospital.' Diana spoke with the imprecision reserved for matters of significance.

'What for?'

'She has had a stroke.'

Diana's gaze let John know that curiosity in such matters was an impertinence. John went to his room and sat for a while. Then he walked out again.

'Can I see her?' he dared.

Austin turned on him the transparent emptiness of his eyes. Diana placed a fork quietly on the sink.

'She is not in any condition,' said Diana

He went back to the bedroom and sat. Austin walked into the bedroom next door. John could hear the rattle of the coat-hangers and the swish of coats. He crept out quietly and went again to the kitchen.

The woman from down the road had arrived. She sat in Austin's chair with a sincere concerned look. Diana served her a cup of tea. No one seemed to notice John.

'Happened just after they left,' Diana explained freely to her friend. 'Everybody gone to work and she was collecting the things to put in the old ice safe when I walked behind her to put away the honey. She stood up. Then her legs gave under her. I caught her as she went down, and the honey spilled on the floor.'

'Terrible.' The woman was entranced.

'I let her down to the floor away from the honey. Then I called next door and he called the doctor and he helped me carry her to the room around the side. Especially made to keep her out of the house and she only got to stay there three weeks.' Diana sounded regretful.

'Yes. Remarkable, it is.'

'I think she's gone, you know, Margaret. The doctor said she'd just had the stroke and she couldn't talk by the time he arrived she couldn't say not a word and she kept trying. Her mouth moved around like this but she couldn't get out any words and her eyes stuck out then she had more, strokes that is the doctor said, and they took her to hospital.'

'To hospital. That's sad.'

'It had to happen but it was so quick and she was out the front yesterday pulling up the weeds as long as I've known her she never had a sick day a day in bed, not a one.'

61

'Not a one.'

'And now . . . the hospital.' Both women shuddered.

'It happens to all of us,' Margaret consoled, or so it seemed.

'But so quick, my mother had pain and she suffered for years she died in little bits slowly with her eyes bad then her legs aching then after all the little things the angina and her chest she wheezed so much even when she sat down then the stroke she held on for longer then the next angina and the next stroke then something else . . . but the only thing wrong . . . with *her* was the diabetes, that scratching!'

'It must have been terrible,' murmured Margaret.

'She loved sugar she never stopped although the doctor told her. She still made rich cakes. German cooking.' The traces of resentment in her voice.

'Lovely cakes they were.' Margaret looked discreetly at the table, reminding Diana gently of the occasion.

'All weekend she was in the kitchen.'

'Slaved all her life . . . a real battler!' Margaret politely agreed.

'Austin's father died young he was a strong man a good fighter now why do you think a healthy young man would die that young.?'

'The time comes to all of us,' Margaret took refuge in a sip of white tea. 'When you've got to go.'

When Austin walked in dressed in his brown suit Margaret looked up with some relief. She whistled.

'That's a nice suit, handsome,' she laughed.

Austin looked around the room with eyes more pallid than usual, the whiteness clear and glowing.

'We've got to go,' he said shortly to no one.

'I want to say how sorry I am,' Margaret stated with dignity as she stood. 'She was . . . is . . . a great woman, a great woman.'

Austin stared at her, as though not understanding her words. She touched his cheek with her lips as she went out.

'Any time you need help, Austin,' she said.

Diana glared as she followed Margaret to the door. John heard her say 'yes' in a voice a trifle too loud, then the wire door squeaked shut. Diana came back into the room. She stared thoughtfully at Austin, who was red but seemed to notice nothing.

'That was funny,' Diana mumbled reflectively to John.

John nodded.

'We've got to go,' Austin repeated.

'Soon as I get my gloves.' Diana moved off to the front bedroom.

'You've got to stay,' Austin spoke seriously and haltingly. 'To look after the house while we go to see your grandmother.'

'I want to go too.' Ellen, who had been sitting unnoticed, suddenly began to wail, giving expression to all the grief which was sensed, unexpressed.

She was still wailing when Diana returned, pulling the gloves straight on her fingers.

'They want to go.' Austin was helpless before the barrage of what he could suffer but not release. 'We should take them. She might be happy to see them.'

'We can't, not while she's in that condition,' Diana said sharply.

'I want to go,' John spoke from the shadow directly to his mother, who was startled, as though a mirror had given voice.

They went to the hospital. John stood at the end of the bed, leaning on the aluminium bed end, staring at Lina as she lolled and stared and moved her vacant mouth. Her eyes watched him through the slack facial muscles, attempting to talk, to mumble, to be human.

When Austin worked on night shifts, the number and intensity of arbitrary beatings accelerated. Crockery and cutlery flew without warning. His inability to grieve, the emptiness afire.

As long as the beatings were confined to the kitchen, Diana did not mind too much. It was easy to clean up the mess on the new plastic tiles. While John was entering puberty he was the main object of Austin's frustrations, but not the only one. Ellen often dived under the table to avoid a punch or a plate. John went through the glass door into the lounge. The glass went over the new blue carpet, which had been there for four years. Plastic strips ran like duckboards across the gaping floral trenches.

After the glass door broke, the carpet was embedded with splinters of glass. Diana took hours cleaning it up. Then the plastic strips were taken away.

John did not fight back, until a Saturday morning, when he was in the shower. He loved the new gas heater and the green enamelled tub and the red-painted concrete floor. He wallowed under the shower. There were no more droughts since a pipeline had been built from the Darling River. Through the small window above the shower he could see the top of the old rainwater tank being encircled by grapevine. Muscatel grapes, nice and sweet. Further around were green grapes, draped along the small concrete room that had been built for Lina.

As he wallowed Austin shuffled outside and knocked on the door.

'Alright, I'm coming,' he called.

He loved being under that spray of water. After a minute, another, more urgent, beat on the door.

'OK,' he called.

He turned off the shower and began to climb out. He had enough time to get his feet on the red concrete floor when the punches began to land.

He knew enough to duck and weave. It was harder for Austin to connect. In order to come under John's guard, he left his chin open. The expression when John speared a straight left onto the chin was a joy he never forgot. Not that the punch hurt much. It was the fact that he hit back. Despite Austin's strength he was surprised. He didn't throw all his strength into the punches after the first flurry. He cooled off. By then, John was just beginning to warm up.

He was doing well, connecting and flailing, when Diana pushed into the bathroom and ran screaming between them.

'This is not happening in my house!'

She had never screamed that way before. Austin dropped his hands and looked sheepish and guilty. John paused, then understood. It was a new weapon.

After the incident, he began to fight Austin. Diana could not favour more than one at a time. Austin needed her. John became indifferent.

He began to dream about Hansel and Gretel. He walked with Ellen into a tunnel. The tunnel was dark. After every few steps, they found themselves in an alcove glowing with light. Behind glass, to the side, was a scene from the play. The children lost in the woods, the wicked witch in black who mechanically moved her arms and looked out at them sideways with a smile as she thrust her hand into the oven to feel the plump little children.

John and Ellen wanted to run, but there was no way back. The scenes behind the glass were compelling. They walked on, past scene after scene. A voice called from above one of the alcoves.

'Are you plump enough yet, my little children? Come forward and let me touch. I love plump little children!'

Behind the glass, Gretel thrust the thin piece of stick forward to be fondled by the old woman's thin fingers.

'Not fat enough yet, my darlings,' came the voice from above. 'You must eat more. Eat well my children!'

The tick bit into his ear. Diana walked him around to the doctor that night, to have it removed.

'There,' said the doctor triumphantly as he held up the stainless steel tweezers with the tick impaled. 'You see it.'

He thrust the beetle toward the end of John's nose. John rubbed the numbness around his ear, then reached for the tweezers. He would taste the tick if he could, and the stainless steel as well. The doctor withdrew them.

'Uh-huh. That's not for you to play with. It might get into you again.'

For an insect to burrow through his skin and wade along his blood, on a pilgrimage to investigate and consume the mysterious organs that were inside! He found the thought intriguing, sensuous, almost delightful. He thought about it at unexpected times later on.

65

PART TWO

PART TWO

Chapter 1

Whether it was after the death of his grandmother, or when he had itching powder poured down his back, or was punished for flinging a sausage and having to eat a plateful of them. Was it at one of the times when Gareth Ham twisted his arm behind his back with a smile as teachers sauntered past, or was it love of his father? What of loathing as he manipulated his mother? Or the constant hypersensitive precious sense of difference, the faces of the men at the rifle club with their rifles across their knees? A teacher's broken glasses, bandages on eyes or knees, no friends or friends who weren't good enough and could never be good enough? Already the corrosion of failure, being locked into a losing duel with his sister which never stopped, not for forty years, a passive fate, and never being able to do anything actively to improve it as he, his existence, was the cause?

Incomprehensible mathematics and untidy writing while his fingers never able to grip a pen felt big and thick except for drawing which was graffiti on the only wall in a span of time and space without distinction or differentiation or colour or joy or dirt. Between snobbery the attraction to dirty stupid boys the inferiority of being unable decently to catch cleanly. Between the desire to taste and the metallic reality, an idiot girl squatting to piss in the road in the dust and the weeping English teacher who came to mark he hit her with a spitball. The wet Anzac Day when a man with a chest full of medals said to his father 'Where's your medals, Aussie?' The startled stubborn look on Austin's face and the man not laughing nicely. Aubrey whining endlessly about sauce bottles and the pension his corrugated iron hut strewn around him. Sharkey flat on the ground with a trickle of blood from his nose smelling of booze the man in the hat leaning over him 'they all belong to mandrake champions and all' sung by Pablo a small dark boy to polite applause the dark

69

Ho Ho of the men at the back. A china dog from the silver city show with a broken nose. A rock in the back from a hedge, his sister flailing with her fists, Ham folding onto the ground outside the toilets, a dead parrot on the bank of the river the skull and crossbones on a pirate hat, the blind man sitting in the corner as John pulled the sheets over his head and breathed his own warm heat. The shovel turning the earth. The trees he hid behind and took off his clothes he was curious he wanted to look until his mother caught him and hounded him back to the house 'put your clothes on you dirty little boy . . .' The trees at the front in the garden, which he felt rub against him, the trees heavy with mulberries and lemons and quinces, the vines twisted on trellises of pipe with bunches of green and black grapes. Austin spraying and pumping and fertilising the garden. Hickey hockey one hickey hockey two the goldfish strewn the chooks gone the fowlhouse was empty there was a dog outside the cot the broken glass mountains glowing in the sun.

On Friday nights, when he walked home from the YMCA, he stole from cars. People left cars unlocked. He went through their glove boxes, their steel vaginas. He didn't like to boast, but once he did. As a result he gained an accomplice.

John didn't want company. He should not have boasted. Mark was flamboyant, and he loved to boast. He strutted behind John, whenever possible smoking a cork-tipped cigarette, and pushing his straight brown hair over to the side. John recalled that he had always been there, unnoticed, in the class photos. John accepted a cigarette. He prefered to indulge his vices alone, and the smoke made him cough.

People parked their cars in the lanes and streets not far from the three theatres near the town centre.

'Pick the ones that haven't been locked.' Mark huffed out a smear of smoke along the edge of the sharp cone from the streetlamp.

'Saves time. There's no noise that way.'

They spoke tersely and melodramatically.

There were no lights in the lane. John hesitated, at the border of a criminal career.

'We've got to see who's around.' Mark waited.

John walked the length of the lane, casually trying the locks of cars, checking the small windows were clipped shut. The door on a big American car opened. He checked that there was no one around, and slipped in behind the wheel.

He felt lost, alone in the huge plush interior of the car. His fingers thrilled as he ran them around the smooth bumps at the back of the wheel. The leather seats gave easily beneath him, and he sank into a much larger shape. He looked out at Mark, whose round regular features stared in at him through the rear window.

'What are you doing?' Mark whispered through the door, which was not quite shut.

John clicked the door behind him and leaned across the wide seat. The glove box opened easily. John scraped out and pocketed a set of women's gloves, a pair of sunglasses, a packet of cigarettes and a box of matches. He left the heavy woollen pullover on the back seat.

'Did you get much?' Mark half straightened as John climbed from the car.

'Not much.'

They worked along the lane, accumulating cigarettes lighters pens and sunglasses. There was a purse under a seat. John stuffed a bundle of notes into his pocket then closed the purse and pushed it back neatly under the seat.

'Let's go,' he whispered to Mark, who hunched between two nearby cars.

As Mark straightened up, a pair of sunglasses rattled on the road.

'Leave it.'

Resisting the impulse to run, they walked from the lane out into the street near the town centre. The peculiar pleasure in being able to resist panic. Cars cruised slowly past them, women ran their gaze indifferently over them, the half-interested question

71

'what are they . . . ?' drifting into the darkness to recede with the rear lights along Oxide Street. Mark was still carrying an armful of sunglasses and cigarettes.

John looked across thoughtfully.

'Where do I put them?' Mark asked.

It was a good question. They kept walking and Mark kept clutching the sunglasses and the cigarettes. Finally they went through them in a corner of the park. They dumped the lot, except for the cigarettes and one pair of sunglasses which Mark liked, even though they might be recognised.

In a milkbar near the Ozone theatre they sat on white chairs at a white table and sipped milkshakes.

'How long you been doing this?' Mark managed to speak while drawing back a solid piece of ice cream through the straw.

'Not long.' John twirled his straw through a streak of chocolate and kept his poker face.

'You're pretty good.'

John looked down to cover the flush spreading across his cheeks. They turned their straws around the far corners of the milkshake glasses, sucking loudly. John paid with a used note which felt strange and pleasant in his hand. The girl behind the counter rang up the till without a glance and handed him back some silver, then she went on polishing the patterned glass along the wall.

John gave Mark half the money as they reached the corner where he would go one way and Mark went the other. Mark stared. He did not know that John had the money. John finally understood why Robin Hood might have robbed the rich and given to the poor.

'See you Monday!' Mark called as he wandered into the distance reluctantly.

Austin was happy that weekend. He pottered in the garden and spread manure around the rose bushes and clipped the dry grapevine, and sat at the dinner table silently and placidly chewing his food.

72

Austin and Diana were becoming friendly with the Bignalls. On Saturday night they went dancing together, while John and Ellen stayed home. George Bignall stood around in the kitchen while Eva and Diana talked loudly and laughed and joked. Eva was small and slight and dark, with a pretty way of turning her eyes around and a voice like a truck straining up hill.

John was in bed late. He heard the car brake at the front gate. He worried at first that it might be the police. The money he had stolen was hidden in a screw-top jar under the house. He had rehearsed in his mind what he was going to say. 'Where were you last night?' 'I walked home.' 'Who were you with?' 'For me to know and you to find out.' He imagined the policeman leaning forward, his huge hairy fist trembling on the table. 'We know what you have been doing! You have been stealing— cheating. We know about you. You are the one who cheats.'

He was still rehearsing in his mind when the wire door squealed and a light switch turned in the kitchen. Whispers. Disconcerting. He strained. There was a woman. He could not hear Diana's voice. Adults, shifting about their large cumbersome bodies.

The light went on in the lounge. The springs of the chair creaked under the weight of bodies. Whispers. There was a silence, then a body raised from the chair. Austin peered into John's room. John was sitting up, prepared for interrogation.

'He's awake,' Austin whispered in the direction of the lounge.

Austin stepped away. John could tell that he was checking Ellen's bedroom. Then the floorboards creaked again, and he moved into the main bedroom at the front. He was still there when Eva Bignall came to John's bedroom.

She paused after a few paces and looked around. The room was large and dark.

'Where are you?'

She groped around tentatively with an arm in front, and touched the end of the bed before he could think of what to say. Then she felt her way along the bed until she touched his shoulder.

'John . . . John,' she settled on the side of the bed and blinked until her eyes adjusted to the light.

73

'Hello John.' He sensed her smile in the shadow. He nodded, to fill the pause.

'Ah John.' Her voice sounded softer and sad and it gave him goose bumps because it was meant to be nice and he was afraid. Another long pause, full of sighs.

'Do you like me John?' She masked the question with a light giggle.

It would have been easier if it was the police. The question of liking or not liking his parents' friends had never occurred to him. They were there.

'Don't worry,' she giggled again. 'You don't have to answer that yet. You know I like you. You're quite a clever boy, aren't you? You keep things to yourself like your father.'

He wondered whether it was true. He sensed that what she was saying was too complicated for him and he wished that she would go away. Then Austin came to the doorway again and stood with his incurious, perplexed look.

'I better drive you home Eva.'

Eva looked back at him, but showed no intention of moving at first. John sensed that she was irritated. He was glad it was dark. He felt her trying to convey something across the darkness. She reached across and touched his hand.

'Good night, sleep tight.'

As they walked through the kitchen John could hear her voice. When they left the house the lights were left on. John got up and turned them off.

He stayed awake until Austin came home, this time with Diana. He was tormented through the night with images of Eva Bignall.

After a few Friday nights Mark and John had become sophisticated in their tastes. They had enough sunglasses to last them indefinitely. Cigarettes were never refused, and lighters were good to give away for small considerations at school.

Mark liked guns. Bushmen came into town to watch movies, and their cars were usually not locked. The guns were left under the seat. John was happy to sell the guns to Mark. Except once.

A short stubby .22 revolver, the sort of gun used in detective stories. So he kept it, despite desperate offers from Mark.

The gun disappeared from the hiding place. A little-used part of the garage, beneath the copper Diana did not use any longer since she had acquired a new Pope washing machine. Mark denied that he stole it. John determined never to tell him anything after that.

With their new riches they began to take days away from school. They took their pushbikes and rifles to the nine-mile dam and spent their time shooting at crows and beer bottles.

It was a warm winter day. John took off his pullover and left his shirt open. The light was clear, a few small stumpy trees had grown around the horizon since all trees had been cleared by the miners and the company in the early years. Not far away, the new regeneration area around the town sprouted bushes and grass. The circle of bush had kept down the dust storms. Rangers looked after the dams and the regeneration area, but the boys had never seen one. The road leading in to the dam curved around a low hill. No one else had ever gone there. They didn't hear the motor as it approached.

It was too late to hide. The ranger stepped out of his old car, a tall man with a broad-brimmed hat and a gut.

'Alright boys,' he grunted in a tone that was half bored and half menacing. 'What do you think you're doing here?'

John leaned sideways and tried to appear casual.

'Picnic,' he answered.

The ranger sighed.

'Under the local ordinances, no one is allowed here without permission. I am empowered from the Department of Lands. It is specifically against the law to use guns on this property. What is more, I doubt that you are old enough to officially use a gun.'

'There is no sign,' John protested.

'We'll see what the magistrate says about that. Prosecution. Gaol is where you're going to end up, if not now then some time in the not distant future. Name and address, please.'

75

'Frank Parker.' John thought for an address. 'Thirty-three Wolfram.'

'Yours?' He turned to Mark.

'George Simpson, from Adelaide. I'm staying with him.'

Mark was very pale.

As they pedalled away from the dam, leaving the ranger in possession, Mark twisted around on his seat.

'The bastard is bullshit.' Mark was still white. 'Let's circle and go up the hill.'

They wheeled their bikes up the rough steep hill. At the top in the middle of the scattered and rusting machinery, there was an old water tank turned on its side. They squirmed inside and watched through the bullet holes as the ranger moved in circles away from his car to collect wood.

He was a long way from his car when Mark began to shoot.

'What if he has a radio?' John asked as the second bullet punctured the car door.

'He hasn't. I noticed.'

Mark giggled as he worked the bolt on his repeating rifle. Slowly and methodically with his single shot rifle, John began to shoot at the wheels and tyres of the car.

It was a while before the ranger worked out what was happening. He stared around at first. When he saw one of his car tyres gradually sinking, he dropped the armful of sticks onto the ground and began to run back to the car. When he was close enough to detect the bullets hitting the car, he paused again. He skipped from one foot to the other, then slid to one side and disappeared behind a small mound of earth.

'He's scared,' Mark laughed. He fired a round which ricocheted from the mound, throwing up a puff of dust.

During the next week, they went to school and quietly waited for retribution. Nothing happened. They did not go near the nine-mile dam again, and together they discussed the possibility that it was only for small crimes that retribution was inevitable. The greater the outrage, the greater was the immunity.

76

Experimenting with the sense of tension, John went out more alone. Austin and Diana sat around playing cards with the Bignalls, and as he went out they waved genially.

'What does he go out for?' he heard Eva Bignall ask once as he pushed through the wire door.

'He's a funny sort of boy,' Diana said. 'He likes to walk out alone.'

'Do you think he has a girl?' Eva laughed.

'It's your turn to deal,' interrupted George. 'I'll have Diana for a partner.'

'Again!' Eva complained. 'That's cheating. You know how good she is.'

John could hear the laughter as he moved out through the back gate into the dark, unlit lane.

He wandered around the town, along the laneways looking through the kitchen windows and at the garages and broken-down cars on blocks. He avoided the dogs and went through the glove boxes of the cars parked near the theatres.

He tried to find significance in the meanest things. A family sitting around a laminex table listening to a radio, the father drinking a glass of beer, the refrigerator left open so that he could see in their lives the contents of their stomachs. The stacked racks of cheese, sausages, chops, rabbits laid out on a rack, potatoes and cauliflower bulging in the bottom. There was a secret from which he was excluded. He strained to hear. The talk was about the mines and the football. The woman gossiped to her teenage daughter about dresses and recipes. This was not it. There was something hidden, something he did not understand, something others took for granted.

He eavesdropped on a minor infidelity in the back seat of a car in a lane. He stepped delicately across two naked entwined bodies in a grove in Sturt Park near the monument to the band of the *Titanic*. When he saw where he was about to put his foot he paused and apologised, before moving off. He was carefully noting the position of the broken column for future reference when a man's voice spoke angrily behind him.

77

'What's he doing around here?'

'I don't know it's only a kid. He doesn't . . .' the woman nagged him back to the job.

Chapter 2

When he left school his parents said they were very disappointed.

'We know you can do better,' Diana wept from her side of the table.

'Why aren't you like other boys?' She declaimed. 'Going out, playing sports, improving yourself?'

John quivered. He *could* not go back.

'You don't have any certificate, no qualification to get a job or anything. I used to think the worst thing would be for you to go down the mines but now I think it might be the best, you're not doing anything for yourself and I don't know how you're going to end!' As she spoke, she waved her hand so Austin stayed in his seat and didn't try to defend or revenge.

He was tight as a spring pushed down. That day, he knew when he saw the teacher walking towards him that he had to go. There was no good in the place for him, and he wanted to kill. The teacher was close, reaching out with his short stubby arms, his grey suit coat flapping open, the shirt cuff drawing back over his wrist. I have you, the teacher's expression said, you can't get away now, you can't win. He was right. There was a window, a long window. It was a short step sideways. He threw his bag over and slid down the wall.

The teacher's voice bellowed behind him as he ran. A dry breeze flowed down the passage. He breathed it. He wanted to run, he wanted to be free, it was enough to breathe. Now, in his parents' kitchen, he could feel the constriction in his throat.

'I'm not going back!'

'The holiday's in a week's time,' his mother stated finally. 'After that, you can go get a job.'

He had accepted reality, but it sounded awful.

Melancholy holidays. He was leaving behind all youth, joy, delight. Life thereafter was to be drudgery. When a job was found, he must be subservient. Disrespect would not be tolerated by an employer. His teachers had to put up with it, at least until he was expelled, or left under such dubious circumstances.

Employers could fire. He would be flushed down whatever sewer society used to flush the failed to oblivion. The loathing and quivering continued and intensified. He tried to swallow it.

Ellen was to continue at school. She strove to be normal, to learn, to behave. His failure was her opportunity.

In the Seventh Day Adventist woman's flat where they stayed for the holiday, Ellen watched with serious, severe and judgemental eyes.

She was not going to get caught kicking back, not then. It was her chance for gold, and she was going for it.

He wandered from the flat to museums. He liked being among bones and artillery and old uniforms. Like being under the stand when his mother played tennis, or under the floorboards of the school. Dust, isolation, bars of yellow light. On that holiday, he squandered what was left of his boyhood on dusty atmospheres. So he swam frantically lap after lap in the pool, and dived into the waves on the surf beach. Instead of wandering along the headlands alone, he hired dodgem cars at the fun park and desperately tried to ram others and run them into the gutters.

He went to the aquarium and censored the thoughts of the sharks as they nuzzled against the glass.

He went to the beach, but with his parents, and tried to enjoy it as they hired fast motor boats. He sat in the back as water sprayed out to the sides and the boat curved gracefully on its side.

He persisted, pathetically seeking his parents' approval. He learned again the truth: it did not matter what he did, his parents did not—could not—like him. He was not a passive receptacle for their desires, so they disapproved. If he was, they despised him. The more he tried, the greater was the sense of inward death. Panic. He was losing time . . . on what?

They might have respected a hardness greater than their own. They could comprehend infatuation with money. They wished himself, or themselves, not to exist. They could respond to fear or disapproval, and not much else.

He was sitting on the seat near the beach looking over at the fun parlour when the girl sat beside him. A very ordinary, pretty girl, with shortish fair hair and serious intelligent eyes.

'Where do you come from?' She asked directly, as she might have spoken to a child.

He told her, stammering slightly.

'Do you study? Are you still at school?'

'I'm leaving next . . . this year. I'm going to get a job.'

'Leaving school early.'

He nodded miserably. She had gone straight to the core of failure. He felt sullen and bitter.

'What do you intend to do?'

'I don't know what I'll be doing yet.'

'My brother works in a garage pouring petrol. He's a bit older than you. It's a part-time job, while he studies.'

He felt childish and ignorant.

'What do you do?' He had sense enough to ask.

'I finished third year this year,' she spoke with her cultivated drawl. 'My parents want me to go to university, but I want to be a singer or an actress.'

To take such things for granted. He was terrified.

'Did you learn?'

'Ballet. Not what I have in mind. Something modern and popular, not so boring.'

She laughed. He decided not to mention his ability with the foxtrot. There was a silence.

'You might be interested in politics?'

He nodded, cautiously.

81

'I think it's awful what the Russians did in Hungary. Just because the Hungarians didn't want them there.'

'Tanks,' John said, because it was all he knew about Hungary.

'Yes, it's awful.' She waited for him to say something.

'Yes, it's bad.'

'Communists hate Catholics,' she said.

'Are you a Catholic?' He looked at her throat to see whether she wore a crucifix.

'Sort of. I don't go to a Catholic school though.'

He wanted to ask why communists hated Catholics, but he didn't dare.

'Should Anthony Eden have resigned, do you think?'

'He didn't win, did he?' John observed gloomily that Eden's political career had finished at the same time as his educational career.

'So has the British Empire,' she said gaily.

When she laughed, she opened her mouth wide and he could see the back of her throat.

'I'm Kate.' She stood and touched his arm. Her touch was warm. 'I'd better go home or they'll worry.'

She stood. He stood also. She showed a bright clean set of teeth.

'They worry because I talk to people down here. They think I will get myself in trouble. Or something. Christ, they worry.'

'Where do you live?'

She pointed to a street leading away from the beach.

'The third house down.'

'No, but where do you come from?'

'The third house down.'

'I . . .'

'Thought people only come here for holidays.'

She laughed then turned and walked away. The way her clothes moved around her graceful and enchanting.

Each remaining day, he went to the same seat and sat. He walked past the third house along and watched for a flicker.

Once the curtains did move, and he hurried away feeling confused and ashamed.

The dreams and nocturnal emissions aggravated him with their pleasure, when he woke thinking of her. It was not her body that he wanted to want, mostly. He ached for that quality that could take for granted education, sophistication, choice. It was imbued with magic and it shook the air around her as she walked.

Chapter 3

In Broken Hill it should not have been hard to find a job, except for his habit of shuffling in interviews and grinning. Employers sensed that something was not quite right. It took him two months before Ken Tighe hired him. There was no one in the panel beater's workshop when John walked in. Cars parked at all angles, the smell of paint thinners, tools stacked neatly in boxes on a greasy workbench. He waited.

After forty minutes no one appeared. He walked to the back, and looked through the maze of car parts. Bumper-bars glistening chrome, mudguards and doors bent and twisted stacked in the corner, a black turret of tyres against a wall.

'What do you want?'

He had to look hard until he found the likely source of the voice. A pair of sandshoes underneath a car. John approached timorously.

'A job,' he kneeled and looked.

A spanner turned on a rusted bolt. The man in the sandshoes grunted.

'Come tomorrow.'

'When?'

'Seven o'clock.'

John waited. When nothing more was said, he stood, then walked away.

The following morning he was five minutes early. The doors were shut. At ten past seven, a young man drove up in an old car, and ambled to the door jangling a set of keys. John stepped forward, feeling the overalls Austin had brought back from the mines pull up tight under his crotch.

'I'm not Ken,' the young man said as he turned the key. A chain dropped to the side of the door. 'I'm passing through. Ken hired me for a month, that's all. Give me a hand with this. He told me you might be here.'

John helped push the wide corrugated iron door across on its rollers. Once the door was open, the young man looked at him thoughtfully.

'Never worked before? Know much about cars?' Then, without waiting for an answer he turned away.

'Tighe is a good panel beater, except that I don't think he could teach anybody anything,' he said to an old Chevrolet at the other end of the shed.

Then he began by showing John what to do. Each lesson was short, and the young man was concise and clear with his instructions. Then he went off to do his own work. He checked each job at the finish, and told him what was wrong. Everything seemed so simple when he explained it.

For the next few days, they were on their own most of the time. Ken Tighe appeared only for an hour in the afternoons. He was short and heavily built, with a dirty red moustache.

He asked Robbie what was happening, made a few phone calls, checked a few jobs, then disappeared.

Robbie talked to him during the breaks when they swallowed thick black tea and sandwiches and sat on old car doors in the sun.

'When I leave here I go back to Brisbane. There's a girl. I done my share of travelling, so I'm going to get married.'

John looked and waited.

'When I go, you better put your arse up and your head down. Work, nothing but work.'

He took a bite of the thick corned beef sandwich and swallowed it without chewing.

'Don't give him a chance.'

After two weeks, Robbie collected his money and went. He almost asked John to go and have a drink, but remembered he was too young. He touched John on the shoulder before he went, and said see you later. Then he went in his old car, down the street and away.

The next day, Tighe had opened the shop when John arrived. He told John to take the door off one car, the mudguard from another, and to sandpaper a small English car for a repaint. Then he disappeared.

By lunchtime the door was off, as was the mudguard, except for a couple of bolts that had rusted on. John was sandpapering the English car when Tighe arrived, and glared around the shed.

'Place is a shithouse,' he commented angrily.

'The door is off.' John did not stop rubbing with the sandpaper.

'Bad,' Tighe commented. 'Bad.'

He picked up the door by the handle and inspected it. Then he swung it around easily and tossed it. The door curled through the air and landed flat in the dust outside.

John thought of what his parents said, and swallowed.

'You think that car . . . has been done?'

'I took the door off.' It was hard to get the words out.

Tighe stepped across and pushed his face in close. His breath stank of beer. John rested the sandpaper on a mudguard. Tighe wiped it off with a sweep of his hand. Putty-pink water sprayed across the floor.

'Lousy,' he said. Or was it lazy?

He waited. John said nothing.

'What you think you were doing?' He belched in the centre of the sentence.

'What you asked. Sandpapering this car.'

'Don't answer me back. How long you been doing this?'

'An hour, about.'

The stink of beer burned John's cheek. Tighe's thick hand rested on the mudguard, beside a spider of cracked and blistered paint. A tiny volcano of bare steel pushed through the duco. John tingled. He stopped himself from hitting Tighe's broad face.

'Two hours?'

John looked out at the door resting in the dirt.

'Two hours,' Tighe screamed, 'and all you did was took off a few bolts!'

'The bolts on the mudguard are rusted on,' a voice inside John screamed. Nothing came out.

'What have you done all morning?'

Nothing. The voice was silent. The silence of his parents.

'What have you been doing all morning?'

Tighe had not cleaned his teeth.

'All morning you've done . . . maybe . . . twenty minutes' work. I could do it in ten minutes. I'll be fair. Twenty minutes. I'm supposed to pay you for the time you spent here?'

John distracted himself by looking away. At the front, the twisted car door glistened in the sun.

'Time you spent doing nothing but drink tea and sit out in the sun . . .'

John swallowed the glob of phlegm that rose in his throat. Another blast of boozy breath washed over him.

'You couldn't work in an iron lung, son.'

He resisted the impulse to grovel and continued to look at the car door. Tighe bored in with his eyes. Small pig eyes, blue eyes, in a chubby freckled face. A drop of spittle hung from the end of his moustache.

'There's nothing I want more than to see an honest lad get on . . . I believe that youth should have the chance to work and improve themselves.'

John did not raise his hopes.

'I don't believe that you want to work. I have watched you closely for several days now.'

'Where did you watch from?' The voice laughed inside John's chest.

'The only conclusion that I can come to—that I have come to—is that you do not work, are not willing to work, and never will work. You, son, are a hopeless bludger.'

The hand on the mudguard closed into a fist. John turned and looked at him calmly. Tighe's face was red, then white. The trick hadn't worked. He shoved the fist down into his pocket and pulled out a handful of banknotes.

He counted out a few banknotes onto the mudguard.

87

'I'm going to pay you—up to now. You come back next week and work out your notice.'

John walked to the bicycle, resting against a pile of bent bumper bars and grilles and headlight surrounds.

'You haven't got any guts!' Tighe's outraged voice nagged on behind him.

John climbed onto his bike before he turned and looked back. Incuriously he observed the red faced furious man.

'I've paid you for this afternoon. You haven't finished yet. You haven't finished until you've rubbed the putty on that car.'

He pointed to the small English car swathed in stripes of pink putty. John was about to push off when Tighe's fist closed around the bar. John's guts sank.

'Get off,' Tighe said.

John climbed off the bike, then stood unmoving. Tighe pressed his face closer, and again John breathed in the sickening smell of booze. Tighe's chest was enormous and deep.

'If he hits you, bite his balls as you go down,' the voice suggested clearly inside his head. He almost swooned at the thought. He noticed pressure on one of the press-studs of the overalls, the excitation before conflict.

He stepped off the bike. Tighe wrenched it away from him and wheeled it out to the back. John walked back to the bucket and the sandpaper on the floor. Tighe was behind him. When John turned to look, he grinned.

For the next two hours he rubbed the putty on the car. There was grim consolation in rubbing again and again, erasing the ribs of pink putty, watching the lines of pink sandy water run over the metal onto the floor. His shoes became wet and the water worked through his socks.

Eventually Tighe wandered past with the pushbike, squeaking across the concrete. John looked up to see the bike rolled against the fence with its handlebars turned.

'Get out!' Tighe said contemptuously. He turned and walked to the rear of the shop.

John let the sandpaper slide into the bucket. It floated unevenly on the pink water. He walked across to the pushbike and pedalled away.

His father was on night shift. Both parents sat around the table waiting when he arrived home.

'How was work dear?' Diana chuckled without looking.

'I'm finished,' he said.

They both looked up at him.

'What did you do?' asked Diana significantly.

'I'm fired.'

'What did you do?' she repeated.

'Nothing. I got fired. For nothing.'

'What did he say?' Diana looked at him without blinking.

'Tell the truth,' snapped Austin.

'Were you lazy?' she asked.

'No.'

'You were always lazy. You never wanted to work mixing concrete,' Austin shouted.

Diana silenced him with a look. Then stood and turned to the stove to go on cooking. Austin looked from John to her, trying to find a cue. He didn't get it. Not that time.

'You'd better sit down,' she said. 'I made stew.'

He never went back to work out his notice.

Tighe owned an eight-cylinder Ford with triple chrome runners along the side. When Tighe drove, he turned on the radio and sat back, wrapped securely in the plastic tiger skin which curved around the dashboard and over the seats. In the rear window, a row of tiny tiger heads bobbed on springs each time the huge car swayed like an overweight beauty queen.

A month after his sacking, John still had no job. At night he wandered along the back streets in the moonlight, sidestepping potholes and avoiding dogs. It was well past hotel closing time when he passed a small pub in a side street. The front door was propped open with an old boot. When he glanced in, he was startled to see Tighe's back. It was unmistakable. Though the shoulders were hunched the familiar large paw was wrapped around a half-empty glass of beer. An impressive row of empty glasses lined the bar.

The car didn't take long to find. It was parked along the street, well away from a street light. John looked back at the quiet hotel. A single bar of light sloped across the footpath from the door.

John touched the car. The passenger-side front window was open. The plastic tiger skins glowed inside, despite the limited light. He reached forward and turned one of the huge knobs on the radio. A small pilot light flickered on.

Girls were made to love and kiss,
Who am I to interfere with this?

John fumbled with the huge knob and turned the voice of the tiger to a guilty whisper. Leaving the door open, he stepped back and unzipped his fly. The need was urgent, and relief was great as he emptied his bladder. He carefully sprayed all over the plastic skins and the radio. He was zipping his fly when light splashed across the footpath from the hotel, as the swing doors pushed open.

The last few drops ran down his leg.

Tighe thrust into the balmy night air. He turned and spoke to someone inside the bar. John shuddered at the thick voice.

Keeping in the shadows, he moved away from the car along a darkened lane. A few gates past the corner, he found a fence which leaned out, held a few degrees from the horizontal by a stick. He wriggled in there and held his breath as the car keys jingled and Tighe approached the car. The car door opened, and he heard the squish. Then the swearing. John swallowed a small delighted giggle.

Tighe's breath rattled as he ran up and down the street. Then he checked the lane. John did not move as Tighe ran past the length of the lane, then back.

'Cunts! Fuck'n cunts!' The words exploded with each wheeze.

Tighe went back to the hotel. John stayed where he was. Tighe brought another man to the car.

'Look at this!' Tighe appealed to the heavens for justice. 'Some dirty bastard's pissed in my car.'

'Mongrel would do a thing like that,' the man agreed.

'I'd like to know, because if I got hold of the gutless bastard ... hasn't got the guts to do it to my face ... hasn't got the guts ...'

'Gutless,' the other agreed softly.

John stayed right where he was, until it was very late and Tighe had been gone for an hour.

Chapter 4

John sat on the front fence. It was Saturday. There was nothing else to do until the football later in the day. The motor bike had been dismantled until now it was a pile of tenuously connected parts spread around the floor of the garage. Austin was painting the roof in the distance. He liked painting. Because he suspected that John might like it too, he never asked for any help. The early crowd was wandering along the far side of the street waving blue and white flags.

'Up Norths!' A girl carrying a blanket in one arm waved a flag at him with the other.

John waved back and smiled. A man waving a bottle pushed the peeling green painted fence on the old house opposite, and laughed when it swayed.

'Don't do that. Someone might live there!' The girl remonstrated.

'Nobody would live there,' the man was genuinely astounded. He resisted the temptation to push it over, but could not disguise his contempt.

'Someone must own it.' The girl did not sound sure.

After the crowd shifted along and became a distant chanting of slogans, John sat tossing pebbles into a shrub.

'Hello!'

John started. He had not heard the man approach. A big man with a bald head and a round face smiled at him cheerfully. John stood and did not know what to do with his hands.

'This where Austin Evans lives?'

'He's up on the roof.'

John turned and pointed.

'You must be John?' The man held out a hand.

'I'm your Uncle Eric,' he laughed as John registered what was familiar about the eyes.

'Please . . . please come in . . .'

'There's something about you that's a bit like old Jack,' Eric said as he strode up the concrete blocks which had been laid over the original path.

'Jack?'

'Your grandfather. You were named after him.'

John had not been told. As he thought about it, it became something of a revelation. It was still opening possibilities to him, suggesting things he already seemed to know, when Eric paused and leaned on the post beside the steps. He looked thoughtfully around the garden.

'I haven't been around here for years.' He sounded a little sad. 'I couldn't wait to leave it. Now I'm getting too old to fly any more and I'm looking for a place to rest my bones.'

John was trying to recollect something about this strange uncle, who had told him something about himself and a distant and even stranger grandfather. He knew all his mother's relatives, and he knew Aunt Mary. He thought about Lina, and wished that she was still around.

'I was in New York when your grandmother died.' Eric seemed to drop psychically on his train of thought. 'Your father sent me a telegram but I couldn't do much.'

The round cheerful face suddenly became guilty and shy.

John was about to take him into the house when Austin's face came over the ledge of the roof.

'Goodday Aussie,' Eric called and his round face instantly glowed.

Austin looked surprised. He swayed dangerously on the lip of the roof before mumbling and making his way across to the ladder on the other side of the house.

'I haven't seen you for a while, stranger.'

Eric was startled when he heard Diana's voice behind him. John did not think either of them was really pleased to see each other, despite the enthusiastic way Eric jumped up the stairs and took Diana's hand.

'It's so good . . .' Eric stepped back and made to drink in her appearance. 'You haven't changed a bit since the day you were married, Diana.'

'That was the last time we saw you,' Diana said a little drily.

Eric paused, but by that time Austin had climbed from the roof and approached with hand extended.

'I just been talking to Flash Jack junior,' Eric laughed as he pumped his brother's hand.

'Ah.'

'Come in, come in,' Diana said enthusiastically, while her body shifted slightly across the doorway.

'It is a long time since,' Eric sighed, and made no move for the door.

'You're always welcome here.' Diana moved aside uncomfortably.

Judging his time, Eric moved forward easily. The others followed his back along the passage. He glanced with just the right lack of nosiness into all the rooms, remarking as he went how nice the place was, how airy after all the little places he was used to in the City.

Once in the kitchen, Diana made tea. She put out the good cups and saucers, the ones that were used for visitors.

'I've decided to settle.' Eric spoke deliberately to his brother. Diana looked up and almost missed a pour.

'I think I'll get a job on the mines. It shouldn't be too hard.'

'You never liked it here.'

'There's a woman in Adelaide. Since Sylvie went I been around a bit, as you know. Italy, Greece, anywhere that wants a pilot.'

'Should have sent a postcard.' Diana pushed a cup in his direction.

'Didn't have much time. Never stayed in one place long enough. The eyes aren't good enough now, so Anna, she says I ought to get a steady job and settle somewhere. Quiet.'

'Would you like a scotch finger?' Diana tipped a plate towards Eric. Eric absently took a biscuit and snapped it in half.

'So here I am.' He dunked one half of the biscuit and swallowed it.

94

The grapevines outside the windows were bare. Eric spoke easily although his hosts never relaxed, and he did not leave until it was beginning to become dark outside.

Austin saw his brother out to the front gate. John sat on the steps. Only then did the conversation become animated.

'You're looking good for married life,' Eric laughed. John noticed how his laughter had become free and musical now that Diana wasn't there.

'Regularity. I go to work each day, come home. Nothing much happens to me.'

'Nothing. Something has to have happened. When I left, the place was poor and there were people living in tin sheds outside of town. Now, as I came up the road I heard someone saying that nobody could own a place like that one opposite.'

He nodded to the tumble-down house with the green fence.

'Things have improved since then. Everyone owns a car. It's only drunks and crazy people like the ones who live over there who don't have a car and haven't lined the inside of their house.'

'Lined!' exclaimed Eric.

'Heaters!' Austin exclaimed back ecstatically. 'You know how cold it was? Now everyone has heaters and no one uses wood-burners any longer or coke and there's aeroplanes . . . you know that . . .'

'Aeroplanes every week,' Eric nodded, a little sadly.

'What happened about Sylvia?' Austin dared.

Eric thought and for a second his face again became thoughtful. Because he normally had a face that made people want to laugh, whenever he looked thoughtful his face became sad. Instantly John felt sad, and had to fight off small anguishes as they tugged gently around him.

'It's what happens when you arrive in a uniform and someone wants to have a good time. That's alright Aussie, so long as you don't get married, because when the good time ends there's nothing left. Shit,' he exclaimed and spat into the dust, 'when it came to sitting around the house and doing the gardening she hated it. It wasn't like it was, for us. Then she picked up with someone and it got nasty and I left, then when I picked up with Anna she started phoning me telling me she wanted me back bad she never wanted anyone except me. I knew it was that she was hurt that I went out with someone, and the someone was having the good time she remembered, and I did take Anna to some of the old places so word got back to her. She started crying then and I hung up the telephone and last I heard she took something and she went into hospital, the fellow she picked up with came and saw me and told me she really wanted me back I should go to the hospital but I wouldn't there was Anna, so there, and we left. She has to sort it out. It isn't any good if I'm around.'

'Sorting it out.'

'That's what I'm doing here,' Eric said.

'It's a funny place to come.' Austin squinted at the poppet heads and the glittering slag heaps on the horizon.

'It's home.' Eric smiled and slammed the gate behind him.

Diana was doing the washing when Austin came back. He walked into the kitchen knowing, and tried to sit and not say anything.

'I hope he doesn't think he can stay here,' she said.

'I don't think so.'

Austin hesitated.

'He didn't pay for any of Lina's funeral. He didn't pay anything. When he pays for his share of that funeral, then he can stay here.'

'It's not his way,' said Austin.

The brothers did not see each other often, although Eric got a job on the mine and Anna came from Adelaide and they lived in a house not far away. When the brothers did meet, it was strained. Diana made little secret about her feelings for her brother-in-law and Austin submitted to them.

About a year later, Eric's divorce was final. Anna and Eric decided to get married. It was a quiet wedding. ('He'd be ashamed

96

to do it in public after the way he treated poor Sylvie,' Diana said cuttingly to Austin, who looked away.)

Murray Cox came with Mary from Sydney. He was still neat and dapper although his hair was becoming thin. Their two daughters were left with John and Ellen at home during the ceremony, because it was so simple, not a public occasion at all really. The two girls sat in the kitchen and talked with Ellen while John wandered out along the lanes and played with a centipede he found in the middle of the path. Finally he took it into the house in a bottle, and the two cousins shrieked.

When the adults returned they sat around the kitchen and the men loosened their ties and the women huddled at the other end of the table over their gin slings while the men passed a bottle of beer, although the occasion was important enough for them to use glasses. John was old enough to stay, as he was old enough to have gone to the ceremony even if it was not really public, but by tacit consent, he was left to his own devices.

Nobody really minded when he left and went outside. His sister and the cousins sat at a table under the vines in the shade, and sipped lemonade and talked in low voices. John sat on the ground near the window and flicked pebbles at a line of ants marching along the corner of the concrete verandah.

Eric was telling stories inside. From the silence at the women's end of the table, John could sense the looks from Diana. Austin was laughing and calling for more stories.

'It was good those days,' he said a little too loud.

'Bullshit it was good,' Eric bellowed. 'This was the driest hottest coldest dustiest most boring place I ever been in. I couldn't wait to leave.'

'Why did you stay?'

'I didn't stay. Except for the old man I wouldn't have stayed as long as I did. Him. Sitting on that verandah with those books and mum, she didn't care anything about the things that mattered to him.'

'What a thing to say about your parents,' Diana remonstrated.

'It's true.'

'It doesn't matter if it's true. It's not good to say things like that about relatives. It doesn't matter if it's true, it doesn't.'

Anna laughed. Nervously. John picked up a small stone and ran his finger around it, feeling the smooth sandy chunks and the sharp edges of stone.

'Doesn't matter . . .' Eric slurred slightly. 'It doesn't matter . . . who doesn't it matter for . . kids find out, they know. Everyone knows . . . what then? You might as well say. That way they don't find out you're a liar as well.'

'You ought to . . .' Anna tried to interrupt and direct the conversation elsewhere.

'I been in the mines three months. I walk to the cage to go down and the cage jumps as the man in front steps through the gate. Goes down, squash.'

Eric thumped the table with his fist.

'That's his head,' he looked at the spot.

'That soon after you started.' Austin looked frantically to Diana.

'I want to see more of the bush around,' chirped Anna. 'I haven't seen desert, ever.'

'There isn't much to see.'

'The space . . . it must have grandeur.'

'There was a travel short on at the pictures last Saturday night about the Grand Canyon. That was interesting although I don't like travel shorts much.' Diana paused and looked at the others, who could not tell whether she was being nasty or not.

'I don't like those shorts,' grumbled Austin 'They pad out the pictures so you think you've had a big night.'

'Why did you come back?' Asked Diana.

'He didn't like to be lonely,' Anna answered for him.

'It never worried him before . . .'

'During the war I was running a shop. A little shop but it was going alright. Marriage OK, money OK. When the Japanese was coming they called me in and there was two of them sitting behind the desk with rows of medals and one of them said "You—learned to fly. Kingsford Smith taught you to fly. We want you."

I said "I got a little shop and I'm happy, thank you." So, they say "You got a choice then. You join the Air Force or we've got a good infantry unit in New Guinea you'll like, and you won't have no choice in the matter." I thought about it. "Alright," I said. "Sorry about the shop," he said, he wasn't such a bad bloke. Sylvia couldn't run it. She was cut up about it. The beginning of the end for us.'

'That was lonely. In the war,' said Anna eagerly.

'Ended flying Catalinas. Training kids and flying along the coast of Queensland to Port Moresby. Nothing to do but fly. No Japs, no medals. Suited me.'

'Yes.' Diana made it sound spiteful.

Anna patted Eric's wrist.

'It was all green on the ground. Most of it was near the sea. Sometimes I thought about Sylvia, other times about the old man. Even Austin. It was hard on Austin when we were kids.'

Diana stared, unbelieving.

'Not that he weren't willing. The others were too good for him. I took lessons from the old man but they still beat him up when I wasn't around. Couldn't stand it.'

'Long time ago.' Anna sounded frightened. 'Eric, our honeymoon we should . . .'

'Wouldn't hit back . . .'

'. . . go . . .'

'Sylvie left. It wasn't hard those days. Walked along the Fairy Bower near Manly beach, where the Yanks went to get it off. Heard one of the women in the bushes. I was with Sylvie, and I didn't want to hear. "C'mon Mac hurry up it's time to slime." Hurry and slime, that's the way they said it, and I didn't want her to hear.'

'Don't . . .'

'Slime! Slime in me. That's what they call it. Hurry up Mac and slime. Slime in me. Sylvie thought it was funny. She used to say it to me. C'mon Eric slime you can slime in me Eric.'

'Bit rough Eric.' Austin cleared his throat in polite disapproval because it was Eric's wedding.

'Couldn't come at it after that.'

'It was the war,' said Anna desperately. 'It did dreadful things to people. Awful.'

'Awful!' Eric contemplated the word. He turned his hand, as though the word were held there, and examined it closely.

'I'll take you flying some time, young John,' he brightened and spoke up, because he saw John's head above the windowsill. 'Borrow a plane and we'll go up. Eh?'

'He doesn't like flying,' Diana said not quite truthfully.

'I do!' Cried Ellen from where she was suddenly standing in the doorway.

Uncle Eric smiled at her indulgently.

It was late. Ellen had gone to sleep on the lounge. Eric and Anna left the house. Murray Cox, who had not said anything during the night, but listened intently, shook Eric's hand. Eric looked embarrassed but he smiled.

'Wish me luck as you wave me . . .' Anna called through the open window of the old car.

'Ha, ha,' Austin peeled his thin lips back.

'Come again!' Called Diana.

Uncle Eric said nothing. John stood beside his mother and watched as Eric kangarooed the car along the road. Eric turned his head back and smiled. The smile seemed strained, almost ghoulish. His face was white.

'He always was a character.' There was envy in Austin's voice.

'Selfish,' Diana corrected quietly.

As they walked inside, Austin looked ashamed.

Chapter 5

During the fifties the corrugated iron houses grew neat front lawns. Hoses with sprays twisted and swirled through the drought. Concrete Doric columns sprouted on verandahs and while old cars rusted on blocks at the back, new Fords and Holdens glistened at the front.

John plodded past the backyards endlessly, staring around the long clothes-lines draped across the yards and the fowlhouses and the small squares of vegetables pushed up under the fence.

A couple made love on a camp stretcher under a light. Although it was dark he kept his head below the level of the fence and observed through a nail hole, ashamed and excited. He could see the woman's broken veins and the short legs and flat buttocks of the man. John noted the steady rhythm of the movements, and identified the sounds as similar to those made by his parents at night.

After a while he was so ashamed that he walked on. He went past the same place a few times after that, but was never treated to the scene again. He did see the man once through the flywire screen, standing with a singlet covering the spots on his back, speaking to someone inside.

The backyards in Broken Hill were deep. Walking so much, he talked constantly to his own tangible, personal despair.

He was too old for Saturday afternoon matinees. He went to the pictures on Saturday nights when Aubrey was never around, although he was once sure that he saw him in the distance shuffling through a cone of light.

He sat with his parents at the back, in the good synthetic clothes which made him uncomfortable. Under Austin's resentful stare, he discussed the audience with his mother as they trooped in. The woman in a cheap fur, the man in the suit with his shirt out at the back and his shoes unpolished. That woman with her lipstick crooked, with too much make-up. Didn't she look . . . cheap? They giggled together while Austin and Ellen watched silently. Diana was delighted with their affinity of opinion and encouraged it.

'Lookit that one, what do you think?' She chortled.

'Too much eye-shadow!' He judged after scrutiny.

'Makes her look common,' squealed his common-looking mother.

'The eyes would be nice if she left them alone.'

He read film reviews wherever he could. During the week the *Women's Weekly* and the *New Idea* were a source of opinion. The reviews of the local papers were a bad rehash of the studio blurb. The women's papers did express an opinion. With a little practice he came to be able to advise on almost all movies, with reasonable advance knowledge of what films they were going to like.

The preferences were simple. Both parents hated foreign films with sub-titles. Light and bright was great, with sexual innuendo, but not too explicit about it.

Themes of mutilation: Deborah Kerr is blind from the beginning. Like all who are mythically blind, she sees the truth from the outset. Charles Boyer gets his hands cut off by his beastly-coloured countrymen, so that's what happens when you are, 1. too smart by half, 2. a pacifist, 3. used by extremists, 4. coloured and above yourself.

This is a deep film.

The Europeans take refuge in the palace. Somewhere, there is a cache of hot machine guns. Boyer won't tell where they are, not even to individualistic selfish tough guy Alan Ladd. The young Indian boy, whose allegiance and love is striven for by Ladd and Boyer, is killed. So is the old Colonel, a man of action and representative of past certainties. Every aspect of the film is weighed, counterbalanced. Two bad guys, one looks like Heinrich Himmler with his high polished boots, the other sounds

102

like Adlai Stevenson. Beware the intellectuals. Which one cut off Boyer's hands?

A dramatic expression of the balance of power, the pacifist's control of the machine guns. When the forces of civilisation are unable to exercise their technological mastery, they are vulnerable to savagery.

Resolution via violent orgasm is achieved in the final scene, as the savages batter their way through the doors of the palace. Boyer, mature and masculine after the death of his young protégé, uses a machine gun on the attackers. He is joined in this task by the now ennobled Ladd, who has been thoroughly civilised by Deborah Kerr and given courage by the death of the Colonel.

'That was a great film,' Austin breathed out as they walked from the cinema.

The crowd had already moved away. They waited. They didn't have to push, and they watched as other people did. Shuffle shuffle on the carpets. Each still isolated in the little world, their eyes and the square of light. The screen. Away from the protective dark, they are exposed. Crowds moving from a cinema appear stunned. They must reassert their privacy and their defences.

At the small general store near the panel beater's work-shed, the little man talked to John seriously about what it meant to have a business of your own. It was so much better than working in an office all your life.

John nodded, although he could think of no more exalted fate at that time than working in an office. Not to get his hands greasy was the ultimate job expectation.

'You seem a serious-minded sort of chap.' The shopkeeper paused before sliding the corned beef sandwich across the counter. 'What do you think is going to happen when they all leave Africa?'

'Who?' John stared at the corned beef sandwich, neatly wrapped in pale grease-proof paper.

'The colonial powers. Portugal, Belgium, France, England. And the rest of them.'

'I think . . .' John worried. 'There will be a mess.'

The little man looked delighted with this answer. He pushed the sandwich into a brown paper bag then tipped it out, and pushed it into another brown paper bag which was smaller.

'I think it will be bad too. Of course there are intelligent, cultured black people, but they haven't been educated to it yet.'

'A tribal mentality,' John groped for a word.

'Still in the tribe. That's right,' the shopkeeper sparkled as he slapped the bag onto the counter. 'It takes a long time to develop western culture.'

'Centuries.'

An elderly woman came into the shop and stood beside John. The shopkeeper nodded to John to wait, and placed the sandwich back in the refrigerator to get cold. The woman wanted a bottle of milk. As he went to get it, the shopkeeper went on about the need to civilise Africa.

'Whose side are you on?' the old woman growled suspiciously.

'My conscience,' the young owner replied after reflection, during which he placed the milk bottle firmly on the counter and accepted a coin.

'You're not on Menzies' side, that old bastard that sold pig-iron to the Japs during the war.'

'They had not declared war at the time,' the shopkeeper responded with gravity.

'Everyone else with any brains knew about it.'

The old lady took the milk and her change then flounced out. The shopkeeper watched her go with obvious distaste. Although he was only in his early twenties, he had lost most of his hair. He checked John's reaction, which was mainly confusion, then invited him out the back to meet his wife. A mouse-haired female equivalent of her husband nursed a plump infant, who gazed at John with obvious suspicion.

'I'm always glad to meet a new friend of Wayne's. He gets so many friends.' The woman smiled thinly as the baby began to wriggle and cry. 'You must excuse me. I have to put Delilah down.'

'Anne is a wonderful woman,' the shopkeeper said with feeling as he poured then passed John a cup of luke-warm tea. 'It's good to have someone like her, who will stick with you and support your efforts to improve yourself. Do you agree?'

John agreed.

'You're young to know yet,' he said with obvious satisfaction. 'It won't be long.'

He looked at John's hands, as an afterthought.

'You work?'

'Around the corner.'

'You ought to study. I thought you'd still be at school.'

John was impressed, but he admitted that he wasn't good at school. When the shopkeeper asked why, he shrugged.

'Winston Churchill wasn't good at school either. You must be creative,' he said.

John enrolled at the Technical College to learn oxy-acetylene and electric welding. Not that he needed it. The classes got him away from the house at night and stopped him from wandering the lanes.

The class was a veteran of the Korean War who wanted to learn a trade, a couple of boys like John and a buck-toothed boilermaker who welded alright just that he needed to know the theory that was what he was there for. Most evenings while the others desperately tried to lay welds uniformly and neatly, he sat back and talked about hypnosis and the occult.

When he got tired of talking about that, the next favourite subject was sex, especially homosexuality.

'I knew one of them when I went through Sydney,' Rodney the boilermaker opined while gazing through the grimy windows of the iron hut. 'Didn't seem bad. Used to ask him why he was like that. He reckoned he couldn't say. It was like an illness or something he had all his life. Couldn't get it out of his head. Went to see a psychiatrist. Didn't do him much good. I asked him couldn't he get a woman. Ever tried them? Didn't interest him.'

'It's weird,' commented Tom the veteran as he dropped a used welding rod onto the table and struggled to pull his gloves off. 'There were a few like that in the army. Everybody knew. Hanging around the toilet blocks and the showers. They never did anything, to anyone else, that is. Except one. He got a dirty discharge.'

'I tried hypnosis on him once to see if it'd do any good,' Rodney went on. 'He was willing, because he said he hated it. Wanted to be normal like everyone else. But one principle with hypnotism. You can't get anyone to do what doesn't agree with their deepest principles. His principles were a handicap. He got belted most weekends for putting the hard word on someone in a toilet. I asked him why he did it. He was made that way, he reckoned, just like some people got flat feet.'

'Women hate men like that,' Tom added sagely.

John watched and listened from behind his electric welding mask. There was little he could add.

A few times he sat in the passenger seat of Rodney's old Ford after the college closed, with a steaming newspaper of fish and chips. It was late, but Rodney wanted to drive and talk, and so they went to the airport and back, then around the sheds of the Silverton Tramway Company. Then a quick trip to Railwaytown, to cruise past the darkened corner shops, while Rodney talked constantly about hypnotism, women and the power of the unknown. Until the night when they were sliding the car around a corner into Argent Street, and he confided that he would like to get out of Broken Hill and live in a city, any city.

'Not much hope of that, now I'm married,' he complained irritably as the car swayed into the centre of the road then straightened up.

John did not know what to say. When Rodney looked at him for a reply, he stuffed his mouth with a potato scallop.

'Now I'm married, there's no chance,' Rodney repeated bitterly. 'Best to get it all over with before you marry. Everybody in this town gets married. As soon as they leave school they marry the girl they sat near in school, then start banging out babies because there's nothing else to do. They just don't know, they don't know anything . . .'

His voice trailed and he looked sadly at the sheds of the Silverton Tramway Company. John wanted to ask what it was they didn't know, but he didn't.

Rodney pressed the cigarette lighter on the dashboard in and fiddled around in his coat pocket for smokes. It was winter. Although it was night the light on the horizon was clear. The packet of fish and chips on John's lap felt warm.

'There's some brandy in the glove box.'

John unclipped the glove box and took out the bottle. It was half empty. He unscrewed the lid.

Rodney blew smoke across the windscreen. John took a sip and allowed it to trickle down his throat, little by little. He passed the bottle to Rodney, who wiped the throat with the palm of the same hand that was holding the cigarette.

'You ought to get out,' he took a sharp swig. 'This is no place for someone who is a bit curious about things. All you got to do is chat up someone in the street and everybody here talks about it for weeks. There's only tarts and old women and the Barrier Industrial Council. If you want to do something you go to the two-up, or drive to the airport and back. It's no life.'

The brandy was back in John's hand. He took another sip.

'I'm trapped. You're not.'

He let this soak in, along with the brandy.

'At least not until you put some little bitch up the duff. Her old man comes around. Then you're stuck with a job underground and forty years to do it in.'

'That what you did?'

'What?'

'Get your wife pregnant? Did you have to marry her?'

'Worse than that. I fell for her. A pretty face and them big eyes that look up at you, and the touch of her hand. That perfume. Christ, I had a hard-on but she seemed so innocent. I couldn't believe it the first time I heard her fart.'

He sighed.

'I know what I should have done. Would have been better all around. It's a high price to pay for getting your end in.'

107

Chapter 6

'I want to leave,' he told his parents over dinner.

They both looked.

They expected him to be defiant or guilty. He was.

'Why do you want to leave dear?' Diana asked sweetly. 'You're not seventeen yet.'

'Just turned sixteen.'

He was used to his mother's trick of putting his age up or down a year or two to suit her purposes.

Ellen watched from the other side of the table. She had just left school to take a job at the big corner grocery which was expanding, and she prickled with responsibility. Austin immediately looked nowhere. The only one who didn't want him to go was his mother. The others would support her because:

a) it was morally correct,

b) they were competing with one another for Diana's favours,

c) his departure in spite of their protests would confirm his eccentricity,

d) above all they loved to be right.

'You can't do that,' Diana chuckled reasonably. 'What would you live on? You haven't finished your apprenticeship yet, you're too young to get a decent job.'

'I'll never be a panel beater,' John stated the unstated truth.

'You can't go,' Ellen sniffed priggishly.

'You can't leave . . . your mother,' Austin accepted the cue instantly.

'She has you,' John said cruelly. 'Both of you.'

Austin and Ellen were furious. John had stepped out of the contest when they were winning. They had been tricked but they didn't know how.

'You'll find yourself in the slums . . .' Diana rapped the table and gave him the long-suffering-mother look.

John was impatient to make his own mistakes as quickly as possible.

'I can't leave soon enough.'

'We know you've never been happy,' his mother said with visible distress. 'You ought to stay for a while, to make sure.'

'You don't know how to look after yourself,' Ellen dared.

'The sooner I learn the better,' John quietly agreed.

His mother wept frequently for weeks. The house became gloomy. Austin bullied and thrashed, acting as though he wanted John to stay while at the same time ensuring that he went.

'Stop it, stop it,' wept Diana.

Austin couldn't.

Two weeks before the annual holidays when he planned to leave, he sat down and wept. He was at work. The boss drove him home and touched him on the arm as he got out of the car.

'Take a few days off,' he said.

John sat in bed and hardly left it for several days. When he did, he wept uncontrollably.

'Why are you doing this?' Diana asked.

If Ellen and Austin had not been around he would have told her. Apart from which, it felt good. He didn't feel weak when he finished crying. Most of the time it felt good.

It was others who got embarrassed.

He sat in the back of the car as they drove to Sydney for their holiday and tried to ignore Ellen's bitter looks. When they arrived, they stayed with the elderly Seventh Day Adventist woman who sat in her chair and sipped tea in secret. Diana found the name of a psychiatrist, and they went.

The family sat around the table. The psychiatrist looked them over.

'It would be good for him to stay here for a while.' The psychiatrist looked over his glasses at Diana.

'Is he sick?' Diana was afraid. She raised her bag to her chest to ward off the blow.

'Not really.'

She looked relieved. John was sick, so he needed to stay in a hospital. It was not their fault. John was not really sick. It could not be their fault.

His father parked the car outside the gates of the hospital, then carried his suitcase as though he couldn't do it himself.

Papers were signed and Diana and Austin talked with a doctor quietly for ten minutes. The suitcase was left beside an aluminiun bed in a long room full of aluminium beds. He walked around the grounds with his parents. They wandered into a gully where it was cool and there were palm trees and European shrubs and small rivulets full of large golden fish. They crossed a stone bridge.

'Really well-kept gardens,' Austin looked about, admiring.

Although the place was beautiful, they were sad, and resentful. He might be staging a clever escape and humiliating them, but they could not say it. It was not the right place.

It was not the right place for John to form into words the sensations and intuitions that crammed and jostled his imagination. It was early January, high summer, and the coastal grass was growing thick and damp in the heat. They sat on the bridge and watched the fish and the round stones on the bed of the creek, and no one said anything of importance.

'Look at them down there. I like the fish!' Diana chuckled as a fat carp scuttled through the clear shining water.

Through the lawns long artificial mounds had been placed strategically to create a well-ordered garden, various and harmonious. As they walked slowly from the gully the appearance of a long single-storey barrack ward nestled in low among the pines and shrubs hardly disturbed the impression.

They walked about the grounds past the lawn-tennis courts where two middle-aged overweight men shambled and hit slow lobs back and forth over the net. Finally they arrived at the gate. The latest model Vanguard car was parked outside. Diana kissed him wetly on the cheek and Austin shook his hand. Then they drove away without looking back.

Only then did John notice that Ellen had not been there.

110

The first night he spent in the ward was hot. Steamy heat, not the sort of heat he was used to.

Most of the patients were war veterans. There wasn't much to do, and the heat might have reminded them. For each other's benefit they decided to replay the war of 1939 to 1945.

The fat man stomped between the parallel rows of glittering aluminium beds.

'Present arms!' He bellowed.

'Left right left . . .'

Several of the others stood to attention between the beds with their pyjamas tucked in and their slippers and bare feet shut tight on the bare plastic-tiled floor. Until another veteran had a better idea and threw himself under one of the beds.

'Fuck'n stukas!' He yelled.

'Into the trenches!' The others cried, and all of them dived under blankets and beds and one sprawled across the space between the rows with a bedpan on his head.

'Fuck'n,' the man who had called 'stukas' before peeped up from under the bed and gazed about no-man's land morosely. 'The bombs are getting closer. They're going to bring artillery down on us.'

'Insubordination!' Called the fat man from under the next bed.

'Call our own twenty-five pounders. Give it to them back,' the man with his head under the bedpan peered to the side and bellowed.

'Cowardice in the face of the enemy.' The fat man slithered round from bed to bed.

Against the wall, a schizophrenic Austrian huddled against the wall in his pyjamas. He stared at them all and softly hummed a lullaby in German. The fat man leaped up and pounded him as he rolled along the floor. The Austrian kept singing softly in German.

'Boche!' Yelled the fat man as he punched at the kidneys.

The Austrian rolled against the legs of the next bed.

'This trench is occupied. You can't come in here,' cried a tremulous voice.

'It's the latrine anyway,' another bellowed with laughter.

'No room for spies, not even in the latrine trench,' the fat man puffed.

'Leave him alone. The Afrika Korps are good fighters,' the man under the bedpan whistled.

'He must be an Italian,' the humorist called.

A coloured South African jumped up onto his bed at the end of the corridor:

Hi jig a jig,
Fuck a little pig,
Follow the band.
Follow the band a—ll the way.

'Piss off Gunga Din!' A boot flew past him as he started on another verse.

The fat man looked across at John's watching face. He stopped hitting the Austrian and pushed him away. The Austrian crawled against the wall and whispered his song on and on.

The fat man wriggled across to John and put his mouth to John's ear.

'Don't worry son. We're allowed to be mad here. The war was bad, and we never get a better time than when we remember it.'

'Is this living?' John asked.

'Remember hell and enjoy it,' answered the fat man, whose face streamed with sweat.

'Were dive-bombers like that?' John indicated with his head the men spread along the floor, so like corpses.

'Yes,' laughed the fat man with mordant wit. 'Real pilots imagined they flew in them. Their memory is now catching up with their imagination.'

A male night nurse finally appeared. He wheeled in a trolley full of dark glowing bottles and medicine glasses.

'Largactil,' he called cheerily and imperturbably to the bodies scattered around the ward. 'Come and get your largactil!'

He smiled cunningly and held up a medicine glass, as though tempting a naughty child with a new toy.

112

'He'll try and double the dose to quieten us down,' the fat man said loudly to the ward.

'You'd take four times the dose so long as it was a drug,' the nurse laughed with good humour.

'You want some?' The nurse looked across at John, who did not line up with the others. He might have been handing out chocolates.

John refused politely. He did not want to miss anything.

The nurse wheeled the trolley away. The largactil didn't slow anyone down. A young man, about his own age, walked past along the corridor in nothing but a hat resting securely on an erection.

'Look at this, look at this!' He called as he twirled the hat.

'I've seen bigger ones than that,' called the fat man who was engaged in an arm wrestle with the occupier of the next trench.

'If you bring it here I'll show you something else to do with the hat,' sneered an alcoholic from the end of the ward.

Nobody gave him the electric shock therapy that was being given to the others. He walked around the grounds during the end of summer and part of autumn, stunned by the beauty of the changing seasons and the colour of the dying leaves. He sat for hours on the bridge and watched the carp. He sat in sunny rooms. He watched women make baskets and tried to imitate their patience.

After four months, he was sent for by the doctor.

'You can leave any time,' said the doctor. 'What are you going to do?'

John sat back and looked out at the paths, aflame with dried golden leaves.

'Stay in Sydney.'

'How do you feel?'

'I needed the rest.'

'I think you made the right decision,' the doctor nodded quietly after making an appointment for him with the social worker.

Because of a promise made to his parents, he returned to Broken

Hill for two weeks. He was relieved that his sister ignored him, and Austin almost ignored him.

'You ought to stay for your mother's sake,' Austin grumbled, but they both knew he did not mean it.

He returned to Sydney by train and kept the appointment with the social worker.

'I am surprised,' she said.

After the interview, he did exactly what his mother did not want him to do. He found a room in Darlinghurst and a job as a storeman. After two weeks, he told the head storeman to get stuffed.

Because he was poor, he shared rooms. He learned to be wary of his room-mates. He lost an electric razor, a small radio, a gold ring, a portable record player and a suitcase to his room-mates.

There were times he went hungry. He held a job as a third-class fitter-machinist for one summer, making trailer axles in Alexandria. The welding he had learned came in handy. In every factory there was a public performer. In the axle factory it was a part-Aboriginal who worked a turret lathe and sang rock 'n' roll all day.

There were other jobs. In a suitcase factory he played darts and joined the cricket team and dropped suitcases from the top floors to a utility below. He graduated to a handbag factory, and stood behind a curved glass window cutting patterns out of plastic while the trains went to and from Central Station across the road. The foreman worked beside him and talked constantly of the troubles he had with the wife, and what it was like being manic depressive. Then handbags weren't selling well. The foreman felt bad when he had to fire John.

'It's a recession, son.' He gave John a sorry look, the same kind of sorry look he had when he talked about the affair his wife had in Western Australia.

Once a week, John wrote a formula on a card then put a stamp on it and sent it to his parents. Writing had not become any easier. The pen was thick and clumsy in his hand and his writing was childish and untidy.

Once a week, he received a letter from his parents. Diana transposed her chatty style and talked about who was seen with who, who was getting married, who was getting on. Austin's style was more ponderous:

> Hello son. Your mother has finished the washing now and she is hanging it on the line. We talk of you often. I think your mother misses you a great deal. She says that she wishes you were here. Bob Simmons on the mines is about to retire and there are rumours there might be a new foreman, but I don't think it will be me. I don't stand much chance since I became president of the bowling club. Diana played well on Saturday in the fours. Kath says she might become as good at bowls as she was at tennis. That would be good eh.
>
> I must go now because the car ought to be washed. It is Sunday morning and Ellen wants to go for a picnic so I better get a move on. It will sure rain when I wash the car.
>
> Dad

He was living in the dusty converted kitchen of an old terrace house in Forbes Street. The landlady was a large retired madam who tied her wiry hair up around her forehead with a bandanna. There was no heater and the breeze blew through the louvre windows along the wall.

Because the room was so cold, he went out as often as he could. He was out the morning Diana arrived. She had not told him she was coming. He was walking along Pitt Street when he saw her. It was so long since he had seen her. He stared.

'It is you!' She cried and ran to him and took his hand. 'It was meant to happen! I was meant to meet you!'

He was not so sure that it was divine transportation that had taken his mother from Broken Hill and placed her firmly in Pitt Street. He checked closely for transparent features, and found none.

'I came down.' She kissed him.

'I had to come to see you. We were worried about what could happen to you . . .'

She was weeping. He was already uncomfortable and resentful.

He asked her what made her come so urgently, once they sat at a corner table in a coffee lounge full of office workers. She fiddled through her purse. He was disconcerted to see a bundle of all the cards he had written, held together by a rubber band. Diana withdrew the top card and showed him.

For more than two years, the reality of his earlier life had receded. He did not think about Broken Hill, not even when he wrote those dutiful careless notes once a week. Comments about the weather. The pen stuck in his lumpish hand. Heavy and strange and difficult as he pushed it across the page, lifting and turning pieces of verbal rock and clay.

> . . . I'm going well now. The weather is good. Much wetter than back home. I lost my job last week. I didn't get on with them and they asked me to go. I think the foreman was sorry, as least that's what he said. He's the one I told you about from West Australia. He said he'd give me a good reference. They gave me a week's pay and some holiday pay, which was alright. I'll get another job. Not much else has happened. The same old crowd I guess.
>
> > Yours truly,
> > John

He re-read the letter. His parents' last letter was crumpled in the hip pocket of his jeans. He smiled.

'Your letter is here.'

He took it out and bought time by reading it.

> . . . The Zammit girl from around the corner you remember her? she was the one you used to fight a lot when you were little, but you liked her I think. One time she hit you with a piece of mud so you came home bawling, you didn't think it was funny not a bit, well I did. She married the other day the boy Brown

116

from the south I think you might have known him from your year at high school he was somewhere near you. He works in the office at the mine. Dad tells me he has good prospects. They got married at the chapel and she looked lovely in white with her family and she was crying. I said to her gee every time I see you your crying and she laughed. They had a lot of nice presents the underground manager went too. They are going to be well set up that's good . . .

Only now it reached to him, tugging him back to the past.

'It was a nice wedding,' Diana sniffed. 'I didn't want to write you another letter before I came so I could find out how you were really living.'

Gradually she recovered.

'Those trousers won't last more than another week,' she observed accurately. 'Why do you stay?'

It was John's choice. He stuck to it.

'There is a job going back home that I thought you might like because your voice is so nice. The ABC radio there wants someone to read the news.'

This was a surprise. It appealed to him. He thought about it, then said alright, just for a while, if I don't get the job. Diana reached and touched his hand.

'I missed you,' she said.

He withdrew his hand.

They went to Grace Brothers' where Diana bought him a new set of clothes. He walked out of the store with his old jeans in a bag. Too late he noticed that the new trousers pulled tight in the crotch. He stretched. The nylon fabric stuck to his skin.

'Drop the old ones in the tin,' Diana said.

'They might come in handy. Besides, I think these ones are too small.'

'They look nice.' She checked the fit closely. 'You can't go back looking as though you sleep in the gutter. If you don't believe me go ask Mrs . . . Mrs . . .'

He knew she meant his landlady.

Chapter 7

The railway platform was cold. A few people greeted relatives and friends. Kisses were exchanged and backs were slapped before they moved back into shelter then away in the waiting taxis. John looked around at the black dull heaps of dust and the familiar poppet heads along the horizon.

His father and his sister waited at the far end of the platform. They did not move towards him, but stood motionless together. Only then did Austin work his way steadily forward and hold out his hand. John shook the hand, aware of the false smile on his own face. Ellen skipped forward and pecked him on the cheek.

This time, John had his bag firmly at his feet.

'Is there anything else in the van?' Austin grabbed at the bag but John gripped it firmly and turned it out of reach.

'No. He's got everything,' Ellen said meaningfully.

They walked to the only car parked nearby. Everybody else had gone, except for two station assistants still wheeling parcels from the van. Diana peered from the passenger seat of the car and smiled.

'We got a new Vanguard,' Ellen said.

He nodded and waited while Austin unlocked the boot.

As they drove home, Ellen confided that she had a boyfriend, who reminded her of John. He did not know what to say.

The manager of the radio station was short and bald and busy. He handed John a sheet of paper and sat him in front of a microphone.

'Turn that switch before you read. When you're ready,' he said from outside the soundproof room.

John read the article out loud. There were words he did not understand, which he pronounced with a French accent. Then he sat and waited. Through the sheet of glass he watched as the manager adjusted his headphones and moved a switch several times. He sat back and gazed at the ceiling before he took off his headphones.

He beckoned to John, then told him to sit.

'You have ability,' he seemed surprised.

'There are other applicants with experience in journalism. You don't have many qualifications . . .' He looked encouragingly, then leaned forward and startled John by touching him on the shoulder.

'Whatever, you ought to try this again. If . . . you don't get it . . . which I must say at this juncture is likely, then please don't give up.'

When he went home, he told both parents the result.

'I always thought you had a beautiful voice,' Diana said proudly.

'He didn't get the job, did he?' Austin raised his head above the *Barrier Daily Truth*.

He stayed for a while. The store where Ellen worked was bought out by Woolworths, and big trucks rumbled regularly into the new loading bay. A few times the store needed someone to unload. John did it, for cash in the hand. He did not mind the work, but he hated it when Ellen stood near the gates and talked loudly to the storeman, saying she always knew he could work when he wanted to.

'Seems alright to me,' the storeman said, and John was grateful.

He resurrected his old pushbike and went on some days to the railway station and talked with Kerry, who was a receiving clerk. A few times when he came home, his father was talking on the telephone. As he walked in, the telephone went down. He was too old and too big to be belted but the pressure was beginning to build. Conversation was strained at the table. On the night Ellen came back from the pictures twenty minutes late, Austin knocked her down in the hallway and kicked her.

'She's eighteen,' Diana ran from the kitchen screaming. 'You can't treat her like that.'

The screaming and arguing went on until late. John decided it was time to get a job, or go.

He was at the railway station two mornings later. He arrived at five minutes to eight. The assistant station-master looked at him when he reported for duty.

'Good,' he said.

'Yes?'

'Yes?' The assistant station-master stared as though he was stupid.

'Should I start work?'

'Yes.'

'What should I do?'

The assistant station-master glared. He had thin red hair pushed across to hide the bald sweep of his skull. He heaved his short, thick body from the chair and led the way onto the platform. A bundle of keys jangled on his belt. There he opened a small cabinet and handed John a broom and a brush.

'Anywhere,' replied the receding voice of the assistant station-master. 'Do the platform, then the steps. Then you can go along the tracks if you like!'

John swept and swept and swept. He swept and cleaned the platform, then he swept and cleaned the steps. He climbed down and looked closely at the tracks, then began to sweep, listening all the time in case of an approaching train.

A few men in dirty jeans and armless shirts wandered past carrying tools. A diesel locomotive nudged along a nearby track. Parcels were delivered outside the parcels office with a thump. Two boys wobbled their pushbikes along the edge of the platform. When John looked up, they turned their handlebars and pedalled casually away.

John paused and looked around. In the distance to the west, between the glittering iron tracks, a figure in blue overalls and a hat was approaching. John watched from the side of his eye as he worked. Dwarfed at first by the cranes and the locomotives, the figure became large and clear. An oily rag hung from a pocket.

Stubble came through the spaces between the oil smudges on his face.

He stepped up onto the platform easily and followed the smooth line of concrete with his toes. He glanced at John incuriously but did not speak, then disappeared into the cluster of offices.

Two minutes later he reappeared. A tall man in a uniform covered with as much braid as a Field Marshall walked beside him. It was the first time John had seen the station-master.

'We need someone else down there,' the man in overalls spoke gruffly. 'Otherwise it's too much for us. There could be an accident.'

'Who is that ... person ... down there? What is he doing? Sweeping the tracks? The railway tracks? Take him! Take him!' Shrieked the station-master as he flailed in John's direction with a thin pointed wrist.

The station-master retreated as spectacularly as he had arrived, in a blaze of colour and braid. The man in overalls stepped to the edge of the platform and looked down wonderingly at John, and silently shook his head. Then he jerked a thumb in the direction he had come from, the land of locomotives and cranes. John rushed to put away the broom first, then followed the broad phlegmatic back.

John remained a pace behind. They walked past gangs of shunters with ground sheets over their shoulders and gangers with heavy hammers. An empty rail truck ground along the tracks silently as a shunter ran alongside in shorts and a baseball cap. A mobile crane ran between two sets of rails, lifting pallets from one truck to another. At Broken Hill goods were transferred from the broad New South Wales gauge track to the narrow South Australian gauge. All along the cluster of lines, diesel locomotives pushed and shoved back and forth beneath the metallic hill of skimps.

The man in blue overalls plodded on unswerving. Past the crane, they came to a small corrugated iron hut. Smoke poured from a rough stone chimney at the side. The man in blue overalls brushed the door of the hut open.

'Go in.' He paused and stood back.

Two men, also in overalls, sat at a rough table. There was a stove in the chimney and a shelf with an electric jug and a row of identical neat floral tea-cups and saucers. Apart from the chairs, there was no other furniture. Both men looked up at him without speaking. A pack of cards was not yet opened in the centre of the table.

The man in blue overalls pushed gently past him and walked in with ponderous dignity. He stopped at an old steel office chair which had been hand painted bright blue. The paint was beginning to peel.

'Do you know how to play cards?' He spoke viciously, then allowed himself to subside into the chair.

Most of the time John lost. He was careful and polite. The men said little. The snap of the cards as they thumbed, the whisper as they were shuffled, the controlled breathing as they checked the cards in their hand.

Every forty-five minutes John emptied the teapot around the corner and made tea. Only once another man in dirty jeans came in without knocking and handed the man in blue overalls a slip of paper. The man in blue overalls took out a pen and signed it without comment, and handed it back. The man in dirty jeans nodded at the others around the table.

'You got a new man on the team,' he dared to comment.

'He'll learn.' One of the other men looked uninvitingly through his cards.

'It's not all as hard as this,' the man in jeans smiled. 'Make the best of it.' Then he left, without closing the door.

Next day he sat on top of a bag of grain in a rail truck, ticking a sheet of paper as Greeks and Yugoslavs heaved bags from one truck onto another.

'It's your job to sit up there and tick the paper,' the man in blue overalls instructed him from the ground. 'It's theirs to lift the bags. You lift a bag and everybody goes on strike.'

The Greeks worked in one line and the Yugoslavs worked in another. Both groups talked among themselves in short guttural sentences. Every few minutes one gave a sly look in John's direction. It was a warm day and he wasn't wearing a hat. John felt miserable and alone. It was harder to put a mark on a piece of paper than to lift the bags of wheat.

The Yugoslavs broke into a particularly long burst of conversation, although no one paused in their work. Then one of the men broke the line and stepped out of sight behind one of the trucks. The other Yugoslavs laughed and the Greeks watched thoughtfully.

'Present for you.' The Yugoslav stepped into John's vision again. He was a short solid man about thirty, with a dusty blue collarless shirt, and a single deep line beside his mouth on the left. He held out a hat of folded newspaper.

John accepted the hat. Aware of being watched, he tried it on. The Yugoslavs laughed. The Greeks laughed. John laughed.

He met Eric in the street. His uncle was looking plump but the lines of his face were tired.

'Hello Uncle Eric,' he presented himself boldly and held out his hand. Eric smiled although he looked puzzled.

'John.'

Eric's face brightened. He invited John to have a drink. In a hotel in Argent Street, John was surprised to be served by Robert Sharkey. Sharkey grinned and his lips spread unevenly across his face when he saw John start.

'Two schooners gennulmen.'

'I saw you fight a few times,' John explained as he placed a note on the bar.

'Did you now?' The smile might have been mockery.

'At the show. I was there the time you got beaten.'

'The big Maori,' Sharkey nodded. He was more interested. 'Not my best fight.'

'You know Sharkey?' Eric asked when Sharkey moved to another customer at the far end of the bar.

'I think it was his last fight.'

'That's what happens to most of them. A few years of glory.

Then they serve beer in a place like this, until they end up in a park pissing down their leg.'

John didn't know what to say. He filled the space with a gulp of beer.

'Worth it to live for a while. Die some time. Same as me.' Eric set his brows and glared around the room. 'I couldn't wait to get out of here and now I'm stuck.'

'You can leave.'

'Something about this place is hard to leave. Years I lived away but I was always here. Never left it.' He laughed dramatically and tossed down the rest of his beer.

'You look alright.'

Sharkey took the glasses and replaced them. John noticed the way he stared off in the distance, at the glass rectangle above the door.

'Not this marriage,' Eric grumbled. 'Nothing to do, nothing to say, nowhere to go, nowhere. Nothing.'

John nodded, and kept watching Sharkey, who wandered about the bar picking up glasses. Whenever he found himself in a shaft of light, he stopped and looked up at the glass over the door. It always took him several seconds before he moved again.

'You can never resist at the time. The power of the pussy.' Eric clenched and unclenched his fist, and laughed.

Austin and Diana were taken aback when John got a job. For doing so unexpectedly something of which they could not disapprove, they sought a punishment. They were delighted when he could not become permanent.

'What did you do to them?' Austin asked, certain of wrongdoing. 'What did you do wrong?'

'They won't hire anyone permanent with a heart murmur. I've got one,' John replied leadenly.

'You'll do anything to get out of it!'

'It's like his colour-blindness,' Diana stated mournfully. 'When we went to the optometrist, he argued about the number in the pattern.'

'I can't be permanent if I'm colour-blind,' John added.

'Ah!' Austin accepted the evidence as irrefutable.

'The optometrist said it was passed down through women, although it comes out mainly in men,' John observed ingenuously.

'You can't blame me for that!' Diana protested furiously. 'That's the trouble with you, never accepting any responsibility for yourself or anyone else.'

Diana squirmed. Maybe it was her fault, the genes and things. She turned on Austin.

'Let him talk! Maybe they won't hire someone who has a heart murmur or if they're colour-blind.'

Austin was astonished and angry at the injustice of the remark. The truth was simple. This was inconceivable.

'How do you work at all?' He sneered.

'I'm casual. They don't have to keep me on.'

'Breaking down conditions. They always do it,' Austin ruminated bitterly. 'They shouldn't get away with it, not in a union town.'

'They'll put me off when there's no work.'

'The mines,' Diana spoke melodramatically in a voice just above a whisper.

Small huts were dotted about the railway yards unobtrusively, each with a small stone chimney. As John walked past, a man with greased brown hair and lined fair skin put his head through the door.

'I put the tea on when I saw you coming,' he grinned.

The man with lined fair skin waved him to a chair.

'I used to see you at school,' he laughed. 'You was a miserable yard of pelican shit. Always wandering about looking constipated. Never knew whether you was or whether you hated it. Me, there was no doubt. I hated it.'

The kettle was boiling. The man with the fair skin had settled down onto a chair and his feet were already comfortably crossed on the table top.

'I'll make it.' John moved across graciously.

'Just drop another teaspoonful on top of what's already there!' The man with the fair skin ordered gaily.

'What's your name?' John asked as he looked into the teapot, which was half full with murky cold water and limp stewed tea leaves. He added another spoonful of leaves and poured in the boiling water.

'Steven.'

John thought about this as he turned the teapot around three times then poured the dubious liquid into an equally dubious looking teacup.

'I know you, though,' Steven spoke evenly. 'You went away for a while, didn't you?'

John nodded as he passed him the cup.

'You were lucky,' Steven went on blithely as he stacked several spoonfuls of sugar into the cup and stirred. 'I stayed. Worked here since I was fourteen. Put my age up and dummied a birth certificate. They never checked. I been married three years and we got three kids. She's alright but she says it's all my fault I can never stay off the nest, so she's always got a bun in the oven. She could of seen Australia but for me, she says. Not while you're on your back you can't see nothing except the ceiling, I said. She thinks that's funny, most of the time.'

He took out his false teeth and placed them on the table. Without the teeth, he looked like an old man. The lines creased deep into his face although his eyes were bright and shrewd and lively. He scraped his elastic-sided boots along the table to get comfortable, then flicked a used cigarette at a closed window, and lit up another one.

'If you want to we can move around, I said. Not with you always trying to climb in, she reckons. What difference does it make? I ask her.'

John smiled and sat down, and invited Steven to boast some more.

'Four times a night, six with the rags on, and she loves every bit of it.' He drew back with satisfaction.

126

Steven introduced Serge the crane driver to John.

'See that,' he pointed from the ground to the steel cabin of the crane that rumbled along between two widely spaced tracks. 'That is Serge.'

With Steven, significance was always hinted at. John looked up and waited for significance to be revealed.

Steven stepped nearer to the crane and dramatically cupped his hands around his mouth.

'Hey! Come out wog bastard!'

'What?' Answered a heavily accented voice from above. A shaggy head appeared at the window of the cabin.

'You midnight mutton muncher! You great stuffer of destitute dogs!' Steven cried dramatically. Then he remained where he was as the engine whined ominously above. The crane hook began to move slowly down and across from where it had been suspended above an empty rail truck.

The heavily accented voice swore from the cabin. Suddenly and abruptly the hook swung across toward Steven. Steven jumped over the wheels of the crane as the hook dragged the ground and ploughed up dust. Steven stood, safely out of range, and dusted off his jeans. The shaggy head glared down at him.

'Missed again you great pussy-eating wog!' Steven laughed.

'I kill you fucka bastard!'

'You don't take any notice of that,' Steven chatted to John as they wandered away. 'He gets over it real quick.'

John was hired for a few weeks at first. Then he was hired for a few weeks more. He was happy to work in the patch of garden facing Crystal Street. The garden was more important to the station-master than trains or timetables or goods or track maintenance. All of these gave him more time on his garden.

When they were taken away from gumming stickers on parcels or ticking sheets of paper, and given a shrub and a bucket each, most of the men complained.

'Yes,' the station-master raised a finger to his lips. 'Those natives

127

are a little scrubby at the front. I think something new, perhaps European . . .'

'He'd plant petunias between the tracks if he could,' Steven grumbled in a stage whisper as he slid a plant from a pot and onto a shovel.

'Untangle the roots a little. That one's pot-bound,' called the station-master.

'Nothing matters to him, except the garden and when the train comes in from Sydney he puts on his hat and parades along the platform!' Another man thrust a shovel viciously into the soft dusty earth.

'He's got something to live for,' John whispered.

At which the others looked at one another meaningfully.

Chapter 8

Serge did not like John. Despite Steven's assurances, Serge never got over it. Although John did not jump out under his crane and call him a midnight mutton muncher or stuffer of dogs, Serge loathed John. He might have found someone he could pick on, so he pedalled after John on an ancient pushbike.

'You come with me,' he called repeatedly. 'I find the little boy for you'

'Mad wog,' John said over his shoulder when anyone was watching.

The job he was doing finished. Then someone went sick, and he had a few more weeks working on the Comet. Broken shifts. Three in the morning to six, then eight to midday.

Everyone cleaned a carriage. All the vomit was cleaned from the floors and the lolly papers collected and the seats cleaned and the windows polished and the bits of ice-cream cleaned from every small crevice. Then the floors were vacuumed and the toilets scrubbed. At five in the morning, they stopped for a cup of tea. That was when Serge appeared.

'Eh! I did good last night. None of them they don't know how to play cards. Not like the Australian eh . . .'

'Then you'll be able to afford a sandwich of your own today.' The man who spoke leaned on the sill and watched the fire outside where the billy was boiling.

There were always a few who stood around the fire, no matter how cold it was, with lumber jackets pulled around their ears and caps jiggling as they clapped their hands above the flame.

'You very funny man. No I haven't got the sandwich. You got lots of sandwich and cake from your missus. Very nice cake. Because you give all the night good jig jigging she is very happy so she gives you cake.'

'Watch it.' The man turned away.

'Sorry, but I haven't got the wife. None of us wogs got a wife. No jig jig, no cake, no nothing. So you give me a little . . .'

'Get yourself a wog wife!' The man exclaimed.

Despite this, someone would eventually give him a sandwich. After he settled in and everyone had started to read, he noticed John.

'Eh you tell me. What is it like to get your finger or something else into the tight little boy's arse?'

John flushed and ignored it.

'I meet the man like you in Europe. Only they are older than you and I hate them. When I am with the friends at the pictures and we see the young boy. The man has been playing with his parts, he says. So we go. We catch him near. The other hold him down and I cut his balls off.'

He flung a set of imaginary testicles to the fire outside.

'He does not do this to the young boy any more. That is how I treat you.'

John tried shifting away and ignoring it. He told him to shut up. Everyone else told him to shut up. No use.

On the fourth night John found a used tampon in the women's toilet. He also discovered a gift wrapping and a bow. He took a peanut-butter sandwich from his lunch and tucked the tampon neatly between the slices of bread, then wrapped it.

Serge came in at five. John wondered how he could be so voluble and energetic, day after day, night after night, then work all day on his crane.

'This was left. I don't feel hungry tonight.'

John offered the parcel casually.

Serge looked at it closely. Turned it up and moved it from hand to hand and inspected the ribbon that circumnavigated the parcel, and the thick purple bow.

'Poofter sandwiches,' he said suspiciously. Everyone groaned.

'You wrap it yourself? You make someone nice little bumwife some day.' He grinned at the man who sat near the window.

'No jig jig, no wife, no cake, no fucking brains,' grumbled the man beside the window.

Serge brightened when he knew that he had successfully aggravated someone. With unaccustomed delicacy he began to unpick the ribbon.

A piece of string was hanging from the back of the sandwich. Serge did not inspect the sandwich, but raised it immediately to his face. His mouth clamped shut around two-thirds of the thick white bread. When he met with resistance, he sawed with his teeth. Then pulled. The chewed tampon dropped from his mouth. Doughy chunks of bread still moved around on his tongue as he stared at the object on his lap.

His jaw moved as he comprehended. John was running swiftly through the back door of the carriage. Half-chewed bread sprayed over the chairs as Serge leaped after him.

The prophet worked as a fettler some of the time. Although he walked off the job dozens of times, the foreman always hired him again. The prophet wore a rough bush hat and a dirty sheepskin coat no matter what the weather. Steven told John that he slept in Sturt Park, although no one could say they had ever seen him there.

He was tall and thin and walked with great strides. He stared straight ahead with undeviating intensity. The local kids tried to tease him, but he kept going and they did not persist. There was something scary about the way he kept looking straight ahead.

The prophet did not rave or demand attention, so he was one of the few eccentrics treated with respect. In a mostly Protestant town, he was allowed to keep his relationship with his god private.

He went back to the foreman whenever his god, or his stomach, insisted that he work.

'I need a job,' he said to the foreman without apology or excuse.

Like Serge, he might have been a Croat, but if anyone spoke to him in a different language he ignored them.

While the foreman thought about the request, the prophet stood with his legs apart and looked into the distance. The foreman was a big middle-aged man with glasses held together by wire.

As he stared at the prophet the glasses worked steadily down his nose.

'I don't know why I should hire you. You're useless even when you're around, you know that?'

Still no answer.

'Tomorrow.'

The prophet nodded, then turned imperiously on his heels and walked away.

'I don't know. I don't really fucking know,' the foreman complained to himself and pushed the spectacles back up his nose.

Every day for a few weeks, the prophet arrived. He took a hammer. Silently and methodically he did a job. If he spoke it was the irreducible minimum.

'Spike.' He straightened and extended his hand.

'Enough,' when a job was finished.

Then he stood where he was and waited patiently for the next job. Finally, after several weeks, he stood extra straight. His face became rigid and his beard quivered slightly. The other workers stopped and leaned on their tools and smiled to one another. When he couldn't hear the constant sound of picks and shovels and hammers, the foreman also turned. With the terrible grin of one accepting an unsympathetic fate.

'God has told me that I must stop.' The prophet spoke quietly without ostentation.

'Yes! Well, next time it might be God that has your job!' the foreman remarked sharply.

The prophet gently rested the hammer on its side and walked away.

Rowley was Ellen's new boyfriend. He called around to the house often, even when Ellen wasn't there, to drink black tea and talk. John knew that the job at the railways would not last much longer, and the atmosphere in the house was becoming tense.

Plans had to be made or he would find himself working underground. He was afraid of being lost down in the darkness,

132

in the shifting earth. His snobbery or his fear of losing himself, it did not matter, it was fear.

Rowley thought about it. Then told John that he had worked for a few months in the shipyards. It was easy to get a job there. John asked him what it was like.

'Food and a room and they wash your clothes, and the work isn't that hard,' he said slowly. 'So long as you don't mind being thought of as dirt. Not that they treat you bad. They just think you're dirt, and that's all you get.'

'They hire anybody?' John asked.

'They don't think it makes any difference. None of the ordinary workers are anything. They hire anybody. If you're slack that's what they expected so it doesn't make any difference. If you're good they don't care.'

John thought about it.

'I'll go there.'

'Won't hurt, for a while.' Rowley pushed his cup forward for a refill.

Chapter 9

He was a few months short of twenty-one when he arrived in Whyalla. The first thing he did was walk to the employment office of the steelworks, a low red brick shed on the main road, away from the cranes and foundries around the shipyards.

He was surprised when the plump young man in a white shirt and blue tie told him there were no jobs. Everyone knew they hired anyone. They hired the gangsters who had left the eastern states when they needed a few dollars to get them the rest of the way to Western Australia. Then, when things had cooled down for them and they were on their way back, the steelworks hired them again. The plump young man gazed at John with frank distaste.

'I told you, there are no jobs. Not today.' He said it in a way that sounded like, for you, never.

It was John's first meeting with BHP.

Back at the town he booked into a cheap boarding-house and stood under a shower for forty minutes, washing away the dust of the bus ride. He traced a figure-eight in the steam on the glass, and wondered how little money he had left from the railways.

Someone rattled the door of the bathroom. He dried off and walked past a row of middle-aged men wearing towels and holding toothbrushes. Then he sat in the tiny room which used to be part of the verandah of the old house and counted his money. He had enough to pay the rent for a week.

On the fifth day he got a job as a casual tyre changer. During the three weeks he was there he became friendly with Walsh, the burly owner of an old eight-cylinder Chrysler. He took John drag-racing along the side streets of the town.

First, a visit to the hotel for a dozen cans of beer. Then on to a bush track outside town, to sit and drink the beer and listen to the radio.

Slowly they got drunk. Walsh rambled endlessly about the girls he had been with, the girls he wanted to be with, and the girls he didn't want to be with. He had ideas on sex and marriage. The ones you fucked weren't good enough to marry. The one you married never fucked anyone, including himself.

'I couldn't take it,' he wrinkled his nose up. 'Knowing that someone had been in there first.'

'Um,' John swallowed a mouthful of the bitter South Australian beer.

'It'd make my stomach turn.'

Walsh went on turning the subject over, obsessively repeating the same thoughts in the same way with the same acute pain.

'What if you never find one?'

Walsh stared glassy eyed and unbelieving.

'What if you never find a virgin?'

'Never get married,' Walsh gripped the steering-wheel and shifted his backside.

'What if she does it with someone else after you get married?'

Walsh shook his head, as though such a possibility, such pain, would not be possible. There was a place in the sun, even if it came with a mortgage, where the expectations of Hollywood were realised and love and sex did not compromise.

This was the warm-up. Once they were really pissed, Walsh drove the Chrysler to a paddock for an hour of figure-eights and slides. Each time the car slid, the doors flapped open. The dust drifted through the cabin and John coughed and held onto the seat while Walsh whooped and yelled.

The dust still swirled as Walsh eased the car to a halt and let it idle. While the doors still hung open, he flopped back in his seat and stared at John with deep orgasmic contentment.

'Fuck,' he laughed, 'that was fun . . .'

Then to the grand finale. Into town, then to drive for a few blocks with one set of wheels in the gutter and the other on the path, weaving and twisting past the shrubs the Council had been thoughtless enough to plant there. Until a quarry wandered along. A girl. Two girls. The Chrysler charged straight at them, then weaved at the last moment. The quarry shrieked as Walsh slid past, whooping. A U-turn at the end of the block then back at cruising speed to a near stop alongside.

The girl in the pastel dress was calm. By the time the Chrysler rolled along in first gear beside her, she was moving at a steady trot, with a contemptuous nod to the side. The girl beside her was more nervous. She looked in the other direction and held her handbag close against her chest.

'Don't try and chat me up, you pair of morons.' The girl in the pastel dress directed her remarks at Walsh's cheeky boyish smile. 'You think you're smart. Well piss off!'

'So you want a lift?' Walsh continued imperturbably.

'I said piss off.'

'Where do you live?'

'Piss off.'

The car nudged forward with an irregular little cough. The girls passed through the cone of a street light.

'I know. You live in the one on Livingstone Street, with the bushes at the front. Your old man drives a Holden.'

'None of your business.'

'You got a brother?'

'If you knew me that well, you'd know that he's twice as big as you and he doesn't like his sister being chatted by cheeky smartarses in old cars.'

'Got to be cheeky in this life to get anyone to take notice,' Walsh stated philosophically.

'Jeez you're big-headed. Got tickets on yourself.' But the way she looked it was not serious.

'You can get in the back. Nobody's there. You can look.'

She looked closely and suspiciously. Her friend stopped and looked over her shoulder tremulously. She let the handbag fall on her arm and stepped closer.

'Straight home?' The girl in pastel looked sideways at her friend.

The door slid open. The girl with the handbag climbed in first. John turned and smiled. Walsh was a natural but John was acting, and he was not funny. Before they could get uncomfortable and change their minds and climb out, Walsh touched the accelerator and the car dragged away from the kerb into the road in a cloud of dust. He was not going in the direction of Livingstone Street.

'Don't get smart,' the girl in pastel warned. 'The old man is expecting us and he'll come after you.'

'Just a ride, around the block,' Walsh turned up the volume on the crackly car radio.

From a jack to a king
From loneliness to a we-edding ring—

Once around the block, then Walsh let the girls out. The house in Livingstone Street was quiet and dark, except for a solitary light at the back. A blind rattled in the front.

'I played an ace and I won a queen . . .'

'See you later girls!' Walsh called gaily.

Both girls waved nervously and giggled as they went through the gate. The car accelerated again.

'For just a little while I thought that I might lose again . . .'

John tossed a can over the hood of the car. It rattled against a fence.

'Just in time I saw the twinkle in your eye . . .'

The night ended as they sat in the parked Chrysler outside the boarding house, drinking the last of the beer, becoming more maudlin and sad, staring up at the cloudless sky listening to the radio on the significance of life and love.

The day after he finished at the tyre service John went back to the steelworks' employment office. He walked down from the town, over the bridge above the railway line, through the saltpan flats, as a crane turned smoothly on its narrow base and swung out over the wharf.

He lost sight of the crane through the scrubby line of trees before he arrived at the red brick shed.

The plump man behind the counter wrinkled his brow when John walked in, as though trying to remember a familiar face.

137

Before John could speak, he asked whether John had filled out a form.

'I might have last time,' John began to lean his elbows on the counter then straightened up.

'Last time? You didn't tell me you worked here before?' The plump young man had changed his tie and his shirt, and his voice was harsh. His eyes closed suspiciously.

'I didn't work here. I tried for a job a few weeks ago.'

'Why did you leave? Two weeks ago . . .' He went on doggedly as he stepped back to pick up the telephone. He did not wait for an answer before dialling a number.

'Records? We have someone here. Want to run a check . . . might have been here before . . . Name . . . What is your name?' He raised his face and bellowed at John, 'Evans, John Evans, yes, birthday . . . What is your birthday?' Raising his face again. 'Date of birth . . .'

During the few minutes' pause, John allowed his elbows to rest on the counter. The plump young man turned on his heels and rested his backside against the desk and looked out through the venetian slats at the crane in the distance, pivoting slowly with a piece of steel hanging from its prehistoric jaws. The handset rested against his shoulder and he dropped his head to one side as he tugged a packet of cigarettes from his pocket.

Finally he straightened, gripped the telephone with his hand and repeated 'yes' twice. Then he turned to John.

'We don't have anything on you!' he accused, with the telephone still hanging from his wrist.

'I never worked here before.'

'You said you left.'

'I tried . . . I applied for a job a few weeks ago. You wouldn't give me one.'

The plump man quietly thanked the person on the other end of the line and dropped the telephone back in the cradle.

'Why didn't I give you one?'

'I don't know.'

The plump man looked at him for several seconds with an expression of frank distaste.

'I think we might have a job for you,' he almost whispered.

There were steel wheels resting on their sides in the sandpit, and tubs and curved plates, all caked with sand. As the sand was broken away with jack-hammers each shape was lifted onto a trolley by crane. Then the trolley was wheeled into a shed and cleaned. When the trolley was dragged again into the world, the wheels and plates were pitted gunmetal blue. The shapes were lifted again and the welders cut away the plugs where the metal had been poured, then the grinders with spinning discs ground the metal smooth and shiny.

There were no breezes and the corrugated iron foundry held in the heat. In winter, bitter winds blew constantly across the flats. Although the doors were closed the wind came through the gaps. As he worked in the sandpit, John's chest dripped with sweat from the hot cast iron while his back was chilled by the wind.

The pit was reserved for the criminal, the retarded, the eccentric. They were issued goggles and safety boots and a black safety hat—the badge of the lowest rank. Many jobs in the steelworks were easy. It was hard in the pit, turning the jack-hammer into the corner of the castings. The sand stuck in the small corners and had to be drilled away slowly.

The BHP was not so much incompetent as immobile. No government department had it so good. With subsidies from a government which wanted to encourage free enterprise so long as it was neither enterprising nor free, the company hired (almost) everybody. Shipbuilding was encouraged by tariffs, subsidies and protection, and the company prided itself on its enterprise.

The same company that had discovered and mined the lode at Broken Hill. A hill of the richest lead and zinc in the world, where they didn't have to dig for it. When that became hard, they made steel when workers were cheap and coal was there

139

begging to be taken, so long as you had enough money to take it, and the Broken Hill had given them that. No one could ever say that the Broken Hill Proprietary did not know how to take an opportunity.

The company believed in the pioneer ethic. Civilizing the wilderness, they encouraged married couples to come to Whyalla. Civilization came in the form of endless credit. The wilderness was covered with pre-fabricated houses. Cupboards covered in plastic wood were piled inside. Bed ends and mattresses in eggshell blue with fine floral patterns were unloaded from semi-trailers by sweating men in blue singlets and stacked in hallways beneath fluorescent tubes.

It helped if you became drunk with moderate regularity, because you were more certain to stay, and if you were disgusting you served to confirm the company's opinions about you. So long as you dropped your card into the time clock within two minutes of starting time, you could sleep it off for the morning.

In the shipyards, hundreds of men disappeared into the hulls of ships. A man in a black hat pushed a broom around a corner. The crane creaked and swung on its slow melancholy axis, lifting a bundle of pipes into the empty blue sky. Another man bustled past with a pot of whitewash and began to energetically drag the brush along a white line that was still stark gleaming from two days before. People with white hats appeared and strode purposefully across spaces with charts and maps in their hands. Then men in green, yellow, red, brown and black hats appeared working steadily at various points around the shipyard. The men in coloured hats moved briskly with relief after the hours of nothing, and the foremen barked orders and wagged their tails like dogs proving how good they were for their masters.

Occasionally a person in a white hat would pause and gaze with glazed disinterest, but most of the time they walked on masked in sightless superiority. Of course they knew the workers did not work. It was an immutable and unchangeable condition of workers' existence that they did not work. There was nothing anyone in a white hat could do about it so why trouble? It was

140

much easier to talk about diagrams and share the smug incompetence of their kind.

What would have happened had a worker been proud of his work, interested and responsible? Impossible! To seriously suggest this was to question the nature of authority itself. If the workers worked, without the drive and innovation of management, the heavens would tumble. The innovators would be left with nothing to do but to innovate without excuses or lies. If the workers were involved? If they were drawn on for creativity and resources? Unthinkable!

There was an ideas box in each section of the works. Every worker knew the story of the man who had an idea for a release mechanism for slipways. He wrote it down and put it in the ideas box. The idea was used. The man demanded payment, recognition. He was fired for being a troublemaker. The ideas box remained empty except for crude remarks. As the men in white hats screwed up the papers and dropped them in the tin, they glared out at the sullen men hiding in the corners behind the brick stacks. What could you expect? They asked each other, and nodded, without exploring the question.

The man with a white hat had already noticed the white lines still wet on the ground, the bunches of unused welding rods, the clean overalls of the young man with the broom, the obsequious smiling foreman. Authority had been seen. The man in the white hat walked away slowly, holding his plans behind his back, a mannerism common to members of the British royal family.

The job in the sandpit was for the untouchables. It was hard and dirty, reserved for the outcasts and no-hopers from whom not even laziness was acceptable. The moulders and welders, most of them British migrants, sturdy and independent unionists who believed themselves the equal of any man, would never speak to a worker from the sandpits. Not unless it was absolutely necessary, if it was the only way they could stop their wives from kissing a Greek.

The next level down was the Australians. Mostly of Cornish extraction, from some place around the Gulf. The foreman was one of these. Short with thin auburn hair, he kept his false teeth in his silver-threaded green coat pocket to be placed in his face only when a white hat was near. His deputy was the heavy man who worked the shot-blaster. With his leather clothes and apron and pits on the back of his neck, he looked like a butcher. Although he must have been fifty he could lift pieces of cast iron easily that usually had to be lifted by crane.

He was called the deputy, not only because of his relationship with the foreman. Many of the expatriate hit-men believed that they were acting in their very own western.

He liked the name.

The quiet tight-lipped farmer came to the steelworks when things were hard. He hated wearing a safety hat and always leaned on a crowbar. He could have been the fragment of a sentimental painting, with rows of wheat in the background and a dog at his heels. The others said he was going to go back to the farm when he paid off his debts. He never said anything.

Medium sized middle-aged balding men with round expressionless faces standing in a circle quietly behind the brick stacks. A parade of characters wandering past, pausing and stopping, imprinting something of themselves on John's character.

The migrants were the level below the Australians. Mostly Yugoslavs, a few Greeks, a few Italians and a German. Sometimes the Yugoslavs talked to the Australians. Because the Australians sat quietly, they thought they got on well. Until there was nothing there, except the Australians watching blankly with the slightest mockery in the glances they exchanged with each other. Drawing slowly on their cigarettes, sipping the black tarry tea, assuming conventions that the newcomers would not understand. Despairing and baffled, the Yugoslavs went back to their kind. Where they talked, waved hands in the air, touched.

The Australians watched and nodded. When they spoke quietly there was distaste in their voices.

The Australians and the migrants were united in their distaste for the labourers in the sandpit. Mostly itinerant, often tattooed, all named Johnny or Pete, they didn't hang around long. The tattoos assured them of a place in the sandpit. Nobody lasted long in the sandpit.

During lunch, the workers at the sandpit sometimes went outside to settle their differences. No one interrupted or objected, as long as a white hat wasn't around.

'With luck they might kill each other,' John overheard the foreman muse.

'Three to one that the trucker belts Johnny in three minutes,' the deputy almost smiled as he sipped his tea.

'Ha! Five on that!' One of the Yugoslavs immediately accepted the challenge.

Most of the time the deputy was right, but he lost the occasional one, to keep the bets coming.

'Shit that Johnny he's a real seed, a fuckin' seed,' the foreman rambled.

'What was the trouble? You drink too much Johnny? This is the third Monday this month you had off.'

'No,' Johnny chewed his words slowly at first and stretched his big shoulders deliberately so his shirt stretched. 'It was like this, Mr Neeble. The mates . . . Peter over there will bear me witness . . . went to the pub Saturday alright and we got a few in. Couple of chicks come in right and we asked them and they sat with us they agreed, right, to go with us after on the Iron Knob road. I was in the back seat with this one and I kept at it. Managed a finger at the top and I worked at it, alright?' (He held up a large and hairy finger and bent it slowly at the knuckles.) 'So after she said alright Johnny I'll give it to you but I don't want to take on the rest of them. Fair enough so I said "Let's get out and take a walk in the moonlight" and I climbed out. You ever been out in the scrub there? She said "But there isn't no moonlight Johnny." Hell it was dark. "It's nice though let's have a sit anyway." "Alright" she said and sits. We seemed to be getting somewhere when she started crying she didn't have a Frenchy and I said eh don't worry I'll only put it in a little way and I put it in a little way and she was saying "don't" and crying. So I drew back and pushed. Halfway and I skun me knob raw. Her yelling she was a virgin. The first I ever met. It hurt so much I could hardly stand up, nor could she. The bastards in the car had driven home and left us. Fifteen miles, I walked fifteen miles with a skun knob. That's why I had a day off yesterday, Mr Neeble.'

'Ah,' Neeble stared speechless.

'Wasn't so bad,' Johnny gave one of his charming toothless grins. 'She gobbled me when we got to the edge of town.

'Who . . .' stammered Mr Neeble.

'Not going to tell you that, Mr Neeble,' Johnny smiled as he crushed the enemy. 'I don't want you having Mondays off.'

John had been there for a few weeks when he went to Adelaide for a weekend. One of the Peters from the sandpit went with him.

'We can buy a bike,' Peter said.

'You lost your licence.'

'Don't matter. Salesmen don't want to know about your licence. They don't check with the police on who they sell it to, not if they want to sell their motorbikes.'

It took a morning looking through suburban backyards at broken down machines, before they agreed on a small 250cc machine.

Peter was disgusted. He wanted something powerful.

'This one goes,' John insisted.

'It'll take all weekend to get back.'

'I've got relatives on the way.'

Peter was startled. Nobody had relatives near this place.

'Aunt Una and Uncle Charlie. In Port Pirie.'

'Port Pirie is a hole,' muttered Peter.

'So is Whyalla, and Adelaide,' John paused, 'except there's more pinball machines.'

They put their bags on the motorbike and they left. All day they drove, taking turns. Every sixty kilometres the motorbike

144

stopped. The sparkplug had to be taken out and cleaned, and the machine cooled down, and they sat beside the road and waited. Peter complained.

'You want to flag down a car and go, you can go,' John told him.

'I don't leave my mates,' Peter said angrily, too angrily, because having said it, he couldn't.

The dark was coming as they drove into Solomontown, on the outskirts of Port Pirie. They stopped at a telephone box, and he phoned his aunt.

'I'm passing through,' he said. 'Do you mind if I call in?'

'I haven't seen you for years!' Una shrieked. 'Of course I'd like to see you!'

The motorbike was ready to have another rest as John turned into Charlie's front gate. He pulled in the clutch to change down and the clutch cable broke. The motorbike screamed and took off. Peter pulled his shirt so tight that John could hardly breathe and yelled something in his ear.

Charlie was down at the club at the time, which was lucky. There was no car in the driveway. Instead of running into the rear of their old Holden, the motorbike accelerated into the garage and out through a wall of kerosene tins and corrugated iron. Timber was rare in Solomontown, otherwise John would have broken his neck. He didn't think to switch off the ignition. Trying to brake, he laid the motorbike onto its side, so that it pushed easily through the wall and dragged the length of his aunt's washing line.

Una ran from the house to find her washing demolished and a motorbike howling and spraying oil. The washing line was wrapped around the front wheel of the motorbike.

'Oh! Oh! Oh!' Cried Aunt Una.

'Hello Auntie,' said John amiably from the centre of the mess.

John offered to repair the garage when Charlie returned. Charlie gazed thoughtfully at the damage, and with dubious grace declined. It would only take another kerosene tin, and he didn't have to buy kerosene for that, because the corner shop left them out the back and it didn't take much to lift the catch. Meantime it would be best to keep John as far away as possible.

They stayed overnight. John sat at the table chewing cold corned beef with lots of fat and watery mashed potato, listening to his aunt as she talked of the old days, the days when his mother played tennis and he sat on the front verandah and she showed him books on the Indian Mutiny. Charlie said little, offered a can of beer, then with a quick apology went.

'He's not really going to cousin Brett's, you know that.' Una leaned across the table conspiratorially. 'He's going to meet Brett at the front gate and they're going to the club. That's where they're going. Brett tells her that he's coming here, too.'

Peter, who was thin and carried a hip-flask of spirits in his pocket, stared at this relative who did not approve of drinking. Una watched them both closely with her cunning conspiratorial look.

'He takes my pension cheque down there, and he drinks the lot,' she snarled.

'What do you live on?' John stared at a large flake of peeling paint on the ceiling.

'Not much.' Una's voice developed a practised whine. 'He doesn't leave me much. It is bad the way he treats me.'

John grunted sympathetically. Peter laughed next to him.

'I know a bloke like that. Lives in Fitzroy. Mother's pension cheque arrives so he waits for the postie, takes in in, says "Mum it's time you sign it" and if she doesn't she gets a belting if she does she only gets a little belting but she always says no so she can get the belting out of the way first then she says "alright I'll sign it so long as you go" and she signs it "that's what I intended to do" he says and comes down to the club and cashes it.'

'Oooh,' whined Una.

'Not a bad friend though,' Peter reminisced to the wall, forgetting how the conversation had begun.

'No way to treat a woman. His mother!' Exclaimed Una.

Peter agreed although he was far from sure.

The following morning they had a plate of cornflakes and a walk around the garden. The corrugated iron walls had rusted away near the ground. A film of black dust from the smelters spread over the bare yard and the paint on the corrugated iron was pitted and scarred. Weeds and saltbush could not grow there. In a corner, a couple of woody geraniums struggled to survive.

The motorbike clutch had been replaced with a hammer handle and a strip of thick fencing wire. Una stood tearfully at the front gate as they pulled into the street. Charlie had already gone to the club.

'You won't tell Charlie, will you?' She winked as she produced a packet of cigarettes from a loose flap of corrugated iron.

'You don't mind if I have one?' Peter asked.

Una shook the pack and offered it.

By nightfall they arrived back at the single men's hostels in Whyalla. The rear axle of the motorbike was grinding and wobbling and the motor was straining.

'Good fun,' said Peter.

John parked the motorbike behind the hostels. A few days later he couldn't get it to start. It disappeared over weeks, piece by piece.

Chapter 10

Delia was at the boarding house when he first arrived at Whyalla. When he worked at the steelworks he shifted to the single men's hostels, but he still saw Delia.

She was pretty, with a small heart-shaped face and flirtatious eyes. Slowly, timidly, over weeks, he showed interest. Her husband worked shifts.

He went to the house she rented with her husband after they moved from the boarding house. He took gifts of booze. He spent evenings listening to her sweet tingly voice, mostly about sex. The unsure feeling that he could be like the others, like everyone else, talk about it, if . . .

His twenty-first birthday came and he set out for the steel foundry.

He worked contentedly through the day. He smiled at the foreman, accepting his bad temper without objection. He made jokes with the other workers in the sandpit and listened and laughed as the Yugoslavs yelled and waved their arms about.

When the whistle blew he walked back to the single men's hostel, then threw a towel over his shoulder and picked up a slimy cake of soap. He was halfway to the shower when his parents walked through the wire door at the end of the corridor. As they stepped from the oblique afternoon sunlight into the shadow, he stopped.

'Happy birthday!' Called his mother.

'Happy birthday!' Chimed Austin and Ellen together.

All in their best clothes. He walked slowly to them, unsure of what to say.

'The watchman said it wasn't allowed but we told him it was your twenty-first so he let us in. Special circumstances. He was so nice.' Diana smiled nervously.

'Happy birthday,' Ellen repeated as she stepped forward and offered her cheek.

He noticed that she was wearing high-heeled shoes.

'Congratulations son.' Austin cautiously offered his hand.

'I've got to have a shower.' He struggled to hide his sense of aggravation and disappointment.

'Go on, we'll wait near the gate.' Diana's familiar chuckle. 'We can't embarrass the boys on their way to the shower.'

His mother laughed again as he walked, more slowly, to the shower.

They sat around a small table with silverware and plates with scolloped edges. The entrée was prawn cocktails. Austin drank beer and Diana drank gin and lemon and Ellen hesitated then she drank gin and lemon too and John drank everything.

Each of them consumed: a plate of vegetable soup, a plate of roast beef with potatoes and pumpkin and hard little peas that they had to chase around the plate with a fork.

As they gradually became drunk, the waiter came and placed a cake in the centre of the table. In the centre of the icing was a big silver-paper key. A man at the next table wiped the froth from his lips and leaned across and offered his hand.

'Congratulations,' he squeezed John's arm. 'To have life ahead of you. Good parents. Good people. Never let you down, people like them, never let you down.'

His parents beamed.

John smiled. He believed it was true. His parents beamed.

A wandering reporter from the *Whyalla News* noticed the cake and led his photographer across the room. A broad, deadpan face with hard eyes. A blue suit, frayed pockets. Notebook.

The hard eyes flickered over the docile table. John felt the eyes touch his own, then move away. The reporter introduced himself to Austin, bowed elegantly and slightly ironically to Diana. Austin beamed. Diana beamed.

'The family came from Broken Hill?' The reporter flamboyantly opened his notebook.

149

'Yes,' Diana went on happily. 'It was a long drive. Austin took two days off, so did our daughter. We came especially.'

The reporter smiled blandly and scribbled a few notes. During the expectant silence the photographer took two photographs.

'You work for the company?' The reporter did not look up.

'The steelworks, in the foundry.'

The reporter looked up, almost curious, puzzled at a contradiction.

'A bit hard.'

John managed a thin smile.

'All my family work hard.'

'Yes,' the reporter agreed drily.

The cameraman packed his camera away. The reporter shook everyone's hand. The eyes looked harder at John. Austin beamed. Ellen beamed. Diana beamed. John looked across at the silver-paper key which had been lifted and twisted from the centre. Much more interesting. The circle of tiny silver balls around the base of the cake twinkled.

'I won't say life is just beginning,' the reporter smiled.

'Will there be something in the papers?' Diana asked eagerly.

'I think so. If one of the photographs comes out alright.'

The photographer was impatient. The reporter turned away.

'When it comes, you send the paper to us,' Diana insisted.

'Keep an eye out,' Austin added.

He wasn't drunk by the time the waiters were stripping the cloths from the tables nearby. Everybody else had gone. His father paid the bill and they wandered from the room, waving and smiling to the waiter. John left them as they began to climb the staircase to their rooms. Diana gave him a wet kiss. Austin shook his hand again. Ellen kissed him on the cheek, a dry suspicious kiss.

Diana turned on the step of the curved staircase. Ellen was beside her and smiled down, stiffly.

'Good night darlin'.' Diana spoke in her authentic voice, but sentimental. 'Look after yourself.'

Both women turned and walked around the curve of the staircase arm in arm. Austin followed with his precise slow plod.

John did fast talking to get some bottles from the bottle shop.

'Sorry mate we're closed. We lose our licence if we sell out of hours. You ought to know that.'

'Yes, I know. It's my twenty-first birthday today . . .'

'The last bloke tried that on, said it was his grandfather's funeral and they wanted some Guinness for the wake.

'I'm serious,' said John.

He remembered the paper key, wrapped under his arm. He unwrapped it.

'See.'

The man looked at it. John placed it on the counter. The man reached across and touched it. Half of his forefinger was gone. He prodded with the stump. A piece of icing stuck. He tasted it.

'Fresh,' he said.

He put half a dozen cans in a box. John took out his wallet.

'Keep it.' He turned. 'These are on the house.'

He staggered along to the rendered-cement bungalow on the corner of a lane. As he went up the front path, he could see the rise and the railway bridge. From the top the steelworks at night resembled what it was called, the octopus.

It was getting late. A light was on. He knocked.

Delia came to the door. She was wearing a plain dark blue dress and although she was not wearing make-up her green eyes seemed to sparkle in the light. She smiled, half tired, half voluptuous. A strand of hair dropped across her face and she brushed it back.

'Nobody has been to see me tonight. I thought you would have come earlier.'

'My parents came.'

'That's nice. You could have brought them over.'

He ignored that.

'I've got some drinks,' he said.

She led the way to the kitchen, and took out two glasses and handed him a tea-towel. He wiped both glasses.

151

The sat opposite each other at the laminex table. The moon was just past full. In the light, the weeds and bushes in the yard, and the trailer, and the old car on blocks. Nobody ever cleaned the yard. The kitchen itself was only superficially tidy. The table edge was sticky with grease. A few plates and a frying pan rested in the sink, waiting to be washed. A plastic SEPPELT'S ashtray was half full with butts and ash. The house smelled of cooking fat and stale cigarettes.

They drank in silence. He was afraid and self-conscious.

'You're quiet tonight.' She flashed her eyes and her untidy thick hair shook. 'What's the problem?'

'I'm twenty-one today.' He swallowed.

'You shoulda told me,' she yipped and jumped around the table and gave him a kiss. 'We could have had a party.'

She sat on his lap. He felt himself getting hard. She didn't move.

'I didn't want to.' He felt miserable. He wanted to get away. 'My family came down.'

'You said.'

She wriggled.

'I'll sit on your lap any time to see what pops up,' she giggled.

She kept sitting there. They drank through most of the beer. Every now and then she gave him a kiss. At first they were short playful kisses. They gradually lengthened and became more passionate.

'Oooh that's nice. I had no idea you could be so nice . . . so forceful.' She thrust her tongue down his throat and squirmed slowly sideways and around.

'This way.'

She directed his hand around the top of her pants as she allowed herself to be taken to the bedroom, all the time protesting how forceful and nice he was.

They made love several times on top of the lime-green bedcover.

'Now you're my lover,' she mooned as she lay back and looked at the ceiling.

He looked down at her. He felt strong and important. He allowed

152

himself to believe, and this happened. It was nice. He had allowed himself to believe in his parents. They had staggered up the staircase to their bedrooms happy. He felt kind and strong and resourceful.

He was about to make love again when she slipped out from under and got up briskly.

'I have to make the bed.' She giggled again. 'He will be home soon.'

'I can help.'

'No. I always leave it a little untidy or a stain somewhere, so that he can see it. It teases him and makes him worry.'

John stared. It was hard to understand.

'If he doesn't quite know, he likes it.' She strapped on her bra impatiently as though explaining something obvious to an extremely slow child.

'I better go.'

She let him out, with the smallest affectionate kiss at the door. He wandered off, happy and sentimental, over the bridge towards the steelworks and the hostels.

John was sitting in a patch of thin grass and red dust near the hostel's administration block. A few hardy trees had survived and grown tall. He was listening to a debate between the Dutch gardener and the alcoholic homosexual ex-teacher from New Zealand.

The debate on homosexuality was endless. John had heard it dozens of times before. It was a hot afternoon and he half listened to the voices in the background as they rose, whispered, apologised, feinted, attacked.

He was determined not to go to the hotel that afternoon. He was getting a thirst and it was hard not to go. Alcoholics from the hostels went to work for the Commonwealth Railways in the desert from Port Augusta. It was for the desperate, the ones for whom everything else failed. John wanted to beat it before it developed too far. The thirst was strong. If this was the beginning, he asked himself, what would it be like at the end? Endless craving, a sexual thirst for tingling alcoholic love, warming, bathing, terrible and wonderful disintegration. The mysticism of alcohol.

He had played four games of ping-pong and guzzled jugfuls of orange juice and tins of Coca-Cola. Litre tins of pineapple juice and the dry bitter taste of mineral water. He was sitting there, half listening, thirsting. Delia's husband was working during the day. There was nowhere to go. He stared at the light, hungry for redemption.

'Here comes Johnny,' the Dutchman's voice chimed clearly out of the fog of insignificance.

Johnny? There were lots of Johnnys. He had become a Johnny himself in the sandpit. He had taken to wearing the uniform of a Johnny or a Peter. The tight blue jeans and sharp shoes, the western shirt. What was it made him look expectantly into the bars of light between the trees?

The sunsets were sometimes exquisite, when the red spread over the west and grasped at the south and north as though to drag them, too, down into the daily enacted configuration of tragedy, the passing of fathers into sons into fathers, the birth and death of the mysterious mother moon, her regeneration into another daughter inseminated by light. The beautiful humble everyday from which the great sought their desperate doomed freedom, dark to light, glowing red to blue, through which a Johnny ambled easily and deliberately, unconscious of the way his auburn hair grew a terrible halo in the light shifting and dancing through his hair. A shirt was slung carelessly across one shoulder.

'What a beautiful body that boy has!' The former school-teacher whispered sincerely.

Neither of the others chose to disagree.

Johnny's heavy work boots kicked up the dust as he walked. He came closer and dropped unexpectedly to his knees.

'Nothing here is prodigal!' He proclaimed with Biblical fervour.

John glanced to the others. They didn't seem to know what the remark meant either. All three waited.

'Nothing there, all combustible, none prodigal!' The man repeated.

John looked from the man, so seriously spouting nonsense, to his audience, who so willingly drank it in. The Dutch gardener introduced them.

John leaned back and did not offer his hand, as was the custom among those from the sandpit.

Johnny dropped his head and may have been trying to look at the small bird tattooed on his sternum.

'Ignominious,' he remarked.

John watched him closely.

'You know Aristotle? Most prodigal.' The man shook his mane of red hair. 'I get it out there, when I restant unpostal at Her Majesty's pleasure-dome I read there *The Roots of Heaven* and insights essential gained there, law irrespective. When they say "Go" I take the book three months non-parole behavioural excellence.'

He took a battered paperback from his hip pocket and weighed it on his palm before dropping it. To ignore the book was a deliberate insult. John picked it up and read the cover, *The Roots of Heaven* by Romain Gary.

He nodded cautiously and put the book down.

'No longer is Gertrude Street the prodigious fun-stained mile of youth. Seeking I walk refunded not by trucks except twice to the desert. Pie-eyed I wend the main road deft and clear. Assault or armed robbery temptation I defer determined not although I live on lizards at Port Augusta. Sixty-six days there before I oblige then grief return to the skimps of houses unenlightening hunger . . .'

'To be caught behind the fowlhouse there eating the farmer's chickens,' the former school-teacher chortled.

'The book was my defence,' Johnny nodded to the book resting on the dust. Errol Flynn's face smiled up from the cover.

'I show it to the Magister and say I seek the prodigal. He thinks amusingly I have seen the film memorable Trevor Howard no fine for you Johnny seeker although guilty you go to Whyalla shipyards and work there six months or once again inside, contemplation yet again of your dreadful record etcetera.'

155

'He'll be inside if he doesn't stick the job,' the former school-master translated.

'Another two weeks only,' Johnny added quickly.

The thirst was terrific and tormenting. For days John sat in the tiny room and read *The Roots of Heaven*, swallowing pineapple juice and Coca-Cola.

Some nights Johnny called and sat around, talking conundrums and puns, the conjunction of words and world. Then to the common-room where older European men played chess through the night and younger ones played cards and table-tennis.

Between sweating games of table-tennis, John told him about Delia. Her husband was still working day shift so John was spared that temptation with the alcoholic one. Johnny looked at him puzzled, then understood. That somewhere John was innocent like him, only different.

'The estranged prodigal,' he sympathised. 'The itching cock is the worst for some.'

'Not like that.'

'Collapse of a vacuum in a paper bag. Exeunt of prerequisites, planted in drugs of reason.'

John sucked through a straw at some more pineapple juice. The cold abrasive liquid slashed his throat.

'Ambiguity in exaltation if you want to come when I reunify classificate inward and leave from here.'

'Where?' John was startled by this lapse into comprehensibility.

'The islands to Crusoe Friday week rafting collapsed pines vine strung heat prodigality thence to trade in wonder. Check the seasons unmonsoon departing no cyclone radios warning static still across waters waves rising not.'

'I must think.' John looked down, afraid.

'The balls toll the air around you.'

He smiled and began to get up. He made sudden unexplained exits.

'Johnny the salt sanguine taste of terror mother's earth milk is wine needed, not the craving of booze.'

156

It was pay night, the second Thursday night of the fortnight. It was early. The Europeans were drinking flagons of cheap wine and arguing in languages he did not understand, sometimes breaking into coarse English, swearing and laughing. John was alone.

The single men had surged to the four hotels. For the married men the compulsion was different, the loneliness chosen.

In the hostels the single men lived in barracks made by the company. Each brick was labelled, the corrugated iron was made by a subsidiary. In each cubicle the neat iron bed and the steel cabinet and the plain painted steel frames of the table and chairs and the laminex table top and the plywood chair seat were made by the company.

The clothes, your own clothes, marked with a room number were washed free. In the canteens within lunch times, you could eat as much bulk food as you could consume. Three huge men sat at the tables for hour after hour, stuffing themselves with pie and bread and butter custard and cream and prunes. No women.

Waitresses, chosen to be old and ugly and preferably deformed. Ugliness was superficial but nastiness wasn't. The company managed to select unerringly.

Only in one regrettable case did they slip.

Although she was single, Myra was so fat. Whatever agency hired waitresses on the basis of singular unattractiveness thought Myra so repulsive that not even the desperate men of the single men's quarters would be interested. Her manner on acquaintance seemed coarse and abrasive. The bluntness soon wore off. Myra was a happy person. As she walked cheerfully between the tables her massive hams shifted with majestic dignity. She picked up plates easily and deftly, accepting with grace the homage offered her, because the men would never cease belching and farting or swearing for any other waitress except Myra. She managed an easy impersonal side-step and a withering glower should any become too familiar.

New arrivals watched with distaste as Myra went her regal

157

way between the tables, followed by the gaze of dozens of frustrated drooling men. Within a month or two most of them joined the droolers. When John did not join the droolers, those who were interested decided that: a) he was getting it somewhere else, or b) he was queer.

The former school-teacher was regarded as a useful temporary outlet for frustration. To minimise conflict, his pay and sexual favours were arranged during the days prior to pay-day. His money was divided, including overtime. He was a cheap drunk. A few beers and a mixer of some sort and he could hardly stand up. Then he was taken into the back lane and divided up appropriately. If no one wanted the remains they pissed on him. Or a primate evolving painfully towards self-consciousness would brave the mockery and take him home.

Open homosexuals made bargains. They secured relationships and privileges, occupied adjoining rooms, asserted dignity.

There were other alternatives. In the camp at Port Augusta, Aboriginal women went for a bottle of beer, and on pay Thursday and Friday night rows of vehicles revved along the highway north, screaming and weaving. The broken glass by the roadsides grew into banks, and small hills of glitter littered the plains.

John sat quietly at the table after Johnny left him. The noise was building outside, as a group wandered past singing and yelling on their way to the game. He waited until they had gone. The Europeans sat stolid and immobile, the chessmen at attention under the light. One man made a move with a bishop and looked at his partner with a smile. The partner moved his eye around the board. He was older and he did not glance up.

John walked across to the counter and bought another large can of pineapple juice and four bottles of Coca-Cola. A small woman with strong body odour and a huge nose thrust them at him across the counter. He asked for a bag.

'You know we don't give bags,' she snarled.

'I see why,' said John as he scooped up the cans and bottles into his arms and left.

In the hostel block, six men played skittles using full beer bottles and themselves as targets. As the bottles broke the floor became slippery and they skidded and rolled in the broken glass. A big man was too slow and a bottle hit him on the side of the head. As he rolled against the wall, he never stopped laughing.

John could not get through to his room. He sat out in the open air and drank slowly one of the bottles of Coca-Cola. Not far away he could see the police raiding the gambling school in among the trees. Men were running through the trees, snapping branches, puffing, screaming, followed by torchlight beams. The police were clever. Many ran straight into the arms of another patrol. The vans were backed up at the entrance to the steelworks and the rear doors were open. As the vans filled, the doors crashed shut.

The police were still moving around, flashing their torches on anyone who wasn't inside. John went inside. The man with a broken head lay against the wall still, except that his legs were curled up and his hands rested around his head. He groaned loudly and flailed with one foot as John stepped past. The others were inside the shower and toilet cubicles at the corner of the block. John glanced through the doorway as he walked past. The door had been ripped from its hinges. The men were leaning over the wash-basins vomiting and one lay on his back pissing into the air. A small fair man with fine features sat on the toilet floor with his trousers down around his ankles and gurgled and swore as he smeared vomit and shit in patterns on the floor.

John almost slipped on the beer and the glass and blood outside his door. Once inside his small musty room, he instinctively flicked on the light. Before he could turn it off, someone beat against the window.

'Let us in,' a voice begged urgently. 'Please. They're getting close.'

John hesitated, then slid the window open. A figure climbed through, smelling, trembling. Then another. Then another. Altogether, seven men climbed through the window.

'No more!' John pushed the window as another pushed a foot over the sill.

The possessor of the foot tried to come in. The others already there yelled No more! Get! Find your own! Then they pushed the foot out and closed the window. The figure outside might have thrown a brick, only he didn't have time. A flashlight probed nearby, and he ran. 'Get them,' someone yelled. He took off.

The police cruised slowly past in their truck. The lights probed across the window. The first man to climb into the room began to recite the Lord's Prayer.

'It's not that serious,' another man whispered.

Another whispered a brutal Shut up.

' . . . will be done on earth as it is in heaven . . .' the voice recited remorselessly as a light crossed the room and blazed for a second against the ceiling.

The rest whimpered and kneeled closer to the ground.

They stayed where they were for forty minutes. The police had gone. Already, others had crawled out from the hostels and hiding places and brawled and yelled. The game began again amongst the trees.

'Why do they bother?' John asked.

'Statistics. They've got to get them up somehow, or they lose their jobs,' one answered.

'Or they might have to look for real criminals, the ones who pay them off!' Another grumbled.

'Can't have that. Can't have that. How would the steelworks operate then?' The first speaker answered.

'It might produce some steel ships,' the first snorted.

'All clear out there now,' another said impatiently working towards the door.

'They won't come back again tonight!' Another giggled as he sipped from a bottle of someone else's whisky.

'They did once. Got more second time round than they did the first.' The first speaker gazed out through the window.

'Back to the game! Back to the game!' The others chanted.

John stepped across and opened the door. He went into the corridor to check. The man who had been hit by the bottle was gone, although there was still blood, and glass, and the smell of stale beer, and the vomit and excrement from the bathrooms.

'All clear,' he called.

The men trooped out one by one, some jaunty, although the first man was still trembling and he left last.

The first speaker stopped and thanked John for opening the window.

'Any time you need a favour.' He scribbled a room number on the back of a cigarette box.

One week later the newspaper still hadn't published his twenty-first birthday photograph. His parents wrote and reminded him. He went down to the newspaper office, where he saw the reporter sitting at the back with his feet up on the desk.

It took him a second to remember John, then he dropped his feet heavily on the floor.

'The one from . . . yes . . . the one with a sense of *irony*.' He leaned back. 'Come through here . . . what can I do?'

John sat on the other side of the desk stiffly.

'My parents were asking about the story.'

'We couldn't publish it because of the photographs.' He clucked a little at the back of his throat. 'Not that they didn't come out . . . here, I'll show you . . . I thought you would have known . . .'

He opened his drawer and fiddled through a pile of envelopes, string, pens. Then he withdrew a wide light buff-coloured envelope which had not been sealed, and dropped it on the table in front of John.

The man watched him closely as he opened the envelope, the sense of eyes probing around his head. He withdrew two photographs. In the top one, Diana and Austin looked rosy-cheeked and so happy. Ellen had a superior tilt to her chin, and her brittle smile, so that John thought he could detect the broken edges around the cornea of her eyes.

The second photograph was almost the same. Father looked soberly fatherly, mother looked warmly motherly, Ellen looked formidably sisterly. In both photographs it was John who was the problem. His eyelids veiled his eyes, making his expression

161

demonic and retarded. His lip raised unevenly to one side, suggesting conscious malevolence and evil.

John stared at both of them. By the time he looked up, his face was red, aware of the reporter's merciless scrutiny. After looking at him closely, the reporter turned to one side.

'You didn't mean it, eh? You didn't know,' he turned and checked John's glowing features again. Something, nothing.

'Well, we can't publish them. You can keep them. Send them back home. If you're game.'

John thanked him politely, wishing that he knew how to respond with a reply that was at once polite and bitter, brutal and clever. He picked up the envelope and stood.

'See you again some time.' The reporter raised a foot and dropped it on the desk top again with a clunk. John noticed then that one of the shoes had worn through to the frayed brown sock underneath.

'Yes,' the reporter was still not looking up. 'You can tell from the photographs that your parents are good, honest people. Workers. Honest workers.'

He looked straight up at John.

'I don't think you are though. Good luck!'

Pay Thursday night. John had dried out. He no longer needed pineapple juice and Coca-Cola. Delia's husband was on night shift. He held out for a few hours before he went.

Delia's brother had shifted in with a girlfriend, and a Canadian was living there. He sat across the table and popped cans and glared at John and mouthed 'cunt' whenever he thought nobody else was watching.

When he met Delia in the corridor after he went to the toilet, she kissed him affectionately and gently tickled his balls.

'You like my brother?' She whispered.

He nodded and fondled her breast.

'Jean is nice. So sexy, isn't she?'

He thought for a second. It was true. Jean, the brother's girl-friend, was sexy. She had one of those backsides that would be

162

heavy and broad by the time she was thirty, but in her early twenties moved with delectable suggestiveness. He agreed.

'Jock?'

'He doesn't like me.'

She shifted a little in shock. Her breast tautened just out of range.

'He's nice, a regular guy,' she imitated the Canadian accent. 'You get used to him, then you love him.'

'He staying here?' John asked casually after his status.

'We needed the money . . . a boarder.' She tweaked him playfully on the chin then turned away.

He followed her into the kitchen a few seconds later. The brother and Jean sat on a plastic kitchen chair together, giggling and feeling. Jock had slipped onto the floor and looked as though he was going to stay there. The brother slipped Jean from his lap and stood up, self-conscious and proud that John saw his erection. Then they moved off into a spare room.

Delia began to flirt immediately Jock rolled onto his side and began snoring in the corner. Soon they went to the bedroom and made love on the bedcover, but John could tell there was something different.

She leaned back and yawned.

'You better go before buggerlugs gets home.'

John went to the toilet. Jock was awake in the kitchen. He dragged himself onto his elbow and mouthed 'cunt' at him again.

'Do that again and I kick your teeth in,' John said deliberately.

'Not a way to treat a guy . . . a visitor from another country . . .' Jock tried to sound angry. He pushed himself upright, and reeled against the sink for support.

As he left, John heard him stumbling around. Lights went on and off. A chair scraped and fell. he was sure that he could hear Delia's voice, and the Canadian's, raised in argument.

Back at the hostels, the brawls and the gambling among the trees were in full swing. Johnny was sitting on the floor against his door with a bottle of vodka.

'How?'

John took out his key and put it in the lock. Johnny shifted across slowly before allowing him to pass.

'Come in,' John said, although he was already in. John took two tin mugs from the steel wardrobe.

'Preference is absteamed from the bottle thanks.'

They sat side by side on the bed. The chair was covered with dirty clothes.

'It was alright,' said John to an unasked question.

'Parole is circumlocuted beyond reasonable doubt tomorrow. Six months I have spent. Then undelayed and undenied not yet mourned I depart.'

John nodded sadly. He did not want Johnny to go, although he felt instinctively it would not be right to ask him to stay. 'What for?' would be the question, and he was uncomfortable with the sensations of answering.

'The elocution of abstemiousness is by now intolerable. The preferences of their honours have now been perversely satiated in the ovens of the company, the bowels of ships, *Seaway King* and *Seaway Queen* must always bear their tiny piece of human me in rusting bolts and weld insufficient.'

John laughed, then straightened at the seriousness with which he was being addressed, the sober beauty of Johnny's face.

'Waif me.' He held up the bottle and poured vodka into John's almost empty mug.

John sipped and felt the warm drink settle down.

'Wandering and waifing wanting wanton I seem to spend nights simmering singing in soul wondering whether such response isolated deems me terror of nothing, hero nothing, lust nothing.'

'I smell of cunt,' said John. 'I'm not going to have a shower out there, with that.'

The sound of beer-bottle skittle smashing against a wall.

'Cunt has always been preferred, generally.' Johnny took a sip of vodka, then leaned forward and held John's head and spat vodka through John's lips.

John swallowed. Warm vodka and spittle, the taste of Johnny

164

behind his teeth. He opened his mouth and accepted Johnny's tongue. Johnny's body pressed forward and their belt buckles ground together. Johnny pulled back.

'Erectile I lust and wonder at the responded privileges delicate and unqueer,' he laughed.

John thought he should get up and pull the blinds. The light was already out but he could hear the police crashing into the gambling school, the screams of running men, the lights turning like a fan on the ceiling.

A man's flat voice was singing loudly along the corridor.

Right sed Fred
climbing up the ladder
with his crowbar
resting in his hand . . .

PART THREE

Chapter 1

Rowley and Ellen were married. Everyone looked pleased, and Diana cried over the sink while they were in Adelaide for their honeymoon. She recovered quickly after they returned, when Ellen came each day to talk.

Rowley was a slaughterman, and he needed a temporary assistant. The Broken Hill abattoirs was out of town, on a side road. John needed a temporary job, to live on and to get away again. He wanted to go back to Sydney.

He had never been in a slaughterhouse before. He might have hated it, felt sick, disgusted. He was surprised when he was indifferent.

The sheep never worried although they were lined up behind the steel gates in rows, nudging each other placidly forward or skipping to the side. Rowley cut their throats with an efficient swipe of his knife as they watched with their incurious eyes. The cattle bellowed when they smelled blood. They kicked and tried to turn as they were forced by the pressure behind to go forward into the narrow steel box. They were killed (mostly) with one hit from the spiked hammer on their brain case, just above their eyes. When they fell, the slaughterman pulled a pin and the floor dropped. The beast rolled onto the floor, and a hook was put through its heel. Then it was raised on a block and tackle. Alive or dead, the throat was cut and the blood swathed onto the sloped concrete floor.

Pigs were killed in a smaller, circular, pen. The slaughterman balanced in the centre of the pen and swung at the pigs as they ran squealing around the sides. When there was a break, the men collected to barrack and cheer.

At four-thirty a.m., the slaughter-room was empty. The meat inspector sat in his small glass cube and stared down at papers on his desk beneath a solitary naked light. The hooks from the rails in the ceiling, the fluorescent tubes glaring onto their reflections on the wet concrete.

The slaughtermen and their assistant offalmen stood around the steel gates sharpening their knives and talking. Then the gate was lifted and the first sheep was pulled forward. Once the headless carcass was raised onto a hook, then John sliced open the gut. He lifted the liver and the intestines out and let them slide into a steel chute in the floor, then stripped the skin.

Steady rhythmic work. The other men shouted now and then and competed to see who could slaughter the fastest. The steel rails rang as the carcasses slid along.

The meat inspector walked from his glass case and moved silently along the lines of white bodies, gazing closely at the stretched thighs, the congealed lumps of fat on the body.

John thought about his sister. Rowley talked about her often. He wondered why she had stayed, why she was a good girl, why he was not a good man. Who was a good man? Austin.

Ellen had sent the telegram. He came back.

His mother would be walking along a beach in Sydney, perhaps along the promenade around the pool. There would be a breeze. The ferries would come and go to the pier. His mother would sit and drink a glass of lemonade on the wharf.

He looked up. The meat inspector was standing a step away, tapping his brogue shoes on the side of the chute. Suddenly self-conscious, he heaved a handful of large intestine at the chute and missed. The inspector swore and jumped back. The liver slithered across the shoes.

Rowley laughed. The meat inspector glared and resisted the temptation to kneel and clean his shoes. John apologised and retrieved the offal, then stuffed it into the chute.

'Mr Thomas,' the meat inspector intoned.

Rowley finished killing the sheep he had against his knees before he looked up. Rowley was tall, he took a while to straighten. He remained bent and looked up at the inspector from the side.

'The one along here,' said the meat inspector, then turned and walked with slow measured pace along the row of carcasses. Rowley hobbled after him.

The meat inspector tapped a small bruise on the thigh of a sheep. Rowley looked bemused and scratched his head.

'Not acceptable, Mr Thomas.'

'I'll cut it out.'

'Not first class, Mr Thomas.'

John lifted a carcass onto a hook, and neatly cut the belly open. So like a human. From the pelvis to the sternum, down in one neat slice. His father, sitting at home, crying he was sorry he didn't mean it. Eva thrown against the wall. The mirror. You ought to leave, I'll look after you I can, Ellen's incomprehensible desperation. Diana stepping through the railing onto the white sand of the beach, there was no one there, walking along kicking the sand between her toes.

When he heard the men yelling, he skipped up the stairs. A bull had survived the hammer and stood. It was in the centre of the pen, trembling and shaking. The slaughtermen jumped through the fence and leaned across with their knives, slashing at the animal's throat, legs, rump.

The bull began to turn in circles. John looked across at Rowley, who was just drawing his knife across a sheep's throat as the bull turned and hooked with its horns at the fence. A slaughterman withdrew his knife quickly and laughed. The bull skidded and broke into a trot, then launched itself over the fence. Rowley swore and jumped behind the sheep gate. The slaughtermen who ran to get out of the pen now dived into it.

John stood where he was, near the door, watching as the bull ambled angrily through the white carcasses. Once it stopped and raised its head and lowed at the ceiling. Then it took out its fury on the glass wall of the meat inspector's office. The meat inspector climbed under the table. The slaughtermen bellowed applause from the far side of the room.

The animal raised its head and looked around. Then John became aware that there was one direction out of the building, through the door he was standing in. The bull watched him closely with red pain-crazed eyes, and might have had the same idea.

It was too far to go to the fence. John turned and galloped down the stairs. The bull clattered behind him. At the bottom of the stairs he jumped a concrete embankment. The bull kept on going through a wall and into the side of the meat inspector's car. Then it shook itself, trembled, and clattered off to a nearby field.

Cautiously the slaughtermen moved down the stairwell. When they saw the bull in the paddock, they gathered and laughed. There was a moment's embarrassment as the meat inspector came down and saw his car with the side caved in. One of the slaughtermen drove him back to town.

Rowley had a rifle in the back of his car.

'Let's go,' he said to John.

John drove the car. Rowley shot the bull.

'He's not much good for anything except dog food now,' Rowley shook his head regretfully.

'We can make some money on the side,' Rowley suggested. 'Buy a bomb and go out shooting the kangaroo.'

They found an old red Ford utility, with no lining in the cabin and plain timber seats. Rowley could not read or write so John signed the papers. While John signed, Rowley looked across the used-car lot at an old Willys jeep parked over the pits.

The Tibooburra Highway was a dirt track, distinguished from other dirt tracks by being wider and better graded. The abattoirs only worked three or four days a week. From that, they earned enough money to survive. With the profit from two nights shooting kangaroos, they could become rich.

While John saw a lot of Rowley, he didn't see a lot of Ellen. She came to the house when he was away, or working. He told Rowley that if he was trying to improve his standing in the family by befriending him, he was choosing the wrong person to do it. Rowley laughed. One ally was better than none, so John left it as it was.

Rowley was a friendly sort of chap. Most of the time he wouldn't hurt anything. He loved guns and he loved killing things.

While John drove, Rowley sat with a small armoury stacked around him. A Lee Enfield .303, a .222 hunting rifle, a .22 automatic (for rabbits), a shotgun (for ducks), the knives from the abattoirs and boxes of shells scattered around.

They set out at three in the afternoon and cruised for hours as the sun gradually set on the left.

'My old man was an alcoholic,' Rowley confided dreamily to the horizon, 'not like your old man. You old man is a decent fella. My old man, he used to come home from the pub pissed most nights, then he'd beat up mum, then he'd come in and beat us kids up, then he'd go in and beat mum up in the bedroom again.'

'Eh?'

'He'd beat her up first because she wouldn't get it off with him, then he'd beat her up when she did.'

He blew a thin stream of smoke from the cabin.

'You don't know how lucky you are with your old man,' he meditated. 'I know I drink a bit. Sometimes more than a bit, but I never beat a woman now. It's not good to beat a woman.'

'No,' John said absently.

'Your sister's alright, she's a good woman. She knows how to stick by someone.'

John hid behind the mirror and agreed.

'She's a good worker.'

'Yes.'

'She's a trier.'

'Yes.'

Rowley was puzzled. He looked around and worked his prominent cheeks, then pushed strands of greasy fair hair back from his face.

'I mean . . .' He brushed the strand of hair back again. 'Your old man. He's a good bloke but he has tickets.'

'Tickets?'

'On himself. Thinks he's good, better than everyone else on

173

the mine. I know some that work with him. No sense of humour, nothing's funny. Never plays jokes.'

'The way he is.'

John wondered how Ellen managed to keep the family secret. From her husband? Why?

At twilight, they stopped and made a fire. John sat on a log listening as Rowley told stories, and he laughed at his jokes, and sipped thick black tea. Behind them the bush rats scuttled and insects rattled and a bird called once from a creek.

When it was quite dark, Rowley stood. He might have been regretful. The moon was waning, but there was enough light to touch the tips of the bushes and outline them. John collected the billy and the steel and kicked dirt over the coals. The flames smouldered and burned defiantly for a few seconds, then surrendered.

Rowley knew every track. John cruised along with the utility in low gear, as he held a search-light over the cabin. The light turned in a low, slow arc across the bush. He glanced quickly along the beam, then back to the track he was following. Then the track ran out and they bounced and rolled over bumps, rabbit burrows and bushes. Small trees cracked and fell as he drove through them.

Rowley followed the beam unblinkingly. He picked out details and patterns in the bush that John was blind to.

'Stop!' He called. 'Back that way.'

The steady beam would settle on an emu, or a rabbit. Rowley swore and they drove on. The old car ground and complained, but kept going.

They went from field to field for hours. John settled into the rhythm of it. He liked the slow jolting of the utility, the cool night breeze and the edge of the window shivering under his arm.

'Stop.'

John stopped, and looked along the barrel of light as it probed

174

a small stand of trees. Nothing. Then two lights. Eyes, reflecting the light, glittering and still.

Rowley leaned the .222 across his chest and aimed. John felt the recoil spring across his chest. The kangaroo flopped down.

'There could be a family. Look around,' whispered Rowley.

The light moved, circled. Two more kangaroos. The same limpid trust as they stared into the light. The same result.

They drove over slowly. Rowley played the light around as they went. The two kangaroos that had been standing together were both dead. Rowley found a joey in a pouch, and dashed out its brains on a rock. They tossed the bodies in the back of the utility. They were going towards the other kangaroo when it stood. A small female, a blue flyer. The kangaroo would not look into the entrancing barrel of light.

As they bucketed across the ground, the kangaroo began to lope off. Irregularly at first, then gathering speed. It veered and turned. John accelerated and Rowley leaned from the cabin and fired, but the utility jolted and the shot went wild.

'Let me drive,' Rowley screamed in frustration as the kangaroo weaved about through the wavering light.

The car was still bumping along in first gear as Rowley climbed out and ran around the cabin and jumped into the driver's side. John threw his legs across the trembling gear-stick and climbed into the seat vacated by Rowley.

Rowley drove faster. He skilfully chased the kangaroo's turns and changes of pace. The utility gained on the kangaroo. Then, when it seemed inevitable that the kangaroo was going to be run down, it tacked sharply to the side. Rowley swore and hauled the steering-wheel around and the old utility slewed across the dust.

The next time the kangaroo tacked, Rowley leaned from the cabin and tried to shoot the kangaroo as it ran alongside. When the animal veered, her entrails were spilling and dragging on the ground. John could have leaned and touched it. Or shot it.

It took forty minutes to run down the kangaroo. Rowley was elated.

'A bit of sport!' He called as he tossed the ragged corpse into the back.

In the morning they gutted the animals. The smell of raw flesh and gas was stronger and sweeter than the warm bland smell of the abattoirs. They had been driving and killing all night. Rowley seemed depressed.

'Friggin' women,' Rowley complained sharply. 'I know she's your sister but they're all like it. She hates it when I have a few drinks, but it's not the same when she goes out with the girls.'

John nodded his head in neutral and tried not to glance up.

'I got home the other night. No more than fifty minutes late, and she goes at me. "What about when you go out with the girls?" I ask her. "You get pissed then, I know I seen you." "Not the same as you," she reckoned, "besides if you don't like it then you can piss off." You know what, I think she meant it.'

Rowley looked at him so directly and long that John was forced to say he didn't know. She always had a temper, though.

Rowley's mood became blacker. By the time they were finished dressing the kangaroos, he was stabbing at the corpses and ripping away the skins. They climbed into the car and John drove silently toward the town. For fifteen minutes they went along, and in the silence it seemed as though the pressure of Rowley's fury could have lifted the cabin.

With forty kilometres to go and Rowley's mood becoming darker, John was surprised when Rowley finally asked him to turn into a side road. No sooner did he turn and the old utility was grinding slowly along the dirt, than Rowley stuffed his shirt pockets with cartridges. He climbed through the window and rested the guns across the roof of the utility.

For twenty minutes, Rowley hooked his knees into the sides of the door, and fired one of the guns each for three or four minutes. He managed to slaughter four rabbits, a wild cat, an

176

emu, and a sign that said SHOOTING AND TRAPPING OF ANY KIND ON THIS PROPERTY IS PROHIBITED.

John glanced to the side after one shot. He almost expected Rowley to drop to the side from the recoil. The empty brass cartridge cases rolled glinting and sparkling from the roof.

'Slower!' Bellowed Rowley as they rolled across a pothole. 'I felt my piles come up my throat with that one.'

'It was the grapes you ate for dinner,' John replied good-naturedly.

When Rowley dropped the rifles into the cabin and slid onto the seat on his back, he was smiling, cheerful, happy. John turned the utility around, back toward the main road. Rowley whistled and sang. They never bothered to pick up any of the rabbits.

Chapter 2

Eventually the train arrived. Diana stepped from the carriage. She wore a blue floral dress and her face was pink and round and fresh although she had been in the train all day.

She leaned forward and pecked Ellen on the cheek. When Austin half stumbled forward, she stared through him. He flushed. Rowley went to the office to pick up her bags. John accepted the small suitcase she was carrying, and the blanket tucked under her arm.

'You're a good boy,' she said somewhat splendidly.

John sat in the back seat of Rowley's car. Ellen began to say something to Rowley, who was driving. Then stopped herself.

'Mum looks good,' she finally whispered back at her brother, in a way that suggested significance.

'Had a good holiday,' Rowley interrupted cheerfully. 'Ought to look good. The beach and the sun, and the good life. That's what you go to Sydney for, isn't it eh?'

John coughed guarded approval.

'I've got a surprise for her.' Ellen stared unblinking at John. The broken lines of her iris fluttered.

'I'm pregnant. I heard about it last week.'

Rowley let out a whoop.

'He already knows, so he shouldn't lose control of the car.'

'Congratulations. That's great,' the things he should have said unspoken.

Ellen looked at him coolly.

'She should be pleased to be a grandmother.'

When they arrived, Diana was sitting at the table. Austin was making the inevitable pot of tea. Both of them were silent.

Ellen sat at the end of the table, in the chair Austin usually used. Rowley sat beside her while John lounged against the door.

'I've got a surprise,' Ellen cooed.

Diana looked at her blankly.

'I'm pregnant.' Ellen smiled at her mother her small bitter smile while the tiny coils and wires in her eyes weaved and touched but never quite locked together.

Diana exclaimed and reached out to embrace, her smile warm and sincere. Then at the last second she drew back.

'Isn't that wonderful!' She exclaimed, but there was something artificial about the way she exclaimed.

'You're going to be a grandmother,' Ellen went on comfortably, only half aware of Diana's restraint. 'I thought you'd like it.'

'Of course I like it,' Diana said unctuously, as though half repelled by the nakedness of what was offered.

'You going to have a baby?' Austin looked up slowly from infusing the tea. He looked from Ellen to Rowley as he turned the pot slowly on its base.

'The miracle of life,' Ellen murmured ecstatically.

'An accident. We decided it was great.' Rowley almost whooped again and his chair scraped across the floor. He stopped when Diana gave him a look.

'There's sherry in the cabinet, and whisky.' Austin placed the teacups back on the rack.

John was relieved to get the sherry and the glasses from the mirrored cocktail cabinet in the next room. He placed the glasses along the table and filled them.

'You can leave work in a few months' time,' Rowley was saying. He poured beer into a glass and watched the froth intently as it settled.

'I don't want to leave work for good.' Ellen looked at the settling froth sharply.

'Have to for a while,' Rowley murmured, disguising the intensity of meaning.

'For a while,' Diana nodded assent to a compromise.

'Wouldn't you . . .?' Ellen switched her gaze to her mother.

'I brought up my own. I don't want to go through that again,' Diana added firmly.

'It's marvellous . . .'

179

'We could . . .' Austin stopped when Diana gave him a frigid look.

'Maybe my mother,' Rowley said listlessly.

'She couldn't,' snapped Ellen. 'She doesn't have time.'

'You'll have to give up work then.' Rowley became almost smug.

'Only for a couple of years,' Diana spoke soothingly. 'You can go back to it.'

'Your friends can come and see you,' Rowley said, not happily.

Ellen turned away tearfully and looked around for a cause, a victim. She gave John a poisonous look. John leaned against the terrazzo and sipped his sherry.

'I like working.' She spoke the innocuous words venomously. 'I believe in keeping myself.'

John crossed his legs. Rowley turned the glass in his hand and gazed thoughtfully through the window.

'A good thing too, for a woman,' Diana murmured.

'I've never had much to do with babies. I'll have to learn,' Ellen despaired.

'Lots of women have done it.'

Diana sounded pleased.

The Menindee Lakes had been salt pans, empty for most of the year. Then they were dammed. Market gardens began. From Menindee, a pipeline flowed with water in the droughts.

Broken Hill people brought small blocks around the lakes and built holiday homes on weekends. Rows of new corrugated iron sheds lined the beach at Copi Hollow. The road was sealed with a smooth unbending strip of tarmac along which a line of cars undulated on the weekend, with water-skis strapped to roof racks. The wide backs of caravans swayed around the centre of the road and boats rattled and bumped on newly painted trailers. Aerials with tails and football flags rippled. A huge Pontiac driven by a man in overalls and sunglasses cruised easily past the old utility. A little girl waved to John from the back seat. John waved back.

If yooo
Needed somethin . . .
I wanna hold your hand
I wanna hold your haa-and . . .

John sat up on an old mattress in the rear, all around him eskies of beer and frozen chops. Rowley turned off the sealed road past the small rounded stone grave of Burke's and Wills' camel driver. It was a tourist attraction so the Council had cleaned off the word WOG that had been carved into it, and repainted it and surrounded it with a new bright picket fence.

It was a short bumpy drive to the lake. Once there, John wandered away and found a place near a thin strip of mud, and stayed for most of the day, watching the motor boats rip along the listless water. The ripples ran in and filled holes in the soft mud where swimmers had trod and felt their way. A thin man on water-skis waved as he was towed in a long slicing circle. The swimmers waved gaily back and laughed. Ellen paddled easily out and began to swim, not looking back.

Diana yelled at Austin. 'She shouldn't do that, not when she's pregnant,' but Austin looked down helplessly.

Rowley followed Ellen into the water, and lazed along on his back, kicking and thrashing, and calling back there was nothing he could do about it. Diana glared and walked back to the picnic blanket and poured herself a cup of tea from a thermos.

'She's his wife,' she resigned herself to the worst. 'If anything happens it's not my fault.'

The thin man on water-skis circled again. The motor boat continued on a wide circle, but the thin man let go of the rope and with a clumsy turn of his bony knees let himself drift in to the shore.

'Watch out, girlie,' he called as he glided past Ellen's head.

The skis gradually lost momentum and sank. The thin man stepped off awkwardly onto the mud and recovered the skis.

Families lined up to use the barbecue racks. Diana sat and watched. Ellen waded back to shore, and flopped down onto the side of the blanket and wiped the hair from her eyes.

181

'I brought some fried chicken.' Austin looked pleased. 'We don't have to line up.'

He fiddled into a bag and drew out the pre-fried chicken in the aluminium foil, dragged out another two plastic buckets of coleslaw salad and a glass salt shaker. He beamed across at Ellen as he produced a thermos flask of coffee and a tube of condensed milk.

'There's tomato sauce and sugar in the bag too,' Austin smiled.

'I would have fitted in a few more cans,' Rowley ran up and shook water over Diana as he towelled himself. He was surprised when Diana did not laugh.

A line of ants began to invade the blanket. Diana brushed them away.

'They aren't worrying me,' Ellen protested.

'They'll get into the food,' Diana growled.

Everyone began to eat quietly, until another family laid out a blanket nearby and turned on a radio. A little girl crawled towards them, then pushed herself upright.

'You want to walk to me?' Austin held out his arms.

The woman from the next group approved and smiled as the little girl wobbled unsteadily across. Austin picked her up when she arrived. The little girl giggled and beamed.

'She doesn't do that for everyone.' The little girl's mother settled back onto the blanket. She was young and her eyes flashed.

'He's good with children,' Diana said drily as she wiped a chunk of hard butter into a piece of thick bread with a knife.

'You can tell when they like children,' the woman stretched out her legs. 'Kids know.'

The man twiddled with the radio dial.

'There isn't much choice,' the woman snapped at him.

The man settled back on the original station.

'Here's a great one,' burbled the disc jockey. 'A new classic . . .'

Diana placed a slice of tomato onto the smear of butter and passed it to Rowley, who swallowed it easily in one bite and washed it down with beer. The little girl wanted to go back to her mother. She thrashed and began to cry. Austin stepped behind her to help her walk back.

When the little girl fell and cried, the mother jumped up and brushed her dress down over her legs. Austin stood dumb and resentful.

'It's alright dear. Mummy's here.' The woman let the little girl haul herself up on her dress.

Austin smiled tightly but did not move.

'She must be tired.' The mother smiled and flicked her hair from her face.

The man behind her rolled onto his stomach and stared out at the motor boat still roaring past on the lake.

'I'm going to get one of those soon,' he yelled in Rowley's direction.

'Wish I could afford one,' Rowley laughed.

'It's easy to get a loan.'

The woman turned her face to the ground. Diana sliced another tomato, and a sliver fell onto the blanket. She carefully picked it up on the blade of the knife and put it onto a piece of crumpled newspaper.

'You can pay it off in five years. We wouldn't have a house if we didn't go to the bank,' the man said softly.

They left in the evening. Most of the cars and caravans had already gone and the lake was quiet and flat. A few water birds flapped around nearby and a light from one of the weekend houses glimmered on the far side of the water.

'I like it after everyone else has left,' said Diana, looking at the empty spaces which had been full of blankets and families and the smell of chops.

The dishes had been washed under a convenient tap. The blankets were rolled and put away in the boot of Austin's car.

John climbed into the back of the utility. The others regarded it as a relegation, but John wanted to look back at the road as it spooled out behind.

They were halfway to the town when the differential crunched under him. The motor shuddered and strained and the rear of the utility rocked. Rowley stopped and they looked but there wasn't much they could do. Ellen walked off into the bushes.

'Where are you going?' Rowley called after her.

'To have a piss. What do you think?'

When she came back, neither of them spoke. They climbed silently back to their places. At first the utility ran more smoothly, then after a few kilometres it was running as badly as before.

John wriggled his back against the cabin instinctively. Inside, Rowley and Ellen sat apart. Ellen's arm rested on the window and she stared out at the blackness. Rowley kept driving.

As the lights of the town came across the horizon, fragments of the smashed galaxy into which they were directed, the steel along the differential screamed and howled. Rowley accelerated. John guessed that he was angry, trying to get Ellen to respond. The more she ignored him staring out into the blackness to the side, the more he pushed the old utility towards the lights. The back of the car swayed and dragged across the road. Another car passed them easily, running across to the far side of the asphalt. The man in the passenger seat leaned from the open window and swore. The tyres threw up pieces of gravel, then the car pulled sharply across, almost running the utility into the side of the road. Instead of slowing, Rowley tried to accelerate more.

The back seat of the receding car presented a bare and hairy backside to the swaying lights of the utility. Someone flipped a bottle into the air, which bounced from the bonnet of the utility. The car slowed and moved from side to side, forcing Rowley to slow. John put his head into the cabin on the driver's side, not quite knowing why.

'I should put a bullet right up that fat date!' Rowley exclaimed, indicating the hairy rear which still moved invitingly against the back window.

John laughed. This was enough for Rowley, an excuse for him to laugh and drop back. The car tried slowing even more. Rowley slowed, Only then, the car took off, as the owner of the hairy

184

date rubbed his fingers along his perineum then flattened his testicles against the glass.

The car sped ahead, until the tail-lights were lost in the cluster of stars from the town.

As they drove into Rowley's family backyard the utility was crawling. Rowley's mother came out to watch. When the car rolled to a smoking halt, Ellen stepped from the cabin and walked into the house without comment.

'You don't have to drive me home.' John started to walk to the back gate.

'We're going to split! Your sister and me!' Rowley hissed after him as he pulled the gate behind him.

Chapter 3

'It isn't as hard as that,' Diana was saying. 'It's nothing. Thousands of women have done it. Everybody has been through it, one way or the other.'

She laughed at her own joke.

'Does it hurt?'

'It's been a long time since I had children.'

'You remember. You can remember everything else.'

'It just happens. If you're a woman, you have babies like all the other women. It's your job.' Diana sounded uneasy and resentful.

'Men can't do it,' she tried another joke.

'When it comes out . . .' Ellen implored doggedly.

'When it comes out you open your legs and let it.'

Diana turned to wash the cups and dishes. Ellen might have been crying. Diana did not turn.

Ellen's voice, when she spoke, was level and flat.

'Why did you get married, mum?'

'He asked me. He asked me half a dozen times before I took it seriously.'

'Why?' Ellen persisted.

The dishes rattled for a second.

'Because he was nice to me. He brought me flowers and chocolates and asked me to the pictures.'

Her voice did not sound at all ironical.

'He hung around, and he hung around. He kept asking me and he seemed nice there was nothing else for me to do so I said yes.'

She placed a cup precisely on the drip tray and sank her hands again into the soapy water.

'He was nice and I could have done worse, and he never got drunk much and he never looked like he was the type to beat

186

me up and he needed me and I could have done a lot worse like Una did when she married Charlie.'

Ellen leaned forward on her elbows on the clean laminex table top.

'It isn't fun to be an old maid, it might be different now but I was almost thirty and I didn't want to be alone. Looking after other people's kids while they go out dancing and to the pictures, too old to go dancing, too old to play tennis, too old. There was a maiden aunt used to come and visit for a weekend every few months, one of dad's sisters. We gave her a bad time, a cruel time. When we saw her in her trap going along the road we jumped out and ran and yelled at her "Ugly auntie Rosie got a big round nosey, no man will pay a penny for her big round fanny, ugly auntie Rosie", we cheeked her bad and she looked hurt. Whenever I saw her she looked as if she was going to cry and I felt sorry for her but I couldn't it only made it worse. She never told mum about it or we would have got a beating but she looked so sad and sorry for herself as though she was just waiting to get beaten. We couldn't help it although I felt sorry when I was on my own I couldn't stand being treated like that, no I couldn't.'

'I hate being pregnant.'

Diana looked at Ellen sharply.

'Some women like being pregnant. They glow, they look lovely, they bloom. Myra Lehmann would have stayed pregnant all the time if she could have.'

'Did you feel like you bloomed?' Ellen scrutinised her mother, who shifted uncomfortably.

'It was you that did it. At least you had some part and you must have said yes.'

'I'm not glowing. I feel awful.'

Diana looked at her desperately.

'It was something I put up with, because that's what women have to do, and men are built that way.'

'Was Myra Lehmann built that way? Was Austin built that way?'

187

'I don't know how . . . what's in people's minds, how do I know? If they think about that all the time.'

She was exasperated. Her voice was raspy and hard and the plates rang as she dropped them onto the drier.

'We'll get it going again.' Rowley spoke as though stating a piece of conventional wisdom which everybody liked to hear and nobody believed any more. He was discussing the red utility, the tyres of which were gradually settling as it stood in the corner of Rowley's family backyard.

'We could save some money,' he went on after a pause. 'Buy a freezing unit and let someone else do the shooting.'

John pushed a plate of Iced Vovo biscuits across the table. Rowley took one and dunked it in his tea.

'Johansen (or was it Johnson?) tried that a few years ago. Good shooter he was, eyes that could see anything. Made a living then decided to go into business with a freezer. Offered better prices than the big companies.'

'Had an accent,' John smiled. 'Like this: "vot is it you vont yah?" '

'Like that,' Rowley accepted the amendment into the story. 'Made a profit for a while, gave the big companies the shits. Then he disappeared. The big freezer left standing in his backyard, nothing wrong, all his things in the house, all his clothes. Food was still there, so was his wife. Except his dog, a savage old brown mongrel. Nobody heard of him again. After six months a bloke from one of the companies called and offered his wife a fair price for the freezer unit. She had a kid and no job, so she took the money. They towed the freezer away that day.'

John took an Iced Vovo and broke it in half. He dropped the uneaten half onto the saucer.

'What happened?'

'Johnson and his dog, they cut them up and boned them and sent them to Sydney with the kangaroo meat. Made him and his dog into export quality pet food, him and the dog got reduced and mixed in with kangaroo and canned. Bones and all.'

'The one with extra marrow-bone jelly.'

'You got a funny sense of humour, you know that? But I used to think about setting up for myself the way Johnson did, because I know everything from the abattoirs and I know the shooters. I'm not game. I wouldn't want your sister to be a widow. Eh.'

'You're telling the story.'

A chunk of Iced Vovo slid down his throat. Rowley looked at him undecided as he took a long sip of tea.

'The Aboriginals got a good one. They used to hunt the sheep because they were easier than the kangaroos, so whenever they skewered a white man they wrapped him in kangaroo skins and buried him so nobody would look close.'

'You could still tell.'

'Not if they broke up the bits and burned the body in a fire. Burn the kangaroo as well.'

John thought about it for several chews of Iced Vovo.

'The squatters would be more angry about losing a sheep than a man anyway,' he said.

'That's right,' Rowley broke up laughing. 'The Aboriginals were too dumb to know that though!'

Rowley became more bad-tempered. Ellen had a bitter haughty look and pursed her lips each time Rowley spoke to her.

'I got to get out of here,' Rowley said.

Which meant, that he had to kill something.

He borrowed his brother's old eight-cylinder Ford which dragged at the back and skidded on the corners. He collected John from where he was sitting, staring at the branches of the vines where they twisted on the rusted pipes. John was not surprised at the desperate manner of his brother-in-law.

'Let's get out.' Rowley could scarcely control his voice when John asked him whether he wanted a cup of tea first.

The Ford hadn't been washed for months. John rubbed his finger across the thick dust on the windscreen. He refused to go until he washed it. Rowley accepted it with bad grace and

189

sat under the canopy of vines while John hosed the car, then rubbed with a ragged piece of chamois.

'I didn't know you were here,' Diana called cheerfully from the house when she saw Rowley.

'Going to hunt.' Rowley said it as discouragement, a part of the world which was alien to women.

'You don't see much of her now she's pregnant,' undaunted, Diana probed for the soft spot.

'It's not my fault. Every night she goes out with her girlfriends.'

'It's hard for a woman when she's pregnant, Rowley. You've got to be a bit kind.'

'No pregnant woman ever gets moods like this. It's not like a woman, pregnant or anything else, to go out drinking with her friends every night.'

'Only men supposed to do that when their wives are pregnant,' Diana stuck the needle in.

Rowley glared angrily.

'It's not much good complaining now. You married her and when you said "to love and to cherish from this day forward, in sickness and in health, for better or for worse", that's what you get.'

'The worse!' Snarled Rowley. His gaze shifted around the back fence. If there had been a rabbit there, he would have killed it with his eyes.

'Ooh!' Diana exclaimed.

'I don't think she meant it,' Rowley withered Diana. 'Not the way she goes out with her girlfriends they go to the pictures and they get drunk and they giggle. It's not the same as the men going out together. It matters too much, more than her baby, more than the marriage. More than me.'

Diana swayed then pushed back.

'I don't want to say anything against my daughter, who is a good girl. She's a good girl, she worships the ground . . . I know Rowley. She told me so herself. Now what do you think about that?'

'She's got a funny way.'

190

'Aren't you ashamed of yourself, saying things about that girl?' She crowed valiantly, wiping suds from her hands in the apron.

Rowley turned his head away sulkily. Diana turned and walked back into the house, having talked herself into believing. John stood back and squinted at the windscreens.

'It'll get dirty in five minutes,' Rowley grumbled as he stood then unzipped and pissed under the vines.

They drove back to Broken Hill in the morning with one kangaroo carcass in the boot and burn marks across the top of the car.

'He won't worry about it,' Rowley said of his brother. 'I'll give him a few bucks. He'll be sweet.'

Rowley was happy. He whistled and called to Diana as John left the car. Then he shifted to the driver's seat and dragged the clutch, leaving a pall of dust.

'He is so stupid!' Diana coughed in the dust.

John said nothing.

'He can't read or write, can he?' His mother asked rhetorically. 'He must be stupid.'

'I don't think he's stupid.'

'You always liked the dumb ones, the simple boys,' Diana went on.

'I didn't marry him.'

She laughed at that.

191

Chapter 4

John had a few days' casual work at one of the bulk stores when he saw Rowley on the far side of the road. He yelled, and waved the hook he was using to stack bales of wool.

Rowley ambled across with a self-conscious smile. Then he leaned on the loading bay with his elbows and scratched under an armpit.

'She just had a boy.'

John finished turning the bale before he grunted an ambiguous congratulation.

'The boy alright?' He asked cautiously.

'Everything's there.' Rowley stopped scratching under the armpit and leaned his head sideways on his hand.

John was about to stick the hook into another bale when the men working with him decided to have a break. They offered the same reserved congratulations, and a cup of tea.

Rowley vaulted to the loading bay and squatted. Everyone else sat on a bale. John filled an electric jug from a tap outside and plugged it into the power point in a corner.

'What you going to call him?' One of the men asked as he rolled a cigarette.

'Pluto.'

The man kept rolling the cigarette but he looked up and his eyebrows arched.

'Like the dog?'

'It's named after a god.' Rowley suddenly sounded depressed.

'Funny name.' The man twirled the cigarette into his thin lips and struck a match.

'Not that funny,' Rowley grumbled. He was beginning to look angry.

'No offence.' The man looked down at the floor, which was greasy from the sheep hides.

They changed the subject. Rowley looked happy when the man described a kangaroo that had jumped in front of his car and frozen in the headlights.

'I missed it by that much,' the man brushed his palms together.

'That much,' Rowley chuckled.

No one knew what to make of that. They sat sipping tea and grinning awkwardly until Rowley jumped up. He tossed the slops from his cup through the doors, and handed John the cup. With an abrupt wave he jumped to the road then stamped away.

'Moody fellow, your brother-in-law.' The man watched Rowley's back receding along the street.

'It's his first.'

'I've known some that didn't like it. They went and got drunk then found a woman for the night. The ones that did like it did the same, only they were happy about it.'

John tossed the dregs of his own tea onto the concrete drive and picked up his hook.

'Alright,' he said, not knowing exactly what he meant.

They walked along the hospital corridor. Austin walked ahead with a bunch of small yellow flowers in grease-proof paper. Diana held John's arm and skipped along, smiling and nodding to the nurses. They avoided looking into the wards, until John glanced to the side to see a tall woman standing at the end of a bed occupied by an old man resting back on a pillow. His deep-set eyes looked back at the woman from a skull that was completely hairless. A small tear was running down one cheek.

He wanted to stop, but there was no time. They hurried on, not staring at beds or trolleys, smiling idiotically at nurses carrying stainless steel pots and bundles of soiled sheets.

Ellen was sitting up in bed. As her parents walked in, she greeted them with a thin smile.

'How does it feel to be a grandmother?' she asked smugly.

'You didn't do it for me!' Diana leaned across the bed and embraced her daughter.

Ellen chuckled deeply, in a way not dissimilar to Diana's

193

chuckle. She looked carefully and questioningly into her mother's eyes.

It was her mother she was seeking desperately.

'It was easy, wasn't it?' Diana asked.

When Ellen agreed, Diana looked a little disappointed.

'It was beautiful though, just lovely,' Ellen beamed to her mother when Diana patted her arm with gentle approbation.

'What is going to be his name?'

'Yes, tell us!' Austin exclaimed from the rear.

Ellen sucked her cheek in for a second, and glanced to the side. A male nurses' aide wheeled a trolley with rattling bottles and tubes past the door.

'Cain.'

'That's from the Bible.' Diana furrowed her brow. 'It's good that it comes from the Bible.'

'It's nice, isn't it?' Ellen shifted on the pillows stacked behind her and winced.

Diana looked as though she might disagree.

'It's a good enough name to me,' Austin grunted. 'He can change it later if he isn't happy with it.'

'I thought it was Jewish, or something.' Diana squirmed before Ellen's gaze.

Although she was smiling, the small lines around the iris of Ellen's eyes began to shift. Diana almost recoiled.

'I suppose it's alright,' she agreed.

'He's a lovely baby.' Ellen sat back and composed her face. 'The nurses all say so.'

The pattern of little broken sticks within her eyes swayed and touched. Then they separated. Ellen looked straight into her mother with her smile. Diana noticed the cold. She leaned away, helpless with distaste.

'I can leave hospital tomorrow. They'll keep the baby here for another night.'

'You can go out with Rowley and celebrate,' Diana strove to be cheerful and chirpy.

'The girls from work came a few hours ago. They gave me

those.' Ellen indicated a bassinette full of baby clothes and blankets.

'We could give you those!' Diana blurted resentfully.

'This one is nice.' Austin picked up a pair of pink booties and twirled them from his fingers.

'They're the wrong colour.' Diana spoke sharply.

Austin replaced them timidly.

'How do you get on with the other girls?' Diana went on bravely. She looked sideways at the other beds, full of young plump women propped on their pillows, holding hands with husbands and gossiping with families. 'The one down the end looks lonely.'

'She isn't married and she won't tell who the father is. Her father won't come and her mother cries all the time, so she likes being left alone.'

Diana took the opportunity to glare at Austin, who shifted his weight to the other foot.

'Rowley came earlier,' Ellen changed the subject.

'He's been celebrating, I suppose,' Diana laughed. 'We haven't seen much of him.'

'He doesn't want me to go back to work.' Again the small transparent sticks floating rippling across the blue of her eyes.

'Married woman shouldn't take a job that a single woman could have.'

'Nobody will get married then!' Ellen snapped at her father, her husband, men, and her mother who failed her.

Austin looked at his watch.

'I'd like to see the new arrival while there's time.'

Diana stood uncomfortably and looked down at her daughter. She wanted to say something that would make her feel guilty, but couldn't think of what. She twisted her mouth in a forced smile.

'We'll go now and see . . .' Diana tried to gurgle. It sounded sad.

A nurse moved past along the corridor with a towel. Her footsteps clanged on the tiles.

'The new grandson,' Austin smiled. It felt much easier to be a grandfather than a father.

'Cain,' John said obscurely.

'You are going to be an uncle.' Ellen spoke to him for the first time. Her voice should have sounded gay, but did not.

'I will try.'

This was an odd idea. To try to be an uncle. You were an uncle, or you were not. What could you try?

It was too difficult. They bade the new mother farewell and went to see the new boy, the new generation, the new son.

Chapter 5

The night before he left, Rowley came around to visit John, who was sleeping in the side room. It was late and Austin and Diana were asleep. John was sitting in his bed reading. The smell of fresh leaves drifted through the louvres and the grapevines were beginning to shoot. Rowley kicked his way noisily through the branches of the lemon tree at the front.

Hoo-ray for Johnny,
Hooray at last,
Hooray for Johnnie
For he's a horse's arse . . .

'You'll wake them up,' John whispered to the shadows in the garden.

' . . . hooray at last . . .'

A window screeched up in the front of the house.

'Go home to your wife and family. Stop coming around here this late at night in your drunken condition!' Diana bellowed.

'Sayin' farewell to . . .'

'Say goodbye tomorrow morning.'

'Last time he'll be stayin' in that house. Your house, didn' you know that? The last time!' Rowley's voice oozed sentiment.

'Your wife and baby home waiting for you, the way she looks after you when all you do is run around drunken like this waking people up when they got to go to work in the morning even if you don't that's all you do you ought to be ashamed . . .'

Diana was building up steam when Rowley interrupted contritely, or so it sounded.

'I know I'm too dumb for your loverly daughter, Mrs Evans,' his voice shook. 'I know I never read a book. You want me to read a book, Diana? Johnny, he can read a book. I'm dumb Mrs Evans too dumb for your daughter I . . .'

'Go back to my daughter then.' Diana spoke crossly, deftly sidestepping an admission.

"Why doncha let him go somewhere where he can be smart and read and leave me where I can be smart where I'm happy and your lovely daughter is happy and then you can be happy and you don' expect me to be Johnny and Johnny isn't me neither . . .'

'I don't care where you go so long as you stop stepping on them plants!'

John let Rowley in. He staggered under the weight of four full bottles of beer in a paper bag to the gelignite-box chair, but it was too narrow to support him. He slipped off the edge and sat heavily on the floor. The box, with its lacy cotton veil riding up, fell the other way. John and Rowley stared at the exposed white timber.

John passed a pocket knife with an opener. Rowley let it drop to the floor then opened a bottle with his teeth.

'Nobody has teeth after they're twenty. Nobody that's Australian.'

John ran his tongue around his almost full set of teeth before accepting the bottle. He gulped down a mouthful of the gassy beer, then rubbed the lip and handed the bottle back.

'Have a few,' Rowley belched open-mouthed. 'I've already had a few.'

John was trying to swallow the third gassy mouthful when a torchlight wandered across the curtains. The door opened and Austin pushed his head in. John and Rowley looked at him. Austin went red, then looked embarrassed.

'You want one Aussie?'

Rowley began to ease the top from another bottle with his teeth.

' Austin hated being called Aussie. He shone his torch unnecessarily into the corner of the room, skipping the upturned gelignite box. The bare whiteness of the exposed timber.

'No no no,' he said quickly, then just as quickly withdrew.

They listened as he plodded away.

198

'You know what I think of y' sister,' Rowley slurred when everything was quiet again.

'Yes,' said John dutifully. The gas rose to his throat and he passed the bottle over to Rowley.

'Do anything for 'er.' He took the bottle and drank without bothering to wipe the neck.

'I'm not what she wants, though.' He put the bottle on the floor with a distinct plink. 'I'm not what she wants. She wants something . . .' He looked up at the ceiling, at a mosquito which had been let in by Austin, which was just beginning to home in on his skin.

'What she wants is something your parents want.' He slapped unsuccessfully at the mosquito, which withdrew just out of range.

John accepted the bottle watchfully. Rowley belched again.

'She wants me to be you.'

John stared.

'Only she doesn't know what you're like either.'

'Ah.' John flailed at the mosquito that was dancing and buzzing in the space between them.

Rowley eventually fell asleep on the floor. He curled onto his side and pushed the empty bottles away. The mosquito, which had drunk its fill, rose heavily into the air unimpeded. John drew an old blanket over Rowley, then went back to the old iron bed. He stared at the ceiling and listened to the steady wheezing of Rowley's breath. The room smelled of beer. The bed, which had been his grandmother's, then his, then his grandmother's, then his again. He peeled a piece of paint from the head. Austin was going to retire soon, then the family would shift. It was the first time he thought of the loss of the house he had grown up in.

Through the leaves of the grapevines, he could see the sky beginning to lighten. He stepped from the bed and slipped into a pair of sandals left near the door. He paused as the wire door squeaked and Rowley groaned and shifted.

He shivered. The pallid moon was not quite full. A few steps away he could see the split in the fence where he had peeped through at the blind man. He bent and peered. The white concrete of the verandah glowed with the moonlight. His sandals slapped along the paths, the blocks of concrete that his father laid over the pebble path which had once swarmed with locusts. He circled the garden, indulging the memories that came to him. The small quince tree he touched for the second time. When he was small he had crawled from the sparse patch of lawn across the ridge of a garden bed then tried to pull hmself upright, gripping a hollow in the tree. The hollow was there still, not far above his foot.

He sat in the curve of the mulberry tree which had served him as a pirate ship. The street had been graded along the edges and there was enough bitumen for two cars to pass. Across the road the houses gleamed in the dawn with a charm and freshness he had never noticed before. The lines of corrugated iron softened and in the distance the lights still gleamed softly on the poppet heads. Far away, it was hard to say how far because noise carried on the desert air, two cars revved their engines and squealed around corners.

The smell of burning rubber. The thick dark shadows of the fig trees on the other side of the house had looked that much like a jungle when he had looked through the synthetic curtains on the side windows.

Miserable remembered nights, when he walked obsessively alone along lane-ways, looking into backyards for the answers to questions he could not formulate.

As he walked back to his room he brushed against the leaves of the lemon tree, which were still damp with dew.

Rowley drove him to the railway station in the morning. Austin had already gone to work and Diana was angrily doing the washing.

'Have a good time in Sydney!' She called to John as he went.

John turned to see if she had relented but she had already turned back to the washing machine and fed a dripping sheet through the automatic wringer.

Rowley had a hangover. His tongue was dry. They had an hour, so John did not object when Rowley suggested a drink.

Although the hotel was not officially open they went to the side door. Rowley let himself in with confidence. The bar was almost empty. Three miners sat around a table looking bleakly at one another. One of them turned and nodded to Rowley, who smiled back and jauntily approached the bar. The publican's daughter waited in her school uniform. Her school case rested demurely on the bar-top. She topped up two glasses and placed them side by side on the damp towel. Rowley gave her two dollars and ignored the change left on the counter.

'What are you going to do this time?' Rowley spoke seriously, knowing both of them understood that he was referring to John's departure.

'Same as last time.'

'What about life?'

'I'll live it.

'Why does everybody think that the only way to live is by getting married and staying in the same job for forty years?' John grumbled.

'Your sister, she worries. She says you always end in trouble and everyone worries because you don't know how to look after yourself. Life goes on.'

'I don't give a stuff whether it goes on.'

The second glass was going down slower. The schoolgirl behind the bar gave him a disinterested stare.

'That's a bad thing to say!'

One of the miners farted. The schoolgirl didn't blink.

'Terrible,' John agreed as he searched his pocket for another two dollars.

Rowley placed a five dollar note firmly on the bar, and two more glasses appeared.

'Your sister and me, we're going to split. I love her and we're goin' to split,' Rowley sobbed suddenly.

The schoolgirl watched with a flicker of interest. John pushed one of the glasses into the vicinity of Rowley's paw.

'Fuck the union!' Rowley waved his arms.

The miners shifted on their chairs.

'What have they got to do with it?' John asked timorously.

'The unions stop her from getting on in this town. She says they keep everyone down on the same level so no one can really get to the top, and they don't want her to work now she's married.'

John looked at the clock above the bar.

'She's smart. If she was a man, she could get somewhere. If she was a man.' The idea made Rowley thoughtful.

The girl put up another two glasses, and counted the price from the change left on the counter.

As they walked out of the hotel onto the verandah, the miners' voices started to hum. The light was stark. They paused to blink.

Rowley's brother's old Ford, with gleaming blue plastic seat covers, was parked out from the curb. As John climbed in, the warm covers slid unpleasantly beneath his bottom.

'Not much time,' Rowley coughed as he dropped the clutch.

They cruised heavily around a corner. There was another, before the station. As the car swayed on its suspension, John looked across at a dark-haired boy crying and pulling against his mother's arm under the verandah of a shop. The mother was red-faced and heavy. She dropped a parcel on the ground and raised her arm to slap the boy. Rowley was leaning across, fiddling with the dial of the car radio, trying to get it on the station, when the boy tugged away and ran out. He was screaming, although John could not hear it. Then the car bumped and the scream stopped.

Rowley straightened slowly. He was driving on, his gaze fixed on the station on top of the rise ahead, the higher rise of the black skimp dumps beyond.

Everything seemed quiet. John's voice dropped from his lips onto the plastic seat covers. Rowley looked, then glanced into the rear vision mirror.

The car braked slowly.

John wound down the window. Rowley stepped into the street

and stood there, watching the woman who was trying to pick up the little boy. People were coming out of shops.

Rowley and John walked back together. An elderly man on the footpath was picking up the things in her parcel. He packed them precisely and put them beside the woman.

'I think these are yours,' he said politely.

'How did that happen?' A shop assistant asked Rowley. 'We called the ambulance.'

The train was pulling out. It clattered indifferently through the crossing, building speed.

'It was like hitting a kangaroo,' Rowley said. Matter-of-fact, distant, detached. Only his mouth was open.

'It wasn't his fault, darling,' Ellen insisted quietly. 'It could have happened to anyone. The child ran in front of the car and I don't think there was anything he could do.'

'I know it is a terrible thing to say,' Diana's voice was raised. 'But he should have been at home instead of gallivanting. If he had been then it wouldn't have happened.'

'It could have happened just as easily. If John was driving it could have been easier because he's not as good a driver.'

'He wouldn't . . .' Diana was stunned by the daring logic of it.

'He would, if he had a chance,' Ellen extended the logic of hypothesis and predestination.

'No!' Diana knew something was wrong.

'What if he was driving the car?' Ellen demanded, inexorably partitioning the pie of guilt and blame. 'He was gallivanting too. He was drinking.'

Diana sullenly refused this logic.

'Rowley is very upset,' Ellen went on soothingly. 'He has dreams about it and he wakes up sweating.'

'A bad thing when a man wakes up and cries,' Diana agreed, changing the subject. 'Men don't cry.'

She thought about it, and observed feelings of genuine outrage.

'I know they shouldn't, darling.'

'A bad thing,' Diana accepted.

'Rowley was up late. John could have driven,' Ellen nagged on gently.

'He should have been back with you and the baby. What do you expect? He can't read!' Diana exclaimed viciously.

Ellen went silent for a second.

'At least he keeps me and the baby,' she added without raising her voice.

'If John was married . . .'

Diana paused at the frank suggestion of a sneer.

'He would stay home.'

'With his wife, and baby?' Ellen's voice was mocking.

'What's wrong with that?'

'Nothing, darling. Nothing. I'd adore to see it happen, really sincerely I would!'

'You shouldn't have married him. Rowley. Not that he's bad, he can't read or write. That's all.'

'He is very upset.'

Diana hooted, not sure whether the hoot could penetrate the discomfort of her daughter's indifference, or her own fear.

Chapter 6

Dear John,

There is so much going on and the house is busy now your father is retiring. Everyone is calling around to see the house and say goodbye. We all have a cup of tea and Austin isn't working now so he walks around with a hammer in his belt. He had to shift the back gate it was so old it was set in the ground it is so long since we shifted it last it must have been one time we went on holidays. I bet you never would recognise the place it is so different now. Elsie Tomms from down the road says it is a pity we are going but I said you've got to go on haven't you and she said yes I suppose but it is a pity. The place looks so nice with the new paint and I will miss you Di, ever since the tennis they were good days we've known each other a long time haven't we? I said yes we have but you better not talk about that too much or everyone will think we're getting on a bit gee I don't like that much. She laughed we had lots of good laughs together over the years. There's been some customers come around and look at the place I have to go out when they're here I can't stand them going over the place putting their hands everywhere looking to see if I cleaned the sill, I saw one of them do that. If I stayed around I would have said Hey look here I clean my windowsills good as anyone you'd be pretty good if you cleaned yours as much, true eh? A couple of the men from the mine came around with their wives to have a few drinks with Austin they all said what a good man he was underground, very fair, they all respected him and they meant it I think. They drank a toast and some of those that had been in the bowling club they made speeches too and at the North mine they gave Austin a watch. An Omega it has his name on the back and it says for forty years service he loves that watch he'd hate to lose a watch that expensive but I don't think he ever will. I heard the other day that Jill Brookes from Brazil Street you remember her? She married the boy Allie from the South well she left him the other day and went to Adelaide. They said he has another girlfriend everybody wonders who it is but nobody knows yet although there are rumours (you know who I mean). We went to the dance on Friday night and everybody was happy to see us we did a waltz around the floor and the band played our music especially and everyone clapped. It was so nice we are getting spoiled, but it isn't so bad after all these years is it? We stayed back with the Brewsters and had a drink and a game of cards. Austin didn't have to think about going in to work or anything. This is the first day of his retirement so he might as well relax and make the best, I'll be dead in six months if that's all I do Austin said, gee I laughed. But I still got up early and did the cleaning in case anyone came to look at the house. I feel sorry the grapes are so good this year, I almost picked them to make some jam the same with oranges and the lemons a while ago it makes you sad but that's life you've got to get on with it I never liked Broken Hill you know I hated it almost as much as you sometimes but I feel sorry to be leaving after all these years. Getting sentimental in my old age but the weather has been beautiful not too hot I thought as I was dusting the venetians in the front room remember the old days with the dust storms? We haven't had a dust storm for years not a bad one that's because of the bush growing around the town. Ellen and Rowley took us to the river Rowley says we should buy one of those huts there and settle but I want to get out of this place and do some living and its hard when everyone talks the way they do around here eh? Rowley keeps going off shooting only he goes by himself now doesn't take his brother or anybody you can hear him when he's near shooting and shooting and when he comes back he's only got a few rabbits or a kangaroo I don't know what he shoots the rest of the time. Ellen says he wakes up and he keeps talking about the searchlight turn it this way turn it that way he yells, Ellen feels sorry for him, I wouldn't stay around when all he does is drink. Mostly he does that alone, doesn't go to the pub with his mates any longer or goes in the car and gets pissed on his own that's bad I keep telling her, no way to bring a boy up but she doesn't worry. If we sell the house soon we'll be in Sydney looking and that will be hard we'll see you then but that isn't an excuse not to write. See you later and love.

Mum

Everybody thinks that cleaners have an easy job. All they have to do is polish knobs and sweep, so that it is normally a job reserved for the old and injured. The old man gripping a rag in his arthritic fist, hobbling past with his eyes turned to the floor. When John was hired as a cleaner he was ashamed.

When he arrived, he found that they needed one able-bodied man at least. He was it. The heavy circular polishing machines were as difficult to use as jack-hammers, and as easy so long as the correct balance was gained: it wasn't pleasant when the apprentices went past singing 'Sadie the cleaning lady'.

He started work early and finished early. The factory was near the city and he liked walking the streets when everyone else was at work. He stopped often in Eddy Avenue to watch the light as it played through the plane trees on the other side of the road. The air was fresher when there wasn't too much traffic around, although the skyline was altering and concrete and glass towers were rising around Circular Quay and on the far side of the harbour. It was progress and the light still played through the plane trees and the harbour sparkled in the sun.

He lived in a room at the back of an old boarding-house full of drunks, but his room was some distance from the main house, so he could hear the singing and fighting in the distance. The room was painted high-gloss orange and glowed with the smallest light, but it had a gas-ring which worked and a tiny verandah and it was cheap. He did not stay there during the day often. Instead he went to Manly by ferry, sitting next to the warm turbines and watching the spray as it dashed over the rails.

In Manly, he looked at the lines of seaweed on the sand and the bits of wrapping paper and Coca-Cola tins left by the tide.

He was thinking about something. Sometimes he wondered what it was.

John,

The house is sold. We got a good price and we are staying in a flat here until we find another home. Austin is looking but it is very hard to find a nice place. We know you are busy but phone us up. The address is on the back of the envelope.

Love,
Mum

Mum,

I'm glad to hear the place is sold and you are down here at last in the sun and the surf. You can have a holiday all the time now, if you want. I know dad doesn't want to because he thinks that if he stops working then he will be dead.

I've been having a good time going out with the fellows from work. Clubs and places like that, good ones of course where everybody has fun. I haven't got a girlfriend at the moment but I'll find someone who is interested and alright for me. There are a few around who seem alright but I'm taking my time.

My flat is pretty good for the price. I have a nice view of the city and if I went to the floor above I could see a bit of the harbour and the top of the bridge. It's an old style place but its been recently painted and it has all modern conveniences. The stove is a good one but I'm not much at cooking so I eat out with the boys. The people here keep to themselves, which I suppose is the best way. If I need a cup of sugar I can always ask.

I don't have a car yet but you don't need one in Sydney. You can walk everywhere and it is hard finding a place to park. I'm saving plenty of money in case.

When you find a place please drop me a line. I know a real estate agent or two.

Love,
John

Dear John,

We are so glad you're doing well with a nice place to live and friends. Austin thinks we have a place. It is near a hill and not far away from the water, with beautiful views, and it is just what we want. If you want to come and see us, phone any Saturday.

Just a note, Love,

Mum

'I hear you've got a house,' John spoke into the telephone with forced good humour.

'We lost it,' Austin grumbled. 'Someone else put in a higher price after we accepted, and the owner took the high price and exchanged contracts.'

'Bad,' John clucked.

'They told me it was legal. It wasn't ethical so I told them and I didn't swear once.'

'You could have.'

'I don't believe in swearing, not when there are women around. When I finished he just said "That's business". "Not where I come from," I said and I told him what I thought of his business.'

John grunted.

'Nice garden. Looked out on the sea. Three bedrooms for when Ellen and Cain come down.'

'When's that?'

'Holidays. We're going to another house now. About to go out. There's got to be others out there.'

'If there's one, there's got to be others.'

'There is a house that's waiting. Our house, just right for us.'

'With room for Ellen and Cain, and a garden like the one in Broken Hill?'

'I wouldn't like a garden that big again. Too many trees. People don't live that way in 1969.'

'Some like it.'

'Old fashioned. You've got to keep up. I like the roses and the lawn . . . but trees. Progress. You can't stand in the way of progress.'

209

Dear John,

You're not going to believe me after the false alarm last time but we've got a house. I don't like it quite as much as the other one but it has recessed fluorescent lights and you can see the water from the front verandah if you stand on your toes. There's a little shopping centre up the road. Phone us when you have time of course dear lots of love,

Mum

The house was on the slope of a hill not far inland. It had a white painted picket fence and a concrete drive and a garage and a concrete verandah and a neat white metal letterbox, and it was painted light green. As Austin climbed from the car he jingled the keys happily in his hand. He stepped across the verge of the close-cropped lawn bravely and took the steps firmly and decisively, as though asserting rights and possession.

'We got the keys from the agent especially,' Diana made an aside. 'He didn't mind because we'll be in it in a few weeks.'

John trod carefully around the barren trimmed lawn. Austin smiled and asked his opinion.

'It looks good,' John said miserably. He preferred his room in Darlinghurst.

The smile slipped away. John recalled his disappointment over his father's first car. John also would have felt more comfortable in that old car than in the new Holden now shining on the concrete drive.

'It's a nice house,' he went on hopelessly while the little voice behind his face was saying 'It is a boring fibro bungalow without imagination or style or character'.

The inside was painted eggshell blue. Wardrobes were built in two of the bedrooms.

'There's a septic tank,' Diana chirruped from the kitchen. 'The sewerage will be here in a year and a half.'

'That wall.' John looked at an expanse.

'We've got something for that.' Diana bustled out to the car and returned with a box. Then she unwrapped and carefully hung a row of plaster emus and kangaroos. At the top, a fine plaster

Aboriginal looked out over the expanse of eggshell blue with one hand covering his eyes and a clean piece of cloth wrapped neatly around his waist.

'We haven't got the new carpet yet, but we've picked it out. Blue, matches the wall.'

'It's us that has to live here,' she added.

'Easier to keep up than the old place.' Austin flicked a switch on and off and watched the light shiver against the wall.

'We stayed a couple of nights with Ellen, then we drove past the old place,' Diana answered something unspoken. 'They'd already pulled out the trees and the plants. There was a tractor there and they waved and we stopped. You know how big the front was? A small field. That's what they treated it like. "It's all yours now," I said to them, "you do what you like." Then I told Austin to drive away because I didn't want to look.'

'The paths would break their tractor.'

'They left the paths,' Diana said innocently.

PART FOUR

Chapter 1

In 1970, he went back to Broken Hill. His parents weren't there any longer. He was quite happy to stay in a hotel, but Ellen sent him a letter saying she would be offended.

Rowley met him at the station.

'Ellen's working,' he said.

There was something meaningful in the way he said it. Rowley dropped his suitcase in the back seat. All the members of his family assumed he could not lift a suitcase.

'I'm only going to stay for a week,' John said deliberately. 'Just got a bit homesick, that's all.'

'She wants to go to Sydney all the time. Every chance, she goes there for a holiday. She talks about nothing else.'

'You didn't marry the family.'

'No offence.'

'I didn't want to be married to you either.'

Rowley laughed. He reversed the car dramatically. John noticed that his driving had not become cautious.

Not quite twilight, although the harsh summer light had softened. In January the temperature was hot, over forty degrees celsius for days at a time. On the train John had stood for hours at the door, letting the hot wind blow on his cheek. He preferred that to the stuffiness inside the carriage.

'It's been hot. You want to go for a drink?'

'I haven't had much to eat.'

'Plenty at the club. Ellen don't like to cook. Probably won't be back until late, out with her girlfriends. Never gets back before late.'

A significant whisper, as another clue was being offered.

'Alright. The club.'

'The Musicians' Club,' Rowley gave an expression of joy. 'The Musos, that's where. It's the best.'

The Musos was a barren hall with grey laminex tiles on the floor and rows of poker machines aginst the walls. Lines of overweight middle-aged men, the same age as himself, stood before the machines with glasses of beer, feeding coins one after another into the slot. John sat in reverie as Rowley waited at the bar to get the first round of drinks.

'When's the dinner on?' John asked when Rowley came back with two full glasses of beer.

'Be on soon. For sure,' Rowley said airily before taking a mouthful of beer.

Although he did not drink heavily after he left Whyalla, John made a point of going to the hotel for a few drinks with the people he worked with. Enough so that he wouldn't be thought snobbish and not so much that he got drunk. He had a feeling Rowley was going to try and push him beyond those limits.

One of the men standing at the poker machines was watching him carefully. A tall, big man with a lined face and an almost bald head. A ridge of brown hair was cut in a semi-circle around his ears.

There was a moment of panic as the man approached. The walk was familiar.

'Good day.' The man sat down on a spare chair beside Rowley and put out his hand.

'Hello Pieter.' John accepted the hand.

He introduced Rowley to his old school friend.

'I seen you around here before,' Pieter grinned.

'I seen you before too.'

'I known John here since he was in school. We was good mates. Haven't seen him for years. What you been doing John?'

'Working.'

The banality of the comment, the desert of inadequacy and failure it implied.

'What you do?'

'Storeman. Cleaner. Whatever gives a living.'

'Is the same here. I'm working on the South. I got married. Three kids. You got any kids?'

216

'No.'

'That's a pity. I always thought you would be good with kids. Yes.'

'Never worked out that way,' said John.

'I'll give you my address. Call around any time.'

'Any time?'

John smiled. Pieter looked uncertain.

'Yes, whenever you're around.'

'I'll do that.'

He knew he wouldn't call. Pieter knew he wouldn't call. Pieter printed the address slowly in pencil on the back of a grubby envelope.

'Here you are.' He handed John the envelope.

John looked at it and turned it in his hand. The envelope had been sent from the gas company.

'I'll call around.'

'I told Eadie about you. She'll be glad to see you.'

John made a mental note to actually go there, to do what he said he was going to do. Very simple, to do what you say. He felt his courage falter, his persistence fail.

As Pieter backed away, John felt his face fall into one of the old hypocritical smiles.

'I'll be around.'

'Eadie will be glad to meet you.'

John downed another glass of beer. Two more glasses appeared miraculously.

'I'll be back.'

He had to go outside, across a red concrete path. The toilet itself was made of red-painted besser brick. A fat man was standing at the concrete urinal.

'Lordy Lordy Lord,' the fat man leaned back on his heels and sang to the ceiling.

'Ah.'

'It's like I can feel myself pissing away. It's lovely!'

'Yes.'

John went into one of the cubicles.

'I wish someone would put their mouths around it. Lick it run their tongue along it Lordy Lordy.'

John bent over the toilet and put his hand down his throat and vomited. The beer spewed into the bowl. When he felt empty, he straightened up.

The man was still there as he came out. Standing away from the urinal and zipping his fly. He looked at John curiously.

'The big spit.'

'That's right,' John moved around him to a stainless steel washbasin. 'The big spit.'

'I never seen you here before.'

John flicked his hands. There was no towel. He thought about wiping his hands on the toilet paper, then decided against it. The water sprayed up the red-painted besser brick wall.

'Where you work?'

'Out of town. Away.'

A heavy hand descended on his shoulder.

'I know you from somewhere.'

As soon as he felt the hand descend, John knew. He turned around and stared into the face of Garry Ham. For an instant, he felt his fear of the bully. His voice caught in his throat.

'No.' He sensed himself faltering.

Ham's heavy hand still rested on the shoulder. Sensing the repugnance, Ham left it there.

'Where?'

'Let go.'

Ham let go. John turned.

'No offence, or nothing,' Ham said. 'It's just that you look like . . .'

John strode out. Rowley was waiting back inside. Another round of drinks was already lined up on the table.

'Getting to you already, is it?' Rowley beamed.

'Not used to it.'

'Drink up. You'll get used to it.'

John drank. After another three glasses of beer, he decided to visit the toilet again. Ham followed him in this time. John

218

went straight into a cubicle and vomited, then walked out again. Ham leaned against the door. He watched John as he again washed his hands.

'I been watching you, from the other side of the room. I think I remember where I knew you from.'

'Where?'

John flicked the water against the wall.

'You used to go to school with me.'

John did not dare turn around.

'You were a smart little kid. We had a fight, like kids do. That right?'

'Don't remember.' John flicked his hands again to remove the last few drops of water.

'What do you do now? I haven't seen you for years.'

'I worked in Sydney for a while. I came back for a holiday.'

'What's it like in Sydney?'

'Alright. Like anywhere else.' He ignored the obvious leer in Ham's voice.

'Girls? Plenty of girls? They easy?'

'Same as anywhere.'

He wondered what it was that made it hard for him to walk out.

'Lordy wouldn't I like to go there sometimes. Get it up one of them with big tits and a big sloppy cunt. That's what I like Johnny. A big sloppy cunt.'

From the side of his eye, John could see the gestures with both hands.

'There's two sizes. Big ones and canoes.'

He laughed. John almost doubled over.

'What about the Cross? What they do, those queers around the Cross. What they do?'

'Never been there much,' John lied desperately, although his feet were heavy.

'Never been there! Everybody that's been in Sydney goes there. Where else you go for women and that?'

'Only if you want to pay,' John said cruelly. 'If you can't get it any other way.'

'Everyone pays, one way or the other,' Ham smeared. 'I don't mind paying for what I want.'

John flicked his completely dry hands at the wall.

'See you next time.'

He moved to the door, and was surprised when Ham didn't try to stop him.

'See you next time,' called Ham.

He went into the toilet cubicle and slammed the door.

Rowley looked up at him. John was feeling quite sprightly He had got rid of two stomach-loads of alcohol. Rowley's eyes looked bloodshot. A stupid, suspicious look.

'There's another beer,' he said.

'Thanks.'

John sat down and began drinking.

'It might be flat by now.'

'I saw someone in the toilet. Someone I went to school with.'

'Call him over, to have a drink.'

Rowley's words slurred.

'Alright. When he comes out.'

Rowley leaned forward onto his arms and stared at John, as John calmly took a few medium-sized mouthfuls. He watched Garry Ham walk across the room from the side of his eye.

'That's him. Hey Garry!' He called.

Ham froze in mid stride and looked around with a smile. Rowley half raised his head and turned. Then he beckoned.

'C'mere. Have a drink.'

'Someone's waiting for me.'

'Bring them over too,' bellowed Rowley.

'Sorry.'

Ham teetered for a second, then waddled away.

'Don' look like he's got somebody over there!' Grumbled Rowley. John downed the next glass of beer and looked at Rowley expectantly. Rowley had only taken a few sips from his glass. He looked at John in confused and dim disapproval. He picked up the glass and put it to his lips and began to drink. The glass drained slowly. John sat there, watching the slow ripples along Rowley's neck.

'Lovely!' Rowley gasped as he shoved the glass across the table. He looked green.

'How about another?'

'Any time.' Although Rowley didn't look as keen as all that.

'I'll get them then.'

As John stood at the bar waiting to be served, he was gratified to see Rowley stagger out towards the toilet with his hand up to his lips. He looked around the room. As he met Garry Ham's eyes, Ham dropped his gaze and checked the table top in front of him. A couple as fat as Ham sat on the other side of the table. All three of them looked terrifically bored. The woman stood and walked across to a poker machine and fed a coin into the machine.

Rowley was gone at least five minutes. Ham went out to the toilet again. As he came back he paused.

'Your friend in there, doesn't look so well with his head in the trough.'

In the toilet, it was not exactly as it had been described. Rowley was sitting in a cubicle with the door open and his head resting on his lap. John tapped his shoulder.

Rowley looked up. His jaw hung open.

'Time to go,' John said.

''Nother drink,' murmured Rowley.

'We better go home.'

'No home. We gone to split, your sister and me. Wez gone to split. Nothin else. Good woman, great woman. But split.'

'I haven't seen her yet.'

He helped Rowley up and walked with him through the long hall of the Musicians' Club. Rowley burbled and dribbled. The spit ran down the sleeve of John's coat.

Someone opened the glass swing doors and held them open. John could feel the cool breeze on his face. Behind him, he could hear Garry Ham's laughter. He shuddered.

Chapter 2

Rowley turned the car into the drive. The back wheels slid across the gravel. John leaned sideways in the seat.

'Always does that,' Rowley giggled. 'Every time. Then it grabs on the bitumen. 'S alright.'

The car did grip the bitumen. As it went across the gutter the bumper scraped concrete.

'Does it every time.'

Rowley stopped the car and thrust the keys into his fob pocket.

'Come in and meet the missus,' as though John had never met her before.

Rowley jumped from the car and led John in through a back door. The lights were on but no one was around. In the kitchen, Ellen was washing dishes with her back hunched over. She didn't turn.

'Brother's here,' Rowley mumbled.

Then he walked across and tried to give her a peck. Ellen waited until he was beside her then turned easily around the other way, so that she faced John and had her back to Rowley.

'Hello darling,' she said smoothly. 'So nice to see you. Here for a holiday.'

'Yes,' John said uncomfortably.

'You're welcome. Any time. I see Rowley has already been showing you the town. No problems, darling, no problems at all.

'You'd like a cup of tea, as long as you can fit it in with all the rest,' she chuckled in a manner which was not at all amused.

'We 'ad a few,' Rowley asserted defiantly.

'So I see.'

'You had some yerself last night. Never got back till later than this.'

'Yes, darling. But I had not promised that I would look after the child as I seem to recall you did.'

Rowley shrugged as though the accusation was proof of his manhood.

'As I do not wish to embarrass our guest, I will ask that you show him to the spare room. He can leave his things. By the time you return the tea will be made.'

'She always talks to me like that,' Rowley whispered to John as John put his suitcase down beside a narrow camp stretcher.

John looked around the room, which was a closed-in verandah. There was a small chest of drawers with peeling timber from being left out in the rain. Curtains and yellow and blue linoleum on concrete and louvre windows. He liked small rooms.

'Goes out every night on the piss with her girlfriends. Never gets back, never does any cooking. I cook rabbit stew Mondays and that lasts, then for the rest of the week it's fish and chips or Macdonald's.'

'I don't mind doing a bit of cooking,' John slid around the point.

'Not the cooking I'm worried about.'

John looked at him, but he didn't go on to say what it was that he did worry about.

'Tomorrow we go to the anabranch.'

John nodded.

'We got some meat, we got some bait and ammunition. June and her family they want to go. Maybe Leddy.'

'That would be good.'

When they went out, Ellen was laying a clean table-cloth. Rowley went to the other side of the table and smoothed a wrinkle with his finger.

'Sit down.'

John and Rowley both sat as Ellen went out, then returned with an aluminium teapot and teacups perched on an enamel green plastic tray.

'I saved this for you.' She placed a mug before John which he looked at closely.

The mug was coloured white, with a stylised set of twins, facing each other.

'I remembered your birthday.'

She smiled sweetly. John never remembered anyone's birthday. Except for Ellen's. He gave his parents a card and a present, dutifully, on Father's Day and Mother's Day.

She poured his tea first, her own second.

'You have milk dear,' she said as she added it to Rowley's cup after the tea had been poured.

Rowley looked gloomily at the murky streaks of milk.

'I'm a bit sick in the guts.'

He pushed the cup away.

'What's life been like in Sydney?' Ellen asked solicitously. 'Have you seen much of mum and dad?'

'I've seen a bit of them, now and then.' He was not able to escape a twinge of guilt. 'I've seen the new house now that they've got sewerage.'

'They sent me a letter about that,' Ellen mused. 'They said that they could wait another year and they would get sewerage free, or they could pay and have it connected.'

'They chose to have it connected.'

'It was expensive, but they deserve it. They're a marvellous couple. Just beautiful. Aren't they beautiful?'

'Sure.'

He did not have the courage to say 'No. They are not beautiful at all'.

'I think they're really wonderful.'

There was satisfaction in the way she said it.

Rowley pushed his chair back on the floor and stood up. He did not bother to yawn.

'I feel stuffed,' he said.

Then he stalked off to the bedroom.

The following day, a caravan of old cars assembled outside John's window. The men walked to the front of the house. In the distance he could hear their intermittent swearing and the loud covert sniggers. The women moved around in the kitchen, packing hampers and looking after children. He could hear their voices clearly, the tone of cool censure as they talked around the distant bullying voices of the men.

'He's still sleeping in,' he heard an unfamiliar female voice.

'Always been like that,' said Ellen.

'Has he!'

There was an unstated 'well, no wonder!' in her voice.

'Yes darling but he's very clever.'

'Have to be, to like the cot as much as that. No wonder he never got married.'

'Someone will get him.'

'No offence darling, but who would want him? I mean, it's alright being smart and that. I know ours aren't that smart and they get drunk, but they do leave us alone, where it matters. Don't they?'

'He's not that bad.'

'I like them out of the house and out of the kitchen. Working, or playing football, or shooting kangaroos, or drinking with their mates. I couldn't stand one that hung around and got under my feet.'

'He keeps out of the way.'

'Never know what's inside their heads if they're too much like that. Our boys, you always know what they're up to. That's what they are. Just boys, when they're doing things you don't like.'

'You haven't met him yet.'

'Sorry Ellen. I know he's your brother but I don't think it's natural for a man to sit around and think. They go bad when they sit around. Got to have something in their hands and not much in their heads and they're happy.'

'Even if it's your nipple?'

'Keeps them busy. Empty them out each night and they don't have much left to give anybody else.'

John turned over and listened idly to the conversation. Men in general. It was a limited subject that had been explored before. They went on to talk about the things to take for the picnic.

225

'I'll take the blankets. They're clean. We dry-cleaned them this week,' said the woman.

Ellen was silent for a long second.

'Not that your blankets are dirty or anything, Ell. Just we got them done only two days ago.'

'Better wake him up soon.' Ellen sounded discontented.

The cars cruised slowly out of Broken Hill. The anabranch was miles away, off the road to Mildura. John sat silently in the back seat of the car with Cain strapped into a baby seat beside him. Ellen sat beside Rowley and spent the time gazing coolly out at the countryside. It would have been easy to cool Rowley down. He wanted to be cooled down. Ellen had become harder, more detached.

Rowley sat behind the wheel and looked meanly at the road. His look was deliberate and set. Ellen wasn't going to play.

The old car was the lead car of the convoy. He began to speed. When there was no response, he accelerated. John noticed his thumbs begin to bend and twitch on the wheel. 140 kilometres an hour. Rowley moved a shred of phlegm along his throat as he worked the accelerator. The frame of the car began to rattle and shake.

Rowley had not shaved. The more he sped, the further he leaned back in the seat. Ellen remained exactly as she was, with her head turned and motionless, watching the bushes in the distance. The closer bushes moved faster.

Cain began to cry.

'Should I pick him up?' John was glad of the excuse to break the silence.

The car slowed down slightly and the shuddering eased so Rowley could hear the reply.

'He'll be alright. Give him this.'

Ellen passed a cup of milk over her shoulder. As John took it, the car speeded up and the rattling began again. While he held the cup up, he looked out the rear window. The other cars were straining to keep up. He could see the grinning face of Rowley's brother, sitting behind the wheel of the nearest car. His wife, the large fair woman who had been speaking to Ellen in the kitchen, turned to his side and spoke. Rowley's brother looked sulky, but the car slowed and dropped back.

Cain was sick. He complained and pulled his head to one side. Then he vomited the milk straight up the back of Rowley's seat. A few drops touched the back of Rowley's head.

'Fuck'n cunt of a kid.' The car veered across the road.

He straightened in time to let a farm truck pass from the opposite direction. With a stealthy grin, he looked over his shoulder at Ellen. When he saw her indifferent back, he clenched his teeth and worked the accelerator pedal again.

He turned from the highway onto an unsealed back road. The car shook and rattled, and he had to slow down. Abruptly he stopped. They sat, as the dust billowed then settled around them. Cain was kicking and howling. John gave up trying to wipe his lips with a towel he found on the floor.

'You fuck'n drive.' Rowley stomped out.

He went to the boot and took out three rifles. The same three rifles. Ellen shifted to the driver's seat and waited.

Rowley climbed back and handed her the keys. He looked as though he would have liked to throw them, but didn't dare. Then he put his body through the window and rested the rifles on the rooftop and waited. Ellen started the car and let the clutch jump enough to make Rowley grip the inside of the door.

''Kin watch it!'

Ellen might have smiled, but it was hard to be certain.

They had not gone for more than three minutes when the shotgun fired. Ellen slowed down.

'Go on! Go on!' Called out Rowley.

John looked around. He could not see anything. Cain had stopped crying beside him. The gun went off again. This time he saw a crow disintegrate on top of a bush.

Ellen did not bother to slow.

The .222 fired, twice. An emu staggered off into the bush. The rifle fired again and the emu flopped. The car kept going.

227

Cain looked around. His eyes gleamed. He reached his fingers up and touched John's face. His face creased and giggled. The gun went off again, and again.

Each time time John looked up a bird or a rabbit was shot. He strained his eyes. There was nothing out there, nothing left to kill. Then one of the rifles went off again, and a rabbit leaped into the air. Years before, he had walked off a road. He had been aware then of living things all around him, thousands of them, invisible. They were not invisible to Rowley. Foxes, rabbits, emus, crows, lizards, snakes, sparrows. Nothing was unworthy of a bullet. The guns fired, one after another. Then the sounds of other guns. John looked back. Through the dust, he could see Rowley's brother doing the same. Further back, he could hear another rifle. Doing the same.

The sun was high. It was summer. The light shimmered across the blue flat horizon. Parrots rose in a cloud from a line of trees. The guns fired more rapidly. Here and there, a parrot fell. Rowley laughed loud enough to be heard in the car.

'Good one!'

Shortly after, he tapped the roof of the car. Ellen stopped. Rowley slid back into the cabin, and rested the rifles against the seat. He was smiling, happy as a young boy.

'Sport,' he gurgled. 'Sport!'

Cain responded with a small shriek, and kicked his legs and pulled with his chest against the strap.

Ellen stopped the car.

'Don't leave the guns in the cabin. Not when Cain is there.'

She said it simply and crisply. Rowley looked. He might have climbed onto the window again. But then something happened. He realised it wouldn't work.

Humbly as a small boy being punished, he took the guns out to the boot.

'I need the keys,' he said from the rear.

Ellen took the bundle of keys from the ignition and hung them out the window. Rowley walked forward and took them.

The jingling as he walked away echoed across the empty landscape.

The cars parked under the trees. The men erected tents while the women unloaded pots and pans and food. No sooner had a fire started than the men decided to go hunting.

'We got to get something to attract the flies away from the camp,' Rowley said.

'There's a lot out there without killing anything else!' His sister-in-law settled into a camp stretcher.

She laughed at the disappointment on his face. A silver-grey battery radio rested on a stump beside her. When Rowley walked away, she turned her attention to the radio and twiddled.

'I can't get 2BH out here at all,' she complained. 'Only the frigging ABC.'

She glared as the notes of Mozart's Requiem floated out over the gum trees.

John moved quietly to the other side of a tree, where he could listen and be unobtrusive.

'Why didn' you go with the others?'

He sat where he was, hoping that the question would not be repeated.

Jean groaned. She deliberately forced her large frame from the canvas chair and tromped steadily over the cracking sticks and dry leaves.

Her shadow fell across him. He looked up at her, trying to smile.

'Why didn' you go?'

'I didn't want to, and they don't need me.'

He felt like a naughty boy being scolded. He wanted to huddle or move across into the sun.

'Your sister is alright,' Jean said ambiguously.

'I'm not.'

'Eh. And why aren't you like her, or the rest of them, come to that?'

'I don't want to be.'

He felt as though he was putting out his tongue. The shadow moved further over him.

'Think you're better than everyone else?'

John did not move.

'Your father always acts as though he is, but I didn't think any member of the family would be game to say it.'

When he accepted that he wasn't likely to get any peace there, John grudgingly stood up. He was relieved that he was considerably taller than Jean. He leaned back against the trunk of the tree, determined to enjoy as much distance as he could get.

'What can I do for you?'

'Just tell me what you doing around here?'

'Minding my own business.'

'Do you work?'

The radio dropped from the log and the sound went off the station. Ellen walked across from the group of women sitting with babies who were all listening intently on the far side of the fire. She picked up the radio and set it back on the stump.

'What are you both talking about?' She called in mock innocence.

'He's telling me why he doesn't work.'

'I'm telling you nothing.'

To his surprise, Jean leaned back on her heels and let go another peal of raucous laughter.

'At least he's got spirit,' she cackled. 'Your old man would never come back like that.'

'You never seen him,' commented Ellen ruefully.

'That's true.'

The men returned. Rowley's brother smiled as he dragged the carcass of a kangaroo from the back of the utility.

'Dump it over there. Downwind.'

He hauled it across the edge of the camp by the legs, letting the heavy tail catch the side of a rug. When the women called out, he brightened up.

'That stirred you,' he smiled. Most of his teeth were gone, except for a single canine and incisor on the upper left side of his mouth.

Rowley walked behind him, unneccessarily, except to show the guns, which he carried under his arms with their muzzles pointed down.

230

Ten minutes later, they were bored again. They walked in a group to the bank of the anabranch and tossed empty bottles into the air. Clay-shooting, with Rowley's shotgun. The women carefully ignored them, and remained sitting in their chairs or on blankets, looking after babies and knitting.

The men had a shot each. Then they had another shot. Then they stood there. For variation, Peter lobbed a bottle into the water. Rowley shot it with the .22.

'Good one!' They all cheered.

Then they all had a turn.

After the second turn, they began to look bored again.

'Give Johnno a shot!' Rowley called.

'Give Johnno a shot!' The others all repeated, pleased at this extra bit of sport.

John allowed himself to be persuaded. He knew that he would be tossed into the water if he did not. He rested the gun barrel in the fork of a tree and waited. The first bottle landed in the water, not far out. John took his time, then fired. The bottle shattered and the ripples ran out to the side of the water.

'Further out! That was an easy one!'

The next bottle landed in the centre of the broad, still stretch of water. Again John smashed it. He released the dead cartridge and waited. Another bottle sailed into the air and landed far away, close to the distant shore. Again he smashed it.

He handed the gun back to Rowley.

'It's a good gun,' he said.

He was about to walk away.

'How did you never shoot kangaroo, years ago?' Rowley asked.

'Why did he never, you mean,' he heard Jean's voice from not far away.

The light had softened and the shadow of the trees angled across the still water. John walked away from the camp and changed into an old pair of shorts. The mud moved under his toes. His feet were tender. He thought about the yabbies in the mud and the pieces of glass and drew his feet back.

231

The water was cold. Plucking up courage, he thrust himself forward. He swam slowly and lazily into the centre of the great anabranch. Away from the trees, the water still glistened. Muddy fresh water. He felt himself become a yabby, he would allow himself to sink to the bottom. Then he would burrow and make his own cave and stay there, sliding out and sidestepping across the mud to find something to eat, fascinated by the sparkle of the light on the fine brown flakes of sand, the slimy film on the pieces of half buried wood.

He lay on his back and splashed. The sun was moving down to the horizon. He looked at it with tiny button yabby eyes, and wriggled the little feelers at the end of his nose cautiously around. The hard segmented shell cased around his body moved and allowed him to breathe. He moved his hard brittle tail and stretched.

How, he wondered to himself, would a yabby think to himself? He pulled himself along, letting his body move in time to the motion of the water.

'What's it like in there?'

He turned over on his back and waved an arm to the hazy figure on the shore.

He had not taken more than another half a dozen strokes when he heard the others splash into the water. He was shifting along in his modest yabby way, when the others, with their long bodies in their single sheath of armour, caught up easily.

'Not a bad idea!' Rowley trod water and flipped a bunch of fair hair out of his eyes.

'Fuckin' good one,' agreed Peter.

John was so content he just turned over on his back and slithered and gurgled. The line down the centre of a yabby's underside, the weak spot where they could be cracked open. White meat.

'What you laughing at?' Rowley was puzzled.

'It's just . . . it's just . . .'

But he didn't really know.

232

Chapter 3

The woman held out her hand.

'Good day.' She did not smile. 'I heard of you.'

The handshake was firm and mannish. There was a furrow across her chin which she made no attempt to hide.

'Good things, I hope.'

'Not all of them.'

'Ethel works with me.' Ellen had already made the tea and placed the pot in the centre of the yellow laminex table.

John noticed that she might have been apologising. He also noticed that Rowley had left the room.

'On the taxis?'

'The only job a woman can get here.' Ellen spoke hastily.

'Only if she's married,' drawled Ethel. 'No trouble if you're single. The Barrier Industrial Council is encouraging people to live in sin.'

'Are you living in sin?'

'Not regularly.'

Ethel and John exchanged glances. John smiled.

'Doesn't hurt, does it?'

'Never does anyone any harm. Now and then.'

They both laughed. Her jaw moved when she laughed so the furrow became more obvious.

'How long have you been driving taxis for?'

'Six years.' She shrugged. 'Went to Adelaide for a few years before. Worked in a factory. Hated it. Assembly line, putting screws into cars. General Motors.'

'I worked for Leyland for a while. In Sydney.'

The front door slammed. Ellen jumped on her chair.

'The old boy going out?' Asked Ethel.

Ellen didn't answer directly. Instead she went in to check that the child was still asleep.

233

'She's lucky to get a job, with the baby,' Ethel went on. 'The parents are still here, so I come back, when I got sick of General Motors, and a bad affair of the heart. If you're from here, you always come back.'

'Here I am.'

'It's not so bad, as long as you don't get married. Then you're stuck with babies and the husband who comes back pissed and there's nothing here for you, nothing. You see the way the wives sit together, the expressions on their faces, the way their lips turn down at the sides by the time they're thirty-five.'

She pulled the sides of her mouth down and made her face bitter and resentful.

John nodded.

'They sit at their end of the table with their knitting needles and their cotton. Each time they knit one, purl one, they put it into the husband sitting down the other end of the table, sharing the jug with his mates.'

'How do they like you?'

'Some of them don't. Rowley, he can't take me. Some of them just accept it when I sit there and there isn't any man that can put me down, they go along. But I know if I was to get married, then it'd be the other end of the table for me, no fun, just bitching.'

She paused and leaned back on her chair.

'You smoke?'

John took one. She scratched the match against the box toward him and lit his cigarette.

'It's not a bad life so long as you don't weaken.'

'You reckon you'll have kids?'

'Doubt it.' She turned her head and watched a perfect smoke-ring drift to the ceiling.

'It's not that funny,' she said when John giggled.

The air was cool and the footpaths full of people who sat on their fences and talked to one another in low voices and stopped as he walked past and held cans of beer against their chests and slapped mosquitoes. Everywhere there were radios, and black

234

and white televisions on verandahs, and records being played in the background. Some he remembered. The old Country and Western music that he had heard when he was a child, but there was also Beatles and Jimi Hendrix and Rolling Stones.

Highways went to Adelaide and Sydney and Melbourne. The railway trucks were still there. The crane was working, but the days were numbered for the Silverton Tramway Company. He stared at the crane as it lumbered along the tracks in the twilight but he could not see the driver. He was afraid to go and see whether Serge was still there. Not afraid of Serge, but afraid of the reflection of age he would find in himself.

His life had not gone very well. Then, he had never expected very much from it. He was entering middle age with no career, no steady job, no education, and only a vague and negative ambition to escape a place and a family. Yet, as much as he sought freedom, he found himself again walking the same place, restless and restricted as ever. Nothing restricted him now, he realised. Except memory—and habit. His parents had outgrown him. Broken Hill was a prosperous, comfortable sleepy town. What did it want to know of his private torment?

His life was as he wanted it. To have had a job, a career, a family, would have involved compromise with *his* family. He was more attached to them than they were to him. He was in conflict with the shadows of his childhood. They leaned over him as he was an adult, disapproving and reproving, and he was caught in their images. Cars, parked across the footpaths, each one of them a personal insult. The crackle of voices, their tone implying a judgement. The dry salt smell, the dust. The light on the tallest poppet head.

He walked back to the house. The light was clear enough for him to see. There were no trees. The garden was gone. The house was bare and shrunken. He placed and remembered. Yes, there was the loose piece of iron beside the front steps which he could lift away to climb under the house. There the small room at the side, which he had built with his father for his grandmother. The louvres were still stuck in the same place. There was the path. The concrete steps rising grey out of the earth. He sat on besser bricks he had made. Everything had been bulldozed and flattened and graded. No bushes, no beds of flowers, the weeds graded over.

The house was so small. A miniature of the one he remembered. Stripped of the layered world that surrounded it, a place which could not give shade. His father had painted the corrugated iron grey before he left. It was still painted grey.

'At least it is honest,' he said to himself.

No, he debated. There would have to be evidence of some introspection for it to be honest, some form of endeavour. That it was barren in a barren landscape was an accident. The woman who had planted that garden had tried to design something. To put such a garden in such a place may have been silly. It was human endeavour, it was work, it sought consciousness, it had the artifice of wisdom. It was only a convention somebody accepted that they should survive there, with a car and a television flickering under the front door. It was a necessity that they lived, that they worked underground for so many hours a day, and built things in the hours left to them. What else was there?

There were certain conventions he had accepted. He had not been wanted. He had not wanted himself. He had not attempted to transform what was around him. His own work was a means by which he remained within conventions. The stripping of the garden was as much about himself as it was about the rest of his family, as it was about Broken Hill, as it was about the Broken Hill Proprietary, the great violent father who, when he looked closely, was the rather pompous shade of himself. A corrugated iron shack in a small desert.

Further along, a spray of fine water wet his boots. A small boy was running away from another boy. John sidestepped. The boys rushed past, calling out and not stopping.

There was someone familiar sitting on a verandah.

'Hello,' he called.

'Who's that?' Asked Kerry's mother.

'John. Evans.'

236

'Who?'

'John Evans.'

The figure on the verandah stirred. She had become mountainous and immobile.

'Come up here then, and have a cup of tea.' The woman who squinted at him in the sunlight was old.

He jumped the fence easily and walked across the newly laid concrete front yard. A tree sprouted from the small rectangle of dirt on either side of the steps. He could see the old woman's face, with the drawn sagging skin on the throat and the dark shadows under her eyes.

'What do you do these days? Where do you stay?'

'Away. Sydney. I been working as a storeman, most of the time.'

He was conscious of the relief as he slipped into the old accents.

'Eh. We'll have to get you a cup of tea.' She shifted and her legs tautened, but the effort was a bit too much. She let herself down again. She looked up at him, timidly. Something of panic. Wondering why, but confident and easy, John smiled down at her.

'There's no hurry.'

'Cup of tea.' With a great effort she pushed herself up. Then waved away John's proffered arm.

He followed her along the corridor. Then he noticed that although her bulk seemed great when she was sitting, when she was standing the clothes hung from her frame.

She put the kettle on the stove. The room hadn't been repainted. The old woman made sure that the tea leaves were in the pot and the pot was set within reach on the table before she allowed herself to settle.

'Married yet? You got any kids?'

He wagged his head.

'Better to play the field, isn't it. While you got time.'

She laughed, but there was something in the way she spoke that made him afraid.

'Came up to look at the house.'

237

'Different now, to the way it was.'

'They spoiled it!' He was surprised at the feeling that rushed into his words. 'They messed the whole place.

'They should have done some improving. Like they could have laid some concrete once they pulled out the trees. Better than letting the weeds grow.'

John didn't know what to say.

'How's Kerry?'

'Not so bad. Works on the Zinc now, gets into trouble same as he always did. Still married. He's got a couple of kids now. They're going to school. They look like him, ugly buck teeth and all.'

She smiled, deliberately showing the remains of the prominent front teeth she had bequeathed her son.

John laughed.

'I see your sister sometimes, from the front. Tears along in her taxi. Drops off Mrs Ryan when she goes to the doctor's each Wednesday. Opens the door and lets her out real gentle and helps her up the path, then runs down. Throws a wheelie in the middle of the street and she's off. Nothing but dust and the smell of rubber.'

John laughed because he wasn't sure of what to say.

'Kerry always said the only thing she didn't have was . . . you know what I mean.'

The kettle boiled. She leaned across and lifted the kettle and poured, then dropped the kettle back on the stove. She was putting the lid on the teapot when someone pushed through the back door.

'Guess who's come to visit?'

'Good day Evany,' Kerry said calmly from the door then sat down as if he might have seen John every second day.

His mother poured a cup of tea and pushed it to him. He added a heaped teaspoonful of sugar himself.

'It was a good game on Saturday. Wests got done,' Kerry addressed himself to John, half of John. The other half, the half that belonged away, was dangerous.

238

Despite his calm, Kerry was warding off the other half. He smiled and invited John into the discussion, the old friendship, on certain terms.

'I read about it.'

A cup of tea slid within range, saving the moment.

'Here's the sugar,' Kerry pushed the bowl with the Railway Refreshment Room teaspoon across.

John smiled as he looked at the engraving. The spoon was tarnished.

'Don't have sugar.'

'Sweet enough as it is.' The tired woman boomed from the corner.

There was something different. John lifted the cup to his lips and surveyed the room. When he looked at the shelf, he knew.

'First time I ever been here the radio isn't going.'

Kerry looked cross, as though he had been caught out. He grunted and leaned back and turned the radio on. The Simon and Garfunkel version of 'Bridge Over Troubled Water'.

It was not right. John knew it. Kerry knew it.

'You could try the ABC.' Kerry's mother said.

It would not do.

'We never listen to the ABC.' Kerry looked miserable.

'How's Elaine?'

He shuffled on his seat and looked bashful.

'Not too bad. Do alright. Still manage to get it up every night.'

'You've had enough kids.'

'Can't help it, though. Go to bed thinking "no go tonight give the old boy a rest" then soon as I get to the cot I jump straight in the saddle.'

'He never changes.' His mother tried to laugh but rocked back in her chair instead.

'What do you think it's there for, fuck it?'

'You're dreadful.' His mother gave a giggle.

'I don't care. It tickles and that little furry bit feels nice once you're in there.'

'John isn't married.'

239

'Well, he wouldn't know what it's like, would he?'

He waited a minute.

'Don't get married mate. From what the mates tell me you get less of it then than you do when you're out on the loose. Then they want to get you, and you know the only way they can do it?'

'Cuntpower,' his mother said automatically.

'Oath.'

'You're disgusting, you know that, Kerry?'

'Course I know it. Wouldn't have it any other way, not like them hypocrites go to church and get it up each other on the sly. You see that cunt who runs the Zinc? Walks around like his shit doesn't stink.'

'You ever smelled it?'

'Never got the old brown nose close enough, what with all the shift bosses and foremen get in first, tongues lapping.'

He made lapping noises with his tongue hanging out.

'I don't know why I put up with you.'

'Because I say what you think but you never say it.'

'You know he's really a good boy, don't you John?'

John took the opportunity to take another sip of tea. 'Bridge Over Troubled Water' had finished.

'. . . now with the compliments of Ryans' Economy Store the family store that has served groceries to all areas of Broken Hill for eighty years branches in Patten Street Oxide Street . . .'

'Have another cup of tea?'

'I'll get it.'

She did not object. John leaned across and poured.

'. . . home deliveries to all areas in the city . . .'

John looked around at the changeless room, the changeless house, the spots which needed painting on the ceiling. Past the sink he could see through the small window on the verandah a streak of light as the sun inched its way across the bare red dust.

Already there was so little to say. Kerry smiled, sure of the restrictions he had imposed.

'I don't drink any longer,' he said. 'Not since the accident.'

'The accident?'

'Oath. A couple of years back. Big time gun miner me, bust me fuck'n guts showing off how smart I was. All went on me. Down me back. It hurt, mate. Shit it hurt. The doc, he said, "Stay like that for long and it's in there with the fuck'n knife," and I asked him what then? "No more jig jig for you Kerry." He thought it was real funny. "Very fuck'n funny," I says. "Well you go fuck yourself with your knife." "Not if it gets any worse it'll be you that gets fuck'n with the knife," he says. I don't like it when he keeps smilin' at me like that, so I take it easy. Watch the nest instead of rollin' into it every night. She says, "What's up with you can't get it up no more?" "Just makin' sure that stupid doctor don't get into me with that knife," I said, "or I won't be able to get it up again, ever."'

'You're a foul-mouthed bastard.' His mother rocked forward on the chair.

'Always was. Trained by a master.'

'Aah.' But she sounded as if she didn't really mind.

Still grumbling, she forced herself from the seat and walked out.

'Somebody's got to do some work,' she whined.

'No one in this family.'

'Still a cheeky bastard. Never changed.'

'Got a bit better after that, so the doc took his knife and I went back to work. No more big time for me, they can get stuffed far as I'm concerned. No more contract gun mining, no more lifting. The shift boss comes along says, "Hey Kerry how about a shift overtime?" "Piss off. I got better things to do with my time, the family to look after." "Problem with you is you want to get in the nest so much you got feathers and I don't mean the nest you keep the pigeons in down the back." "Least I get something from life, not like you with your head up some engineer's arsehole." "That's not called for," he says. "Take it to church then," I said, "all of you. The day of rest and you make more deals on who gets on at the church, when you're

241

in your suits than you ever do on any report. So long as you get the right church. Watch it Snowy, because I heard it that the next underground manager is a Catholic." "Trouble with you is you got a big mouth," the boss says. "You think you're smart but you watch it one of these days you're gettin' into big trouble." "And a ramma ramma ding dong," I says.'

'You got a good future.'

'Another sarcastic bastard,' Kerry said.

He followed John's glance after his mother.

'She's not so good,' he dropped his voice.

'Thought so.'

'Cancer.'

'What they reckon?'

'Not so good,' he repeated. 'Not that long.'

On the front porch, John turned and touched the old woman on the hand. It was the first time he had ever deliberately touched her. She looked up from her chair startled.

'See you later. I got to go.'

The old woman looked at him closely. She smiled and leaned back. She realised he was saying goodbye, but he was one of many.

'Sorry the house changed so much.'

'The way things go.'

'Say hello to your father and mother for me.'

'Call around,' Kerry yelled from behind him.

'I'll do that.' John dropped the handle on the gate with a clink. 'Some time.'

It was almost evening. As he walked back to his sister's house, he could hear a cricket in the dark.

'What have you learned as a result of your trip?'

Ethel sat on the other side of the table and looked at the smouldering end of her cigarette.

'Lots of things.' He shook his head.

242

'That's funny. I alway know what I learned and what I think about things.'

'Sometimes I do.' John felt a little miserable.

'Your sister knows where she's going.'

'Everybody says that, even before.'

'I don't think lover boy is going to keep up. He won't be part of it.'

'Rowley?'

She watched him without answering or moving her head.

'Where you think she's going?'

'I don't know, but she's going there.'

'What about Rowley?'

'He's not going. He doesn't even know anything's moving. He says they'll break up alright, but he hasn't got the brains to think about why.'

'Why?'

'Because he can't move and he knows nothing and he thinks he knows everything and he can't think at all.'

She stubbed the cigarette methodically in the bent tin ashtray.

'I like you.' She reached across decisively and rested her hand on his.

'I'm leaving tomorrow.'

'What do you think I am?'

The hand withdrew and her nose turned.

'Ellen won't mind,' he said, although he wasn't certain.

'She already knows.'

Chapter 4

He had not been in Sydney for more than three months when he received a letter from Ethel. He had started another job and shifted to a flat in a different part of the inner city. He did not usually give a forwarding address.

He was sitting in the sun under Captain Cook's statue in Hyde Park, idly watching the old men playing chess on the tables under the trees, when someone called his name. 'Mr Evans, that is you?'

He rolled over. His former landlord was standing over him with a pleased uncertain smile. His wife was the usual run of East Sydney landlady, with a heart of gold. Her husband had always looked at him solemnly over his glasses from the front room as he walked out, and said nothing when his wife called to him to bring back the rent today, or get out please. This was no place for the unemployed person, please. Only people what worked here. Please. The husband must have liked a lot of lodgers in that house, because his wife hated them all, except for Mr Hocking who had worked in the post office for forty years but had now retired, and who had a pension cheque each fortnight. Mr Hocking spat in the corridor and farted loudly outside John's door, and the landlady trembled at his approach.

'Goot morning Mr Hocking,' she said each morning as he stomped slowly on his wobbly legs down the stairs.

'I hope so, Mrs Jowanovics, I hope so,' he boomed.

Then he would walk straight past her. For him alone, she withdrew the mop she normally let flop insolently across the path. Once at the door, Hocking spat, loudly, across the doorstep.

John quickly acquired a job, as a storeman in Surry Hills, packing boxes of kitchen-ware for housewives who had been sold them by door to door salesmen. The salesmen were on commission. They had to get the signatures. The women who signed tentatively for the kitchen-ware had to get out of it. With his first pay, John left the boarding house.

'We keep you until you get the job. Then you bloody leave!' The landlady complained.

'That's gratitude.'

John was sure he saw the landlady's husband smile.

Three weeks later, he sat in the sun in Hyde Park, and the man stood over him.

'I have the letter. For you,' he held up the envelope and smiled, sure that it would justify the intrusion.

John looked at the childish writing.

'Where from?'

'I have not looked at this.'

Mr Jowanovics sounded slightly indignant.

'How did you find me?'

'I think: yes, I could send the letter back, but there is no address on the back. So I put it in my pocket, just in case. Then today I see you here, with Captain Cook.'

He smiled, as though he had just said something enormously witty.

'Thank you very much.'

John accepted the letter. Mr Jowanovics still hesitated. John invited him to sit, which he did.

Dear John,

Surprise. But I couldn't stop writing because I wanted to say I told you so.

Your sister has given Rowley the big 'A'. She went out with a couple of the girls one night last week, and we got a bit drunk and so she got home late. Rowley was really shitty. Ellen says he belted her one. He doesn't normally do that. So she took the kid and shifted.

Rowley came around here a couple of times looking for her, but she was too smart to stay here. He said he just wanted to see how she is, and maybe make it up. He tried to look like it didn't matter much but he didn't look real happy. I told him I didn't know where she was, and he looked at me and stopped

245

himself from saying bullshit then he laughed and went. We never got on. I don't think we're going to get on any better, especially after the other time he came around. He was a bit under the weather, well he could hardly stand up. I wouldn't have answered the door if I saw him coming but I was too late and there he was.

I want to know where she is, he says as soon as he gets into the kitchen. Oh yeah I said, what you asking me for? Come on tell me, he says. You want a cup of tea or coffee? I reckon you need coffee most? I asked him, but then he reached across and grabbed me by the butt. Piss off what do you think I am I said and he took his hand away. He looked at me as though he didn't expect that. You let some of the others, he said, looking hurt like I really did something bad to him. That's my business I told him, now you get out or I'll start yelling and I pushed him out the door. He stood there for a while on the verandah but I wouldn't open the door not even when I heard him pewking over the verandah. Then he went away. He left a mess. I didn't feel sorry for the bastard. I don't know how she put up with him so long.

I suppose you've already heard this from your family. Your mum is up here helping Ellen look after the little fellow, but I'm not going to say where she's staying just in case. If you told shithead Rowley where she was living Ellen would never speak to me again. The weather here's been good and I like driving taxis alright the other day I got a fare from a cocky farmer wanted to go to Cobar so I took him. It was a good drive and he paid. As I was coming back it was night and I thought how lonely it was going to be in this place without your sister, now I think she's going to go to Sydney to live with your parents. They will think it's alright. I even thought about you. I miss you too I don't know why. So when I got back I decided to write. As good as talking in a way isn't it?

It's getting winter so when I'm not working I come back home and put my feet in front of the heater and feed the dog. The girls don't come around so much now. Lots of them are having babies and they're busy and in a few years time they'll come and look me up so I can be aunty. Not so bad I think it has compensations.

246

If you come back for another holiday you can stay here if you want. Bugger the next doors.

Love,
Ethel.

John re-read the letter, then he looked up. The shadow of the trees was creeping towards him,

'It is important?'

'It is important.' John swallowed and smiled at Mr Jowanovics' eagerness. 'I'm thankful you found me.'

'It was nothing,' said Mr Jowanovics.

He stood up and brushed a few pieces of grass from his trousers. John was afraid that he was going to extend his hand. He didn't. He said goodbye, and he would see him again. John thanked him. Mr Jowanovics waddled off, away from the quickly setting sun.

Austin answered the telephone immediately.

'I thought you'd be working.'

Austin had a light duties job packing detergents. He couldn't stand sitting around for long.

'I stayed home to work around the house.' Austin had a slightly guilty croak.

'Where's mum?'

'She went to Broken Hill for a while.'

'Did she?'

John could hear Austin wheeze at the far end of the of the line. He wasn't cunning. If he couldn't frighten you, then he didn't know what to do.

'Ellen's having trouble.'

'Sick or something?'

'She's left him. We told her not to marry him. He wasn't smart enough. He can't write.'

'What did he do to her?'

'Came home late. Punched her, hit her around the kitchen. She took the little boy and left while he was asleep. He must have been drunk.'

'Out like a light,' John said glibly. 'What's she going to do?'

Austin didn't want to tell him, but he was never good at telling lies. 'She's got to come here and stay. Get a job while we look after the boy. I can't think of anything else.'

'A bit hard on you.'

Deep thought on the other end of the line.

'Oh no. I can't . . . think of anything else.'

'Bit old for this.'

'If you've got a family. That's what families are for. We always wanted a boy.'

Palpable silence.

'That what you want?'

'You . . . we wanted . . . it didn't work before . . .'

'Three times lucky.'

'I won't be around to do it three times.'

'Never know. I might get married yet . . .'

'We'd be pleased if you got married.'

'How long before they get back?'

'Diana said on the phone they have to stay longer. So everything can get tied up.'

'Legally.'

'Otherwise you don't know what he might say in court. Diana says he walks around all the time looking for them. He yelled names at Ellen in the street.'

'Embarrassing.'

'It's no good to cause a scene, not in public. Everybody watches in Broken Hill.'

'Who . . .'

'There's still people we know there. Not all of them have retired yet. They stay there. They keep staying there, or they live at Sunset Strip and they go to Broken Hill to play cards, or bowls. I got a new car a month ago. Sold the old car. Another Holden, a new one. Next time you come.'

He paused.

'I can drive you, to Manly.'

Austin hated anyone else driving his car.

248

'What . . . when I have a weekend.'
'You working?'

Dear Ethel,

Thank you very much for your letter. You know I hate writing anything, so take this as proof that I think you're OK. It is that every time I say anything nice, then I'm using Austin's voice. I hate it. The only way I can shake it is to swear and yell, because that way I can get something that sounds like the truth coming out. I feel like spewing.

There isn't much good talking if the only thing you do is avoid saying something. Austin hates words because they tell the truth about things, some things, even when they are used to tell lies.

It was interesting news about Ellen. Nobody had told me that she left Rowley. Not that it is easy to let me know, but they know where they can leave a message. They don't want to, because I will know the truth. So do they, only they don't want to say it, even a lie would let the truth in. That's why, when I phoned up, he had to tell me the truth. That way, I might go away. I feel bad because they want me to be, it's the only way they can be right, and it's the only way I can live with myself.

Hell I'm morbid.

They want a boy, that's because they want to prove that it wasn't really their fault, they can turn out a tennis champion or something. If they're right, it hurts and I'm jealous.

Don't know what you're going to make of this.

Ellen will come back to Sydney. Austin and Diana will get another try at bringing up another tennis player. Rowley might be a bit of a bastard, but his problem is not that he can't read or write or that he's dumb. He's in the way.

Your letter got to me because a little guy who lived in the bloodhouse I was in put it in his pocket and walked around until he found me. I think he did it because he hates his wife, and his wife didn't like me. Along with the rest of the human race.

So I shifted. I'm working at a different job and I'm living in a different house in the next suburb, but it's closer, and I like walking

249

through the parks. The trees are bare now but they haven't cleared the leaves, so each day I walk to work and the dry leaves crackle under my shoes. At nights I sit in bed and read. Sometimes I watch the old television, but its fuzzy and on Channel 10 you see double. The foreman where I work takes me for a drink some Friday afternoons, and he tells me about his marriage. He hates it. We escaped that, so far. Austin was always telling me that I should get married and have kids. What the fuck for? I asked him. He looked at me in that goggle eyed way, and says, that's what people do. I guess it is.

When I say to the foreman I ought to get married he thinks it's funny but he thinks it'd be a good thing, like they all believe in it, although the belief is what makes them miserable. They can't talk with one another because it would mean being in a lousy job with a mortgage and a bad back might be real, and if it is, then where would they be? That's what people do.

This is a lot of writing for me. I'll try not to write as much next time, if there is a next time. Send letters to me care of the Post Office. I go past every afternoon. I can ask.

> Yours in the shit,
> John

Chapter 5

'We've left it to both of you. Half to Ellen, half to you.' Diana scraped the bottom of the cup across the saucer.

'I never asked for it.'

'It's what is fair. We decided to be fair.' Austin sounded important. He smiled and his cheeks, which had become ruddy as he grew older and put on weight, reddened.

'I'd take it. Soon as we're gone you better get in for it, or she'll have it. She's swift, I tell you,' Diana added.

'She's got enough now, she doesn't have to worry.'

'She worries alright.'

'It is your money. You worked for it.' He strove to maintain distance.

'No good unless you leave something,' Austin smiled broadly. He loved being benevolent.

John took a sip of tea. An unpleasant, sticky feeling.

'Ellen will come in soon for lunch. We better cut out talking about this.' Diana looked at Austin slyly.

'She thinks it will all go to her,' added Austin.

Diana put her hand across and touched her son on the wrist. She gave a giggle.

'She'll get a shock, won't she love.'

The old sly sparkle in the eyes.

'You've always been a battler, so you deserve it.'

'Never been lucky, have you love? Never got a girl that stuck around, never got much money. But, you know, I reckon you're not such a bad catch. For a decent good girl, nothing flash.'

'Nothing flash,' repeated Austin agreeably.

'She's flash. Your sister.'

'How?'

'Thinks she's important. You know, she owns a flat down by the beach at Manly now.'

'I went in to the office during the elections. Liberal Party how-to-vote papers in a box by the door. "What's this?" I asked her. "You vote the way your interest is," she said. "You think you're up there with the capitalists?" "Yes, or I will be soon." She was cool as you please.'

'She'll be home soon,' Diana said nervously.

'Doesn't matter. I can say what I like.'

'He will, he'd tell her. They'd fight all the time if I wasn't here.'

'She thinks she's smart.'

'She's not as smart as she thinks. Not when Gough got elected.'

'She says he won't last. All he'll do is mess the place up for the likes of her, so she says.'

'I don't reckon he will,' grumbled Austin.

'Just that they're used to getting it all their own way. They don't want to lose anything. They want every last little bit of it and they think they're hard done by when they can't get it.'

'All of it,' Austin repeated emphatically.

'That's why we left half of it for you, half of it for her.' Diana poured herself another cup.

'She's only a salesman, but she's a good one.'

'I don't doubt it, not a bit. She always could talk. Sell anything to anyone.'

'We left some money for Cain.'

Diana looked at Austin crossly.

'That's only fair,' she added.

'That's only fair. I left it so he could get it when he's twenty-one, because I don't think we'll be around.'

'Not then we won't. I don't think. Austin would have left it for him when he was eighteen, but I talked him out of it. He won't have much sense when he's eighteen. Not with the mother he's got.'

'Goes out drinking every night.'

'With her girlfriends, every night. We bring the kid up, I tell you.'

'Not that we begrudge it.'

'No,' it was John's turn to smile.

'He's a lovely kid.'

A lovely kid.'

'But the house. We left it half for you, half for her.'

'Including the contents.'

'Make sure you get here quick though, she'll have the lot,' Diana cackled.

'How was your holiday? You haven't told me yet.'

'Great love. The boat! It was so good. The service we got, the food. It was such a good time.'

'We liked Japan very much. The Japanese were very courteous. Always courteous.'

'Do anything for the tourists.'

'They're the ones who pay, they know it too. The customer always right. Not like Hong Kong.'

'It was so dirty. All these people, running along the streets. All talking ying tung ying tung and everything smells.'

'Cain liked the Japanese best too. He knew.'

'He did too. He walked around and looked at everything and he listened and he talked.'

'Smarter than his mother.'

'She'll be here any time.'

Diana looked up guiltily.

'I made some extra dessert for you.'

'I like the Sunday dinner your mother makes,' Austin nodded.

'Still the same as Broken Hill.'

'I'm glad we're out of that place. I never liked it, you know. I'm a bit like you.'

Ellen's car pulled up in the drive. Austin prised the venetians apart. Ellen glanced up and smiled before she turned her knees and stepped from the other side of a new red Triumph sports car with bucket seats.

'I don't know how she takes passengers out in that!' Austin whispered.

'It's so small.' Diana patted John's hands as though in compensation.

253

'It cost her a lot. She's still paying it off.'

It was hard to tell where admiration and envy left off.

'Hello brother.'

John nodded as Ellen strode in and sat firmly with her legs apart on the chair at the end of the table. Diana was already in the kitchen spooning out the food.

'How is . . . business?' John asked.

'Going wonderfully darling. Great guns. There's lots to be made there. You ought to try it.'

'I don't have a sales personality.'

'No dear,' she chuckled. 'I don't think you do. There's something you can do though to make money. You're smart enough. You just haven't found it yet.'

Diana came out and put down a plate of food for John. Ellen stared at it. Diana went out and brought in another and put it in front of Ellen.

'One for you . . . and one for you . . .' Diana sang as she went back in for Austin's serve.

Last of all herself.

'One for you . . . that's lovely darling,' Ellen said to her mother with a sweet smile.

'I don't want to go without.'

Diana pushed the mint sauce across the table to John.

'He's my boy,' she said slyly. 'Boys need to eat more.'

Ellen winced.

'I'm not that hungry,' said John.

'You've got to eat.'

'Later on I'll show you the minerals.'

'He got them sent down from Broken Hill. He went up there for a dinner at the North Mine and they gave him a glass case, to put them in.'

'Long piece of wood, all varnished. Expensive.'

'No more than they owe you, all them years underground.'

'You're living alright now. Lots of fun. Aren't they great?' Ellen turned the full glare of her innocence on John.

'It was great on the *Oriana*,' Diana interrupted.

'Never forget it,' added Austin earnestly. 'Never.'

'I don't think you ever will darling. It is a pity that John couldn't come.'

For a second, panic showed on the faces of Austin and Diana.

'I didn't ask to go.' John dabbled a fork in the mashed potato.

'He didn't want to go,' Diana asserted.

'See!' hovered above the table.

Austin silently chewed at a minute piece of lamb. Diana clattered her fork down on the side of the plate as she chewed and looked around with a defiant expression, from one sibling to the other.

'It was nice though, wasn't it.' Ellen spoke quietly and looked through the window, where she might have been able to see the chrome front window surrounds of her car.

'It was nice.'

'I'd go there again, except that you get the opportunity only once in your life.'

'Some people go to England every year. I don't know where they get the money.'

'Some people work for it.'

The silky comment floated past. Diana pretended not to have heard.

'Some people don't work for it,' said John.

'People get what they deserve.' The silky voice again.

'Themselves.'

John smiled spitefully as the barb went in.

'It was nice, especially in Japan. It was so clean.' Diana's eyes clouded over.

'They are so polite, they helped us when we arrived and there was no one there to take us. We went to a counter and asked. They were the opposition, they said, but they telephoned the company. For the tourists from Australia we want to make them happy, they said, and made sure we had a taxi and a guide. We've got a photo of her.'

'She was so nice! A young girl but so polite.'

'You can't tell how old they are, they look young but then

you find they are about thirty-five. That happened in Hong Kong, we thought she was young. She's on the slides too, but she wasn't as nice.'

John nodded agreeably and ate. Ellen finished first.

'Dears, I must go back to work!' she announced.

'The sweets!'

'I never eat them. You know that.'

'You do, I've seen you, I'm sure of that.'

'No she doesn't,' Austin spoke carefully. 'She never eats sweets.'

'I was sure.'

Diana looked bewildered.

'Just forgetfulness. I'll see you later.'

Ellen took the plate out to the kitchen and dumped it on the sink, then kept on going. Austin almost forced John's head around on his shoulders.

'That car, it cost . . . it cost $20 000!' His supremacy with figures unquestioned.

The car revved once, then squealed from the driveway onto the street. 'She'll have an accident, one of these days!' Snapped Diana.

Austin disappeared inside the house, then came back a few minutes later with his collection of rocks. He laid them on the table. Diana was halfway through washing the dishes.

'That's what they gave me.' Austin looked proud.

'And the watch.'

'And the watch.'

'It's a beautiful watch,' chorused Diana from the kitchen.

Above her, a clock face set in a pink ceramic fish moved silently and electrically. John found it more interesting than the collection of rocks.

'That one there, that's galena.' Austin tilted the piece of timber so the light glistened on the fragments in their small glass bowl.

'Like the street.'

Austin looked at him, suspicious of words, those incomprehensible games. Then he thought.

'Galena Street! That's right.'

He laughed.

'They're all named after streets.'

Austin looked suspicious and surly. Although John asked him about the rocks, Austin savoured the hurt and did not lose the opportunity for self-pity.

Finally he went out to water the garden, because the beds had been dry.

'You never got on, you and your father,' Diana ruminated from lounge as she watched the television going on the far side of the room. 'I don't know why you never got on.'

John watched the clock hands in the pink ceramic fish intently. It was two o'clock. He would have to stay another two hours at least, before his father would give him a lift back to Manly wharf. He thought about the bus trip. Endless back lanes and gardens and stops. Not many residents of the area caught buses. Glossy cars trundled past gracefully. No, he couldn't catch a bus back.

'They vote Liberal here,' he said.

'I don't say anything about politics. They all hate Gough. They'd do anything to get rid of him. That's not fair. He was elected, and he is a good Labor man. Isn't he?'

'They think so.'

'Watkins down the road, he said he sent all his money out of the country the night Gough got elected. They'll stuff the economy he said, as if sending all the money out like that won't stuff everything quicker. He said all of his friends did the same.'

On the night Gough was elected, John was doing overtime. Someone had a radio going.

'Make the best of it,' the foreman said. 'They're only giving you overtime Saturday right through the night, so you won't vote.'

At lunchtime, they walked to the school around the corner and lodged absentee votes. Back at work, the boss glared.

'Where you been?' He put his head out the side of the glass case he sat in.

'Voting,' said the foreman.

257

'Absentee voting,' someone added.

The boss slammed the door and sulked. They'd been promised the overtime. The boss yelled at them to turn the radio off but someone listened to the results on the walkman.

'They won!' He called across the room. The plug flopped down on his shoulder.

The storemen cheered. The boss did not look up.

They were packing china, in small cardboard crates. Usually a few plates were broken. That night, not one plate was cracked.

At eleven o'clock, John walked part-way home. Lights were on. In the small inner city terraces, there were parties. He was not in the mood.

He saw a bus when he was halfway along Broadway, and ran to the bus stop. He had caught the bus before. Normally the bus driver was silent and angry. The same bus driver late each Saturday night on the 438 bus. That night, he had a sprig of wattle in his hat band and he swayed in his seat.

'Don' fuckin' pay me,' he said when John offered the fare. 'Let the fuckin' gov'ment pay for this one.'

The bus was three-quarters full of middle-aged couples coming back from a bowling club. The 438 bus danced across the lanes of Parramatta Road. Then the driver took everyone to their front doors. John lived six blocks from the bus route.

The driver offered John a sip of whisky at the door.

'Thanks,' said John, and swallowed.

He told his mother the story, and how the drunken bus weaved along to the end of the street and did a U-turn to go back to the main road.

'They didn't do that here,' Diana said. 'The lights were on alright, but they were all quiet. So quiet you could hear the dials turning on their telephones as they sent their money out of the country!'

'You wanted to shift here.'

'It's alright to improve yourself, so long as you don't get snobby.' Diana looked at him, as though he was the snob.

'You think I'm snobby?'

'I didn't say that.'

They were watching television. Austin was still at the front watering the single bed of roses in the barren lawn-covered front yard. Another car drove along the drive.

'That's Cain being delivered.' Diana stood and turned down the television.

John stayed where he was. His mother went out to greet her grandson. The car started again, a woman called, the car went.

The boy came into the lounge room. A small, fair-haired facsimile of Rowley, round in the face, tall for his age. He looked at John.

'You remember my little man.' Diana walked behind him and gave him a hug. 'This is John. He's my little man too.'

John laughed.

'I better go soon,' John said a few minutes after the clock hand passed three.

'It's been good to see you son.' Diana wiped a crumb from her upper lip.

'Ellen is doing alright for herself.'

'She's not so smart.'

From the side of his eye, John observed the little boy playing with a toy truck on the lounge floor pause, then run the truck over and over on its wheels. Behind him, the television was still going, but the sound was down. Austin looked across at it every now and then and kept chewing methodically on his piece of cake.

'She can start a company on her own soon, she says.'

'How can she do that? So quick?'

'She says she can, soon.' Austin looked across with his pale eyes. He could not tell a lie.

'How's that?' John cut off a slice of cake.

'She's got plans.'

259

'Plans?'

'If they work . . .' Austin chewed for the fiftieth time on the piece of cake.

'She could make a lot of money.'

'She could. Or go broke.'

'That sounds like what they say about our first Labor Prime Minister for twenty years.'

'What?'

'Gough. That's what they say. Either he makes it, or he goes broke.'

'Makes what?'

'That's the problem.'

Cain pushed the toy car along the floor. It crashed into the lounge.

'He likes his car. We gave him that. For his last birthday.'

'Show Uncle John all your toys!' Diana said.

'No.' Cain looked up insolently.

'We gave them to you, most of them. That your mother didn't give you. So you show them to your uncle,' Austin insisted.

'They're mine!'

'But we gave them to you.'

Diana smiled and took John's hand over the table.

'See, he used to be my little man,' she giggled.

John tried to pull his hand back. His mother hung on.

'I'll show them to you, when he goes to bed,' Diana whispered quite loudly enough.

Cain retrieved his car, and pushed it towards the legs of the television.

It was dark. John knelt by the engine room in the warm and watched the pistons thump steadily and remorselessly. And he looked out, through the windows that would not close, across the harbour at the lights in the suburbs where the rich and comfortable had it all, culture, power, choking in it. The water slopping the side.

Further along the bench, the only other customer, a huge middle-aged man in shorts with a rucksack under his legs, smiled at him broadly. He held a portable radio up to his ear.

'Where you come from?' His voice was too loud.

'Broken Hill,' John replied automatically, although he hadn't lived there for years.

'Good Labor town.' The man slid his weight closer along the varnished timber slats. 'I'm a member of the Labor Party myself.'

John nodded, too passive to move.

'I've seen you around.'

'Might have.'

'See, because I don't work, I walk around. I'm dyslexic. I can't read or write. I can't control my fingers or my thumbs to work, so I'm on a pension.

He held up his huge, meaty, useless hands, and concentrated his face. The fingers moved slowly in, then out.

'So I walk around and I sleep where I can. My mother lives in Wollongong but I can't stand staying there, so I walk around the city. It's because I like to look. I remember people. I've seen you around.'

The pistons thumped insistently. John repressed an impulse to yawn and lie down on the seat.

'I've noticed you,' he insisted loudly. 'I seen the way you walk and the way you look. You like to look too.'

'Yes.' John knew he was being addressed with something important. He did not want to hear. He was drowsy.

'People who look, they never do anything. Everything is like a film. We sit there and watch, and then it's over.'

'Life.'

'It's not that you're dumb. I'm not dumb, invalid pension and all. I sit there, outside and inside at the same time, and all I can do is watch.'

'Nothing else?'

'In George Street the other day there was an accident. A car hit an old man in a crossing. The driver had been smoking dope, and he said that the light was green when it wasn't. I was the only person who stayed around. No one else wanted to be a

261

witness. He said, "It was green, it was green, wasn't it?" While I looked down at this old man on his back. I think he was having a heart attack. He started to turn blue. When the ambulance arrived, the driver was still trying to tell me the light was green, and the ambulance men wouldn't shift the old man until the police were there. So I laughed. The driver looked at me and his mouth went open, then he hit me. "You cold-blooded bastard," he said.'

'What?'

'That's what I mean.' The man heaved the portable radio onto his legs.

'People hate people who watch.'

At Circular Quay, the man fidgeted with a purse.

The woman sat and glared. When he found the right coin, he put it through the window. The woman gave him a token. He followed John through the turnstiles, imitating exactly the manner in which John dropped the token into the slot.

'See you some time,' he bellowed.

Still too loud. John could hear the music from the radio as he walked away, in the direction of the Botanic Gardens.

Chapter 6

On the day after Gough Whitlam's Labor Government was sacked in November 1975, John left his room and nodded to the landlord who watched as he went out the front door. The landlord was a veteran of the Great War who had been gassed in France. Because he was so old he hardly left his room, although the door stayed open so that he could see who came and who went. A radio played classical music from the time he woke until the time he went to sleep. When he wasn't listening, he was staring through a magnifying glass at a book.

'Nothing to it,' Clifford wheezed at John. 'All he had to do was fire them.'

John hesitated. He gave a strained smile.

'I heard it on television,' John said.

'They wouldn't have lasted. They shouldn't have tried. They ought to start a revolution or shut up. If you get into parliament, you end up like them, or they fire you. What if he refused to go? What if he fired the Governor-General?'

'I don't know.'

'Scared, I tell you. They're going through the motions. They want to lose, because if they don't, they'll have a civil war, and they'll all get shot. What good is being in parliament if that happens?'

'Never made it there,' John was flippant.

'No friggin' good,' the old man laughed. The thick lenses of his glasses turned to the side. A small scar wept constantly on his left cheek, and he rasped and hacked when he spoke.

'Do you want anything? I'm going down the street.'

'The *Herald.* Not that it's any good.'

'I'll bring it back.'

John was relieved. His room had a balcony and a window, and it was quite large. After he had been in the house for a year, the previous tenant had died, and the old man said he could have it, if he didn't mind cleaning it himself. There was a park not far away. If he stood on the edge of the balcony and leaned, he could see it. The fumes from the cars weren't that bad. But the narrow unpainted corridor and the old man's constant asthma made him want to get out as fast as possible.

The day was cool and clear. He walked down the hill to the railway station. A lot of people were crossing the wide street outside the station. He brought two copies of the *Sydney Morning Herald*, then walked to a small vacant lot near Elizabeth Street where he sometimes sat and read. It was too far away for the drunks and he was usually left in peace. The crowd gathered outside the newspaper offices further along. There was a lot of waving flags, calling out, listening to speeches. It was hard to read the newspaper. John closed it and walked toward the crowd.

A van full of policemen had parked inconspicuously in a lane. A policeman leaned against a wall with a radio. When the policeman gave him a hard look, he walked along.

Three policemen stood quietly together at the back of the crowd with quiet faces and their hands behind their backs. The crowd gathered around the gates. The trucks were loaded with papers behind the closed shutters of the building.

John looked around. He stood next to an older man in a brown jacket with leather patches on the sleeves.

'The printers want to strike, in sympathy,' the man said to John.

'Why don't they?'

'It's them got to decide.'

'If they want to . . .'

A union representative climbed on to a box in the front of the crowd. He had a loud-hailer. He was short, and he wore a black leather jacket.

'We've had a communication from inside,' he bellowed into the loud-hailer. 'The shop-stewards are calling a meeting to find out what the membership wants to do. It's up to them to decide. They're the ones who work in the place. It is up to us, though, to remain here in readiness to support them if they should come out.'

'Tell them to come out here and join us!'

'It doesn't work that way. They work there. There's been a lot of complaints about the conditions in Murdoch's papers. They could find considerable justification for industrial action.'

'Without us!' A woman called from the front of the crowd. 'What about the women who work in there? The typists? The typesetters?'

'It's being put to them,' the union representative answered imperturbably. 'However it doesn't seem they're too keen.'

'Because of the men. They wouldn't go on strike because of the men. They resent the dominance of the patriarchy!'

'We don't want anarchy in there!' Then the representative smiled. 'Sorry to the comrades with the red and black flags at the back.'

'Why don't you ask why the women won't go on strike?' The female voice called louder. 'You might find out why. It's because you want to run everything, you with your big pricks.'

'I don't know why, and I don't ask why. All I know is, a group of female comrades in there have decided not to take action. This has been communicated to me, to pass on to you. The reasons are their business, while I would be as prepared to listen, if they chose to tell us.'

'Fascist authoritarian!'

The union representative flushed slightly but ignored it. As he climbed down from the platform, one of the gates at the end flew up. Nobody was there. A red truck loaded with papers accelerated up the ramp to the street. Several people jumped in front of the truck, then leaped quickly out of the way as the truck kept going. A man in shorts climbed on to the tail of the truck and began throwing bundles of newspapers down. He was joined by two others. A woman yanked at the door, but it was locked. A big man with a red face wound the window half down and put his head there.

'Fuck you,' he spat at the woman's face.

While he slowed to do this, most of the papers on the back were unloaded. As the truck swayed around the corner and picked up speed, the men on the back jumped off.

The bundles of newspapers were stacked in the centre of the road. A short middle-aged woman with no false teeth ran into a corner shop and returned with a plastic bottle of methylated spirits and a box of matches.

'He spat on me!' The woman called.

'He would never have done it to a man!'

'Challenge the patriarchy!'

As the newspapers began to burn, the woman jumped on top of the pile.

'This is what they did to Joan!' she cried.

'The first time I ever sympathised with the church,' the man next to John mumbled.

The union representative again climbed on to his box. He stood with the loud-hailer near his mouth and his other fist resting against his hip. The crowd lost interest in the drenched lumps of smouldering newspapers. One bundle had split apart, and newspapers were strewn across the roadway.

'We have achieved success!' The man on the box called.

There were cheers, and a few calls.

'Are they coming out on strike?' The man next to John asked loudly.

'We have achieved success, because . . . if the newspapers can't be driven out by three o'clock, then the whole day's issue is aborted. Not just an issue. A whole day.'

'What about the printers?' A man called.

'Aborted! What about the women?'

The bulk of the crowd clapped and cheered, albeit reflectively.

'If we remain for another forty minutes, then we will have stopped the power of the Murdoch press . . . for one day!'

John looked behind, and noticed that more policemen had arrived. Standing in a row at the back, with an inspector with a silver-braided hat, and a sergeant whispering into a walkie-talkie radio. The crowd became conscious of the police at the same time, and began to huddle around the speaker. They moved in tighter and closer, and the police herded slowly around the edge.

'Stay where you are! We have only . . . thirty-five minutes to go.' He checked his wrist watch.

'We shall overcome . . .' A woman began to sing.

The whole group began to sing, slowly, hesitantly at first. Then the force of the voices built up. As the singers gained confidence, the crowd seemed to swell again and spread. All together the policemen took an unsteady step backwards.

'We shall live in peace . .' the crowd positively swelled and spread.

The police waited. John moved around the crowd, away from the police, but he could not bring himself to sing. When he looked up at the newspaper building, he saw faces behind the glass. Office workers and journalists, staring down. A window near the corner squeaked open and a cameraman leaned out.

'Come down and join us!' The woman who had jumped on the fire called.

The cameraman took a series of rapid photographs, then he smiled and waved. He was young, with thick fair hair. The window squeaked, but it would not quite close again.

'It is time!' Called the union representative. 'We have stopped the Murdoch press from spreading lies . . . for today!'

John felt the line of police shift and shuffle like a row of horses impatient to race.

'We ought to leave. There is nothing more to be gained here.'

'What about the printers?'

'The printers have not made up their minds yet . . .'

'Whose side are they on?'

'Rupert's rabbits!' Someone else added.

'It is up to the membership . . .'

'Like it was up to the membership of parliament . . . Like it was up to the Governor-General!'

'We have stopped the press from producing lies . . . the printers, the workers, the workers in there, I say, they are in support of us. They must be let to support us in whatever way they choose!' The union representative was speaking with passion. He waved the loud-speaker. It moved away from his face and his voice became thin and reedy.

'Who do they choose, comrade?' Called a woman.

'It is up to us to choose to support them. They have the machines! They have the power, when they realise it. They will use it. No Governors-General, no Rupert Murdoch, will stop them then.'

'What about their overdraft?'

'What about their mortgage?'

'The point is, that we have nothing further to gain by remaining. I must suggest . . . that as you leave, nothing personal against our boys in blue, but it has been known to happen . . . stay together, stay in groups, don't stray on your own. They been known to pick up stragglers. With no witnesses they can do what they like, and say what they like in court!'

John felt the shiver behind him.

He moved away with the group. All around him, people arguing, laughing as though it were a picnic, talking. At the railway station they paused as a group, then gradually disintegrated into the people coming home from work. The women went together to have coffee. Quite quickly, with shy sidelong glances or smiles and waves, the crowd dispersed. John still had the paper under his arm. He took his time and walked through the station, out onto the avenue where the buses ran. He crossed the road at the lights and had just entered the park when he heard someone call.

'Hey you.'

His heart sank. Three police stood nearby, smiling.

His mother answered the telephone.

'Hello dear!' She chirruped. 'What are you doing with yourself?'

'I'm in gaol.'

'We hadn't heard from you for so long.'

'I was arrested an hour ago.'

'Austin always said you'd get into trouble. What were you doing?'

268

'I wasn't doing anything!'

'Then what were you arrested for?'

John turned to one of the three policemen standing nearby.

'What am I charged with?'

'Resisting the reasonable direction of a police officer,' came the unsmiling reply.

'I'm charged with resisting the reasonable direction of a police officer,' John parroted into the handset.

'What did you do that for?'

'I didn't do anything.'

'Go on! You don't get arrested for not doing anything.'

'I need someone to come and get me. I don't know anybody else.'

'Austin is away. Ellen is here eating dinner. She could go and see what she could do . . .'

'She might have to bring some money. For bail,' he added after a pause.

He waited. Diana called Ellen. Her hand was half over the telephone handset.

'He's in gaol, or something,' Diana said.

Ellen was laughing.

'I always thought he'd end up in trouble of some sort,' she howled.

'He's a good boy. He's my son.'

'Better get used to it mum. Your son's a gaolbird.'

'Resisting the orders of the police. That's not that bad.'

'He never could think big.'

'He's your brother.'

'Yes, I know. I'll go and get him out. Where is he?'

'Where are you dear?' His mother's voice came back, clear and unmuffled.

'Regent Street Police Station.'

'How much money?'

'Two hundred dollars bail.'

The police did not bother to put him back in the cell with the

269

wet concrete floor and the timber pallet and the small window where he had spent the last four hours. They let him stay in the office, sitting on the bench.

One of the policemen who arrested him stood over him.

'Most of your type call their mates.'

John stared, not sure of what he meant.

'The Communist Party or whoever organises those demonstrations. They always come down here. Usually a coon, a lesbian or two, and a lawyer. We know them pretty well.'

'I don't know them.'

'That's tough.' The cop smiled like a good guy. 'What were you doing along at that little turn?'

'Saw it happening.'

'You saw it happening?'

'I decided to have a look.'

'Shit,' the cop spat out disgusted. He turned to walk away. One of the other police laughed.

'We didn't get one after all!'

'Just a . . . just a . . .' He couldn't find the right word and stalked off.

'He's been wanting to get one of the big-time stirrers for years,' the second policeman addressed John. 'Don't take it personally.'

'I wasn't charged with being at a demonstration.'

'You were there. That attracts attention. It means you're a stirrer. Most of them that go to these things, they're kids. Going to university. Give them five years and they're solid citizens, managers, teachers, lawyers. That stuff. We get a lawyer in here we used to see at the old demonstrations in 1970. Have a joke about it sometimes. Good bloke. Thinks it a great laugh.'

John forced a laugh.

'The ones that go in for politics, they get to be members of parliament. The only time they go to Redfern to mix with the coons is for the paper.'

'Got to grow up some time.' John held the mirror agreeably.

'That's right. Except you. You're too old for that sort of stuff, so we pick you. Mind if you were a real agitator from inter-

270

state, the last thing you would have done is go walkabout in the park on your own.'

'Why don't you let me go?'

The cop looked around. There was no one else about. He rested back on his chair and put his feet up on the desk.

'How much money you got Johnny?'

'A bit. A few hundred in the bank.'

The policeman sat there quite still, waiting for him to go on. When John didn't he stood and walked slowly and quietly out of the room. The leather of his shoes squeaked with every step.

John looked at the door. He could have walked out. He decided not to.

The police were bored. They stood around talking about their business.

'Did you ever try and join the force?' One of the policemen asked John heartily.

The other police guffawed lightly in the background. John looked at their round faces and smiled.

'Yes,' he said. 'Once I did try.'

'You're big enough,' the cop said thoughtfully.

'That's what I thought.'

'Why didn't they let you?'

'They checked my heart.'

'What's wrong with your heart.'

'Nothing much, except that I was so scared.'

'You don't look the type, no offence,' a younger cop joined in.

'It was better than where I was.'

'Where was you?'

'Sleeping in Moore Park Golf Course under an army blanket. I couldn't get a job. I didn't have anywhere to stay. Used to take the morning paper from a house in Surry Hills.'

'You shouldn't tell us that.'

'The woman used to watch from her window. She thought it was funny. They never wanted to catch me.'

271

'Oh.'

'One day I saw this ad, for police cadets. "Go to the Bourke Street Barracks", it said. So I went to the Bourke Street Barracks.'

'The Training Centre!'

'That's right. There was this big cop in there, real fat, no offence. Sitting behind one of those desks, like that one over there. I stood there for a while. When he looked up, he looked from the top of my uncut hair to my jeans with the hole in the knee to my shoes. From the way he looked I bet he could see the holes there too. Then he said to me "What you want son?" "I want to join the Force, sir," I said.'

The police all began to laugh. John smiled and waited for them to stop.

'That's what he seemed to think. He said "You want to join the Force!" like that. "I want to join the Force, sir," I said. He looked at me for a long time. Then he said . . .'

'You want to join the Force!" Bellowed one of the cops.

'That's what he said. "You want to join the Force." I said, "I want to join the Force sir.' Then he shook his head. He thought about it. Then he took me along the corridor, and every time he met another cop, he'd stop them and say "You see him?" When they nodded, he'd say "He wants to join the Force!" They'd say "He wants to join the Force." I'd say "I want to join the Force, sir."'

'You could be directing traffic in Parramatta now,' said the young cop.

'Or arresting demonstrators,' said another.

'Beating the piss out of them,' said another.

'Then eventually we ended up in the doctor's office. "What does he want?" asked the doctor. "He wants to join the Force," said the copper. "He wants to join the Force, eh," said the doctor, quieter than the others. Then he calls me over. Takes out a stethoscope and listens. Then he looks up at me and he says, "I'm sorry young man I cannot gratify you with that which your heart most desires." "Why not?" the cop said. "Why not?" I said at the same time. "Because you have a slight heart murmur.

272

Did you ever have rheumatic fever?" "I bet he's got a bad heart,"
I said about the cop, who shifted a bit. "Maybe. But he didn't
have it when he came into the Force," said the doctor.'

'He didn't run you in?'

'No. He patted me on the back as I went out, and he said
to me, "Bad luck son. I'll see you later." "Like hell you will,"
I said. It looks as though he was right after all.'

'That's a good story.'

'Try it on the magistrate,' the young cop called as he went
to answer a telephone.

Ellen walked in just after eleven p.m. She did not look at the
clock on the wall or at John, who began to raise himself from
the bench, then sat back again. Ellen was wearing a mink coat
and dressy jeans. She walked immediately to the counter.

'I believe you are holding my brother.'

'What is your brother's name?'

'John Evans.'

'That's him over there,' the policeman nodded in John's
direction.

Ellen still didn't look.

'I would like to get him out.'

'That'll be two hundred dollars' bail.' The young policeman
flushed slightly. 'You'll get it back, when he appears in court.'

Ellen plucked exactly two hundred dollars in new notes from
somewhere in the fur and laid it on the counter. The policeman
counted it methodically, then wrote a receipt.

'Thank you.' Ellen took the receipt. It disappeared into the
fur. She turned and looked at John for the first time.

'I will drive you home.'

She strode mannishly across to the door. John looked at the
young policeman, who for some reason winked at him. Then
he followed his sister into the street.

A yellow six-cylinder Toyota was double parked a few doors
along. Ellen opened the passenger side door, and told him to
get in. Then she let herself in on the driver's side and started

273

the car. John noticed that she had left the keys in the ignition.

As the car took off, one of the policemen from inside the station had wandered to the door and leaned against it. John waved to him.

'See you later brother!' Ellen called as she let John out at the door.

'Thanks,' said John, although he wasn't sure.

He tried to go in quietly, but Clifford heard him.

'What happened to the newspaper?' He called.

'I ended up in gaol.'

John had left the newspapers at the station.

The old man rocked back on his chair and wheezed.

'They're looking for any excuse,' he said. 'What was you doing?'

'Crossing the park by myself, after I was at the demonstration outside the newspaper. They said I was resisting reasonable direction.'

'What did they direct you?'

'To smile when they thumped me.'

The old man laughed and wheezed, all at once.

'It's not funny,' John complained.

'I saw a bit of it on the news on telly. Didn't see you there.'

'What did they show?'

'A truck trying to run everyone down and newspapers being burned in the street.'

'I never saw any cameras. Not television cameras.'

He couldn't remember them being there at all, but there must have been all sorts of things he couldn't see.

Clifford took an interest in John's trial. He sent John to a barrister he knew. The barrister heard his story and nodded.

'Police are good in court,' he told John earnestly. 'They know what the magistrates want to hear, they know the order they want to hear it in. There's always two of them, at least. That way, everything is checked. The story is confirmed. Unless you have a witness . . .'

'Nobody saw, that I know of.'

The barrister nodded. He was a casually dressed grey man, a few years older than John.

'We'll try something. Can you get a suit?'

At the trial, John wore a suit that he hired that morning. It pinched his shoulders and it was too big around the waist, but it looked alright in the mirror. Walking up the steps of the court with Clifford wheezing slowly next to him, he felt the trousers drag down. He hitched them up, despite the intolerable irritation of the coat.

'They twisted?' Clifford said it to slow him down. It was his chance to be involved in the events of the world and he wasn't going to miss it.

Once in the courthouse, he sat around in the corridor. The hearing was set for eleven a.m. John watched the procession of the last night's arrests as they went one by one into court. The little drunk in the crumpled suit and patent leather dancing shoes. The Aboriginal drag queen in an off-the-shoulder gown, with tattoos down both arms and whiskers coming through the make-up. The prostitute with dyed blonde hair and a red miniskirt, who told the cop who called her name to watchit.

'Watch what?' the cop looked down at the miniskirt.

'Watch what you're lookin' at you great blue-bellied prick!'

The cop reddened and took her by the arm to steer her into the court.

'Fuck'n let go!' She squealed and kicked.

Another cop came across and helped.

'Nice place,' Clifford remarked.

Eventually his name was called. John and Clifford both stood and approached the court. A policeman waved them to one side. They went up a set of dusty stairs, into a smaller room with a window looking over Liverpool Street. They had taken their seats when the barrister came in. He was puffing.

'My apologies to the court,' he said as he gave a slight bow. 'I was detained by another client.'

'The court accepts your apologies,' the magistrate said gravely.

275

'They didn't want this to be public,' Clifford whispered.

'Why?'

'There are reporters in the courts downstairs. They do the courts every day, looking for something to happen. They don't know this is on.'

John was surprised. He hadn't thought any great significance attached to his case.

'It's political. If there is a statement that the charge was because you were at a political rally, they don't want the press to know about it. There's enough trouble already.'

One of the policemen took the stand and testified. He had seen the defendant near Eddy Avenue. When the defendant was approached, he had responded by saying that he was under no obligation to tell the constable anything.

'I assured the defendant that he was indeed obliged to give me his name and address upon request. The defendant then swore at me.'

John stared.

'He told me that it was none of my f. . . business. I then requested the defendant to go with me and Constable Thomas to the police station. "On what f. . . charge?" the defendant said. I told the defendant that he would be charged with resisting the reasonable direction of a police officer. The defendant then told me to "piss off".'

'Why did you not charge the defendant with offensive behaviour?' The magistrate asked.

'It seemed to us that there were certain mitigating factors,' Constable Benton intoned.

'What were they?'

'The defendant is previously of good character. Although a manual labourer, he has references from his sister, a prominent real estage agent from the North side of the harbour.' The constable submitted a letter to the court.

'I see.' The magistrate perused the document quickly.

'Constable Thomas and myself were obliged to escort the defendant. He did resist vigorously.'

276

When the barrister came to interrogate the constable, he asked to look at the letter. Then he handed it back.

'Constable Benton, did you see the defendant at any time before you approached him on Eddy Avenue?'

'No.'

'Were you on duty at Kippax Street, Surry Hills, less than an hour before you went to Eddy Avenue?'

'Yes.'

'Did you see the defendant anywhere near Kippax Street at that time?'

'No.'

'Are you aware that the defendant was taking part in a political rally in Kippax Street at that time?'

'I saw the rally. I am not aware of the defendant's participation in that rally.'

'How many people were at that rally, constable?'

'Approximately one hundred and fifty people.'

'How long did you attend the rally?'

'Thirty minutes.'

'You are sure that you did not see the defendant at the rally at that time.'

'I did not see the defendant at the rally, no.'

The barrister sat down. Then Constable Thomas, the young policeman, gave evidence. The story he told was identical to the story told by Constable Benton.

The barrister asked him the same questions as before, and received the same answers. Later on, when he came to speak to the court on John's behalf, he drew the attention of the court to John's demeanour.

'You can see that my client is a quiet man, not given to extravagance in his actions. He dresses neatly and is invariably polite, as his sister testifies in her letter. He did attend a political rally not long before the incident described by Constables Benton and Thomas, but the part he played was very small. You have heard my client give evidence. He saw the rally taking place, and decided to join it in a minor role because of his political beliefs. Without any malice, he claims that he did see both of his accusers at the rally. It is hard to believe that he, an untrained observer, should see both policemen, while they should not register his presence at all.

'My client states that he did not respond to the constables in the manner described by Constable Benton and Constable Thomas. You have heard him speak. He is a man not given to the use of obscene language.'

The barrister sat down. The magistrate and the others in the small room kept looking at him, startled by the suddenness with which he had finished. The magistrate looked down and thought for a few seconds.

'Guilty. However I direct that there be no fine, and the charge be stricken from the record, as the defendant is a first offender.'

Outside the court, the barrister shook his hand.

'Not a bad result,' he said. 'That letter of your sister's . . .'

'What did it say?'

'It said . . .' He wrinkled his forehead, 'that . . . you had always been a cause of worry to your parents . . . that . . if you were guilty, then this would cause your parents much suffering, which they had already had a share of, on your behalf. Despite this, you were always thought of highly in your family home . . . although you had missed many opportunities and this had caused your family much sadness . . .'

John stared.

'You don't need enemies.' The barrister smiled as he walked away.

'Why did she say that?' Clifford asked.

'I don't know.' John looked away at a pigeon walking along the roof of the courthouse. 'She's my sister. I don't know.'

Chapter 7

In 1978 John was fired.

'Nothing wrong with your work,' the foreman said as he gave him notice. 'Just the way things are. The economic climate. Everybody's cutting back. They'll probably fire me next.'

John wasn't too worried. He had always managed to get a job before. He kept staying at Clifford's, because the old man was attached to him. As Clifford became older he depended on John to do the maintenance around the place, to call the plumbers, to fix the roof when a sheet of corrugated iron came off in a storm.

'I'll take it off your rent,' Clifford wheezed.

When John was out of a job, he felt that Clifford wouldn't be too hard on him if he couldn't pay the rent for a few weeks.

He slept in for a few days. Walked around the Cross and sat in coffee lounges and watched. There were more prostitutes. The place seemed sleazier. The prostitutes seemed younger. Or was he getting older? There was always violence. John liked walking the streets when they were crowded, feeling the crowds as they walked past. He liked the edginess, the sense of potential explosion, the hysteria. With heroin users, there had always been a wall. The wall was higher, there were more users with that metallic emptiness, that assumed superiority.

The coffee was milky and tasteless. The cakes were greasy. He did not feel like hanging around more than a few days. He set the alarm to get up early.

He walked the streets behind Central Railway station, near the newspaper building. The area was full of small factories and storehouses. He had never failed to get a job within a few hours in that area. He failed. The small factories had changed. Most of them were storehouses, stocking things brought in from overseas. The ones that were producing things, like travel bags

279

and clothing, were using Asian women on machines. From the way the workshops were tucked away, John suspected they weren't being paid award wages.

'It was Gough that did it,' One of the factory owners told him. 'We used to have this whole floor full of machines. Each one of them had a woman working it, and men stacking the dresses and trousers, and packing them. Hard to get enough workers then. Now, the only business is importing. Clothes, imported from Hong Kong and Manila. Cheaper than we can make them. The ones who survive, they're going into imports. Storehouses. The whole places is full of storehouses. We don't manufacture anything any more. Because we can't compete.'

'What about the machines going back there?' John indicated the wall of hessian, behind which he could hear the machines.

'That's a few casuals. Nothing but a few casuals,' he laughed. 'Most of the work is done by outworkers now!'

'Outworkers!'

'Outworkers. You know, women with their own machine. They sit home when the kids are at school. Earn a few bucks.'

John knew. Outworkers. A woman had rented the room next to him for a few months. She tried outwork. John was kept awake all night by the machine. In the afternoons, he sometimes met the woman, with plastic bags full of clothes. She was thirty, but with her wispy hair and tired eyes she could have been fifty.

He had offered to help her down the stairs with the clothes once. She talked to him after that. Might have hoped to get a husband. Anything, to get away from piecework.

'It's my hands,' she complained. 'They hurt, right up the elbows to the shoulder. I try and rest them. As soon as I go back to the machine they start hurting again.'

She got rid of the machine. She tried waitressing for a while but her shoulders and arms still hurt. After she lost the second job waitressing he found her sitting at the table in the communal kitchen weeping.

'The first one, he fired me when I wouldn't screw him,' she said as John made her a cup of tea. 'This one, I couldn't do it. I just couldn't do it.'

John didn't know what to do, so he made the tea. Then he turned away, because he couldn't face it. Any weakness and she would use it against him.

'Sorry,' he said. 'I got to go out now.'

When the factory manager mentioned outworkers, John controlled himself again.

'See you later then,' he said.

'Sorry I can't give you a job. It was Gough messed it for you.'

Dear John,

You know I haven't seen you now for—what is it? Seven years. Funny that we keep writing to each other. When I close my eyes, I try and remember you, but it's getting harder. Your nose is big and it bends in the centre, and you have brown hair, and I have a feeling about the way you walk. You sort of throw a leg to one side, don't you?

I know you better from your letters now, although I do wonder. You might have gone grey now, or gotten fat, although it doesn't sound it the way you live. Unless you ate lots of junk food or something. For women time isn't kind. I'm getting paid back for all that drinking and those late nights. When I look into the mirror in the morning I can see crows feet. I used to despise women who worried about their appearance all the time. It always seemed so silly. Now here I am doing it. Sometimes when I sit I feel my thighs and they seem so big. Women when they get older get this pear shape, and their bottoms drag behind them.

I don't care so much about men not being interested any more. I pick my mark more carefully these days. It's just that I always liked my body and now I don't any longer. I wonder whether I should have had kids after all. That doesn't make any difference, I know. I go and see the girls and they are just as fat and pear shaped as I am, and they have to put up with more. The urge for immortality dies hard, even with someone so set against the survival of the stupid race as me.

Ellen hasn't written for ages. With her I think it was always a case of out of sight, out of mind. Do you ever see her? You are so different, the pair of you, but there is something about

281

you that is the same. A feeling about things, the jaw line which you both get from your father. Is he still around? He'd be getting on now. You know how he always acted like such a stodgy old bastard. How he used to rubbish Rowley and that, not that I disagree with him there. That time I saw Austin with his car on his own on the far end of Gaffney Street. Well they hadn't built there, and he was revving that car, and chucking wheelies and figure eights and making it skid. You wouldn't have thought it was an old man driving. All on his own he was. I am sure it was him. He didn't see me and I sat there and watched him for ages. Then a few nights later he was carrying on about the way Rowley drives. Like he never had any fun, and there he was, desperate to catch up and guilty about it. I was a bit sorry for him, it was a long time ago.

The taxis are still going although business isn't as good as it used to be. On pay nights, all the drivers hang around the clubs and the pubs waiting for fares. Not many cocky farmers around now. I guess they all fly to Adelaide and Sydney in their private aeroplanes.

All the same if the taxi business gets that bad around here I can take up minding kids. I went to a party at Mavis and Bobs the other night and everybody sat around talking about how their kids are getting on at primary school. The only fun I got was a couple of the fellows weren't game to look me in the eye.

Things are looking crook for the economy, I know. If ever you feel like coming back here for a holiday your welcome to stay. The only condition is you don't bring that mongrel Rowley around. I see him getting around Argent Street some weekends and pay nights. He's given up working at the abattoirs and now he works out at the Pinnacles. They have started the old mine there again.

The most interesting thing is a letter from you. A come-down for the old girl. Write again soon.

Love a duck,
Ethel.

There were no jobs. John went on the dole. He went looking for jobs. He went to the Commonwealth Employment Service.

This went on for months. Gradually he began to stay awake at night reading, then he slept in in the morning. The room was cheap. He could live on the dole. There was a stove on the small verandah, and an old refrigerator. He had never saved much money, and what he had went quickly.

When he received the government cheque, he was careful to pay the rent to Clifford. Several times, Clifford gave him a rebate for this or that job around the place. Then John walked to the nearest bulk food store and laid aside a large parcel of brown onions, a bag of potatoes, two packets of brown rice, two packets of lentils, a cabbage, plus a selection of whatever other vegetables or fruit was available in season. He was not a vegetarian, but meat went off in the refrigerator if he didn't eat it quickly. Two packets of tea and a packet of powdered milk from the corner store.

A few theatre chains let the unemployed in cheaply on quiet days. There were free concerts. He walked everywhere, or went by bus or train. Clothes were available at St Vincent de Paul. He walked across the bridge to more fashionable suburbs, and visited the opportunity shops there. There were elegant clothes, good shoes and shirts. He chose the ones that were practical and obviously plain.

At the end of winter, he began to feel like doing something. He did not know what. He enjoyed sitting in the park. He enjoyed reading. Sometimes he wanted sex, then one day he sat next to a middle-aged woman in a coffee lounge.

The woman allowed him to talk to her. Picking her manner, he talked immediately of sex.

'Do you like me?' She stared at him. Her eyes were disconcerting. Clear and blue, although her hair was dark.

'Yes,' he said simply. Because he was not sure that he was not lying.

'It's what you are supposed to say.'

'Yes.'

'Are you married?'

'No.'

She thought.

'I'm not married,' she said. 'I was once and I hated it. I never wanted to be tied.'

'I know women like that.'

'Middle-aged and frustrated but still happier than the other way?'

John thought about it. There was something in common.

'Men can find women easily. Younger women,' she said without bitterness. 'I don't think it's fair.'

'I never had much luck myself.'

'You don't realise the position you are in. You are at the right age. Not bad looking. If you did things right you could be a gigolo.'

'I don't want to be.'

'What do you do?'

'I'm out of work.'

'What work did you do?'

'Storeman-packer. Anything. I'm thirty-eight and I can't get a job.'

The woman sat back against the beige plastic of the coffee lounge seat. Some people at the next table had left so another table was available.

'What things do you like?'

'I like films. I like books sometimes. I like walking. I sit in the sun and I like that although I think I should do other things with my life. I think I ought to care about a lot of things but I don't.'

'Would you like to come with me to a film?'

'Yes, but I don't have the money.'

'I can pay.'

John shrugged.

'It is a relief to find a man who is not too proud.'

'I am middle-aged and unemployed.'

They went to a European movie with sub-titles.

'What do you think of that?' She asked when they came out.

'It took getting used to.'

'You're funny.' She took the opportunity of sliding her arm inside his.

They developed an arrangement. He called her the day after he had his cheque. They went out, and then they went back to her flat. Between cheque days, she called him, and they went out, then they went back to her flat. Things were leisurely. They did not go to bed together for a month. When they did, it did not change things. They still met at the same times and did the same things. Both of them were surprised.

John came back to Clifford's house late one morning. He had been away all night. The walk from Bondi, through the back streets with the old lacy terrace houses, had been leisurely and uneventful. Winter was over, but the days were still cool.

He opened the front door and stepped in. The corridor was dusty and closed in. The smell of gas. Comfortable and a bit unpleasant at the same time. Every old boarding-house he stayed in smelled of leaking gas and old socks.

He meant to paint the corridor. Had meant to paint it for a year or more. Clifford was quite happy to pay for the paint, and take the cost from his rent. There were always more pressing things.

The door shut behind him. He had taken three steps along before he paused. He listened. Something was different. The music from Clifford's radio. He had taken another step or two before it registered. The radio was not on the station. He had never thought about it before, or noticed it, but Clifford's radio was always on the station. Perfectly and precisely on the station.

He was relieved when he saw Clifford. Sitting at his table with a heavy hard-cover book open in front of him. The magnifying glass resting behind his arm. Clifford turned his head slowly. His face was grey. When he spoke, it was with enormous effort. The weeping sore on the side of his face looked raw.

'Goodday,' he said.

John leaned against the door and thought.

'Something the trouble?'

'Winter. In winter it's harder. Each time it gets harder. You know ... I came out here because of the weather. After the gas got to my lungs. The weather in England was no good for it.'

John looked and thought. He should have done something. He was being called upon to do something. Yet he felt, more than anything else, the greater strength of a calling to observe. To stand and look, taking part only with his eyes, passively contemplating the destruction of himself and all around him. Finding in that process confirmation of the terror of action that he had accepted from his father, and that he had in reaction against his father.

'You know my family were Quakers.' The old man seemed to read his mind. 'My father was a doctor.'

John's mouth opened. His throat had closed. Nothing came out.

'They disowned me when I went to the war. My father said they would. There's a photograph of him, down there ...' He nodded with careful precision in the direction of a drawer. 'My mother begged him. She said it was because I was young ...'

Clifford smiled and wheezed for a while, uncontrollably, as at a painful and sweet memory.

'She was right of course, but it didn't change him. He ... always acted as though he was the instrument of God himself. "Thou shalt not kill", he waved his arm. "You are goin' to take up arms ... to slay ... your fellow man ..." I never thought of slaying anyone. Just ... the uniform ... if anyone was killed it wasn't really people ...'

'Watch,' a voice said to John. Held him to the spot, with his back pushed hard against the door so it hurt his back.

'I never knew. Nobody knew. When I got there the first thing I saw was a hole in the ground. We walked ... past it in a row. It was sunny, but the bodies had been in there when it had been wet. They'd sunk into the mud. It was easy enough not to look. My father had been a doctor, he talked about ... dead people, what they looked like. These were ... further on. It was the smell . . . never smelled dead before. Sweet. Sunny, it was hot. Then . . . never noticed. Lived with it. Jokes. That officer's shit doesn't stink.

'Robert Graves said . . . he . . . couldn't stand to shoot a German . . . in the bath. Gave the gun to Sergeant. "You do it Sergeant . . . it's too ugly . . . for me . . . but you do it". Precious bastards. All like it.'

Small flecks of blood were running from the side of Clifford's mouth. Foamy blood, with bubbles. The left side, the same as the raw weeping scar. Running down to the chin.

'Wasn't there long. Three months. Gas. Head down in a hole. Rag over mouth . . . Pulled my head up too soon. Mouthful. Burned. Sent hospital . . . letter to mother. They posted it. No answer. He got it first. Servant collected mail.'

A drop of the blood dripped onto the table. Another drop flew as he jerked his head and hit his arm. Clifford didn't seem to notice.

'1925 . . . came here. Dry. Better. Was. Winter in England too hard. Winter chasing me.'

Only then, he looked down at the spot of blood on the table. Then conscious of what could have been a melodramatic gesture, he smiled and took a towel from the back of the chair and wiped his lips.

'Done alright with one lung.'

Should he have said something. Like "You've got lots of years yet" or "You're not going to die on me mate?" That was what he should have said. A lie. A game. A hiding of the truth because it was embarrassing or painful. Clifford knew the truth. John nodded.

'I better get the doctor.'

Clifford looked at him with the ambiguous smile, part grateful to him for not lying, part mocking.

'What happens to people when they die?' John heard his own small voice, thin and childish. 'They rot.' His father's voice was so much younger then. The words being pushed out of him as though it were a painful evacuation.

287

Clifford had never been able to afford a telephone. John had to go out. He walked away with a smile from his friend, with whom he had an understanding, to whom he had not lied. His friend was dying. It was time for him to die. A curious sort of ecstasy, a knowledge. He was extended further than ever before.

The receiver of the nearest telephone had been ripped off. Two pieces of wire hung beside the grey frost-coloured machine. The tray which took the coins had also been ripped out. Because it was not far to the nearest hospital, he began to run.

Clifford died two days later in hospital. Two of the tenants upstairs were happy because they wouldn't have to pay rent, for five or six months. At least. Three weeks later, one of them died of a heroin overdose. The other came down to see John.

'Tom is sick,' the man said. 'You come up and have a look.'

John looked at his eyes. A wall. No entry. No reflection in the mirror. Vampires. He laughed to himself. The tenant also giggled.

John climbed the stairs. At the top, there was a small room that could have been used for an artist. A tiny garret with sloping walls and small windows looking over other garret windows and rooftops and pigeons on old guttering and chimneys.

Two girls in jeans were sitting on the floor side by side. The vacant look. Tom was lying on a crumpled single bed, rolled up in the sheets.

'He's been sick for a while.' The tenant spoke from behind. He was wearing slippers and he walked easily. From the strong broad chest, John guessed that he would have been athletic not so long ago.

The man in the bed was cold. John touched him again, then tried to push him. He was hard and stiff.

'It was a few hours ago. We thought we'd wait.'

'He only really complained a little while ago,' one of the girls said.

'He's dead.'

'He's not!'

288

'How did that happen?' Said the other man.

John laughed.

They all laughed, the same empty inane giggle.

'Bad shit,' said John, still laughing.

'I had some of the same shit!'

John laughed again, louder. The girls laughed together.

'You got a car?'

''Sixty-six Holden station wagon.'

'Take him to the hospital.'

The tenant looked unsure.

'Ah shit!' Exclaimed the other girl. Then she stood up and collected her handbag and walked out.

The others stared at each other silently until the sound of the high-heels went down the stairs. In the distance, the front door slammed.

'I'll help you take him down, if you want.'

There were people in the street but no one looked at the three people who carried a corpse bundled in a blanket out of the house. The tenant in slippers ran ahead and opened the back of the Holden station wagon and dropped the back seat flat.

'There's room!' He called.

John was stuck in the door with the corpse's shoulders. The girl was behind him, wriggling around, lifting. It had been hard getting the body down the stairs. Each turning of the stairs was narrow. They had to lift him over the banister. Once he fell down a full flight.

'That makes it easier,' John said.

'He's sick,' the tenant in slippers commented thoughtfully.

From the doorway, John had to call him back. They heaved the body onto the tray.

'Now slide!' John called.

The body slid. A man walking past briskly on his way to work cast an anxious glance as the man in slippers tried to close the tailgate, but the head got in the way. When John looked back, the man looked down and hurried on.

The tailgate had to be roped up because it would not close. There were some ocky straps in Clifford's room. John went and found them, then gave them to the tenant. The top of the corpse's head, which was wrapped in blanket, was held steady with elastic ropes on either side. A shock of brown hair hung from the blanket. The woman tried unsuccessfully to tuck it back. Each time, the hair managed to flop out of some corner of the blanket. She gave up.

'Thanks mate!' The tenant called as he climbed into the car and started it up. The girl jumped in after him.

Two days later. John hadn't heard anything. The room upstairs had been left unlocked. John thought about it at first, then he stopped worrying. He was in bed reading when the door knocked timidly. The tenant was there, in the same clothes.

He shifted uncomfortably from one foot to the other and looked at the floor as he spoke.

'Look. Ah. Where you say that fuckin' hospital was man?'

'You can't find it?'

'Can't find it nowhere man, I been lookin'.'

The false American accent was heavier than before.

'It's . . .' John thought about it. 'I'll come out and show you.'

'All you got to do is point the way . . .'

John closed the door and pulled on some clothes. The man was standing in the same place when he came out.

The girl was still sitting in the passenger seat. The bundle was still in the back. John knew for the first time exactly what Clifford meant when he talked about the sweet smell. The lock of hair dangled from the rear.

'Where have you been?'

The man looked embarrassed and didn't answer. The girl looked at him and sneered.

'We scored.'

'Where?'

'The National Park. That's where we been. The National Park.'

'It's beautiful there this time of year,' the man interrupted.

290

'Cold at night,' the girl added. 'We got a tent. Then the shit ran out and Horace needed a bath.'

'The hospital is over . . . I better go with you.'

He climbed into the passenger seat and gagged at the smell although the girl huddled against him cosily. Horace looked at him suspiciously as he slid the old car into gear. Three minutes later, they pulled into the drive of the outpatients' department.

The tenant stared at the plastic swing doors and the OUTPATIENTS neon sign.

'You better go in and tell them,' John remarked.

'Go in and tell them,' the girl repeated. She pressed suggestively on John's arm.

The man went in through the swing door. John climbed from the car and stood up-wind. The girl followed.

'It's nice out here,' she said.

They both leaned reflectively on the mudguard. It moved easily under them.

'You straight?'

'Yes.'

She smirked. That superior I know things you don't know and never will sort of smirk.

'Never?'

'Never. Not that.'

That was when the man came back. Followed by a nurse in a blue uniform, with a crucifix hanging on her neck.

'He's over here,' he said. 'But he's very sick.'

The nurse bustled over and pulled back a corner of the blanket. She glared at the man and put her hands on her hips.

'Very fucking funny!' she exclaimed.

'See you later,' said John.

'I think I'll come with you,' the girl gurgled and ran alongside.

'I'm not much good for what you want,' John puffed as they got around a corner.

'Nowhere to stay.'

'You'll find somewhere.'

'Let me into Horace's room then.'

'You don't pay rent.'

'Nobody pays rent there. Not since the old man died. It's like a squat.'

'Your boyfriend's room is still open,' John laughed.

'I don't think he'll be back, not for a while.'

She giggled again, that suggestive giggle.

Chapter 8

Dear Ethel,

It took me a long time to answer your letter. Sorry. I've been out of work for more than a year now and I can't say that I've been pushed for time. It is harder to do mundane things (not that writing to you is mundane) when you have all the time in the world. I have to push myself now to get out of bed before midday. Washing my clothes is hard, where before I used to fit it in between working and watching television and writing letters to you and all the other little things with which I delude myself that I am living my life.

You will notice that I have changed address again. Clifford died. Then someone else died, and the place was full of police and newspaper reporters and a television crew. Nobody was killed or anything but the guy who died was taking drugs and they decided to make a big thing of it. Nobody was paying any rent until Clifford's probate was finalised but I decided I didn't want to live there any longer.

There were case loads of things. Paperback books and clothes and a television and a radio and Clifford's old photographs. I don't know what to do with them, but he sort of gave them to me before he died, I don't think anyone else wants them, and I took a copy of *Finnegan's Wake* which he was reading with a magnifying glass before he died. Coincidence. He was always sitting around reading books like that and listening to music, sometimes he talked about James Joyce and Robert Graves and Mozart and the war to me. I liked him. It's a pity you never met him. Now the house is full of smack freaks and prostitutes are working from the front room and the other night a gang of bikies came around and had a party in the room above me and pissed out the window and sprayed on my verandah. Not that it wasn't that way before. Just that it's getting hard to take.

293

Where I am isn't a great improvement. Not much has changed in these places ever since the 1930s. Old people, drunks, stale rooms, dirty socks. The gas in the corridor. One toilet with a broken plastic seat to pinch your bum and it's always wet. This one has a whole crew of alcoholics in residence. My room is out the back, and there is a laundry. I sit here most nights looking at my reflection, listening to them upstairs and out the front, wandering from room to room, singing, fighting. Endless stupid arguments, endless equally stupid expressions of friendship. I read, I think about Clifford.

I did go and see the family not so long ago. They haven't changed much. Austin sits at the end of the table and chews his food endlessly and tries not to look at television. Diana talks, although she repeats herself a lot. Sometimes she talks to me and calls me Cain. Once she called me by her father's name. Austin always corrects her, between bites. She doesn't believe him all the time. Then when she realises that what he says is true, she gets embarrassed and apologises. Ellen comes in at the end of lunch and sits down and eats. Austin tells me she is on the way to being a millionaire, as long as she learns to hold on to her money. She throws it around on her girlfriends. He doesn't like it. She says it keeps him alive. They're both right, I think.

She owns a couple of flats down near the water and a house and two more semi-detached in Balmain now. The only time she talks to me she talks about them. If I say too much it will sound as if I'm jealous, and I probably am.

Are you serious about your offer of somewhere to stay, if I come to Broken Hill for a short holiday? Please say if you aren't, even though it might be hard. I would much prefer to know now, because I am thinking about going there for a week or two, at a time which is convenient. I would like to look around. There is some part of me that is still firmly attached to the place.

Yours with a red face,
John.

It was summer again when he arrived in Broken Hill. Ethel came and collected him at the railway station. They surveyed each other quickly from a distance, then walked briskly and kissed.

'You haven't changed a bit!' Ethel leaned back from the hug and laughed.

'You have. All for the better.'

'You were always almost honest. That's what I like about you.'

John looked up and down the familiar platform. Although quite a few people were standing around and looking up at the skimp dumps on the other side of the train, not many were being met.

'They just pass through on the way to Western Australia— or somewhere,' Ethel interpreted his look. 'We get a few tourists. Most of them come and sit around in the clubs, or they ask for the RSL bar they showed in that movie.'

'A good movie.'

'Chips Rafferty's last.'

'He came from here, originally. So he said.'

'So did you.'

John had to slam the door twice on the taxi before it closed. Ethel cruised out along Crystal Street, then turned and circled the main block.

'It hasn't changed at all.'

'It has,' said Ethel. 'Except it isn't obvious yet.'

John looked at her, but he wasn't brave enough to follow the matter. Instead he gazed fixedly at the old men who sat on the bench in front of the post office. Surely they had always been there. They looked so familiar in that spot. The young men sitting in the milk bar and lounging along the footpath and whistling at girls. That had always been there. The milk bars looked the same. They were furnished the same. The hotels might have had a coat of paint but the colours weren't different.

Ethel did not interrupt his reverie. The taxi rolled smoothly the length of Argent Street, around the Technical College, along past the high school. The high school had changed. Rows and rows of new buildings took up a lot of the open space.

'Where you want to go?'

295

'Anywhere. I don't want to stop you working.'

'Off pay period. Not much work anyway.'

They cruised past a man standing at the footpath who tried to wave them down.

John was pleased to find that he was given a small verandah at the back, with sliding windows and crinkled glass which broke the sunlight into patterns across the bedclothes.

Ethel left him alone. Still, he made an effort to get up early, and he went to the nearest shop and bought bread and eggs and bacon. By the time Ethel got up he was cooking breakfast. She came out in a dressing-gown and settled comfortable at the table.

'I don't wear rollers.'

'Some people don't like to be talked to in the morning.'

John placed a thick cup of black tea in front of her. She heaped in a large teaspoonful of sugar.

'What you going to do here?'

'Nothing much. I don't know why I came. I get a cheap fare on the railway.'

Ethel sat there, looking solemnly into the black tea. John thrust a plate of bacon and eggs before her.

'I though you might have liked me.'

John stared. His impulse was to say 'I do', but something told him it was the wrong thing.

Instead they sat there in gloomy silence for several minutes.

'I'm sorry,' she said with forced brightness. 'I do have you at a disadvantage. It's just that . . . I'm sick of being auntie I guess. Not that anything has changed. I'd be just as much the impossible slut as ever. Fuck it, I'm lonely.'

'I wouldn't be much good.'

'You're better than you think, compared to most of what's offering around this place. Married men, sniffing about for a bit on the side. One of them offered me money. Young kids yelling out "box" at me in the street. Late at night they come around and they yell out, dirty things. Or they throw rocks on the roof.'

John blushed as a memory came back.

'When I was a kid here, we did that. To a woman in Oxide Street. We use to call her "Mole" and put bungers in the letterbox. Really because we were curious and scared. We couldn't control ourselves and we didn't know what to do with it. So we thought up these stories and we picked on her and made her miserable. Some nights I woke up dreaming about her and wetting the sheets.'

'Thanks,' Ethel said doubtfully. 'It doesn't make it any easier.'

John walked for most of the time on his own. In Sturt Park, the broken pillar of the memorial to the sinking of the *Titanic*. There was a mural along Argent Street, outside the old Arts and Sciences Museum. Each section of the mural had been done by a different class of kids in the high school. A blue-painted poppet head on a background of red hills and artificial green trees. A crow on a fence in the corner. A flock of yellow parrots over the blue poppet head. A miner with a granite jaw and a lantern shining from his helmet gazed proudly on the scene.

He was still looking at the mural from the footpath when he felt a hand drop heavily on his shoulder.

'Hello Uncle Eric,' he smiled.

The familiar bald head was balder still, and Eric, who had been a strongly built man, had shrunk and stooped.

'You owe me a drink.' His uncle spoke a little haltingly.

'Come on then.'

They went along Argent Street, past the men sitting outside the post office. The smell of pipe tobacco drifted after them as they went. To the same hotel they'd gone to before.

'What are you doing now?' His uncle asked when they were sitting at a table.

'Been out of work for a while. Came back to look around.'

'Not a place to come to looking for a job.'

'Mainly to look around.'

'How's your father?'

'He's living in Sydney. Went with Diana on a cruise on the *Oriana* around the Pacific. They liked Japan.'

297

'Bloody nip bastards!' Eric swore. 'They shouldn't have worried about declaring war on us. What they should have done is given all their guns to the Yanks and told them to do the fighting. By now, they'd own all the bloody place, not just half it like they do now.'

'Ellen went with them. She's a millionaire, or almost.'

Eric whistled.

'They haven't spoken to me since the time they had to pay when mum died. I never had much ready cash. Your mother has been crooked on me ever since.'

He paused to think over the implications of this.

'If I had known, I would have paid. Ellen a millionaire. How is young Cain?'

'They're sending him to a private school. One where he wears a badge on his tunic and he gets to know the sons of judges.'

'Is he smart?'

'I don't know.'

'You're the black sheep of the lot?'

'Yes. I've been out of work for a while.'

'Join the rest of the family.'

They both laughed.

'I retired a bit after your father. Of course, they didn't pay me off as well as they paid him, him being a shift boss. We live alright. We're both on the pension. Comfortable. I didn't think I'd ever want to be comfortable. Now I sit and watch television every night and occasionally a friend from the mines drops over and he looks at the aeroplane photographs and he says "Ah you were a flyer". "Yes," I say. "I was trained by Kingsford Smith. He showed me how to fly." "Eh," they say, but they don't believe it, and to tell the truth nor do I it was so long ago. It was someone else I remember. "He was a real gentleman," I say although I'm not sure whether I imagined it or not. But I want to prove that I'm not a liar. They nod and they agree, then they change the subject.'

An old man shuffled across and picked up the empty glasses from the table. John looked at him and started.

'Good day, old Bob!' Eric called out.

Sharkey turned and gave a vacant, expressionless, toothless grin. The face strained for a second, groping for thought. Then he sank into the soothing clouds that he floated around on, and he shuffled on, trying to focus his concentration on the task of finding glasses.

'They're good to old Bob in here.' Eric did not bother to speak quietly. 'He used to be the champ. Great boxer, like your grandfather. Except Big Jack knew when to give it up. Eh. He had all his marbles, and he kept them. Old Bob, they kept him here to do the cellarman's work. His hands got so shaky he couldn't pour the beer. They didn't fire him. No way would they do that to a mate! No they keep him here, picking up glasses. Even now someone will square up to him and say "How you going champ". The champ will put up his paws, but they got to watch he doesn't drop the glasses he's carrying, and when he shuffles about they all cheer. You can tell he was a champ, and he forgets what he was doing and he wanders off trying to remember until he sees another empty glass. That reminds him.'

John looked at him, not sure. His uncle looked down expressionless into the glass.

'I don't know why I'm here,' John said to his uncle.

'You need a job,' Eric deliberately misunderstood.

'That's not why I'm here. This is the place I began.'

'A bit the same for me. When I was a lad, it was me that left, and Austin that stayed. Now it's me that's here and him that's in Sydney on the rantan.'

'There's something in that.' John agreed, twirling an empty glass on the table. 'He never had much fun.'

'He was the oldest. When the old man died it was him that became the father, it was him that had to look after his mother. Before the old man died he always seemed to be looking after mum. Like both of them didn't like the way Jack lived. Not that he did much. Sat out on the verandah reading most of his spare time. Lazy, maybe, but it was his way of enjoying himself. They hated that. Not that he wasn't working, but he was comfortable.'

John had put on weight. His jeans pinched. He shifted.

'That's funny,' he said, and did not know quite what he meant by it.

'She's going to be a millionaire.' Ethel spoke out of nowhere, as it were. John was making breakfast.

'Yes.'

John had never made up his mind about how he felt on his sister's success. He looked moodily into the back yard. Ethel had parked the taxi beside the clothes-line for the night. It stood there, solid and appropriate. In any other town, a taxi parked under a clothes-line would be absurd. Every backyard in Broken Hill had its car, usually an old one, set up on blocks. Engines and tyres stacked against disused fowlhouses.

'I've never known a millionaire,' Ethel mused. 'It's funny to think of someone I know being one.'

'I've never known one either.'

'You're family. You would do alright out of it.'

'I don't think it would make much difference. I'm the black sheep. I wouldn't bank on it.'

Ethel laughed.

'I'll have to go back soon.'

'What are you going back to?'

'My own life.'

'Is it much of a life?'

'It's mine.'

'I did it my way,' Ethel broke into song.

'You can come and stay with me, if you like. Any time.'

'Any time,' Ethel smiled.

John had noticed before that the gums around her teeth had receded.

Chapter 9

'Come on and I'll show you the office.' Ellen spoke casually. 'For a Sunday drive.'

'You ought to go and have a look at the office,' added Diana.

John was halfway through the bread and butter custard. He felt no special attachment to the custard. Diana's memory had been getting bad and she often doubled the quantities. The custard tasted doughy and sweet. He did not want to be shown the symbols of his sister's success.

He dabbled the custard with a spoon. Ellen was not patient. She might go back to the office rather than wait.

'You want some more son?' His mother asked.

'It's nice. I'll have a bit more.'

When the plate was returned to him, heaped thoroughly, he dabbled more. Ellen watched him with an amused smile. She was being very patient indeed. She had been waiting for years, and a bowl of custard was not going to stop her. At the other end of the table, Austin chewed his way silently through his own portion of custard.

As there was no way that he could politely escape his fate, he pushed the custard away.

'You should finish the custard,' Ellen purred.

'A bit too much of it for me.'

He grunted, and theatrically loosened his belt.

Diana looked disappointed.

'It was very nice.'

'I'll keep it for during the week.' Diana scooped it up and whisked it back to the kitchen. 'We can eat it then.'

Austin's face did not alter.

Ellen led John to the driveway. Her latest car was parked there. John admired.

He kicked a tyre. 'How old is it?'

'Three months. I've had it three months. 1981 Porsche, still on warranty. In three months it's given me more trouble than any other car. I take it back to them on average once a week. I tell them I'm not impressed.'

'No.'

John leaned backwards in the narrow driveway.

'Last week I went back to Broken Hill. Just for a visit. It broke down the other side of Wilcannia. Along came a 1953 Ford Consul full of Aboriginals. They gave me a lift. I phoned the Porsche dealers from Broken Hill and I told them. This is not good enough, I said I want you to get this car and you fix it. Or I'll go to the papers! It's a prestige car. It shouldn't break down like that. They got it towed in, and they sent it back to Sydney by train. Their expense. They should replace it. I asked them for another one. "No," they said, "it will be alright now." A week later I'm in there again. Out he comes in his little suit. "What now?" He asks. "This is outrageous!" I yell in front of a room full of customers. "The car you sold me . . . this . . . prestige car . . . prestige, you tell me! It has broken down for the third time since I had it, three times, in three months, three times it has broken down, brand new. You won't get me buying another one!"'

'What did he do?' John felt quite faint-hearted.

'He sent a tow-truck, and they towed it from Pitt Street. Pitt Street in rush hour. They fixed it again. "Nothing wrong with it madam," he said to me. "Like the last half dozen times I had it in here, darling. It was alright then." He didn't like me saying that.'

She looked at John, who said nothing.

'The next time I *will* write a letter to the papers.' Her face flushed with the sensation of power.

The real estate agency was small and poky, although it was on a corner.

'Good day darling.' Ellen smiled at the receptionist behind the small switchboard.

'There is a call for you now,' the receptionist said efficiently.

She was twenty and severe and middle-aged. 'There were two calls before, but I put the messages on your desk.'

'Thank you darling. Look, this is my brother John. John, this is Lee-Anne. Lee-Anne, be a sweet and entertain him while I answer it. Don't entertain him too much though. Pop wouldn't approve.'

She giggled and went off into an office behind a small blue screen, the same colour as the carpet. Lee-Anne looked him up and down, and might have said "Well! I know why they don't talk about this one". John noticed that Lee-Anne was wearing a blue top.

'Everything here is blue,' he said.

'Ellen insists. It's like a uniform. The men wear blue shirts and ties, too.'

'Ties.'

'They have to wear ties. It's one of the conditions. Ellen is strict about that. "How can we expect to impress the clients unless we're dressed well?" she says, every time someone comes in who is a bit scruffy. She never hires them, even when they have excellent references. I think it looks nice, though, for a man to be neatly dressed.'

'I suppose,' John agreed drily.

He could hear Ellen's voice. He strained to make out the words. He could tell when she said 'darling' because of the inflexion.

'I have been here three months. Ellen says if I get the licence, then I can have a try at selling.'

'That's how she started.' John wondered if that was the right thing.

'I didn't know that. Although I did know she came from a very honest working background. Pop comes in here and helps with the books.'

'He always liked that.'

'He worries about those books alright. Won't let anyone else see them. Takes them home and sits with them at night, and he gets cross when Ellen has parking fines for double parking in the city. "It doesn't matter," she says, "it saves time. My time is worth more than the fine. Anyway, just wait and don't pay it until they're ready to take me away. That way we get credit on the money." He gets really shirty about that. I can understand how he feels even if it is a bit old-fashioned. "If you paid it the first time, it costs only fifteen or twenty dollars. We end up paying a hundred dollars. It's not you that pays it either, it's the company." He waves the books around and you can hear him yelling half a block away. He gets all red, although I suppose you've seen him.'

'I've seen him.'

'I didn't know there was any others in the family.'

'I'm the one they don't talk about.'

'Are there any others? Just in case.'

'No others.'

On either side of a narrow aisle, sales-people in blue sat behind blue dividers talking softly with clients. Four of them, and one empty desk at the end. Although it was small the office was glassed on two sides and got the afternoon light.

'There's always business here, especially on weekends,' Lee-Anne nattered. 'Sunday is our big day.'

One of the salesmen followed a young couple out to a blue Datsun angle-parked nearby.

'Blue cars as well.'

'That one belongs to the firm. They use it when their own cars are in being serviced. We have an account with the garage down the road and he services all the cars as a job lot, charges by the month.'

Ellen put her head over the divider and called out to John. Lee-Anne nodded.

'His master's voice.'

John was contemplating the remark as he sat on a curved chair with blue covering. Although it looked good, he did not feel comfortable. He shifted his bottom forward and put his elbow on the table. Ellen looked. She leaned back comfortably, inviting

304

him further foward. He wondered what would happen if he prostrated himself on the carpet.

'This is the small office, darling,' she purred.

He rocked forward and felt his knees touch the carpet. The cling of plastic.

'This is the first one. It does an excellent business still, but I am looking to expand. We have the other office, at the shopping centre near the beach. Once it goes it will leave the others for dead. Of course, we need another director, because it will be a separate company. It's the law.'

She looked out through a crack between the dividers at the play of light shifting gradually across the small plaza. Mistress of all she surveyed. John pulled his knees up and smiled sheepishly.

'You could be a director,' Ellen prodded, turning on her most charming, most assured, most successful, smile.

'I never thought of myself that way.'

'Few people do, darling. That's the problem. There are not enough workers around, and too many bludgers. Nobody takes chances. All in unions. More money, they think they have a right to it. You know that! It's not them that takes the chances.'

'I've never seen myself as a person who takes chances.' John questioned himself as he said it.

'Not many people take chances.'

'A lot of people see themselves as taking chances.'

Ellen hesitated.

'The economy wouldn't run if people didn't take chances, darling. If they didn't put their money up to try to get out of the rut. Then everybody drags them down. The "workers" in their unions, none of them individually capable of doing it. But we've got to pay them! Oh yes! That's fair. The government sets up these rules so you have to pay, and pay, and pay. It would be better to give up and join the queue, the endless line of bludgers.'

Her voice became irate. As she spoke she thrust her chin forward. The small broken threads in her eyes swayed, brushed like seaweed, and parted. Their chins were almost touching.

'I'll show you the other place.' She leaned back again and laughed.

As they went out he was introduced to one of the salesmen. He leaned forward and accepted the strong grip and a steady stare from the young man in his early twenties, with fair hair and a neat trimmed beard. He was trying to catch his name, which Lee-Anne had mumbled from the side.

'Gavin is new,' Ellen intoned. 'He has promise though. We were thinking of putting him down in the new office, the one we're going to open near Manly.'

'It has possibilities,' Gavin smiled.

'Only if he sells well.'

He looked back at Gavin, who was gazing from one to the other of them. He, too, had a thoughtful foxy smile.

As Ellen drove the Porsche over the hill toward the beachside suburbs, John looked over the glassy expanse of water. He regretted that he had never been out of Australia, had hardly been anywhere in Australia. Whyalla, the inner city of Sydney, Broken Hill. He felt a bit sorry for himself.

'Gavin is a good salesmen.' Ellen chatted happily beside him.

'He's smart.'

'You can tell!'

The car purred happily as it crossed lanes and turned, down a side road with potholes on a steep slope.

At the bottom of the hill, they turned with the traffic onto the highway. A man wearing blue jeans had his thumb out for a lift near the corner. Ellen signalled to the nearest bus-stop.

The new office still had green carpet and the desks the sales-people sat at with their customers did not have dividers. The receptionist smiled professionally, but she didn't try to make small talk as she handed Ellen a bundle of messages.

The salesmen looked down as Ellen led her brother into the separate office at the rear. The bank of telephones on his sister's desk jingled as she settled down behind them with a contented smile.

'We need a director. For here.'

'What does a director do?'

'Nothing much. Lots of people are directors. If anything goes wrong, they sign a form, and they're off. It is a . . . legal provision, more than anything. There has to be directors.'

He sat, feeling soft inside.

'All you have to do is be there. If . . . it all goes as expected, then of course a consideration will have to be made for your services.'

It had been pleasant for a few years to live in small rooms, with the advantage of the casual sexual liaison. The constant smells that permeate every corner. The change of jobs every year, and finally no job at all . . . for how long?

His sister dangled a dream. It might not be too late. To be important and comfortable and able to command. To have a car. He didn't have a licence any longer, because he couldn't afford it. To have a car with automatic gears, which slid around corners and purred down hills. A car which people envied. A car people looked at as you drove past and you didn't look back.

He struggled feebly. Pieces of his past were sticking, slowing his movements, clinging. He was sinking back. He had not been there for years. It was pleasant. It was not so bad, it had never been bad. Lassitude.

He looked at Ellen. If she had tried to push, then he could resist. She sat there watching.

'Yes,' he said.

'Good,' Ellen allowed herself to move. 'I thought you might go for it. You were . . . nibbling.'

Ellen prepared to make a phone call.

'You don't mind curry do you darling, to celebrate? On the company. It's a tax deduction for directors.'

The first weakness was the greatest. Once the compromise had been made, all other compromises followed, and the final capitulation. He nodded.

She tapped once on the digital pad of the telephone and rested back as the number dropped in.

'Hello darling. I was thinking of going Indian tonight, a special occasion. My brother. I have my brother here. You would like to meet him. The other member of the family. He is very clever darling.'

'Meet the brother,' Ellen waved her hand and the three women already seated at the table looked at him.

'I'm too stunned to comment,' one smiled.

'Another member of the family. Well!' Said the slightly older woman in the corner seat.

'Meet Jean, darling. The one in the corner is Tilda—Matilda really, but we call her Tilda for short—and the quiet thoughtful one there is Bernadette.'

'Hello brother,' Jean waved a pinky from the side of her coffee cup.

John sat down.

'John has become a director, or is shortly to become a director, of Mylady Proprietary Limited.'

'How many more members of your family are you going to produce to be directors of your companies?' Asked Tilda forcefully.

'Worried that you will never get a chance to be a director yourself?' Jean teased. 'You'll have to be content with that motorbike.'

'I bought her a motorbike. She had no way of getting around.' Ellen flushed a little.

'It is a nice little motorbike.'

'We've never heard of you before,' Tilda asked John.

John swallowed.

'What do you do, dear?'

'Anything I can, which hasn't been much for the last couple of years.'

'There must be lots of people on the dole who don't want to work. I've never had any problems getting a job.'

'I've looked.'

'They've come looking for me,' Jean went on. 'I was a legal secretary in the city, I can type, take shorthand, use a dictaphone. They pay me thirty-eight thousand a year, and next job they'll pay me more.'

'I can't type.'

'You could learn.'

'There are laws now, that they can't discriminate. You could learn to type, do office work.'

'You'd have to tidy up a bit,' Ellen added.

The evening went on. They drank a lot of wine. The traffic on the highway outside began to thin. The candle in a small amber bowl guttered and flickered in a small lake of wax. The girls were beginning to giggle and get sentimental with one another. Tilda had taken Bernadette's hand and put it on the table and weepily assured Bernadette that she was the best friend Tilda had ever had. Jean made an odd clumsy gesture to John, waving with one hand across the table.

'You got a good family,' she drawled uncertainly. 'Wha's wrong with you? Smart fellow, nice sister, pop good honest worker. Wha you na got a job? Don' you want work?'

His sister looked at him. In the spidery candle-light her face changed, into the face of a little girl.

She leaned forward and began to stir the candle wax with a satay stick. Clearing a patch for the wick, then stirring the molten wax, picking up the solid flakes of wax and watching them melt from the naked flame.

'You remember the Willyama Hotel?' She laughed, an unfunny guttural laugh. She looked at her friends. 'It was funny. He was a character, real character. Climbed in there with—who was it? His friends . . . Pieter, that . . . idiot. They stole the money, stacked the chairs up, wrote all over the counter. That. Vandalism. You remember? Ha. I told on you. Told the old man. You got it.'

John stared into the face of his sister, the small resentful angry face. As into a dream. The eyes that looked up at him, the eyes of the natural enemy. He remembered.

'The lounge chair? That's funny. You remember the lounge chair?' (The voice was a shriek just held in, scathing and angry. The satay stick prodded around the small, low flame.) 'You broke the lounge chair. Broke the end off. You sat it back there. When it fell off, I was near there. He blamed me. When I said it was you, he wouldn't believe me. He belted me all over with that piece of wood. As he belted me, you stood behind him and you . . . laughed. Each time I said "Look at him! Look at him! He did it and he's laughing!" He turned around and you were looking serious.'

'Do you hate me?' It was a relief to feel the cool stone inside him.

'I don't hate you,' Ellen laughed.

A lump of wax landed on top of the flame. It melted and swamped the flame. The corner of the restaurant plunged into darkness. Until the waiter approached with a match.

'It happens all the time,' he apologised in his musical Indian voice. 'Everyone likes to play with the candles. I will get you a new one.'

'We were about to go.'

'You are welcome to stay of course.'

He found another candle and lit it in place of the other one.

'We were always different,' Ellen half-addressed the others. She had, after all, been telling funny stories.

'You're the same.'

It was the first and only time that John heard Bernadette speak.

PART FIVE

PART FIVE

Chapter 1

'So you have a job?' His sister sounded disappointed.

John nodded. It had taken him eight months, and the job wasn't as good as he might have hoped. He was a storeman again, but the typing he had learned had not gone astray. The goods were listed on a word processor. When paper went out, or paper came in, he loaded it or unloaded it then typed the details into the word processor.

Austin was impressed. It was the mathematics he could understand. Tangible things, quantifiable, stackable, conceivable, and touchable. Reassurance that the world was there. There was nothing dreamy about Austin.

Ellen watched as Austin asked questions about paper. What else was there? Office supplies. Biro pens, pencil sharpeners, erasers, staplers, markers, scissors, tape, stencils, bulldog clips. Bays of racks, all numbered. The small Apple word processor that kept track of everything. Nobody could steal a bulldog clip?

'They get stolen, but we know. They don't disappear. Two other storemen, so it doesn't take much to find out the likely culprit.'

Austin looked pleased.

'We ought to go to the office to see the books. Seeing you *are* a director,' Ellen interrupted.

The roast beef was very salty. John paused.

'Leave him here to eat. You can have him later,' Diana roused herself.

She had lost a lot of weight and looked very tired. She raised her head for a second of defiance, then sank back into her chair.

Feeling the obligation of an old alliance, he stayed.

'See you later then.' Ellen swiftly stood and picked the keys up from the table and walked out jangling. The swing door puffed shut behind her. As the Porsche backed from the drive, Austin apologised. He wanted to go out and look at the roses.

John sat, looking at his mother. The television wasn't going. There was no possible distraction.

'You know what he's done?'

Diana raised her frail little old lady's head. The eyes focussed and gathered expression, humour, the character of his mother.

'He's mortgaged the house. The house we both own. My house. He's mortgaged it, and he didn't ask me. So . . . she could have her business. She asked him for it, and he gave it to her, but he knew I wouldn't agree, so he didn't tell me.'

'When?'

'Two years ago. I tell you, they got no brains, any of them. No brains. He knew it . . .'

'Why?'

'She didn't have enough money, so he put up the house for her.'

'Won't she pay it back?'

'You'll never get it back from her. Get nothing from her. My house! It's my house they've taken!'

She yelled. Her face reddened.

He didn't know what to say. His mother rambled, getting angrier at first, then further from the point, until finally her anger petered out in incoherent grumbles.

'Every night she goes with her girlfriends. Drinking, and I don't know what else. Austin got a phone call last week from the police. Her car in a street in Paddington, with the windows open. Wallet on the seat with hundreds of dollars in it, sitting there. So he took it to the station and called us up. "That's her," I said. "No bloody brains! Owes us this house and she goes and leaves six hundred dollars on her car seat. Next week she won't be able to pay the rent and she'll come and ask Austin and he'll pay the rent out of his pension." I tell him, but he won't listen. That's because he's as silly as she is.'

'Austin keeps the books. He should put money aside for a couple of months. That would be enough.'

314

'He can't.' Diana was almost weeping. 'She walks all over him. He grumbles and he yells, but then she just asks, and he can't say . . . no.'

'Why don't you ask?'

'He won't say no. He won't do anything. Then I can't remember . . . he tells me . . . I know they're telling me a story. None of them tell the truth.'

'Why don't you fight her?'

Diana's face immediately crumpled.

'Trouble . . . screaming . . . I can't stand it any more . . .'

John sat.

'No bloody brains, none of them,' she raved. Already the anger had gone, and the voice had diminished to a whine.

He could hear Diana washing the dishes as he stepped through the wire door. His father was pruning the thin screen of roses between the rectangular trimmed lawn and the street. From the verandah, he could see over the rooftops of the new houses to the high rise coat-hanger buildings beside the shore. The sea was hazy with the dust from the traffic and the factories that still worked in Brookvale.

A pile of twigs had accumulated at his father's feet.

'Goodday,' his father grunted.

'Mum . . . Diana's been talking to me.'

Austin turned his blue eyes around. He was holding secateurs and wearing gloves. For a second, the eyes bulged.

'She always told you everything.'

'I don't care. I never asked you for much. I don't want you asking me for much.'

'We won't ask you for anything.'

'She can afford to give it back,'

He turned and stubbornly began to clip the roses again.

'It was someone else's turn to have Christmas dinner.' Ellen touched Diana lightly on the shoulder. 'We've been having Christmas dinner with you for years. It's time, darling. You know that.'

315

Diana slumped in her chair and glared at her daughter. It was too much trouble. There could be an argument. Diana flinched. Instead she fixed her wavering attention on the view.

From the second storey, where they were sitting, they could see the sails of yachts as they skipped across the silhouette of the bridge. The bridge itself, with its heavy pylons at either end of the sloping arch of steel, hung sulkily, dividing the sky from the sea.

Ellen's building was a three-storey box of red brick on a narrow slice of land surrounded by older, Victorian terrace houses. The entrance was a narrow tree-lined lane. From the street, it could have been the drive to a green-painted late Victorian building with a verandah. There was a barbecue and a hoist, constantly in shadow except for twenty minutes when the sun was at its peak. The view through the wide sliding glass panels to the east was magnificent and saleable. Blue carpet had been installed.

'Beautiful.' Tilda recognised the designer's intention. 'Just like the sea and the sky comes right in to you!'

Ellen beamed and directed modest attention to the table. Plates heaped with duck, turkey, beef, ham, prawns, jellies, lamb, small jugs with sauces, three bottles of champagne unopened.

'You can slice the meat.' Ellen delegated the knife to Austin who was sitting on the other side of Diana.

As Austin began to hack at the carcass of turkey, Jean offered to help with opening the champagne.

'You can't wait to get into it, can you?' Ellen asked coolly.

'That's what it's there for.'

A cork popped, and flew across the table, flying between John and Cain. Everyone laughed. Cain, who was fifteen, did not bother to smile. A lumpish boy trussed into a small school uniform and strangled by a tie, his small eyes glowered morosely.

'Can you take your coat off?' John asked him as the champagne was being poured into his glass.

'No, darling. It's a good school. They like their boys to wear school uniforms at all times,' Ellen answered.

'It's Christmas, darling,' said Jean.

316

'I am aware of that,' Ellen replied archly.

Cain shifted on his seat. John read something of himself in the suet-faced boy.

'Where to later?' He whispered. 'Are you going to take off that tie?'

The boy looked startled. He shifted the chair along the carpet without lifting it.

'That will mark the carpet,' cried his mother.

'Oh go easy,' yelled Jean. 'You got to let them have some fun.'

'Not at the expense of my carpet.'

The boy settled down.

'I always walked the food off,' he tried again.

'There's a James Bond movie on channel seven at one-thirty, if you want to watch it. There's a teeve in the bedroom.'

Because it was past midday, the sun was above the roof and the room was in shadow. It was still hot. Everybody sat drinking champagne, and no one showed any inclination to eat.

'The view from here is lovely.' Tilda swivelled on her chair. 'It's the view that you pay for, isn't it?'

Ellen blushed demurely.

'You better eat up,' she said. 'This is Christmas dinner.'

'Shouldn't we have prayers?' Diana asked, because she occasionally remembered.

Ellen thought about it.

'Let's,' said Tilda.

'Cain can say them.'

Everybody obediently clasped their hands together and bowed their heads. A drop of sweat fell onto the grey fabric of John's trousers.

'Gennul Jees meek 'n' mil' thanks for all that you give us this day our daily bread amin.'

They blinked at one another.

'Let's tuck in!' Cried Jean.

Cain noticed that the time was getting perilously close to one-thirty, and was bolting down a plateful of prawns and sausage

317

rolls as quickly as he could. Bernadette was sitting on the other side, silent as usual, dabbing at the corners of a piece of butchered turkey thigh.

John leaned across and spooned a square of sliced ham onto his plate.

'Eat up mum.' Ellen dropped another prawn onto Diana's plate.

'It's great food.' Tilda leaned across and slapped the old woman on the arm.

'Yes. It is beautiful food. I could not make food like this.'

'Nor could she, darling. She got a caterer to come in and do this!'

'Tax deductible,' Ellen added.

'That was great,' Cain said suddenly. His cheeks were still full of food. 'I think I'll go upstairs and lie down.'

'He hasn't had enough to eat yet!' Exclaimed Diana. 'Look at the size of him, and still growing.'

'That's alright. I'll take a few sausage rolls, in case I get hungry later.'

He carried a small plate of sausage rolls up the stairs. His tread echoed through the ceiling, and John heard a few seconds of the Mars Bar advertisement before the door closed with a slight, heavily carpeted, puff.

'He is such a nice boy,' Diana smiled.

'He's not doing so good at school,' Ellen grimaced. 'He is always in the middle. I tell him he's got to do a lot better than that if he's going to be a lawyer, or a doctor. The teachers say that he is good at biology.'

'You can take a horse to water,' said Tilda in a sing-song voice.

'He is a good boy,' Diana repeated at Tilda, as though she was querying this.

'I don't doubt it, darling.' Ellen poured some more champagne from the second bottle into her mother's glass. 'He's been getting private lessons. Teachers. They get paid . . . do you know how much an hour? Just to get him through their exams. "What do you think I'm paying you for?" I ask them, "When you can't

318

get him to pass, and pass well. That's what I'm paying you for. To get him through, to get him to pass .. I don't want him to be ... another bludger." If they answered me straight, that would be alright. "He can do it," they tell me, so I keep paying them. I pay, and I want results. I want him to be a lawyer. It is what he wants to be.'

'Or a doctor.'

'Or a doctor.'

'Does he have the ability?'

'What else is money for?'

The champagne tasted sweet and warm. On top of the food, it gave John a headache. The light coming through the glass. Sydney Harbour, a large piece of cheap blue tapestry, with the Bridge and the sailing boats and the tall buildings sewn along the shore.

The palm trees planted at the back of the old terrace. The narrow drive leading into the block was lined with trees and shrubs. Ellen's Porsche had been parked in the drive when he arrived.

'They don't object when I park in the drive next to their house,' Ellen had greeted him. 'It gives their house a lift.'

The meal went on. Ellen pressed a button, and Charles Aznavour seeped through half a dozen speakers spaced throughout the house. Everyone looked.

'It was getting quiet.' She held up a small gadget with the button, and smiled. 'I can turn it on from anywhere in the house.'

Austin leaned over to look.

'It's like the phone you brought back from San Francisco,' he said, grasping eagerly.

'That!'

'It's really good,' Austin stared from face to face, looking into emptiness with his empty eyes. 'You can carry it around, up the street. You can make phone calls and get them. There's no wires. As clear as . . . as clear as a bell.'

'To the end of the street, you can carry it.'

'Can you?' chirruped Tilda.

Ellen looked. It might have been mockery.

Everyone settled back and looked at the view while the food settled. Charles Aznavour crooned on.

'What are you doing now?' Jean asked John.

'I learned to type, and I got a job.'

'Eh?'

'As a storeman. Only now I type requisitions as well, so they don't have to hire a typist.'

'He's a director.'

'I don't get any money out of that.'

'You will, when we come in . . .'

'Every time you get some money, you spend it somewhere else,' Austin suddenly interrupted. 'You could be rich—if you had any sense.'

'Goes to show what you know about it.' Ellen sawed between her gums with a toothpick imperturbably.

'I know more about it than you think!' Austin menaced.

'I want to go home.'

All eyes settled on Diana, who looked across the table at John. Her dull shrewd eyes picked up a glow from the sea.

'It has been very nice here, and I am thankful. But I want to go back to my own home.'

Tilda and Jean chorused regret.

'There's no need for you to go.' Ellen gave Austin a meaningful look. Diana stood.

'Thank you very much for having me. It was nice food and the house is lovely and the view but I want to go to my own home.'

It was the first time they had gone somewhere else for Christmas dinner without taking some food.

Austin let her pass before he stood up and followed her. Diana put on a grey coat, and straightened her hat in the mirror.

'We haven't said goodbye to Cain yet,' Austin hesitated.

He walked to the foot of the stairs and dropped his palm on the banister.

320

'Hello Cain!' He bellowed. There was no answer. He called again and went up a stair.

'He can't hear,' he chuckled in the direction of the table.

'The teeve's too bloody loud,' muttered Tilda, softly, so he wouldn't hear.

'We're going now,' Austin bellowed.

A door opened upstairs.

'See you later!'

'See you later.' Austin could not conceal disappointment as he turned away. The door closed upstairs.

'I'll call him down,' said Ellen.

'Don't worry. He's busy studying.' Austin's grey head descended the stairs slowly, step by carpeted step. Diana followed.

'Back in a minute,' Ellen called gaily to the others and winked.

'It was funny they didn't say goodbye to you.' Tilda gave John a searching look.

'They forget,' said John.

'Sometimes Diana talks about you, and she calls you Cain.'

He thought Bernadette was about to say something, but she sipped on a glass of luke-warm champagne instead.

They had been sitting for a few minutes when Ellen came back. Her face had reddened. Tilda stubbed her cigarette and turned an impassive profile to study the harbour.

Ellen stomped into the small kitchen, and returned with a can of beer. She sat and tore the ring top viciously and swigged straight from the can.

'What am I going to do with him?' She asked the room rhetorically.

None of the women looked about to say anything.

'Who?'

'The old man.'

'Why?'

'Don't get me wrong, darling. They're a gorgeous couple. Beautiful, really they are lovely. But he's too old. He interferes.

321

He doesn't know anything about it, but he comes in with pieces of paper and makes a pain of himself.'

John noticed a small strand of grey hair hanging down the side of Ellen's face. Her hair had darkened long ago to light brown. Lines down the side of her face.

He was two years older.

'He's delightful; really the old bugger is. The other day he came down to the office, and I was trying to get rid of one of the salesmen. I'm sure he was feeding my sales off to Brown's agency down the road. Next thing I know, do you know what the silly bugger is doing? He's trying to get them to strike! You ever heard of it? Real estate salesmen on strike! I got in the car and went to the house. "Diana," I said, "you get that silly old coot and keep him home away from me, or I'll kill him. I will. I'll kill him." '

'Delightful,' said Tilda.

Beyond the blue carpet a cloud had gone across the sun and the water was heavy and flaked with silver.

'I tell him he ought to retire. He won't. He says he knows when he will retire, but in the meantime it's giving me the willies that keeps him alive.'

'He's no good with the books any more?'

'He's too old, darling. He was alright a few years ago, even then he was old-fashioned. Now he makes mistakes all the time. The girl at the desk checks his maths all the time. He forgets whole pages, or he doesn't see them. Except when it's some bloody little detail that doesn't matter, like a parking fine. Then he remembers. Drives me mad when I've got important things to do. No sense of . . . no discrimination, no priorities. Details.'

'You definitely don't want him around?'

'No.'

'He paid money to the business?'

Ellen reddened.

'Yes. Valuable at first, but not important.'

'Why not give it back? Then tell him to retire.'

'I tell you what I offered him. I want him to take Diana on

a cruise somewhere. Just go away to the islands, all paid for. She needs a holiday, she's sick. Sit in the sun, talk. They liked that other holiday. Will he take it? Will he go? No way. It's more fun driving me mad, that's why.'

'Why not give him the money? All that you owe him. Then tell him to piss off. He won't have any excuse.'

Ellen stared. She willed it away, just as Austin had willed it away.

'It wouldn't cost you much,' John plunged on, into his past.

The three girls watched him. Tilda with a slightly cruel smile. Jean with panic. Bernadette with curiosity.

'What you'd make on a couple of houses . . . that would be enough. Wouldn't it? Then you could send him home and be rid of him.'

That was not what Ellen wanted. She wanted him to be wrong. To stay, in her power, and be wrong. The face of a baby, with lines and grey hair. The eyes of the enemy.

'Have another drink, dear.' She leaned forward and tipped a bottle of wine.

'Thank you.'

He raised his glass, aware that he had been reassessed. Raised to the status of someone who had not yet, quite, been destroyed.

'You can stay, if you like.' Ellen leaned across the table, which was stacked with lumps of uneaten meat.

'Get to know the girls,' Tilda laughed heartily.

'He knows too much about them as it is, I'll bet,' Ellen calculated.

'I've got a few people to call in on. Because it's Christmas.'

He stood and smiled to the three girls.

'I'll walk down with you.'

Ellen stood also. None of the girls made a move. Tilda smiled flirtatiously through the smudged wine glass.

'That little bugger can come out now too!'

'It doesn't matter,' because it did not.

'That's the problem with him at school. All he wants to do is watch television. The teeve. He'll never get anywhere doing that.'

John paused at the stairs. His sister stomped to the next floor up. A door closed. Shortly after, Ellen came down the stairs, followed by Cain.

'We have decided to see you off, Uncle John,' Ellen said deliberately, looking at her son.

'Thank you.'

John continued down the stairs, followed by a chorus of 'goodbyes' and 'see you laters'.

'We can give you a lift,' Ellen offered.

'Be in that,' added Cain.

'He likes driving. He's a natural.'

'I can walk. One of my friends lives not far away.'

The trees and shrubs planted at either side were cool. He looked with a sense of relief at a stain on the stone wall of the house fronting the street. Ellen was still behind him.

'You know, he doesn't know when to stop. He is too old.'

'Why don't you give him back his money then?'

'It would kill him, darling. He would have nothing to live for. I would feel responsible.'

'He's responsible for himself. Surely.'

'Not really, not at his age darling.'

'You don't want him around?'

They stepped out into the street. The glare was instant and intense. From the sheltered green of the driveway, the road curved away on either side. The walls and the fences had been cut back to the original stonework. Beyond them, they could see the towers of the city in the distance. The afternoon sun glowing from the glass of the new buildings.

'Contrasts,' said Ellen.

John was not sure that they were.

They walked on silently to the main street.

'It's not him being around that I mind. It's that he interferes.' Ellen spoke eventually.

'It's his money that gives him the right.'

Ellen shrugged. A bus was already coming. Ellen stood back as Cain shook John's hand.

Chapter 2

Ethel sat at the table and heard the story quietly. She scraped the cup across the saucer and thought about it.

'Well!' she said.

'There's not much I can do.'

'You can resign.'

'What good will that do?'

'Even if you don't have much, it will say to her that someone doesn't like what she's doing. It might make her think about it. Although I doubt that she's ever been good at thinking—about herself and her own works.'

'Sorry for telling you this, when you came down here on a holiday.'

'Time I saw the big city again. I never thought it was that different. The story you told me proves it. Only, here you can get away with it, and there's more of it.'

John swallowed. He did not want to resign. Something in him wanted—what did he want? It slipped away.

'It's a nice flat you got here.'

'Not as much space as you're used to.'

John was tired of living in rooms which were too small, with shared bathrooms and tinea. When Ethel wrote and said she would like to stay, he found the flat in a two-storey red brick block not far from the water. It had three bedrooms and an electric stove and a bathroom which was all his own. He was at an age to compromise.

He had become used to letting it slide, to letting things happen. To do something—anything—seemed too hard. He shuddered at the thought of conflict.

Ethel shifted into the front bedroom, the one with the small verandah, from the corner of which you could see a little triangle of ocean on a good day. On the weekend, John showed her the shopping centre. They went to the pictures, and they went to a fish restaurant, and sat on the concrete lip of a wall and let their legs dangle and looked down at the sand. It was too windy for anyone to be swimming. A man paddled slowly along the beach with his long trousers rolled up to the knees. He wore a suit coat and a hat and he carried his shoes in his hands. Ethel thought he was funny.

'Is this place always like this?'

'Just the same.'

'Have you written that letter?'

'No.'

'Are you going to?'

'I don't know.'

He phoned Ellen, after he called the company accountant.

'I'm resigning. As a director.'

'Why do you want to do that?'

John swallowed.

'I don't want to be a director.'

'You have reasons.'

'I'm thinking of getting married.'

'Congratulations,' Ellen said drily after a short pause. 'Who is the lucky . . .?'

'Ethel.'

'Is that her name? Charming darling. What does this have to do with you being a director?'

'Your old friend, Ethel.'

Ellen paused.

'Darling, I had no idea that you were so constant.'

There was a moment's silence.

'I'll come in later today, and submit the resignation. The accountant says that it can be backdated. He also says that I should give a copy to you.'

'Considerate.'

A long pause.

'I don't wish to be bankrupt. I think you could be bankrupt

easily. If that happens, Austin will lose the house. I don't want to be part of it.'

'If you want to be a success, you have to take chances.'

'Not with someone else's money.'

The telephone dropped into the cradle.

He was having a day off to settle the matter. He wrote the letter of resignation, in triplicate, and walked down to Circular Quay. The accountant had an office near one of the northern beaches.

It was early January. The sun was beating down by nine a.m. and he stayed in the shadow as much as he could. As he walked along the streets, he was always passing new buildings, or buildings being built, or old buildings being torn down. In a few places, the new buildings included the facade of the old. Coat-hanger buildings with the sunlight flashing from the angles of glass. Square blocks of dark glass, reflecting the clouds. He had felt comfortable in Sydney, because it was so large. It was a relief to lose himself. He loved the sensation of people walking past, and sometimes something more subtle, the sensation of another person entering his skin, touching. Anonymous intimacy.

Was it himself, or them? He could sense himself resist, begin to reverse the drift of years, the abnegation of desire and direction. He was these people, all these people. Now he strove for consciousness. To be aware, to differentiate, to select, to reject.

'Goodday, brother!'

A man in a suit addressed him.

John wanted to keep whatever was himself discrete. He smiled and walked on.

The man in the suit fell into step beside him.

'I work for Grendel Office Furniture.' He spoke exuberantly. 'They're about to go broke. The office is not far away . . .'

He sounded quite happy about it.

'All they're going to do is have a party today, so I'm going to take a walk.'

'How long have you worked there?'

'Fourteen years. Since I left school. I intended to go into the

327

public service, then I got this job as a salesman. I like it. Been there ever since. I'll get another job, easy enough. Contacts in the industry.'

John felt the man tapping, working his way under the skin. He didn't want him there.

'What do they build those things for?' John pointed up at one of the tall coat-hanger buildings.

The man stared at him. He pushed the blue suit coat forward on his shoulders and moved his scapulae.

'You can't stop progress.'

'Why are they there?'

The man screwed up his face. Then his features relaxed, as though with an effort.

'Everywhere has them. America they got them. The firm sent me to Canada two years ago. In Canada they got them. With air conditioning, everybody can work in one place. A place like Sydney, and they can get all the offices in a few small suburbs. Like here, and Parramatta, and Bondi, and North Sydney.'

'But why?'

'It's progress, that's why.'

The man sounded irritated. He turned and walked away, in the other direction.

The bus stop was a few doors away from the door of Ellen's estate agency. As he stepped down the stairs, he had an impulse to stay on the bus and keep going.

'I spend half my life getting away from them,' he said to himself. 'Now I'm going back.'

Because he was. Although he was going to hand in a resignation, the act of defiance was going to bring him into the orbit of his family.

Ellen was standing near the door. There were no salesmen or receptionists in the office.

'They're all out selling,' Ellen said. 'Business is good.'

He followed her into the small cubicle, surrounded by blue.

'You will never be rich if you keep acting this way.' Ellen

328

smiled, although John could detect the shifting lines in her eyes.

'I would rather be rich through my own efforts.'

'We see what your own efforts amount to!'

He had prepared himself. He took the copy of the resignation from his pocket.

'The accountant says it is alright. He says it is alright to backdate.'

As Ellen read the document, her face reddened.

'This is not good enough!'

He said nothing still.

'What do you take me for? Do you think I am dishonest? Is this what you are suggesting? Is that what you think?'

'It doesn't matter what I think.'

'So you do, don't you? Who thought this up? You . . . don't have the courage.'

He pushed the chair back and walked out.

Chapter 3

'That wasn't very brave,' Ethel said after she had heard John's story.

John knew.

'You were afraid of her,' Ethel went on, every now and then looking out of the window.

John, who had hoped that Ethel might be complimented by the suggestion of marriage, felt depressed.

'I always feel bad when I'm with them, as though I never grew up.'

'Everybody feels that way about their family. You were the bad one?'

'So they thought.'

Ethel said no more about it. They went out, that evening, to a restaurant.

At the end of the evening, as they went quietly to their separate bedrooms, she called out.

'It's been a lovely holiday. I have to go on Saturday.'

He felt afraid. She was stronger than he was. The upper part of her face was in darkness, but he could see her chin, and her lips. His face must have shown the extent of his despair.

'You don't have to.'

'I do.' Her lips moved although the chin remained rigid. 'You must be brave, John.'

The sense of despair was real as he entered his room, sat on the end of the bed, pulled off his shoes and socks, and rested back on the pillow. The view from his window was of the windows and verandahs of a newer block of flats. A few lights were still on. A couple was making love under a tartan eiderdown beside a bed lamp. He watched them moodily for a few minutes before rolling under the blankets and closing his eyes. It was not easy to sleep. Images turned over. His father, his mother, his sister.

Their faces. They drifted, looking at him, mouthing words which he could not hear. Strands of seaweed in water. One by one. First his mother, then his father. Finally his sister. Her lips were closed. She stared, with mute hostility. He looked into her eyes. He expected anger, fury, bitterness. There was nothing there. Emptiness.

He pulled his eyes away. The image stayed there, as though waiting for him to look again, to be drawn into that depthless nowhere. Finally, reluctantly, the image shifted sideways and drifted away.

He opened his eyes. The two under the blankets sat in the bed talking. The man lit a cigarette and rolled onto his side. The woman laughed. Her breasts jiggled. He could see her bad teeth. Their condition disgusted him: he was so human. The man leaned across and turned off the bedside lamp. The glow of the cigarette end remained, dull then glowing, dull again, without motion against the dark.

When he slept in the front room, he liked the sense that out there somewhere the ocean was moving.

'I don't think I can do anything.' John scraped a layer of charcoal from a slice of toast. 'It's their decision.'

Ethel nodded. She had taken a bite of toast and vegemite, which she chewed slowly and swallowed before she spoke.

'So long as you know it.'

'What else could I do?'

She did not bother to reply.

'I'm going to miss this place. It doesn't take long to take the water for granted. Every day since I came, I walked along that beach down there. Even when it's raining or windy.'

John left and went to work.

They talked brightly over breakfast on Saturday, but in the taxi there were silences.

At the gates, she kissed him lightly on both cheeks.

'Don't bother to come onto the train. It's too much trouble.'
'We'll write,' John said.
She nodded. Then turned and walked briskly away.

Two weeks later, he took a driver's licence. A week later again he acquired an old car. He had not driven a car for years. There had never been any use for it. Except that he had been working for a while, and he had saved money. So he acquired the car.

A 1956 Hillman Minx. It did not go very fast, and he kept well to the side to allow other drivers through. Apart from going to work, there was little for him to do with it. Then he drove over to see his parents.

Austin was in the garden pruning the thin rose bushes. Diana was sweeping the verandah. He parked the car against the gutter and got out.

'Hello,' was all he said.

The blue eyes. He had always thought they looked into him. Now he was sure he looked into them.

'You better come inside.' Austin pushed the secateurs into his pocket.

'We went and played tennis last Saturday,' Austin said when they were around the table.

He dropped the words so quietly.

'Ellen took us to the courts. She booked them to play, with some of her girlfriends.'

'They all went. Thought it was great fun, they did,' added Diana as she put the teapot in the centre of the table and sat down.

'You played?' John bit.

Austin nodded.

'She made us play. She told them all how good we used to be. Diana was, at least. "Come on, get up and show us," you know how she talks. Then the others all started. "Show us, show us," they all yelled.'

'I didn't want to,' Diana interjected.

'"Come on Diana," I said, "let's show them. It can't do any

harm." "Yes have a hit," one of the girls said. They gave us racquets and we went out on the court.'

'Couldn't hit a ball.'

'I served it. Got one over the net.'

'It's awful when you were so good once, and you could hit anything. Now I can't see a ball to hit. There it was, this little ball, dribbling along the ground. "Hit it!" They were all yelling. I walked off. "What you walking off for?" Ellen asked. "You were just starting." "I'm not doing this to entertain you," I said, "just because I can't hit a bloody ball any longer." "Oh come on mum be a sport," she says. "I'm not a baby and I don't want to be treated like one."'

'I tried to get her back to play. The girls thought it was good fun. Not every day they get to see an old champion.'

Diana squinted at him.

'Old champion, my arse!'

If it wasn't that she had to pour the tea, she would have walked out.

Chapter 4

He had a job. He had an old car. He had a telephone. He kept the small flat near the water. He could afford prostitutes, when absolutely necessary. He acquired a colour television set. In the evening, when he came home, he sat out on the verandah listening to the sea in the distance.

At night he sat and watched television. He was middle-aged.

It was winter, and it was cold and dry. He had not arrived home from his job long enough to make coffee. The kettle whistled on the stove and he was about to pour the water onto the granules of instant coffee when the telephone rang. He hesitated before he picked up the receiver.

'Ellen,' his sister introduced herself crisply.

He waited.

'You must buy their house.'

'Whose house?'

'The bank told me today. They are declaring me bankrupt. There is a new manager. The house will be repossessed in two weeks. There is no other way. You must buy the house.'

'How?'

'Always a chance it could happen the way I do business, darling. Taking risks, I mean. They refused further credit. There was no reason. The place in Beachfront was almost sold. A big contract, to the government. It could come through any day. Enough to pay for the lot and get started again.'

The handset against his cheek felt sticky.

'It's time for you to step in. You must buy their house.'

'I don't want a house.'

'You have had it easy, darling. All these years you had it easy, doing nothing, never working. It is time you accepted responsibility.'

He could hear her breathing.

334

'You have to buy it, or they will get thrown into the street.'
'I must think about it.'
'Do that, darling. Then get back to me, soon.'

'What's that?' Austin was surprised.
'The house is to be sold.'
'Heard nothing. There's a mistake.'
It was three hours later, when he called John back.
'I talked to Ellen about it. You exaggerate, she says. The bank is doing something. Nothing drastic, at least not for another year. I'll go and talk to the new bank manager tomorrow.'
'Why did she call me then? Yes, see the bank manager.'
He did not wait to hear the response.
Twenty minutes later, he was halfway through his cup of coffee.
'When I say something to you, it is confidential,' Ellen screamed. 'You are not to tell anyone else about it. Anyone!'
'It is his house you intend me to buy, and you don't want me to tell him about it?'
'He shouldn't know about it.'
He slammed the telephone down. It was not a good idea to get a job. Not a good idea to have a telephone.

He waited. For two weeks nothing happened. Each night, he walked down near the water. Perhaps it had sorted itself out. Perhaps nothing would happen. He wished it. It seemed as though it was true.
With only a vague sense of dread, he climbed into his car at midday on a Sunday and went to his parents'.
His father sat at the end of the table and ate slowly. His brother, Eric, had died. Last week. He hadn't heard until Eric's funeral was about to happen.
'I decided not to go.'
'He never paid for his mother's funeral!' Diana exclaimed, a memory coinciding with the present.
'We didn't have the money for the aeroplane.' Austin glared at the floor.

335

'How?'

'Cain. He couldn't pay his fees. He has a car. He needed petrol last weekend.'

'I mean, how did he die?'

'Heart attack, quietly in his sleep. Heard from . . . her.'

John waited as they finished the meal.

'Lucky we had the meal left over from during the week.'

The food was heavily salted.

'I went and saw the bank manager, after your last telephone call. He said it was nothing to worry about. It wouldn't arise for at least a year, probably more. Big, bald-headed man. "Don't you worry Austin, it will sort itself out. We were thinking . . . well, someone in head office was applying a bit of pressure. But we're giving her a chance to sell her way out of it. There's that development, the big block they want to build government offices on. That could come through any time. There's a few others. She set up a sale for a big commercial development near the beach . . . there's no way we want to miss out on the profits for that." They've taken away her office, though. She can't . . . she's selling it. They are all in to get it. Once the word goes out that someone is broke, the other agents come in like sharks. Then, I said to him it's young Cain's last year at the private school. Yes, he said, we don't want to stop the boy getting an education. Not when he's such a promising young chap.'

'He's such a good boy!' Diana smiled as she buttered a slice of bread.

'Better than his mother, that's what I think, I said to the manager. He looked up at me and said, "Don't worry about your house Austin. It will be alright. We've given her a chance to sell her way out of it." "She's a good salesman," I said. I don't think she should have gone into business, but she thinks she knows everything.'

'Not selling my bloody house! Not that way! They signed it, those stupid . . . ooh . . . they signed it. Without my knowing about it they signed it. I never thought they would have done it to me.'

336

'The house will be alright. They won't be doing anything, not for a year, they won't.' Austin leaned across. His hand had deep liver spots across the veins. He touched her.

'Without me knowing, they signed it.'

Diana banged the table with her spoon.

'My house. They did it to my house.'

Austin withdrew his hand. He looked steadily into the distance.

'That's what they did, didn't they, the dirty mongrels. They took away the farm. Someone else is there now. They own it. Abos! That never wash, all they do is sit about all day and do nothing. Mum and dad would never stand for it. When I go back . . . I want to go back. How is mum now? The horses, where are the horses out on the paddock? There were some horses left when dad sent the Clydesdales off to the war. Mum's eyes are bad from cutting onions. She would have paddled my bum if she'd have caught me when I threw the slops over the fence and it went all over him. Remember Daphne and the house on the hill? The daffodils they're growing there now although the house isn't there. That's from the bulbs she planted. Still growing there underneath the ground. Where's dad now? In Adelaide in that house full of clocks. They think I don't know about it, but I know. They took all those rings that mum had in the box inside the dressing-table. Jewellery, lovely diamonds. When I wore mum's shoes the day they were out I looked in there. Una stole them. Because I beat her at tennis. But she married Charlie. She could have married anyone, you know, she could have married Brett Wyman he had everything treated her good he had money a gentleman and she went and married Charlie, now what she go and marry Charlie for? Una was always after money, but she married Charlie. What she marry Charlie for? He hated it when she had any fun he broke her tennis racquet when he came back from the pub and she wasn't back from tennis he did it in the street in front of everybody because she wasn't there to make his food. He was always trying to catch me in the bathroom when she was out I never could have told her, but I had to hurry in and out of the bathroom into me clothes so he didn't catch

337

me. You could never tell what he was up to and he was so dirty. The well out the back has sweet water in it the best water for miles and down the road it was so brackish you couldn't drink it, all it was good for was the cows and the paddocks. When I walked the cows home I twisted their tails and switched them with a stick "get on there" I yelled there was no milk in them mum knew something happened but she could never catch me "You done something to those cows?" She'd ask me "No mum, nothing happened mum nothing," and she'd look at me. If she'd ever caught me . . .'

'Often like this now.' Austin looked across at John.

'Where has Ron gone?' She asked. Her voice sounded only mildly puzzled. 'He's got to bring the horses in. Dad is wild because of the way he belts them horses. "That's no way to treat them," he says, but he can't deny Ron is so good with them, they love him. "At least they're livin', not like motorbikes," dad says. But dad never gets real wild at anyone, it takes too much trouble. "Les is down there with his flaming motorbikes, he treats them like they're alive, he plays with the bolts and nuts and takes them all to bits and puts them back again and he pats its petrol tank like they were alive. Then Ron kicks the horses and spurs them and handles them like they're made of steel, and they love him for it. No understanding them."'

'Makes no sense.' Austin looked at her pitying. 'One day she'll be alright, she knows everything, talks to you sensibly. Then next day she doesn't know who I am. Some times she thinks I'm her father. Then she talks to me as though she doesn't know me.'

'Cain is a good boy, a nice boy,' Diana chanted and leaned across and ruffled John's hair. 'He's a good boy. He loves his gramma, doesn't he.'

'This is John,' Austin insisted.

'John! John!' Diana started. 'It is not John . . . You're not John . . . who are you? You're . . . you're . . .'

Her face screwed up and she concentrated, trying to get it right.

'We went to a few doctors. Most of them said there was nothing to do for it. "Premature ageing of the brain," Doctor Menzies said. "Nothing you can do about it. You're welcome to look around if you want, get another opinion." There's this Chinese Doctor, Hung, he says if she takes these pills he reckons it can regenerate the brain. Along with vitamin pills. I left the pills with her. Then she got sick. When I took her to the doctor he found out she was taking too many pills. Forgot she had taken them. Took another lot five minutes later. Now I keep the pills, and I've got to give them to her.'

'Bloody pills!' she exclaimed, and swung her arm in an arc across the table. 'Can't stand the bloody pills. Just as soon they let me die. I'd rather die than put up with this . . . what's the point of livin', if all you got to live for is them bloody pills?'

'You've got to take them, Diana, Di-Di, or it gets worse.'

'Get worse! What could be bloody-well worse?'

'It is because you're not well,' Austin insisted, desperately.

'Want to die then. I want to die.'

'Goes on and on.'

'My house, they took my house. They signed it out from under me, they didn't ask me. I didn't sign nothing and they signed the papers. You're so tall. How did I get someone so tall? Little fellow like me! How did I? I don't know you, don't try that. You can't bloody well go to bed with me. What do you think I am, hard up or something?'

'Time for the tablets.'

Austin leaned behind him and scrabbled in a drawer and found two jars of tablets. He counted three tablets onto his palm and held them out. Diana hit out and they flew over the floor. Austin climbed under the table and picked them up.

'Just because you're an engineer doesn't mean,' she ranted and glared, 'you can come across here!'

Chapter 5

'You can have them if you like,' Austin said. 'I'd rather you have them.'

'How many shares are there?' John asked.

Scraping of a pencil on a piece of paper.

'Two thousand eight hundred and five Perrett Mining, four thousand West Broken Hill Mining, six thousand five hundred and twenty-six Barrett Explorations.'

John covered the telephone handset and coughed.

'They want to foreclose?'

'This is the letter.' His father spoke carefully and precisely. 'It says: "Mr Austin Evans. Dear Mr Evans, Re: variation of your short-term advance from Brash. We enclose herewith epitome of mortgage in relation to the further variation of this short term advance. Please note that the next payment of interest falls due on 26th August 1985 and must be forwarded direct to Mr and Mrs T. Brash of 213 Eckhardt Parade, Karingal. To arrive on or prior to the due date. Please note that the new payment is $162.70. Failure to forward the above will result in foreclosure. Should you have any queries in this matter, please do not hesitate to contact us. Yours faithfully Joseph Simpson and Company, per Jill Legge." '

Austin sounded proud that he read it out correctly.

'What are the conditions?' John didn't understand, didn't want to understand. He asked, desperate for time.

The sound of paper being turned. Austin cleared his throat. His voice sounded thin and old.

'The principal is $11 000 . . . principal repayable 26th October 1983 . . . interest $24.00 per centum per annum, reducible to $17.75 per centum per annum if paid on due dates . . .'

'What was the loan for?'

'Ellen's rent. She couldn't pay three months' rent for the second real estate agency. I borrowed it. It kept her going. She doesn't know how to handle money. Spends it like water. Hangs on to nothing, goes out every night. No money to pay bills but she can go out to party every night, with her girlfriends. Cain stays there when he comes back from the private school. He tells us what goes on.'

The enormity of it, the innocence, the stupidity, the naive greed.

'You still loaned her the money?'

'She couldn't keep going otherwise . . . the house was already mortgaged to the business. She told me the other day I better go down and pay the bills, or I wasn't going to have a house to live in.'

'You've got to let me think.'

'That's fair, but it's a bargain. You buy them, you can have them.'

John had a thought.

'How much are they on the stock exchange now?'

'They've been stable for months.'

'Check it out for the next few days. I'll call you back . . .'

'The next week, or they foreclose.'

'Friday. I'll call you Friday.'

'They're going up. They're rising. They've been jumping up two cents a day.' Austin could hardly control his excitement.

John tapped the telephone handset and thought.

'That's what they want them for,' Austin gurgled.

'It's hard, telling when they're going to peak,' John added.

'That's what they want them for. I got another letter today, saying they're very sorry, but they want payment or they're going to foreclose. Monday.'

'They know that they're going to go up—say, until the end of next week. Then they sell.'

'A tidy profit too. They're very sorry. They say they're very sorry.'

'Here is what I suggest,' said John carefully. 'I have enough money to pay the debt. I have to borrow some. Now, how much do you get at present prices if you pay off the mortgage and sell now?'

The pencil scratched again.

'Let me see—two thousand three hundred and forty-three dollars thirty-nine cents, approximately.' He grunted with satisfaction.

'How about . . . how about . . . I pay the mortgage. Then next week—say Wednesday—we check whether they're still rising. We sell, as near to the peak as we can. Then I take back my money, and you keep the difference.'

'Less interest.'

'How much interest would there be over a few days?'

He meant the question rhetorically, but the pencil started scratching.

'Seventy-eight dollars, approximately.'

'I'll phone the stock exchange and ask around. You don't have a broker?'

'No.'

'When I find the best deal, I'll call back. We'll go and pay the mortgage Monday.'

'The last day!' Austin said gleefully.

'Then we'll check how the prices are going.'

'They stayed steady for ages. Now they're going up.'

Joseph Simpson, solicitor, did get a surprise. He invited Austin into his office and waved them to a small battery of black leather chairs with rounded armrests.

'We're going to pay the mortgage.' Austin smiled.

Joseph Simpson allowed himself to smile. It was a small deal, not enough to get upset about.

'You have . . . a cheque?'

He looked at John.

John placed a bank cheque for the amount on the table. Joseph Simpson reached across and pulled the strings of his venetian blind. It was still morning, and the light from the concrete path opposite dazzled, and the traffic was loud. Later in the day it became quieter. Then, when the shadow moved across the street and the cars belonged to suburban shoppers instead of rush hour commuters, he would open the blinds and look out. The house across the road had built a shield of gum trees and shrubs. The shrubs all blossomed with small delicate white and pink and blue flowers. In a few weeks they would be gone, burned by the sun. Meantime, for perhaps six weeks, Sydney was full of delicate blossoms and perfumes. He liked the strong, sensual smell of jasmine. Joseph Simpson did not think that he was an altogether practical man, because practical men did not like the smell of jasmine. It suggested, even to Mr Simpson, that he had a weakness. Something rotten and decayed, something not right.

He turned back with an effort to concentrate on the matter at hand. The old man was simple. The daughter had taken him to the cleaners and if he had any scruples about taking the old man's money, then his daughter certainly would not.

'We haven't met before.' He smiled at John.

'I'm the black sheep.' The untidy man with dark brown hair beginning to thin at the front and a nose turned noticeably to the left spoke in a sing-song voice.

'That isn't true!' Exclaimed Austin.

John looked at his father sideways. Simpson guessed that John had false teeth. He did not really like false teeth or workmen but he had a growing dislike of Ellen. Once, she ordered him around and called him on the phone in the middle of an interview without apologising. She patronised him, and called him 'Joseph'. An upstart, but it had not been wise to say anything then. He was certain. He had always thought her an upstart. He shuddered that he had been addressed in that presumptuous, familiar manner. He would like her to be crushed, humiliated, destroyed. Meantime, there was his professional reputation to consider. He would be quite happy to see Ellen destroyed by someone with false teeth. As for the money, it wasn't *that* much. It was worth it.

'They used to say I was the black sheep, too.' He bestowed a professional smile. 'Sowed a few wild oats.'

'The shares.'

'The shares, of course. You know something about shares, Mr Evans? Mr Evans Junior, I mean.'

'Not very much.'

'We could perhaps make an offer, take the shares off your hands, for a mutually acceptable price?'

He thought John Evans had an unpleasant, somewhat mad laugh. A lot too loud. Common. It went in the family.

Evans controlled himself with an effort.

'I think we'll just pay the mortgage and run.'

'You're a shrewd man, I can tell, Mr Evans.' Simpson did not bother to disguise his contempt. No other member of the family had even suspected the depth of his contempt, the knowledge of his superiority.

'Modest and not ambitious, I think, Mr Simpson.'

'You have come to the rescue of your father?'

'I am here to give you a cheque.'

The old man went ahead. Joseph Simpson walked just behind him and laughed.

'Well Austin how is the business going?'

'It's a bad business. You know they are trying to get the house? The bank has appointed a new manager. Hard man. He won't take any nonsense. Says the wages have to be paid by him. She doesn't get to look at the wages book.'

'How did it all happen?' He queried with stage surprise.

'The Tax Department. She could put it over the bank. She put it over me and she put it over you, but when she didn't pay the tax she took out of everyone's wages they got her.'

'Never take on the government!' He wagged his head sagely.

'That's what I say. And Diana, she's got . . . Alzheimer's disease . . . premature ageing of the brain . . .'

'Bad. Bad.'

The old man walked on.

'Any time you need a lawyer, Mr Evans,' he said quietly.

John started.

'Any time,' he repeated meaningfully before turning away.

344

It took a lot of practice to know just when to turn away.

For two days, he held off selling the shares. Each afternoon, Austin called on the telephone and told him what the prices were. By Thursday, they began to go down.

John had found a broker. A firm which sold shares as a job lot, rather than taking as their fee a percentage of the transaction. Glen Garden and Company were based in Melbourne, he was told by a rather formal girl on a switchboard, but they had intentions.

'You mean ambitions?' John asked.

'We intend to fulfil our ambitions.' The telephonist responded haughtily.

'Job lots. Seventy-five dollars a lot?'

'That is correct, sir.'

On the Friday morning at ten o'clock John arrived outside the address a few minutes early. He stood on the steps of the new white concrete and glass building. All around him, similar tall buildings shut off the light. It was a cloudy, dull day. The shadows were fuzzy against the walls. Now that the rush hour was over and commuters had mostly gone inside, Pitt Street was dismal and deserted. A fine rain slanted down, spotting the pavement.

His parents arrived fifteen minutes late. His father was wearing his best grey suit and a pair of brown brogue shoes, which seemed very out of fashion. Diana screwed up her face when she saw him. She was wearing a tartan wool dress and a green jumper.

'How are you love,' she addressed John.

He kissed her on the cheeks.

'I been saying that I want to go back home, you know. I've had enough of this place. How about we go home.'

She looked at John firmly.

'She wants to go back to Broken Hill,' Austin whispered. 'She thinks we still know people there.'

'I want to go home,' Diana insisted. She folded her arms and looked up at a company crest above the automatic glass doors.

345

A middle-aged man in a dark suit walked through with a large file of papers, and pushed past. She glared as he went down the steps, his fashionable black leather shoes ringing on the clean polished marble.

'Who does he think he is?' Diana said loudly, turning in a semi-circle to the street so that anybody could hear her.

Austin touched her arm.

'We should go inside.'

'I don't care who bloody-well hears me, I don't.' She stamped. 'Who does he think he is?'

The man was moving across the street lightly, skipping as though there were traffic to avoid. Once across he turned and walked briskly into a small street between two huge buildings, one circular and long and the other squat and square.

Austin looked quietly down at his feet. In a few seconds, Diana's angry expression became hesitant and confused. Austin looked up and registered the change.

'Well,' he sounded relieved. 'We had better go upstairs. To business.'

They walked together to the bank of lifts, past a desk where a man with a green uniform and a peaked hat sat reading a newspaper. Austin walked near enough to be accosted. The man did not look up.

'He has a good job,' Austin remarked once they were inside a lift.

'You have some shares that you would like to sell?'

The young man sitting behind the small desk with a visual display unit and a pad was diplomatic enough to look curious. He might have been nineteen. His suit was light and summery, and even the way he wore his tie gave an impression of lightness and informality.

'My father has some shares.'

Partly grudgingly, almost proudly, Austin took the envelope from his inside coat pocket. The young man opened the envelope and checked the shares.

346

'A good time to sell, Mr Evans.' He looked up and smiled from one to the other.

'Yes,' Austin sounded slightly numbed, but could not stop himself from preening.

The young man touched a few buttons and a series of lines came up on the VDU. He checked them over, and scribbled a note on the pad.

'We can get—let me see—someone in the market for a few hundred of these in Melbourne—the rest at . . .'

Austin leaned forward and gazed intently at the magic machine. His eyes shone.

'Fifteen thousand six hundred and eight dollars and twenty-six cents!'

'Approximately,' Austin nodded.

'Precisely,' the young man responded with a self-satisfied smile.

'Is that enough?' Austin asked.

'They have peaked, I think,' the young man smiled. 'You can never tell of course. Someone could still want them. A takeover in the offing—when that happens there's no saying when it might stop.'

Austin looked at him, stubbornly seeking a certain, the right answer.

'I can't say for sure. Really I can't.' The young man swivelled on his chair and chewed the end of his pencil.

'You think there's a takeover.'

'An offer—but you can't tell when they'll drop it. Then they could go down quicker than they went up.'

'We must sell.'

Austin eyed John resentfully.

'We must,' John repeated firmly.

The young man sat silent until it was resolved.

'It's certain then? Good. We will see how we go. Must get in fast, or someone else could pick up the buyer. A matter of seconds.'

'With the computer?'

347

'Connected up all over Australia. Brokers everywhere can get into it, make offers, sales, buy . . .'

The young man tapped the keyboard rapidly and pressed a button.

'Austin was always good at numbers.' Diana spoke for the first time.

The young man sat back and watched the screen closely. Austin craned his head forward to see. A series of numbers, then a question-mark.

'They are prepared to buy.'

'Yes.'

A little more typing, then another press of the button.

'Done!' The young man clapped his hands together.

Austin was enchanted.

The young man wrote out a cheque for the amount, less the fees.

The drizzle was still falling as they left the building. Austin held Diana's arm in case she slipped on the wet marble. Diana seemed vulnerable, old and delicate. On the footpath they hesitated. A couple of taxis cruised past.

'Where is the stock exchange?' Austin asked. 'I know it is somewhere near here.'

'I think it's along there.'

John pointed to the narrow street between the two buildings.

'I never saw a machine as good as that one up there.' Austin spoke with complete sincerity. 'You could be in Sydney and you can sell shares to someone in Perth, just like that. In a second.'

'You could do it to New York too, if you were rich enough,' John added.

'I want to see.'

The stock exchange was below ground level. They paused at the steps. A magnetic neon tape above ground level ran through the prices of stock. HESSON STEEL LTD 36C . . . TIMOR PLASTICS 25C . . . SIGNOR EXPLORATIONS 41.2C . . .

'That's interesting!' Austin exclaimed.

Diana looked closely. Her eyes were dull and she held onto her husband's arm tightly.

The stock exchange was on two levels. The upper level was carpeted and had a battery of red telephones against the wall, and a few low tables with business magazines strewn across their shiny red surface. The level was divided from the lower gallery by a thick perspex screen. On the wall, the magnetic tape running with prices. On the floor, men played with small visual display units similar to the one used by the young man. The wall below the magnetic tape was lit up with the names of companies and the prices constantly changed and altered.

On the upper floor, Austin worked his way gradually through the cluster of businessmen against the perspex. Diana followed him docilely holding his hand. When finally Austin reached the perspex he pressed his nose against it and stared as the lights moved up and down, the prices, the numbers.

John stood not far behind, tall enough to see, embarrassed again. When Austin turned and smiled at him, he was taken back to the day he arrived home with their first car, his first car.

'Come and look. Look at this!' His father was all boyish delight. Like the day with the first car, only more so. It was joy, those electronic numbers. There was proof. The world did work like that.

Slowly, for the first time, John grinned at his father.

'Yes, I can see,' he said.

Instantly, as though he couldn't stand to be away from it, Austin turned and pressed his nose to the perspex. Diana leaned quietly against his shoulder as he reached up and with his other hand involuntarily clawed at the screen.

Thirty minutes later, he stepped back from the perspex. His face was still flushed. He sat at one of the low tables. A businessman walked past and looked at him, a little oddly. Austin did not care.

'Do you want to have a coffee?' He asked, but reluctantly. There was something else, something more he wanted to do, but he could not do it.

John nodded.

'You can stay here,' he said. 'I've got to go back to work.'

He added 'worse luck' when Austin looked at him curiously.

'When do we go home?' Asked Diana.

Although she did not mean that home.

As Austin led her from the building, he looked back, longingly, at the wall full of electric numbers.

Chapter 6

Dear John,

Re: Property at present belonging to Austin and Diana.

It has recently come to my attention that the abovementioned premises are to be repossessed by the Bank, in foreclosure of the debt taken out by Austin. This would not, I am sure, be an event which any of us would desire to see.

I did previously suggest that you could buy this property. If you are still interested, then I can inform you that you could acquire the premises at an amount significantly below the market value. I would be prepared to offer on your behalf, the amount of $90,000. I have reason to believe that the bank would look favourably on such an offer from a member of the family, which would defray some of the debt. The house would probably be worth $110,000—120,000 at current market value, although if it went to auction then it might go for considerably less than this.

If you are willing to make an offer please contact me during business hours.

Yours etc.

Ellen.

'They told me nothing would happen. At least for a year.' Austin spoke slowly.

'I'll arrange for you to see a lawyer.' John paused. 'I don't have the money to buy your house,' he added.

There was no response.

'I'll pay for the lawyer.'

Dear Mr Evans,

We have now had the opportunity of considering copies of the bank mortgage and the bank charge, which were supplied by your father.

The documents appear to be in order. Given that your parents had knowledge of the nature of the documents and of the poor financial condition of the relevant company, it seems to us that the documents are binding on your parents.

Your suggestion that your parents should seek sympathy from the bank and suggest that the bank defer action under the mortgage for the balance of their lives, was a very good one. We have urged your father to approach the bank along these lines as soon as possible.

We understand that your sister was the managing director of the company. Your father mentioned she had some large deals still to be settled. If those deals started in the course of the company's business, then any profits that she realizes from those deals should be paid to the company. The fact that the company is being wound up does not mean that the company loses its rights to claim those potential profits. For that reason your parents would be well advised to keep an eye on your sister's further activities, and keep the liquidator posted.

We shall now close our file. Our account is enclosed. Thank you for your instructions.

Yours faithfully,
Joseph Simpson.

'He wasn't much good, that fellow Simpson,' Austin complained. 'I called him up and asked him what to do, and he told me there was nothing except to go there with my cap in hand and beg!'

'Perhaps it's the truth.'

'He was paid to help me.'

'At least we know where we stand,' John commented.

Austin wanted to say he hadn't thought of that before. But he had.

'Why do you want to go back to Broken Hill?' Austin sounded very puzzled. 'You never liked it there.'

'I don't really know, except that I have holidays. There is nowhere else to go.'

'They promised they wouldn't be foreclosing. Not straight away.

The manager at the bank told me to write a letter, and I wrote it. Saying that we were pensioners. Where would we go if we were thrown out, and that. Also what would happen if the newspapers wrote about it, wouldn't it reflect badly on them. He sent it in to the main directors. Straight to the top it goes, he says.'

'Nothing will happen in the next two weeks?'

'He says it will be a while before they decide. Meantime, Ellen is still trying to get the money for that big government development. Gavin, that salesman she hired, did a deal with another agency. Now he says they get part of it, and she had nothing to do with it. I told her he was hanging out for more. She should have given him more and settled. Now he's done a deal with another agency. He gets half, they get half, and she gets nothing.'

'What does she think?'

'She knows everything, like always.'

'You can have a key to the flat, just in case.'

'No need!' He protested.

'I had to get out,' he told Ethel over the table at the Willyama hotel. 'It was like going back twenty years. Having my head held under while someone pulls the chain.'

'Weird you came back here.'

Ethel put her hand to her mouth to cover a small belch.

'Back into the sewerage line itself, I suppose.'

'For you. You never left the place.'

It was a Wednesday. Still so cold that he could feel the wind although he wore a heavy jumper. He walked automatically towards the old family home. When he arrived he scarcely paused. A few more cracks had appeared in the slabs of concrete he had mixed and put down with his father. Nothing had been planted to replace the garden that had been ripped out when Austin and Diana had sold.

As he approached the edge of the town, he began to sweat,

353

despite the cold. A few things had changed. A new high school had been placed at the beginning of the track he had followed more than thirty years before with his grandmother. Past the high school, he climbed slowly through a barbed wire fence. A woman hanging out washing in the yard of a red brick house looked at him, but not for long. He walked through the low bushes and stunted trees. The strong decaying smell of the bush, acrid and strong. He followed his senses. Each dried waterbed, each low hill, each hole scooped from the side of a mound and filled with rusting iron, was both familiar and distant. Each item was familiar and each could have been the same as any other.

He was surprised when he saw the ridge made of old cars and broken glass. It was further away and more to the left than he remembered, but the glass still sparkled in the sunlight. It took him a long while to get to the hill of broken glass. He did not allow himself to stop. The prickles caught in his socks and scraped his legs. He had to brush through delicate spider-webs strung between the bushes. Recalling what he used to do, he picked up a stick and waved it before him, breaking the spider-webs as he went.

If he had stopped and thought, with the discomfort of the spiders, the sweat, the smell, he would have turned back.

He climbed slowly to the top of the hill of glass. There, he paused. It was a place he had liked when he was a boy. An earth of ashes, fine and velvet. Nothing would grow in it. The weeds grew from the old car bodies that had been pitched into the gullies on their sides before he was born and still remained there, glassless, tyreless, rusted engine blocks full of drifting sand. Someone had dug a few shallow holes. Old medicine bottles and jars rested on the side. Not many people came there, although a bicycle track weaved around the mounds. What would they have come for? A myth. An impression of the world after a nuclear war. Fine ash. Skimps. Dust. John thought about archaeologists of the future digging at the heap of rubble with toothbrushes and trays. He recalled that he had, once, tried to create the scene

354

of a murder, so that he could enjoy the thought of investigators pecking through false clues.

The smell of decay wasn't as strong on top of the hill of glass. There wasn't anything left to die. Still compelled, he walked on.

The hills became higher. The old mines and chunks of scattered mica spread out. The bushes were taller and the spiders were larger. He stopped. Aubrey's hut had been on a slope, near an old mine. From the slope, he could recollect the old man standing and pointing off at the town in the distance. The pension. He wanted to be able to live quietly and comfortably and not have to walk into town with his varicose veins.

John followed the slope of the hills, checking the sight of the town, waiting for a memory or a clue. Finally he found it. A few broken pieces of glass. An old shaft. A bent piece of corrugated iron. He sat and picked a prickle from his socks, and tried to remember his friend, and wondered why it was that he had come.

Kerry's father leaned against the steel pole at the end of his verandah. He carefully rolled his own.

'While since we seen you.' He licked the paper and looked up. The side of the house was still cluttered with motorbike parts. A new Japanese truck was parked at the side.

'Passing through.' John decided to be equally non-committal.

'How's the old man?'

'Same as ever.'

'Same as ever. He retired at the right time. Got out of town. Smarter than I thought he was.'

'Eh?'

'The skimp dumps over there.' He indicated with a finger the direction of the black mountains of waste that ran through the centre of the town and dominated the skyline. 'They set hard a couple of years ago, so we stopped getting that black dust on everything with the wind. Now the unions are weak. The companies been moving in trucks and hauling it away. You remember how big they was?'

John stared. The dumps did look altered.

'The old ones they're taking away. But if you look over the side, they're building a new one.'

There was another mountain, rising almost as high as the first. New gunmetal-coloured sand, glittering and dull.

'The dust is worse now than it was in the old days. The lead gets into the tankwater.'

'Lead?'

'Mrs Keenan down the road, the old woman although she wasn't that old then if you remembered her, she kept on blowing the fuse in her electric jug. Every month or two she had to get a new fuse. Once she had enough of that so she brought in an electrician to look at it. He looked at it and said, "You're using rainwater eh." "How did you know?" She asked. "It's the best water. Come out of the sky, got nothing in it, no problems." "Problem is the dumps," says the electrician. "I'm not supposed to say it because nobody's proved it yet and the mining companies, they all say it can't happen. Healthy enough so babies can live on it, they don't need mother's milk, they reckon. But take it from me Missus since those dumps been shifted and those trucks been working, anybody who uses rainwater in their electric jug gets trouble." "How does that work?" asks the old woman. So he holds up the core, where it's all corroded. "See that," he says, "if you take that down and get it analysed I'd take a bet they'd say it's lead." "They can't do that, lead's poison," she says. "Don't get angry with me, I didn't put it there," the electrician reckons. Mrs Keenan, she went up and down the street telling everyone, but they don't care. All scared of losing their jobs. For me, it don't matter, I retire in two years. But they got everything on time payment. They can't afford it. When she come up to me she looked real shitty. "They can't do that, it's not legal." She waves this piece of paper at me. "They're doin' it though, and there's not much you can do about it." She always was a bit funny. Used the tankwater because she doesn't like fluoride only now the tap water is healthier.'

While the old man was speaking John ran his eye along the

356

top of the dump. Trucks moving slowly along the top of the skimps, and dust.

'What you doing now?'

'Working.'

'Working.' The old man drew back on the cigarette. His head was almost bald now and his hair was thin. 'That's what we all do. Work. For the bastards that do that, and reckon we're whingeing if we complain.'

He laughed.

'Sound like Mrs Keenan,' John leaned back against the cement brick verandah ledge.

'She's alright, she is. Trouble is nobody will take her serious. They don't want to. I wish I had her guts.'

John tried, but he couldn't remember who Mrs Keenan was.

He looked into the hotel where he had last seen Bob Sharkey collecting glasses. The place looked the same, except that the lino had been pulled up from the floor. The men who sat on stools and leaned against the bar might have been the same men as were there two years before, or twenty, or seventy.

John walked in self-consciously. He felt the eyes on him, and the attention of the barman who deliberately kept wiping glasses with his eyes turned down.

The men sat immobile as he circled the bar, seeking a way to the counter. Finally he found a spot on a corner and insinuated himself, and leaned his elbows on the red plastic top. He ordered a beer. When the glass arrived, a flat glass with a shallow head of foam, he asked after Bob Sharkey.

'Who?'

'Bob Sharkey, the champ. Used to work here.'

'I'm a casual, only been here a few weeks.' The barman retreated.

'Since he left the mines, before they give him the boot,' a man called in a deep laugh.

John turned to see who it was who spoke. The voice sounded friendly enough. Most of the faces in the bar were laughing at

357

the joke, although when he looked, the expression closed.

'You mean old Bob?' A short thickset man in a check shirt spoke from a table behind him.

'Could be.'

'About . . . I don't know how old. Got the DTs, a bit punchy. Would have been a fighter once, yes.'

'Sounds like him'

'They couldn't keep him on here any longer. There's too many unemployed young blokes, can't get on the mines, on strike when they are, so there's not enough money. He went somewhere. Adelaide, I think. Got people down there.'

John nodded.

'A pity it is, because he would have been a good worker in his day. There's not enough money coming in now.'

John felt the murmur of assent around the bar. In a recession, nobody was going to worry too much about Robert Sharkey.

On Friday night, there should have been late night shopping. John walked to Argent Street alone. Ethel looked at him as he went, but made no attempt to join him.

It was never as empty as that, John thought to himself. He stood beneath the statue of the World War One soldier throwing a hand-grenade, less than a block away from where his grandfather had first climbed from the train. The wind blew across the skimp dumps, and fine dust cut his skin. The road before him was tarmac. A few lights glowed dismally from the shopfronts. He walked on to the post office. No girls stood on the corner, no boys cruised past gaily in old cars, skylarking and calling careless obscenities.

A car did pull slowly to the kerb and stop. A woman climbed from the passenger seat and pulled her dress over her knees when the wind tugged. She scrambled across the path to drop a letter in the mail slot, then scrambled just as quickly back.

The milk bars that had not changed were there. Where once rows of girls with bows in their hair and coarse, fresh skin served milkshakes and lime spiders, a single middle-aged man wiped the counter with a rag.

358

'I think I know you.'

John was startled at the voice. A figure appeared from the entrance to an arcade. John blinked and stared. A small, slightly stooped man, of his own age. A fine bone structure with wrinkled skin. He could be old. The form that this man would take when he was old was clear. Yes, the man was familiar. John racked his brain, trying to remember.

'I don't know your name either, so it doesn't matter. You mind company?'

John assented uneasily.

'The place has changed a lot,' the man said as they began to pace side by side.

'I've been away a while,' John answered.

The man nodded wisely.

'I worked in that shop back there for twenty years, since I left school.' He leaned his head to the side, indicating a men's wear shop. 'Used to be seven people worked there. By the time I got the bullet, I was the only one, except for the boss. Except every time he needed a holiday he hired me back again, no casual rates, he couldn't afford that, and the odd few weeks it was busy. Then I was out of work two, close on three, years. He got a motel for his daughter and son-in-law, but they was too useless to run it. So I got hired under the scheme from the CES that paid most of my wages for six months, and I did it all, until the scheme ran out. Then I got the bullet again.'

'Married?'

'I would have gone to Adelaide or somewhere if I was married, but on my own it don't matter so much. I know people here. Never got married, don't own no house or car, no debts. Got a room and a colour television and a video I brought from a school-kid for twenty dollars. Walk around most of the time. When I'm sixty-five I get the pension. I'm forty-four now. I'm waiting until I'm sixty-five.'

'Something to look forward to.'

They reached the corner of Argent and Oxide streets.

As suddenly as he appeared, the man turned on his heel and

walked into the darkness along Oxide Street. As he went through a patch of light cast by a hotel, he raised his arm in farewell. Then he disappeared. From where he was standing, John could see a single couple sitting at the table against the wall of the pub. They were drinking slowly and intently. The man wore a felt hat and the woman was a little too ample and a little too old for the dress she was wearing. There was something bitter in the way neither of them looked at one another.

'Thank you for staying.' Ethel kissed him lightly on the cheeks as he was about to climb onto the train.

'I'll see you next time.' John was aware that he was being quite indifferent to the woman who had been his best friend. He had sat most of the time in morose silence, which she had not attempted to interrupt. Although she liked to talk about the goings on of the day and found great relief in doing so, she had maintained a stoic silence.

There was the shock of standing on top of a hill of broken glass and ash. He had needed immersion in the inarticulate solitude of his youth.

From the platform, he stared up at the new mountain of skimps. When the train began to jump, he pulled his gaze down, and was startled to see that Ethel's eyes were damp.

'See you later darlin'.' She pushed him onto the train and stepped back and waved as the train departed.

360

Chapter 7

John had been back in Sydney for a week. He had dutifully phoned his parents once, and heard that his sister was being declared bankrupt. Austin had talked to the bank manager. Nothing was happening, it seemed nothing more could be done. Because Austin didn't want anything to happen, it seemed that everything would go on as before. It was still spring. Each afternoon John walked around the beachfront, or along the back streets, listening to the growing discontent which came each year with the heat. The lush smell of jasmine was still strong, but before long the small flowers would be scorched by the sun. Families squabbled in flats and the screeching carried through the open windows down to the streets, where couples loitered and held hands and men sat on fences drinking beer.

On Saturday nights there were parties, and on the weekend the coffee lounges facing the beach front were full of people smoking and talking intently over coffee. John walked quietly past, aware of his middle age. Once a young man pushed past him and swore. When John turned, prepared to fight, a girl plucked at the young man's shoulder.

'Come on,' she jeered. 'He's too old!'

In the morning, syringes which had been thrown in the front yard of the flat were collected by the elderly caretaker. She went out with a small plastic bucket. After a few weeks, she gave them to the local member of parliament, who told her that he was dismayed. There were not enough police on the beat, but when his party was in office, that would be changed. Until then, he would draw the attention of the minister to her complaints.

It was a Monday night. He was sitting on his verandah looking at the tiny triangle of water in the distance. It was almost dark, and the street lights were flickering on, street by street, when the telephone went.

'I live next to your father,' a woman with a high voice told him. 'We found your telephone number, and your sister's, on a pad beside the telephone.'

'Yes,' John said, and waited. His parents were at an age. Such things had to be expected.

'Your sister didn't answer. We called a few times.' The voice altered pitch.

'I've never met you,' she added.

'Ellen may have shifted.'

'Your father has had a turn. Your mother came out into the front yard. I saw her there, waving her arms about. I asked her what happened, and she said your father had fallen.'

'I'll come.'

'Not here. The ambulance has taken him to the Point Hospital, with your mother. My husband went with them.'

He was almost on the freeway to the bridge when the car behind him turned his lights up to high beam. John let the car past. An old white Valiant driven by a man with a broad-brimmed cowboy hat. As he passed, the driver glared. John could see his lips move, but heard nothing.

The white car pulled into the lane in front of him and braked. John swore as he also braked abruptly. They continued, crawling slowly across the bridge. Each few yards the white Valiant stopped and then jumped forward. When John tried to change into another lane, the white car moved over also. Once John stopped altogether and waited. The white car moved on a few hundred metres, and waited also. The driver with his hat did not look around. His eyes watched John in the rear-vision mirror.

John was parked beside the first, southern, pillar of the Sydney Harbour Bridge. An electric train screamed past along the track beside the freeway. Other cars turned to the side.

Who was in the white car, what ghost, what power? He could have sat there indefinitely. He could park across the traffic lanes, and cause such a serious disruption that the police would be attracted. He knew that could be a mixed blessing. Police were not sympathetic to middle-aged storemen in old cars.

He began to move again, slowly and cautiously. The white car pulled out in front of him again. They crossed the bridge slowly. Every now and then, the white car accelerated and pulled away, changed lanes, invited him to compete.

'If I don't do anything he might get bored,' John said quite loud. The driver of the white car did not get bored. Instead, he crept along a short space ahead, now and then applying the brake quickly and sharply, then accelerating again.

They drove past North Sydney, with white buildings and neon signs above the sandstone lined with the vertical scars of diamond drills.

He edged his old car across the lane as he came to an exit. The white Valiant slowed and pulled beside him. The driver raised his grey stetson and smiled, then waved and accelerated along the highway.

It took him a while to get to the Point Hospital. The building was near one of the beaches where his family had gone for a holiday, years before. He saw his mother sitting inside the smudged glass doors. She looked up and smiled as he came in. A small man with track shoes and green trousers and a moustache was sitting with her.

'They've been keeping us a long time.' His mother smiled at him. 'Now you are here, we can go back home.'

'We can't go back home yet.'

'What about . . . the cows. We have to put the cows in the shed on a night like this!'

John sat down. The short man offered his hand.

'George Thomas,' he said manfully. 'I live next door. Hope you don't mind me staying with your mother.'

'Thank you for coming,' John mumbled politely.

'It was a shock, to everyone concerned. He . . . they . . . your parents both are regarded very highly in the neighbourhood.'

'Ooh . . . when he fell over I thought he was playing the fool. Get up you silly! I said to him. Then I looked at him. His face was all blue. That's not funny, I said, so I ran outside.'

A television was going on a stand in a corner of the room. An American comedy, where each time the comedian looked directly at the camera, someone turned on the canned laughter. Diana sat with her hands in her lap. George Thomas had to go.

It was an effort to stand.

'Sorry to have it happen . . . sorry,' George repeated. 'Very respected in the community. Everyone in the street knows them.'

John nodded.

The television show went on. His mother took his hand. A nurse pushed through the plastic flaps at the far end of the room and called for Mrs Evans.

An Indian doctor met them. His accented voice blurred as he spoke. He looked from one to the other, then settled his gaze on John.

'We have been trying to stimulate. The muscles of the heart are not working, which is very bad. Very bad. The prognosis is poor.'

Austin was stretched out on a trolley, a plastic face mask across his mouth and nose, but his startling blue eyes stared up. He tried to talk, but no words came out. Then he looked at John, and signalled with his finger to Diana.

'Isn't it marvellous what they can do now?' Diana sensed that an important response was needed. She stood there, holding on to her self-possession and a bone plastic handbag.

Two nurses wheeled the trolley away. John led Diana back to the room with the television and the glass walls, where they sat and drank several cups of cold weak coffee.

A nurse came out.

'He has perhaps fifteen minutes,' she said. 'If you want to go and see him.'

A blue curtain surrounded the bed. Diana stood there, still holding the handbag. The blue eyes followed her through the plastic face mask. Two nurses stood dutifully at either side of the pillow. Weakly, faltering, Austin held out his arms to his wife. Diana stared at him, still self-possessed, confused. Austin tried to speak. The words could not get through the plastic. He felt along the plastic tubes with his fingers, then suddenly gripped the mask and tore it off. One of the nurses leaned forward. Austin heaved himself past her, and threw his legs to the ground. He gripped Diana by the shoulder.

'Remember . . .' he called.

Diana stared, uncomprehending. The nurses grabbed him by the shoulders and pulled him back on the pillow. He struggled a little. The blue eyes were suddenly full of wonder, words that hadn't been said, things that hadn't been done, numbers, blue on blue. Numbers running horizontally down the curtain. Bubbles.

John stepped back, brushing the curtains aside. He turned. Ellen had arrived. John was weeping.

'Do you want to go in?'

Ellen looked at him keenly. She glanced in, then stepped away.

The three of them sat together in a small glassed-in room. Ellen was calm, even cheerful.

'Would you like another cup of coffee?' She asked her mother.

Diana drank another cup of coffee. The old woman looked pleased that someone took so much notice of her. One of the nurses came out and handed her his clothes, neatly wrapped in a bundle.

'They know he won't come out.' Diana picked through the clothes and found Austin's wrist-watch.

'A beautiful watch,' she mused as she turned it in her hand. 'He got that from the mine. Years in the mine, years ago he got it.'

For a short while, it seemed that his mother's personality had returned.

'It will be yours if you want it. We can't wear men's watches.'

'He is dead, if you want to go in,' the nurse said quietly.

'I'd prefer not,' said Ellen.

365

John walked through the blue curtains, with his mother. Austin looked quite peaceful. They held each other and wept. Diana walked several times around the body of her husband. She touched him once tenderly and asked John who this man was, but it was because she needed to know the relationship.

After a little while, John took her out to Ellen. Then he went back.

It was the first time he recalled touching his father's face.

'I'm sorry,' he said.

He was, for all that wasted time.

A doctor and a nurse walked past. The blue curtains weren't pulled across. He whispered some things, then walked away reluctantly, because there was more. When he went out, Ellen looked at him firmly.

'What do we do now?' She asked.

'I was about to ask the same question.'

'Who was he?' Diana asked in a querulous, old voice.

'Austin. He was your husband.' Ellen spoke in the manner she used to speak to very small children.

'It's alright to leave him. You can make the arrangements tomorrow,' they were told by a nurse.

Ellen waited until the nurse had gone. She leaned across and fiddled with the lace of Austin's shoe.

'Is there any objection to having him burned?' Her manner was glacial.

'I think his father was a Catholic. They object,' John said.

'He never talked about it.'

'I heard from Eric.'

'Wouldn't pay for the funeral,' grumbled Diana.

'I'll take Mum home.' Ellen patted her mother on the shoulder. At last they were alone. 'We have some good times together, don't we, Diana?'

'I don't always say what I like,' Diana returned sharply.

Chapter 8

'I have a position with an agency . . . the hours will be (scratch of a pencil on a piece of paper) twenty-two hours a week. The Real Estate Licensing Board wants to take away my licence. I'll fight them all the way if they try . . . I can work, but I need the big money that I can earn . . . the problem was a cash flow problem. We have had a good forty years and now we are having a bad trot—eighteen months or a year of it—but we'll get back. They can't take my licence! I have done nothing illegal. They can't accuse me of . . . what is it called . . . malpractice . . .'

'Fraud,' Cain interjected.

'Yes. Fraud. I'm working three jobs at the moment . . . shifted in here three months ago and they've sold this place, they sold the last place, that doesn't happen when there's no market. I'm holding on here so they'll have to pay my removal expenses.'

The audience was Aunt Mary, Austin's sister. She had never been to see them before, but she came for her brother's funeral. A tall well-dressed woman with pale skin and a husband much shorter than herself. Diana did not like her, but John could remember her saying that she married money, and made more of it. Now she sat in Ellen's flat beside Diana, and stared out of the window at the trees of the North Shore. Uncle Murray made drinks.

The carpet was white and hairy, and the furniture was also white, except for the table, which was glass and chrome.

'The furniture is so lovely.' Mary frowned, as from a great distance. 'How did you find such a place?'

'I could see the ferries passing from the last flat,' Ellen replied. 'It was on the harbour.'

'Wonderful,' the aunt breathed airily.

Name ....

Address ....

Name/address of next of kin ....

....

Pensioner number (if applicable) ....

Medical Benefit Fund ....

The woman was handsome, middle-aged. Severe tortoise-shell spectacles. She stood and walked around the desk to get Diana to sign.

'What newspapers should we put the death and funeral notice in?'

She went back back behind the desk and tapped a pen on the blotter. A large white empty square. John looked into it.

'The *Manly Daily* and the *Barrier Daily Truth*,' Ellen said with authority.

John nodded.

'Yes we have lots of friends.' Diana smiled.

'What profession should we have? Was he retired?'

'He never retired,' Ellen said. 'He was a company director.'

'He was a shift boss on the mine,' John contradicted.

'That was a long time ago.'

'Before he retired.'

'Floral tributes.' The middle-aged woman interrupted.

'Yes. I'll have some flowers, a wreath inscribed "To dad with love from Ellen and Cain."'

'What about the roses from his own garden? He grew them. It seems appropriate."

'A floral tribute is so nice.'

'A single rose is fifteen dollars.' The woman tipped the tortoise-shell glasses down her nose.

'A bunch of three, at least,' Ellen bargained. John was paying.

'Do you wish to see him before cremation?'

There were things he had not said.

'I would,' Ellen enthused. 'They do them out beautifully. You come too, you ought to see.'

Another wonder of the world, another sight, another superficial miracle.

'I don't want to see.' Diana was firm.

Ellen pouted at the continuation of an ancient injustice.

The woman produced photographs of the crematorium.

'The grounds are lovely,' said Diana.

'They are beautiful gardens, excellently maintained,' said the lady with a smile.

'Austin always loved the garden. Do you remember the garden in Broken Hill?'

'The wording of the article,' the lady added gently after a pause. She began to write:

'In loving memory of Austin Evans, in tribute from his loving wife Diana, children Ellen and John, grandson Cain, sister of Mary . . .'

'That's enough,' said John.

John sat at his parents' home with his mother. Neighbours called. A stumpy intelligent woman with a bunch of flowers and an earthy voice, and a young pregnant woman.

'It was so quick. He was so fit to the end.' The pregnant woman sat on the lounge. Small blue veins ran down her legs.

'Yes it was quick. His mother went like that,' John observed.

'He was good to me, he spoiled me,' Diana cried. 'Now I can't remember anything. How I'll get on without him I don't know!'

The stumpy woman threw her arms around Diana's shoulders. But finally, no one knew what to say.

There were his father's papers. In the drawer, the money left over from the sale of the shares, the notes bundled together with rubber bands and tucked neatly into the corner, the coins separated and counted. A cheque account with sixteen dollars and forty cents in it.

Three cardboard boxes, with letters from the bank. Huge debts. Account books filled in, debit and credit in Austin's precise fussy writing, which had become spidery as he grew older. Debts. More debts. Loans. More than a quarter of a million dollars. Papers which were so neat, margins, additions. A small yellow sheet of paper, covered with numbers, subtractions and divisions. In a small rectangle of clear paper, the writing had become so spidery as to be almost indecipherable. "Who's God believe in? No one." "Then he's a atheist." At the bottom of the wardrobe, another small box. Another bundle of papers, coloured red, blue, green. Lottery cards, entries in competitions, win a four-bedroom spacious family home on the Gold Coast, second prize a new Toyota four-wheel drive, plus one hundred consolation prizes. Houses. The first prize was always a house. Coloured pictures of bungalows set back on spacious blocks, views, trees, driveways with lock-up garages, paths, rockeries, lawns, rose bushes, shrubs. Double storey, single storey. Famous tennis players smiling in the driveway. He was astonished and moved to find that they had all been bought in his name.

Then the photographs. Old photographs, some of people he did not know, the photographs that he had looked through when he was a boy. The photographs that he took away. Old, poor, cracked photographs, grey snapshots. Intuitively, he knew that it was the photographs he wanted. He left most of the rest, except for a few important papers, the lottery tickets and the money. He wondered at how precise his father was with papers, and how chaotic was his mind.

Ellen walked in and sat down heavily. In the manner of a Commander-In-Chief she leaned forward and linked her fingers on the table.

'What is the estate?'

'A bit of money and one car.'

'I need a new car now. Leave it in the garage for a while.'

370

'Diana needs the money. We should sell the car.'

'I paid for that car.'

'It's in her name. It should be sold for her expenses.'

'What expenses? She doesn't have any expenses.'

'When the bank takes the house.'

'That won't happen for years—not if I can sell . . .'

'That's good.' He managed a dry bitter tone.

'Let me tell you now why I am working, darling,' She breathed hard. 'Do you know that any director of a company is liable for two years after the resignation?'

'That is not my advice.'

'That is not the point.'

'I don't want to know about your affairs.'

'You've had it light,' She screamed, suddenly. 'You've been sheltered. All your life you've been sheltered, you've had nothing but fun. Never worked. Never cared about anyone except yourself.'

John was not surprised by the loss of control. He sat silent, interested in what was said, the tone of grief and sincerity.

'Responsibility!' She screamed and hit the table. 'All my life I've had responsibility!'

Diana suddenly put her head in the room.

'What's this about? Who are you yelling to?'

'What do you want, mother?' Asked Ellen, suddenly regaining control.

'Leave me alone.' The old woman threw an arm up, as though she was about to serve a tennis ball. 'Up your arse.'

Ellen laughed.

'I think I'll stay tonight,' John said.

'You can, if you want to.' Ellen stood up and walked from the room, stepping lightly. 'So long.'

He could hear her footsteps go down the path, the roar as she started her car.

'I haven't seen Una for ages,' Diana grumbled. 'What did she want to marry that Charlie for?'

'Sex, I think.'

371

John showed Aunt Mary the photographs. The old woman knew who some of them were. She was interested in a photograph of a big old man with a white moustache leaning on a verandah. A dog sat near his feet.

'That's Jack!' She exclaimed. 'Kindest man I ever knew. He died when I was young, that's why I got to like your father so much. When his father died Austin took all the responsibility. He became like the father. No one else to do it. Mum was so tough on him. Kept him working all the time. He always wanted to be an accountant. Never got the chance.'

'Always good with money,' John commented.

'Never had a chance to be anything else. No fun or anything really. It was Eric who left.'

'Eric told me once your father caused a bit of trouble.'

'You don't believe everything that Eric tells you. He wasn't good, Eric wasn't. Not like your father.'

John nodded.

'There was the time in the big strike. Everyone was out of work and the water—you know what the water was like—I was only little then. Big Jack believed in the unions. He sat on the verandah and for days the women tried to talk him into going back to work. I wanted him to go back to work. He ignored it. No time for women in those days. Those men came around at night and they sat about talking. There was an old carbide lamp they put on the verandah and it was mines this and big mine that and the big mine wasn't there any longer, and they'd go on into the night. One night mum was in the kitchen complaining about it. She always thought he should go back to the job, bugger the unions they won't do you any good, she said. If he went back he had enough brains. They'd give him a job on the staff. Then the unions could do what they liked. He wouldn't. One night Austin walked out there with his thumb in his braces, he was thirteen about and he only had one pair of trousers. "My mother doesn't want you around so late." he says, "We want to go to sleep." The men, they all looked at him, then a couple of them laughed and one of them said, "Can't keep the women

372

up all night, eh?" and they all decided young Austin was a fighter like his father to look after his mum like that. That's what he did.'

'Looked after his mum?'

'Always the gentleman, he was. Like his father. Except that his father could talk. When he wanted. Read books, too. I wouldn't mind getting a copy of the photograph.'

He picked the roses from his father's garden. They were in bloom. Long-stemmed pink roses, and a single startling yellow rose. At the service in the crematorium, he laid the single yellow rose on the coffin. It glowed from among the wreaths. It kept glowing as a Presbyterian minister gave a short service and a sermon. The mourners stared at the single, almost obscene, yellow rose, as it sat there, dripping glowing petals onto the casket.

As John walked out, the man who had delivered the wreaths gave him a look. He wore dark glasses and a blue suit.

'A beautiful day,' he said.

'A beautiful day,' John nodded.

'Where is Austin?' His mother asked as they stood outside in the sunlight talking to the neighbours.

'He died on Monday night,' John answered.

'Oh!' She was genuinely stunned. It registered again. 'I didn't know. I'm glad you told me. So glad you were honest because I had to know. I'm glad it is the truth . . .'

She looked at the crematorium.

'If they forgot me I'd never forgive them, honest if they didn't take me I'd never forgive them.'

Cain was standing nearby.

'How you going mum?' he called.

'He's a good boy.' Diana gave him a hug. 'He always looks after his mother, don't you, John?'

The Delhi Road was busy. Cars chewed past blowing smoke.

373

John was about to get into his car. Aunt Mary was escorting Diana along the footpath. Both women wore stockings and good clothes, only Ellen wore black.

'Such a lovely garden, with those trees,' said Diana. 'Every time I see those trees I think of the garden in Broken Hill.'

Chapter 9

'The neighbour gave us your telephone number, Mr Evans,' the manager of the bank said apologetically. 'You see, I went to your parents' house. Your father had put in a request that the bank not repossess the house while they were alive. After your father's death, the bank was told of your mother's condition. We have no desire to throw the elderly from their homes.'

'Without any roof over their heads,' John added helpfully.

'We are not heartless.'

'Of course.'

'Imagine then the consternation I felt when I went to the house to pass on to your mother the good news, and heard that she wasn't living there any longer. The woman who was there had many complaints. She said that she had a lease, which she showed me. I had to explain that as I understood the law, a lease that was made out when the party was no longer the owner of the premises was not binding. She was most upset, Mr Evans, most upset.'

'Where is my mother? I haven't heard anything for more than two months now.'

'Mrs Brady—the woman in the house—did say that a number of the neighbours were worried also. She seems to have disappeared.'

There was a short silence.

'Well, I must tell you that we would like to contact your mother. We had no intention of foreclosing while your mother was resident, however now we have been advised that the best policy is for us to claim the house.'

'From the lease, can't you find out where my sister is living? Through her agent?'

'Your sister has taken certain precautions so that it is difficult to know exactly where she is. While a period of Her Majesty's pleasure would no doubt be instructive for her, the costs would be borne by us with little possibility of redress.'

'I have tried to phone . . .'

'I understand your predicament with your sister, Mr Evans. It is a sad time for your family. I knew and respected your father. A simple and honest man, sir, salt of the earth. Still I hope you understand that I am bound by the instructions of my superiors. Given the turn of events—an illegal lease and money and bond, all taken—the Rental Bond Board have been notified and they know nothing, they have not received the bond, as is the law. Eight hundred dollars, a small amount, but taken in this fashion, not such as to inspire confidence. All told some six thousand dollars, which should be the property of sundry creditors. We are only one. The Australian Taxation Office also has an interest in recouping . . .'

'How long will it take?'

'Realistically, Mr Evans, realistically, I think we will allow the Brady family to serve out their lease. Paying money to us as the legitimate owners, of course. Then we shall foreclose and sell at auction, as is usual in these cases.'

'Hm.'

'That should take, at the most, two months. If there is anything there of value to you I suggest you collect it, although Mrs Brady did suggest that there was little there. A washing machine, a refrigerator. Your sister sold almost everything. The stove stayed, only because the premises would have been difficult to let otherwise. A terrible story, a sad end to a life of toil and duty, Mr Evans.'

'A life of toil and duty!' John exclaimed.

'I will give you my telephone number in case you have any enquiries, Mr Evans. If we can be of service. And of course, the number of Mrs Brady and her family. Two sons. Fine young men, Mr Evans. Do you have any children, Mr Evans?'

Diana was small, thin, weak. He walked towards her, following the back of the nurse. Against the walls elderly men with shaking chins stared at him. An old woman with wispy grey hair raised her arms and reached up to him.

'Rodney, come here Rodney,' she called.

The nurse half-turned and smiled. His mother was one of these broken, aged children.

'Mrs Evans. Your son is here to see you.'

John thrust a small bag of Lebanese cakes forward.

'Isn't that nice,' said the nurse. 'If you want we can take them and put them in the fridge. That way we can feed them to her at dinner time. She had lunch not long ago. They'll get taken, won't they Diana?'

John did not resist as the cakes disappeared into the kitchen. The nurse came back.

'I put them there, with her name on, if you want to check.'

'It's so nice to see you.' Diana smiled up at him. Her false teeth were not in. She took his hand.

'This is my brother come to see me!' She exclaimed to the nurse.

'Yes, it's your son,' the nurse corrected gently.

Diana screwed her face and thought.

'What did you steal?' She asked. 'No, not you, who, John, Johnny, he stole.'

'I am here.'

'He stole. Like Charlie and Una. Never give nothing back. You ready to take me home?'

The nurse turned and walked away. Diana began to walk, leading him by the hand.

'How is mum?'

'She died. A long time ago.'

'I had no idea. When she die?'

'A long time ago.'

Although obviously this was not so. For Diana, her life existed in one turbulent present.

'Are you going home?' She asked slyly, the glint in the eye.

'I will go home.'

'Take me there, back to the farm, back to the yard. I want

my house with the big trees, the well. Remember the sweet water? The pepper trees out the back? Dad?'

'It isn't there any longer.'

The home was laid out in a square, around a courtyard. They walked out onto a small verandah. His mother looked down, at the lower floor, the elderly who were not senile, shuffling about, sitting in chairs, enjoying the sun.

'I hate this place.'

She threw a leg over the side, and dangled it.

'Wish I could die, but I'd only break my bloody leg, then I could never get out.'

She withdrew the leg and leaned against the parapet. John noticed a scar, a scab which had not healed.

'Did they take my house?'

John nodded.

'They shouldn't have taken my house, they sold it, I didn't sign anything, I didn't. It was John stole my house. I know it was him, they told me.'

John nodded again.

'Charlie, he always wanted to get into the bathroom when I was in there but I wouldn't let him. He was such a beautiful baby, lovely kid, I talked to him. Sat up there and smiled as I talked and we sang together. I can't believe it was him that stole that house not after that. I know he is bad but I don't believe it, he couldn't have done it, not to me. Nobody's that hard. The way he smiled and played. When he could hardly talk there was a dog, he threw the ball and the dog used to run and get it.'

'Would you like a cup of tea, Diana?' The nurse walked to the sliding door with a tea trolley.

'Yes. Thank you,' she said.

The cup of tea was delivered. She stayed standing, leaning the tea against her chest with a trembling hand. The nurse looked closely.

'You're not going to spill that, are you?'

'They won't let me play tennis in here either. No good. Left-handed. Mum was standing beside the court, she yelled all the time, "Play with the other hand like you should, you can't play like that". She went up to the school and they belted me until I wrote with me right hand and at home I did everything with my right hand but I wasn't going to do that no matter what. So I practised and played with my left hand. It was like that was what I was, a left-hander, I didn't give a bugger if it was the side of the devil, it was me I was going to do it. Ran every day. Beat everyone, or just about everyone, that was me. I said that to Clarrie. That's me, I said when he tried to kiss me on the side of the hill near the pepper trees. That was me. I don't want nobody to interfere, nobody inside me, put it away I don't want to, and he didn't, went somewhere else for it. I wish I did now because everybody talked they said "That's her that got jilted I bet he did it to her then to that other one ha ha," got to leave the farm. Daddy daddy please go and stay with Una, watch that Charlie Diana, he said, he's a one.'

As he walked to the door, he saw the nurse.

'What does she need?'

The nurse was writing something in a book. She pushed a lock of brown hair from her eye.

'Fruit,' she said. 'That's what she needs. Lots of fruit.'

As he walked to the door, he was followed by three elderly women. His mother held to one hand. One of them held to the other arm.

'Take me with you!' The other woman called. 'You promised to come, you promised to come for so long.'

'Take me home,' his mother implored.

He slipped through the door to get away.

In early autumn, the leaves had begun to yellow, but not to fall. John walked away from the home, down a road, at the bottom he could catch a ferry. He had been seared. Seered? Seer? He had no visions. If hell was the inability to love, his sister was in hell. Time past, the demons, the lovers, the images of his mother's life crowded around her, plucked at her thin weak legs, cried and wept and suffered endlessly without the possibility of

379

exorcism. His father, endless rows of numbers, speech which had never been made. Duty. Toil and duty. Deserving something for his duty, he had been good, it was not fair to have children without having a chance to be childish, to be a secret violent child.

The images of the past, of history, he was caught in them. Untransformed images. Things happened, there was no order in them, they followed one after the other, inevitable only if you looked back. To look forward to the perpetual repetition and variation of images. Coincidences and imposed patterns, mind.

His sister was in hell, his father was in hell, his mother was in hell. Hell was the past without meaning. Only meaning was human. He was in hell.

The stone was turning and cutting inside.

It was Sunday morning. He could hear the old woman downstairs cleaning up the needles. Steps, coming up the stairs. Hesitation on the landing. Knock.

A man was standing there. Tall, neat, with a suit and an umbrella.

'Mr Evans?'

John stepped aside. The man stepped over the piles of unwashed clothes, the box of photographs and papers.

'Were you an acquaintance of a Mr Clifford Gent?'

'He was my landlord.'

'Mr Gent was the recipient of a considerable sum. Did you know that certain of his relatives in England were quite wealthy?'

'Quakers.' John waved the man to a chair.

'It has taken us some time to trace him, and then to trace his will. He did make one out. You are his beneficiary.'

'Eh?'

'If everything is in order, you will inherit a significant sum.'

'What am I to do with that? How much?'

He was speaking more to himself than to the other man. On top of the box of photographs which had been dumped in the hallway, he could see a folder for a lottery. He shrugged, to get rid of the sensation of hell, closing in.

'I could give it away,' John whispered. 'There are thousands of people out there who need it.'

'You can suit yourself, sir. It is none of my affair. It is my experience that there are always far more people than one can give things to. Such . . . saintliness . . . invariably earns the undying hatred of the recipient.'

'I can't get away from it?'

'You can ignore it. There are ways. Investment advisers can use it, give you interest, you don't have to worry.'

'It is not that much.'

'It is . . . significant.'

'I would like to buy a house, an old house.'

The man smiled at him happily, and expressed relief that they had managed to reach an accord.

'A fashionable term in this country at present, I believe.'

'Most people are learning to suspect it,' John answered.

First, he made sure that his mother was paid for. She was shifted to a better hospital, with grounds. Whenever he went to see her, she was still immersed in the images of her past.

He bought the house, and began to rebuild it. Once the man who had given him the news of Clifford's bequest asked him why he wanted to build a dome over a not especially large, single storey house.

'There is nothing else I can think of to do with it,' John replied. 'What should I do? Go on holidays to Hong Kong? Educate myself? Improve? Impress somebody? Build a city? Finance a drug ring?'

'This sounds frivolous.'

John said nothing of his real motive, which was to listen again through the wall to accents and voices of the past, to hide them and observe them and write them down. There was a pattern, even if he had to make one.

Chapter 10

John lay in his room most of the day, listening to the workmen next door. After the death of his father, he began to get a bad back. Gradually it got worse, so that it became hard for him to get up at all. It made no difference whether he lay down or stood, the pain was excruciating. The more tormented his body became, the more obsessively he listened. At night, after the workmen had gone, or in the morning before they came, he listened and watched his recollections and his dreams.

The more his body was unable to move for the spasms of pain, the more the needles threaded the muscles of his leg, the more clear and tangible were his memories. When he went to the toilet, he sat trembling and sweating on the edge of the bowl. There were times when it gave relief; at other times, his bowels remained full and heavy and the pains radiated through his body to his spine and down his legs. The toilet was surrounded with building materials. The roof was a frame with two black hanging plastic sheets. The electric lights strung on thin cords of flex in the middle of the day were inadequate, and the back of the house was dark.

The winds blew from the south. Although the builders put up sheets of timber across the back of the house, the wind came through. Jan the carpenter kept a small electric bar heater going constantly, although it had no effect except to send up the electricity bills.

The plumber did not need to come for a while. Then one day a truck pulled up and workmen unloaded six curved sheets of perspex.

The men grunted as they hauled the perspex along the side of the house. When all six sheets had been put down near a tree at the back the workmen accepted the offer of tea.

'What they want perspex for?' One of the men asked.

'Ah I don't knows,' said Jan. 'We got a madman in here somewhere. He puts it up there. On the roof!'

'Like a skylight?'

'Yes, I thinks that what he got in head.'

'How he going to get it up there?'

'Crane. We gone to hire a crane, and we gone to hire a welder, and we gone to stitch it up there.'

'It's an old house. How can it take that much weight? He's already taken out the walls.'

'That why I'm here. I braces the ceiling with thick pieces of timber, and we put RSJ across from here to here.

'I tells you, more money than sense, that what he gots!'

'Wouldn't mind having as much. Is he a millionaire?'

'That what I hears.'

'That case he can afford to have something like that, and keep you sitting in a job for months.'

'I tell you I likes to get another job, except that jobs are scarce. Him and Wallace and it's so cold here, I tells you. If there is another job I tell him to stuff this job and I say you get another carpenter to Wallace you see how you go. He don't gets another carpenter like me easy, then I go. See how they like it.'

'Where did he get the idea from?'

'I don't knows. Where does mad people get ideas from?'

'Tell him I've got a daughter he can marry any time if he's got that much money.'

'He sits down in the bedroom. You does not knows when he listens,' Jan warned.

The man laughed.

After Jan had gone, John went over the copy of the plans. The architect he hired to make them up had asked him why he wanted to put a dome there, and make a garden. John gave him a steady smile.

'No accounting for taste, alright,' the architect said. 'You're paying, so you've got a right. Just that it helps if you know what the final purpose is. Then you can come up with alternative suggestions.'

John still gave him the steady smile and said nothing. The architect shrugged.

'We're going to need a landscape architect as well, and a structural engineer. It would be much easier to do on a new house. You could build a new house for the cost, if you wanted.'

'I want it here.'

'What for?'

'I like it here.'

The architect had all the measurements. He went over them carefully.

'I know you've already decided, but I ought to warn you. This will be hot in summer and cold as hell in winter.'

'I want it.'

'It's a terrarium, a sort of—do you want to allow for curtains so that you can cut down the sun, or a sliding panel that can act as an ordinary ceiling?'

The architect was good at his job. A thin man in a suit which seemed to pinch, he swallowed a lot and looked guilty when he told the truth. Each time he swallowed, his Adam's apple pressed against his collar and he put a hand up to his tie.

He bent over the plans and wrinkled his brow.

'We could have a whole mobile timber floor, so you could vary the height depending on how or what you wanted to see— the plants or the sky or what—if you wanted that.'

'That sounds interesting,' John said.

The architect looked up.

'Most people, they say they want an original plan. When I was young I designed a house for a couple. They wanted it *avant-garde*, they said. When it happened that way, the woman said that it looked good but nobody could live in it. So I ended up doing it straight and ordinary. The everyday bungalow with a few trimmings. "That's what we wanted!" she said.'

'This is your chance,' John whispered.

'I think I gave up taking chances then.'

The plans had been done well. Measurements and estimations of tensile strength and materials required. Cross-sections with lines of stress.

'We can make it so you can shift the dome, alter the angle and pick up more sun in winter, less in summer.'

'Show me,' John had said.

As the architect showed him, his hands were shaking.

'I never did one like this before!' The architect said.

John looked composed despite the pains moving along his legs and his *gastrocnemius* muscles taut as piano wires. It was hard to focus. He concentrated hard on the paper, accepting what his decision was going to be.

'It looks good.'

'The neighbours won't compete for a while.'

The architect left him with the plans. John stood upright at the door as he went. The architect climbed into his car. The pressure swelled against John's belt. There was no relief. He had already gone through a box of bicarbonate of soda that day.

He closed the door and moved back to his bedroom. He lay down. There was a plaster rose above him. If he turned his head in the right direction, he could see a pinprick of light through the tiles above the ceiling. He wondered whether there was a star he could see through the tiny hole. Slowly he rotated his body around the bed, all the time staring up at where he knew the tiny hole to be. He imagined the hole, and the light. There was no light. The tiny hole concentrated the dark. The densest dark, folding in on itself, tight and burning. He was in it. The gas in his stomach was expanding with the dark, blowing him up like a huge balloon.

Chapter 11

His eyes were getting bad. The optometrist told him that he would have to have reading glasses in the next year. A pain ran up through the joint of his elbow to his shoulder, from where it did a neat circle around his scapula. His seventh cervical vertebra twinged and sent constant messages along the telegraph to the base of his skull. The pain radiated from his right hip to the back of his knee and the outside of his foot. Three weeks before, when the men were working outside heaving around pieces of timber, he hugged the wall listening, and when he tried to stand the pain had transferred itself to his left side. The surface of the skin and the heel became numb, making it impossible for him to run or move quickly. The doctor, a small mild bachelor in an untidy suit, told him it was memory responding to the effects of extreme shock in the fifth lumbar nerve and the first sacral nerve.

'Memory?' he sat up, interested.

'Before you were born.' The doctor was bored and it was late, but he kept talking as he put away his equipment. 'When you were a foetus, the areas of skin which are numb were proximal—close to—the S1 and L5 nerve. The brain can't distinguish between stress as a result of external causes and stress from internal causes. It thinks that all pain must be a result of an external cause—an assault—and responds defensively with the nerves on the surface of the skin. That skin is not related to the area of stress neurologically or rationally in any way, other than by subliminal memory.'

He left John with a bottle of pain-killers, and told him not to wait so long next time.

John limped. Not because of pain, but because of a dermatone. A pain related to another pain through memory. A connection made six months before he was born.

386

When he drove, his foot cramped over the accelerator pedal.

His lower back swayed out where it should have swayed in. His upper back swayed in where it should have swayed out. His neck was a noose and the atlas and axis joints wedged into his skull. His testicles pulled his hamstring muscles up under his buttock.

His blood pressure was too high. He was told to relax to bring it down. Anxiety. He got another bottle of pills, which he didn't take, because he wanted his own pain. He had a right to it. He told the doctor, who laughed.

He put on weight too easily and it was getting harder to take it off. When his lower back ached, his stomach went into spasm. It twisted like a dishcloth being wrung. The doctor laughed again.

'You worry too much, you see.' He offered the tablets again. 'I know you've got a right, but it is so . . . unneccessary.'

John still wouldn't take the tablets, but he kept the doctor, for the self-knowledge.

He went to see a naturopath because his hair was going grey. As a result, he took vitamin B in the form of yeast, kelp, charcoal, pantothenic acid (B_5), zinc, vitamin C, one bottle of Bach remedy drops for anxiety situations, another Bach remedy for 'general balance' plus six drops per day of homeopathic drops. When he got tired of them he began to use a Ventolin inhaler, a Becotide inhaler, neulin tablets, a muscle relaxant and a firm bed. He began to use a backswing which looked like a sexual aid until he got tired of it and left it standing in a corner where the plumber made jokes about it and the carpenter tripped on it and swore.

The zinc, as well as helping in the body's synthesis of vitamin A and B_5, controlled herpes virus type A.

'The middle classes never get herpes on their lips, so they get it on their pricks later,' the doctor smiled grimly. 'There's some advantage coming from the working class.'

'Ha,' John responded automatically.

'You better stop eating all that bran in the morning though.' The doctor sounded both sombre and facetious.

'Bran counteracts the effect of the zinc. If the zinc has any effect, which I doubt!'

'Even you say it's good for the colon!'

'Also good for diabetes and the heart, although I shouldn't tell you, because you will work out some way to do the opposite. Why you see me, I don't know!'

'My moral development.'

'Sometimes I think all you want is to be entertained.'

'You perform the traditional functions of the healer—you tell me what is the moral cause of my troubles.'

'You have offended the gods.' The doctor spoke, only half jokingly. 'You can't escape being human by laughing at . . . us. Do you hope to neutralise pain by mockery?'

The doctor sat in an old comfortable chair near the window. The light from John's bedside lamp illuminated part of his face but his eyes remained dark and hidden.

'I didn't think I was so savage.'

'This is not a medical opinion. You said I am . . . a faith healer. If I was, then I would diagnose you this way. Your mind—your spiritual state—is corroding you.'

John sat up, trying to catch the expression. The doctor's head wove around the small triangle of light.

'You are eating yourself!'

The doctor spoke with feeling.

'It is, of course, a most unscientific diagnosis.' He fell back on the chair. 'There are certain theories about anorexia which are similar. Discredited, mostly, but they always have a following with the gullible. The millions, the people.'

'Coerce me.'

'I was not aware of doing any such thing.'

'What are you saying?'

'You accuse me of being a faith healer. A witch doctor. I think it is you who are the witch doctor.'

John looked at him, at a loss for words.

'When I was young, I spent some time with Christian

missionaries. In Africa, New Guinea, South America. I stayed in Indonesia for years, and left when Sukarno went. I lost my faith gradually, and part of the reason was what I saw of witch doctors. Not that there aren't a lot of frauds. There are a few of them in my own branch of the healing profession. But there were some who were healers, not because they wanted to be, nor for money, but because they couldn't help it. They were not humanitarian. They hated humanity, either as an abstraction or as individuals. They were morbidly sensitive to themselves, and they disliked themselves intensely. They suffered with unusual intensity what it was to be human.'

The doctor drew in a deep breath. John rested back on his pillows.

'They could not deny some knowledge of people, some wisdom in them which was (I think) innate. It was not something they wanted. They often felt themselves victims, having to carry something which set them apart, made them friendless, suspicious and not trusted or liked. One of them told me he had an old soul. An old soul! I asked him what it was to have an old soul. He was a filthy, bitter, obscene man. Could never keep his hands off the women. The husbands and fathers hated him, feared him, would have killed him, except they did not know what sort of revenge would be wreaked upon them, if they did. They needed him. He healed them, even while he loathed them. An old soul is one who is very close to extinction. The last lives as a human are difficult, because the soul must learn to separate from all that men regard as important.'

John looked at the thin stick blind on his window. The light from his room reflected against it. A stray cat, creeping along the windowsill, began to howl.

'I lost my faith there, if not certain elements of my Christianity. Because, of course, the only reason for Europeans to be there, was to be superior. By helping, they

389

reinforced that superiority. It was obvious that no element of my religion could withstand this kind of cynicism. Including, of course, myself.'

'Are you an old soul?' John asked.

'No.' He turned his head nervously a little further than before. 'I am not. I am quite comfortable giving people pills for their problems. It is you who possess the old soul.'

He said the last with a flourish.

'If such a thing actually exists,' he added.

He flicked through the photographs he had taken from Austin's house when he died. It slipped away. A detail he could not recall! He sifted his small heap of images, memories, rejecting those which may have been a fabrication. It had gone. Almost uncontrollable despair. Something had disappeared, he could not recall it, hold it up, renew it, touch it, let it slip through his fingers. Fine ash, the touch of velvet, the glint of broken glass on an autumn day. Perhaps he was always asthmatic. He discussed this with the doctor, the failed missionary, he who had taken the kingdom of the world as a second best when the kingdom of God had already been mortgaged to a gang of heathen holy men.

'You are not a hypochondriac,' the doctor asserted. 'Except of a certain type. You don't want sympathy, you merely want to be sensitive to yourself.'

'Not self-indulgence?'

'You win either way!'

'The art of civilised debate.'

The doctor's lapel shook.

'What did you want to be? When you were young?'

'I thought about becoming a pilot.' He smiled at the childish charm the idea still had for him. 'My uncle was a pilot. Something lots of boys want.'

John shrugged.

'What do you believe?'

'That question makes me panic. I don't know.'

'People who don't think they believe in anything, usually do believe. Except that what they believe is usually stupid, and they wouldn't believe it if they thought about it.'

'I think you're right,' John confessed. 'You have converted me to the way of Satan. I am a magician, a healer, witch doctor.'

'You might be,' the doctor said in a voice which was quite level. 'What was it that caused you to become so ill?'

'The death of my father.' John straightened.

The workmen had almost finished when the doctor arrived. He had not been called.

'This is early!' John exclaimed when he hobbled out to the door to see him.

John had never seen the doctor in daylight before. His skin looked pale and chalky and his suit was pressed. He carried his little bag.

They sat down in the large front room, as far away from the noise of the workmen as they could get.

'I received the test results this morning,' the doctor said. 'They are positive, very positive.'

'What does that mean?'

'Cancer.'

John was not surprised or afraid. He had been waiting all his life, certain that it would come. It was the logic of his life.

The doctor sat there for a while. When it was apparent that John was not going to say anything, he stood up.

'I think you ought to do something, now,' he said before he left.

Chapter 12

The aeroplane took him to Broken Hill in a few hours. There were women sitting near him, discussing children. A man with a wide-brimmed hat. A woman with a parcel, wrapped in brown paper, which she would not let from her lap.

He was not used to arriving so quickly. He picked up his bags cautiously and took them out to a taxi. Then he asked to be driven to a hotel.

'Plenty of room,' said the driver. 'Close to town, or out a bit?'

'Close.'

'Come here for a look around?'

'Yes.'

'There's lots here. You can get a tour down the old mine there, or you can see the Memorial in Sturt Park. To the sinking of the *Titanic*. Lots of people like to see that.'

'Yes.'

The following morning, he watched from the verandah of the hotel, the empty street, the empty shops, a few cars. He caught a taxi to see his friend Ethel, who did not know he was coming.

'Didn't expect you,' She said.

He slumped in a chair. His clothes were too big.

'You lost weight.'

'What's happening?' He asked.

He was looking out at the skyline. The trucks were moving along the ridge, hauling away the skimps. But he saw something else. He had not noticed it before, or taken it into account. There were trees. Old pepper trees and sugar gums, rising above the corrugated iron of the houses.

'Not much. You done anything?'

He stood up and walked slowly to the window. The trees were everywhere. Ethel's house was on a slope. All over the town, there were trees. Corrugated iron and trees.

'I made a dome, out of perspex,' he said. 'On a roof. So I could see the sky.'

He could hear Ethel pouring water into a kettle.

'I decided to come and live a while,' he affirmed.

He dreamed in the afternoon of the lemon tree. Never thought of it with that significance before, although it was behind or near many things he recalled from his childhood. The huge mulberry tree near the front fence. The three parallel beds of roses nearer the house.

The garden had been planted before his parents shifted to the house when he was a few months old. It was there, already full grown. Each year, Austin sprayed the new fruit on the tree with insect killer. White milky fluid in a bucket. He drooped a long brass spraygun into the bucket, then gently drew back the handle until it was full. Then again after each long spray. The spray was fine and delicate and sticky. Khaki trousers and steel-toed mine shoes.

He preserved the plants already there and planted small flowers in beds around the trees and shrubs that already existed.

There were other trees. The front garden was deep, sloping up from the corrugated road and the single gum tree at the front. The wild mulberry tree had an enormous base which forked into three large branches. The leaves overhead never quite cut off the sky. An orange tree against the fence on the far side, and a small quince tree in front of a lawn. Two large fig trees on the western side of the house, and a grapefruit tree next to a patch of raised ground where each year Austin had tried to grow tomatoes, and each year was beaten by the frost. All of these he remembered easily and placed simply in a corner of his memory, each with meaning and suggestiveness. Not so the lemon tree.

In his dream he was small, crawling under the lemon tree. The leaves almost touched the ground. He sat near a fern which caught a little speck of light through the leaves. There was no meaning there, and he was afraid. He called to his father, who bent from where he was spraying outside. His father stared as

John fondled the fern. A few traces of fine milky fluid dripped from the leaves.

'You shouldn't be here,' his father said. 'The spray is poison.'

'There is no meaning here,' John complained.

Austin looked puzzled.

'It is important that you find your own meanings.' Austin spoke, hesitant and afraid.

John crawled from under the lemon tree and walked back to the house and sat on a step. The lemon tree was quite perfect at that moment, symmetrical. His father drew back the handle and the pump guzzled the milky fluid.